It's

A whimper escaped her as Dane brushed his lips—so gently, so slowly—from one corner of her mouth to the center to the other corner and then back again, barely touching her, yet touching her more deeply than had his passion a moment past. More completely than she'd ever been touched before. Her fingers dug into his shoulders. Her mind screamed *"No!"* as every vein in her body seemed to vibrate with a low thrum at the feel of his arousal pressed against her. Her heart warmed and rolled over in pleasure even as she refused to give in to the beauty of his tenderness and the need to encourage him to go on and on until his kisses turned to passion once more and she felt him inside her, filling her . . .

Other **AVON ROMANCES**

ONLY IN MY DREAMS

EVE BYRON

AVON BOOKS ◆ NEW YORK

AVON BOOKS, INC.
1350 Avenue of the Americas
New York, New York 10019

Copyright © 1998 by Connie Rinehold
Inside cover author photo by Shea Balika
Published by arrangement with the author
Visit our website at **http://www.AvonBooks.com**
Library of Congress Catalog Card Number: 97-94768
ISBN: 0-380-79311-3

First Avon Books Printing: June 1998

AVON TRADEMARK REG. U.S. PAT. OFF. AND IN OTHER COUNTRIES, MARCA REGISTRADA, HECHO EN U.S.A.

Printed in the U.S.A.

WCD   10 9 8 7 6 5 4 3 2 1

Prologue

London, 1802

She had it all—a title of her own, wealth, a grand estate, and the physical attributes by which men set such store. Unfortunately, she had it all on a grander scale than the other debutantes of her generation.

Lorelei, Baroness Winters, hadn't known that she was different or that her stature and the accompanying proportions would make a difference until she'd begun the interminable walk through the throngs of aristocrats on her way to be presented to the king.

She raised her chin a notch and then another, the better to avoid having to meet anyone's gaze. Ironic, really, that she'd spent her entire seventeen years waiting for the moment when she would leave the rarified atmosphere of her existence as cosseted heiress and neglected orphan and enter the world where dreams came true.

She would make her bow at court, dazzle everyone at Almack's, and live happily ever after with the man of her dreams. She would have a family of her own.

A family. She really had no idea what such an institution entailed, but after observing the affection and comfort exchanged between the tenants of her estate and their relatives, she'd been determined to have one of her own—a husband who would call her his "love" and whisper naughty suggestions in her ear as she'd seen a footman do with a parlor maid.

Never again would she stand outside of life, watching and wishing . . . and wanting what she'd never had.

How silly she had been to arrive in London with her heart thumping in excitement and her mind overblown with quixotic expectations.

Lost in her disappointment, Lorelei took one step too many and stumbled as one of the courtiers flanking His Majesty hissed at her. Lord Havers, a trustee of her estate acting in her late father's stead, halted abruptly and yanked her back. Titters fluttered in the air, barely muffled behind ladies' fans and gentlemen's gloved hands. She stared straight ahead, acutely aware of how ridiculous she looked, rigged out in a voluminous gown and every jewel she owned. Feeling like an open parasol adorned with paste beads and crowned by enough plumes to keep a flock of ostriches warm for the winter, she forced herself to ignore the snickers and whispers to concentrate on surviving the occasion without her weighty headdress pitching her forward at the king's feet as she made her curtsey.

Panic seized Lorelei as she rose and turned to walk the gauntlet once more, refusing to look at the malicious grins and expressions of pity thrown her way. With each step her extravagant headdress swayed on her head, threatening her balance and making each step she took at Lord Havers's side seem like a slog through mud a foot deep. Despite the layers of clothing draped over her frame, she felt naked beneath the lewd and assessing stares bestowed on her by the young bucks grouped near the open windows, as if they planned a hasty escape as soon as the show was over.

Humiliation and disappointment blurred the rest of the proceedings with impressions that she couldn't separate from herself. Every whisper seemed focused on her. Every casual glance appeared critical or reproachful. She kept wanting to tug at her bodice or check the back of her gown to make certain the hem had not somehow become caught up, exposing her backside. She felt like a caricature of herself, a pretender in the midst of so much nobility and splendor.

The moment it was permissible, she left the crowds and the laughter and climbed into her carriage, barely able to thank Lord Havers and send him on his way, barely able to speak at all, much less shout for the coachman to hurry away. It wouldn't do any good. Already scores of coaches clogged the streets in front of the palace, giving no hope of exit. They would have to wait their turn in the queue.

Until now she'd believed that her large eyes and pretty smile would be attraction enough, that her intelligence and wit would impress enough to blind the bachelors of the Upper Ten Thousand to her height and Rubenesque proportions. How certain she had been that her stature would be accepted by the sophisticated and civilized society of London.

How naive of her.

Drawing the curtains over the windows, she ripped the headdress off and sank back into a corner of the seat, shattered by the realization that it did make a difference. Why hadn't she known? Why hadn't someone warned her that she would be viewed as less than attractive simply because she was not small and dainty and "discreetly curved"?

But then, who had there been to warn her? Family? She'd had none since her parents had died fifteen years past, unless one considered an army of servants, solicitors, and trustees as family. She had only an elderly distant cousin who acted as chaperone, and an indifferent one at best. Families hugged and shared and even squabbled. Judging from her observations of the tenants on her estate, family life seemed both chaotic and comforting. Her life had been neither. Only her bosom bow, Harriet, hugged her and advised her, and since they were of an age, her friend knew no more about the ways of the *ton* than she.

And Harriet had not told her that the current fashion did not suit her ample frame and in fact exaggerated her proportions. It wouldn't have occurred to Harriet. There were a thousand rules and rituals dictated by invisible powers, all scrupulously followed by obedient masses.

Lorelei had never been required to obey anyone but herself. At Winterhaven, she was the ranking official. Only in matters of education and deportment was there a higher authority than she. Since education was a pleasure and proper deportment necessary, she had learned her lessons well. To her, they were the coin with which she would acquire passage into the broader world beyond iron gates figuratively maintained and guarded by the stiff-rumped men of business appointed by her late father so long ago.

Men, she realized, whose power over her would diminish greatly after her eighteenth birthday tomorrow. In that, she was fortunate. Few women in England actually inherited a title, and fewer still were allowed to manage their own funds. Her father's will had stipulated that after her eighteenth birthday the trustees of her estate would advise rather than manage—a titular role to satisfy the laws governing women.

The door opened and a man climbed inside with languid grace, pulling the door shut behind him. Favoring her with a grim look, he took a seat across from her. "Never allow them to drive you into a corner, my lady," he said gravely, as he reached over to wipe a tear from her cheek with his gloved fingers. "And never allow them to see you weep."

She sniffed loudly, too stunned to respond. She knew this elegant man who outshone the grandest duke with his trim figure and fine yet wholly masculine features. His waistcoat of dove-gray damask was perfection itself, and his neckcloth was tied in the notoriously impossible folds of the Mathematical. Yes, Lorelei knew this highest arbiter of fashion and social detail. Who didn't?

"I would not have taken you for the speechless sort," he commented. "A young woman with a title and more wealth than the king should cultivate . . . an attitude, shall we say, of unshakable confidence. A certain sangfroid. No one need know that beneath the facade you are trembling like blancmange." Breaching every rule of formality, he carefully pulled off one glove, then the other—to put her at ease, perhaps?— as he angled his head to regard her closely.

"You are not beautiful, but you are potentially stunning, given the right fashions and coif. In fact, you *are* stunning, even in that abominable costume." He shook his head in exaggerated despair. "Really, those ostrich plumes are too long, and satin—particularly pink satin—forgives not the slightest flaw of form. Who on earth dresses you?''

''My chaperone,'' she said in a small voice.

''No, no, my lady. Speak robustly. Laugh robustly. There is nothing so grating as a voice that does not match the woman.''

He had called her a *woman*. He had called her *stunning*. He, whose every motion was polished and superbly confident, even as his amiable smile and the twinkle in his eye softened his impeccable image. And he liked her; she knew he did. George ''Beau'' Brummell, bellwether of London society, never spoke to those he didn't like.

Lorelei supposed she should think it odd that he was here, speaking to her and chastising her as if he had the right, but it didn't seem odd. It seemed natural, as if it were an occasion meant to be and only wanted the proper time to occur.

''We will begin immediately,'' Mr. Brummell said conversationally, as he settled into a studied sprawl. ''I know a modiste who will deliver a wardrobe within a week, if I request it of her. And your chaperone should be no impediment—Lady Bertha Winters, am I correct?''

She nodded, fascinated by her unfamiliar sense of being taken care of—not for wages, but out of interest. Why else would the prince's confidante and advisor ignore propriety to sit alone with her in her coach?

No one but Harriet had ever been interested in her.

''Your last relative,'' he astutely guessed. ''No doubt, the woman is as old as Methuselah and should be retired to a cottage where she might read her ghastly Gothicks and sip her port in peace.''

''How did you know?'' she asked.

He shrugged. "It's a common enough situation. I also made some discreet inquiries. The moment you entered London your life became public knowledge among the *ton*." He gave her a rakish grin. "Unfortunately, descriptions of you did not prepare them for the reality, fools that they are."

Wishing she could melt into the cushions, Lorelei sank back, then caught herself and simply sat with back straight and head high. She had never allowed the servants at Winterhaven to see her in a state other than pleasant equanimity. She had refused to display her distress at court. She would not cower in the corner now. Not in front of this man, or anyone else, for that matter. "It hadn't occurred to me that I was so. . . ."

"Overwhelming and impressive, my lady," he supplied. "Few men are so tall, much less women. Fewer still are so magnificent as you . . . or as you shall be with my tutelage."

Magnificent. Lorelei blinked, overwhelmed by his compliments.

She kicked the hated headdress out of her way and leaned forward, needing to challenge him and what he was convincing her to believe. *Stunning . . . a woman . . . magnificent.* Odd that she'd not thought of herself in any terms at all until she'd walked among her peers. Only a few moments in her life to form distasteful perceptions of herself. And now, only a few moments more with this man to question those perceptions.

"My . . . um . . . upper limbs have ripples," she confided, needing to test the verity of his statements, needing to know if they were facts as he saw them or merely embellished flummery. "And they are plump."

"Really?" he said with a somber air, not at all put off by her blunt speech, but then he was reputed to be rather outspoken himself. "Is there anything else I should know before I take you on?"

"My weight goes up and down at will," she said crisply, voicing concerns that had been little more than fleeting thoughts before today, concerns that appeared to preoccupy the very society she sought to join. Now, by necessity, they preoccupied her as well. "I have a bit of a stomach that never goes away." She sighed. "I am too forthright for my own good . . . obviously."

"I strongly suspect that beneath their corsets and yards of fabric, most ladies have similar imperfections. They have simply learned to direct attention away from them by drawing the eye to their attributes. You need only learn to do the same, and under my tutelage, you shall succeed magnificently."

"I require a husband," she blurted, thoroughly entranced by his casual acceptance of her, throughly entranced by . . . him. An idea formed and gained dimension. A practical idea, which, she realized, was her first deliberate step away from the realm of girlish dreams.

He nodded. "You require a man who will cherish everything about you and see all the beauty in your countenance, my lady."

"I think you should be that man," she said, certain she was right. "Will you marry me?" Taken aback by her own boldness, she sat very still, her breath stalled, her eyes wide and fixed on the man across from her.

He arranged the folds of his neckcloth, as if he tried to divert, with more shallow concerns, the sadness that suddenly clouded his eyes. He sat forward and took her hands in his. "My lovely, proud lady, I have no doubt that you are a woman worth having. If I had any sense at all, I would employ all my considerable charm to court both you and your fortune. You would never bore me and I would revel in the sparks we would strike together. You are one of the few truly genuine people I have come across, and your bluntness is a delight. Even the thought of your . . . er . . . dimpled 'upper limbs' inspire in me some rather inappropriate interest." He gave her a look of regret which quickly changed to feigned humility. "But I have no sense beyond fashion and frivolity and have loved another for more years than I can recall. You deserve better than me for a husband."

Lorelei stared at him, completely caught up in the admiration he expressed—one particular part of his speech standing out from the rest. "Inappropriate interest?" she repeated. "Do you mean lust?"

He smiled with a mockery that did not offend. "Quite so, my lady, though I would caution you to find a suitable metaphor for that word—at least in company."

Awed by his confirmation, she was again rendered mute as she digested his speech, believing every word whether she ought to or not. She was not hideous or freakish, as she'd begun to believe while at court. She was not unappealing. She inspired lust—*inappropriate interest*—in a man such as Beau Brummell. Lorelei trembled as warmth radiated throughout her body. She feared rejection, hated it, was decimated by it, yet this man's refusal of her proposal sounded like approval, respect. "We do not always get what we deserve, Mr. Brummell. That, I have known all my life."

"Yes, I daresay you have." He gave her a cocky

grin. "You do, however, deserve me as a friend and a mentor. I am, by all accounts, a most exemplary friend."

A friend. She'd only ever had one—Harriet, with whom she had so much in common. They were both orphans, each titled in her own right, each wealthy and searching for a place to belong . . . a family. Now she understood why Harriet had said it was a frightening thing to be a lone female set farther apart by the status of wealth and a title in a society that felt threatened by, and therefore abhorred, such distinction.

Early on after meeting at school and being avoided by the others because of said titles and wealth, she and Harriet had formed their own family of friends and remained so ever since. Now this extraordinary man, who had gained the confidence of the future king, was offering his hand in friendship as well as to play the role usually occupied by a father or a brother.

Somehow, she found that to be more valuable than a husband. "Why?" she asked bluntly.

"Because I liked you the moment I saw you." He shrugged. "And I have been touched by you in a most profoundly unsettling way, Lady Winters," he said, as if to himself. "By the vulnerability you displayed as your expression changed so gradually from anticipation to realization to utter devastation. And by the loneliness I observed as you straightened and walked so proudly as if you knew you could count only on yourself. Never have I witnessed the transformation from naive young ingenue to sophisticated woman accomplished so quickly or so dramatically." He gave her a dark, brooding look followed by an odd smile—sheepish almost. "And because I need a friend as badly as you," he said baldly, then cleared his throat as if recovering from a momentary lapse of sanity. "In any case, I have need of a worthwhile project to allay boredom. If I do not stun society at least once a year I feel unfulfilled."

Worthwhile—a word she had avoided all her life. A question about herself she'd dared not contemplate since she'd been old enough to realize her parents had cared more for adventure and each other than the child they'd spawned then abandoned to a wetnurse and servants before she was old enough to smile. When word had arrived that they had died while exploring Egyptian tombs, she had been so long alone that she thought she was hearing of the unfortunate loss of two strangers who continued to live in her world as they always had in layers of paint on the canvas hanging above the mantel. Yet now she understood the loss she had suffered during infancy. Now she realized what she had never had.

In Brummell's countenance she saw compassion and a caring that was astonishing, coming from a man to whom she had not been formally introduced. He asked for nothing, yet offered her everything in the hand he held out to her.

"Do you really think it possible?" she asked, recalling the barely veiled rejection she'd suffered at court. "I have just now learned to give up childish dreams, you see, and feel quite without direction."

Again he shrugged, careful not to displace his artfully arranged neckcloth, or the hand he held out to her, palm up. "With my help, you will have them all lapping at your heels."

Her shoulders heaved and tears flowed freely down her cheeks as she ripped off her glove and placed her hand in his, soothed as his fingers closed around hers, warm and reassuring. She saw the sincerity in his eyes, and heard it in his sigh before he again donned insouciance much as she donned pride as a shield against the overwhelming loneliness the world pressed upon her.

Squaring her shoulders, she met his gaze through her tears. "It would be absurd for me to try to fit in with society," she said firmly. "Instead, I fancy making them fit in with me. Rather than trying to conform, I would much prefer being a nonpareil." She gave him a watery smile. "In any case, I am already that and it would take the least effort to accomplish."

Brummell chuckled. "A nonpareil, and, I suspect, an eccentric. Society loves nothing so much as an eccentric, myself being a prime example." He sat on the edge of his seat and kissed away the tears from her cheeks. "Forgive me, my lady, but I really must. . . ." He pressed his mouth to her cheek, then a soft brush over her lips.

She cried harder, sobbing into his mouth at the beauty of his gentleness, the comfort of it. She had never received such tender affection by anyone for any reason before.

"What a dashed inopportune time to develop a conscience," he muttered as he drew away from her, a sad smile curving the corners of his mouth. "And if you had displayed any hint of passion just now, it would have likely beat said conscience into submission and trotted me down the aisle before I could properly adjust my waistcoat."

"We might get on very well together," she said, as an uncommon sadness grew inside her at the dawning certainty that Beau Brummell was right. He was not the right man to be her husband, though it would have been nice to have both mate and friend in the same person.

He shook his head. "You, Baroness Winters, are the answer to my prayers, yet I cannot do it. You are too special to be so ill used. Instead, we shall be bosom bows and I will make it my quest to find for you the perfect man."

"There is no such thing," she murmured, shocked at how far she had strayed from her dreams during her brief encounter with the *ton* that afternoon.

"Not as such, but perfection is a matter of perception. Never doubt that there is a perfect man for you who will think you the perfect woman for him. I will not allow you to settle for less." Donning his gloves, he sat very properly straight in his seat. "Now, if I may prevail upon you to deliver me home, I will prepare for the assembly at Almack's tonight, where I will ask you to dance a scandalous total of three times. The tabbies will be shocked, all London will be agog, and our plan will be well on its way."

Lorelei said nothing as her heart again thumped in anticipation, her mind firmly rooted by determination. So she was tall. So she was a bit plump and had more womanly endowments than was fashionable. She possessed a comely face and grace and intelligence and wit. She also had enough wealth to order a new wardrobe designed to flatter rather than accentuate, and to expect delivery within a week. What did it matter if the garments were not in the current style? The ones she'd begun with hadn't served her. At least she ought to feel good about her appearance, and if it shocked the *ton,* she told herself she cared not a whit.

She could do anything. Rippled thighs and lofty stature aside, she had strength and pride and a small family of friends. She would manage whatever met her in the strange world she had entered because she always managed. She would endure whatever cruelties and disappointments lurked in her path because she always had. She would have what she wanted because, as Brummell said: she deserved nothing less. All that was left to do was set her illusions aside and want what was sensible rather than what was unattainable.

And, one way or another, she would believe that to be true, for if she fell to the persuasions of her own uncertainties and fear, she would deserve to have nothing.

Chapter 1

England
Late July, 1812

Adrian Rutland had heard it all and seen it all—
the strained courtesy with which he was received, the heated political discussions and snide
comments that immediately sprang to a dozen lips
when he was within earshot, the mixture of forced
indifference and barely concealed fascination of the
young debutantes he was vetting for the position of
his wife.

At least he'd thought he'd heard it all until Lady
Harriet, Countess Saxon, had invited him to the house
party she traditionally hosted every year before the
Little Season began. Lady Harriet had been one of the
few people who had sincerely welcomed him upon
his arrival from America and subsequent introduction
to society as Viscount Dane, heir apparent of his uncle, the Marquess of Wyndham. Because of her genuine kindness, he was less startled by her inclusion of
him onto her select guest list than by her bluntly
stated reason for doing so.

"I've a fancy to indulge in some matchmaking," she'd said during a visit to his uncle's London townhouse.

"And who is the victim?" he'd asked.

"Perhaps both of you, depending upon how you get on with one another."

"Then I suppose my question should be: who is your intended victim—besides myself, that is?"

Lady Harriet had frowned as she studied his expression, an expression he suspected was more indulgent than interested. Then she'd shrugged, risen from her perch on the marquess's brocade sofa, and secured her reticule on her wrist. "I do believe I'll surprise you. It will be interesting to observe your reaction . . . very interesting, indeed." She patted his arm on her way out. "Don't fret, Lord Dane. If you live up to my high opinion of you, I daresay you will immediately know her to be the right one." Again she shrugged as she paused in the doorway to glance back at him. "If you do not, then I will know you and she do not suit and will do my utmost to see that your paths do not cross again." With that, she'd descended the steps and approached her waiting carriage with the jaunty walk for which she was famous. Equally famous was her habit of taking for granted that no one would say her nay in anything, particularly when it involved a coveted invitation to one of her fêtes—an engaging arrogance when combined with the countess's youth and gentle nature.

Less interested in her invitation than in his own curiosity, Adrian informed his uncle that they were expected at Saxon Hill three weeks hence. He kept Lady Harriet's motives to himself, preferring to speculate in private as to the identity of the woman whose impression on him would determine whether Lady

Harriet would continue to hold him in high regard.

Every day since her visit, his imagination had run rampant, parading all manner of females through his mind—each more pale and dull than the last. Yet he had found not a single pert and pretty miss to his liking, and liking and respect mixed with a healthy portion of lust was far more desirable to him than simple aesthetic and material considerations—another attitude that did not find favor among the aristocracy.

His introduction into society had been less than auspicious, his success notable only by who deigned to do more than politely nod before bustling off to rip his character to shreds. He'd been quickly labeled too brass-faced for his own good—a brash American upstart too full of his own consequence to pay his respects to theirs. Who did he think he impressed with his arrogant stance and soft voice? How dared he set himself apart from his betters rather than mingle, thus affording them the opportunity to make a fool of him with their superior wit and worldliness? And really—how pedestrian of him to don those ghastly spectacles when he needed to study something closely, as if he were a mere secretary, when any man of breeding would use a quizzing glass. Worse, how could the Marquess of Wyndham—a thoroughly likable and solid fellow—bring an American into the *ton?* Better to let the name die out than pass the title and estates to one such as Adrian. After all, hadn't that young man's grandfather eschewed his heritage in favor of taking up residence in a country that even now was on the brink of war with Britain? Hadn't the marquess recognized the error of his own father's ways by leaving his family in the Colonies and returning to England, therefore embracing the king and country of his forebears?

But not so the upstart who would succeed him. He still traveled between England and America, straddling the fence rather than jumping to one side or the other. He engaged in trade, of all things, owning shipyards and a merchant fleet with his cousins and actually taking part in the enterprises. And he attended every social function only to stand apart, silently observing the *ton* as if *they* were the Curiosity of the Season instead of him.

And as he observed them, his curiosity grew as his every foray into society revealed yet another layer of the aristocracy in all its stages of wealth and power, another nuance to the games of romance and intrigue and social politics. He'd wandered the elegant parks scattered throughout the exclusive neighborhoods and prowled the warrens where the poor survived in ramshackle dwellings and filthy gutters, not to experiment in the many entertainments to be had but to learn about the country to which he now owed allegiance. After completing university in England—actually studying rather than carousing—he'd spent three years traveling the Continent, absorbing the nuances of European politics and culture, then another three years wandering throughout His Majesty's realm, seeing it all.

At least he'd thought he'd seen it all until *she'd* walked into the ballroom, not with the mincing steps of her contemporaries, but with the powerful glide of a stately ship cutting through the waves.

A very tall ship with very proud proportions.

It disconcerted him to suddenly meet her gaze not across a crowded room, but above the heads of the people crowding the ballroom. Never had he seen a woman with such height. But more than that was her presence, the sheer magnetism of it. Fascinated, he watched one person after another gravitate toward her as she reached the sidelines and turned to smile at the assembly in general.

The air seemed to come alive with her smile that held nothing back as lines bracketed her generous mouth and radiated from the corners of the largest eyes he'd ever seen. Eyes that sparkled and regarded everything with what seemed to be wry knowledge, as if their owner thought—and accepted—that she might be the subject of a cosmic joke.

For some reason, that acceptance disturbed him.

Adrian sauntered to another vantage point in an effort to have a better look at her and propped his shoulder against the framework of a door separating ballroom from outside terrace. She had to be over six feet tall, and her figure . . .

She was a veritable hourglass of feminine curves, though on a more ample scale, with full breasts and wide hips separated by a thicker-than-acceptable curve of waist. From what he could see, added to what his imagination supplied, she was likely described as plump or dumpy, though her long-waisted torso and regal carriage scarcely gave credence to such a description. As she shifted to listen to a young fop in puce satin breeches, the skirt of her gown molded to very well-rounded thighs topping off legs that appeared to begin at her aforementioned long waist.

Each time his gaze settled on a different part of her anatomy, it was quickly drawn back to her intriguing face. A face of patrician bone structure covered by the most beautiful complexion he'd ever seen. A face that appeared to have as many expressions as the sea, sparkling as she grinned, or lively as she laughed with a deep and hearty sound that seemed to make the air ripple, or soothing as she listened to a clearly dis-

tressed friend and murmured what Adrian imagined
to be advice and comfort. Her expressions were un-
contrived and completely honest. Completely disarming.

Completely, incredibly stunning.

The longer he studied her, the more everything else
faded in comparison. She did not slump in an effort
to diminish her height, or hunch her shoulders forward
in an effort to hide her generous figure, or cringe on
the sidelines in an effort to be inconspicuous so as
not to offend the current standards of beauty and
grace.

In his eyes, she *was* beauty and grace. A real
woman, rather than merely a female.

Even her attire was imposing. Her gown followed
the current fashion with its empire waist, but there her
concession to conformity ended. Rather than being
overtly pastel it was a soft, dull gold silk that draped
rather than flared out from just under the bosom.
Rather than being delicately scooped or off the shoulder, it rose to a high collar that embraced her neck
and flowed into tight long sleeves that seemed to
merge with her matching gold gloves. Over it all, she
wore a long sleeveless tunic-like affair of royal blue
satin embroidered with an oriental design of chrysan-
themums and exotic birds in gold and red and purple
that fell from her shoulders in a long column to the
tops of her feet. Her deep brown hair was pulled
sleekly back from her face and wrapped in a thick,
coiled bun on top of her head, the wisps around her
face natural rather than frizzed and artfully arranged.

He imagined that hair set free to fall around her
shoulders and down her back, straight and silky and
as abundant as her extraordinary body.

Though her costume was far from ordinary, it

suited her perfectly. In fact, he thought she would look absurd in the usual uniform of shy young debutante. Shy, she certainly wasn't. Nor was she as young as the misses gathered around her, all chattering at once.

She couldn't be real, yet there she was, impossible to miss, impossible to ignore, and, he suspected, impossible to forget.

Now he understood what the *ton* meant when naming someone an ''Original.''

He reached into his jacket pocket and retrieved a pair of wire-rimmed spectacles. Placing them on his nose and adjusting the earpieces, he blinked at the change in focus and stared more intently. With the improvement in his slightly nearsighted vision, he realized the lines that had appeared when she smiled were permanently etched at the corners of her eyes— such beautiful eyes—as if she'd smiled from the day of her birth. A birth, he judged, that had taken place at least five and twenty years ago, perhaps more.

Where had she been during the Season several months past? In mourning for a parent? Or a husband? Or did she simply prefer rustication to the diversions of the city?

One by one, she spoke with those who approached her, always bestowing that unrestrained smile as each took leave to join another group or accept an invitation to dance.

As popular as she obviously was, not once did she dance. From what Adrian could see, she hadn't been asked. Alone now, she observed the activity in the room with that same wry smile of amusement rather than resignation.

He muttered a curse as Lady Harriet rushed past him in the direction of the source of his interest. His mind rooted in fascination for the creature across the ballroom, he'd forgotten why he'd been invited to attend in the first place. Yet Lady Harriet had made no effort to introduce him to any of the females he hadn't yet met and all the young ladies were occupied.

All but The Original.

"Our hostess has gathered an impressive array of debutantes this year," his uncle said, as he took a place at Adrian's side. "You have but to choose." He heaved a sigh. "Sadly, our English beauties seem to hold little appeal for you."

Adrian's mouth quirked at his uncle's feigned aggrievement. After Adrian's failure to find interest in any of the potential brides paraded before him during the Season past, Uncle Robert had abandoned subtle hints in favor of blatant statements regarding his nephew's need to marry. That method had since given way to expressions of dismay and small criticisms of Adrian's impossibly high standards. And though he didn't give a damn what others thought of him, Adrian cared greatly for his uncle's feelings, which included concern for Adrian's solitary way of life.

"I am quite willing to honor my duty to marry and provide you with an heir, Uncle Robert," he said, perversely allowing his uncle to wallow in disappointment for a while longer. "I do, however, feel that a certain degree of interest is required if one is to pledge one's life to another, not to mention that a certain degree of lust is helpful in the act of procreation."

"Would that the males in our family were less discriminating," Robert said with another sigh. "Our contemporaries have no such problems."

"And if the law allowed, they would be quite content to hire women to breed their heirs, then go merrily on their way without the shackles of matrimony,"

Adrian commented, as he continued to stare at the Original. "But as you have often pointed out, Rutland men have a sense of romance bred into them. We do not settle for anything less than sloppy emotion coupled with raging lust."

"Still, England has a lovely assortment of young ladies," Robert said. "Surely you can find one who inspires both."

"I have—" Adrian broke off as his hostess suddenly turned and favored him with a brief yet penetrating glance, then slid her gaze to the object of his interest with a triumphant smile.

Realization hit him like a good swift kick. Lady Harriet aspired to pair him with The Original—a possibility that had not occurred to him. And as predicted, he'd immediately noticed the female half of Lady Harriet's plan. More than noticed, he amended. The moment he'd seen The Original, he'd indeed known she was the right one for him. He couldn't explain it, and with the sight of her to occupy his mind, he had no inclination to work it out.

A far more interesting puzzle at the moment was that such a woman required help in being paired. Her imposing presence aside, she exuded warmth and good disposition and an intriguing air of mystery—

"You have what?" Uncle Robert prompted. "You have given up your search? You have decided to return to America to find a bride?"

Taking pity on his uncle, Adrian gave him a fond smile. "I have found what I want."

"Found what?" Robert blinked. "A woman? Here?" He glanced around the room. "Where? Who?"

Placing a hand on Robert's shoulder, he turned his uncle toward the two women—one average in height and bright with vivacity, the other too extraordinary to describe easily. "There, Uncle. A woman worthy of the name."

Robert stared at the two women, then at Adrian, comprehension widening his eyes.

Favoring his uncle with an arch of his brows, Adrian smiled wryly and nodded toward The Original. "I want that one."

Chapter 2

Lorelei, Baroness Winters, better known as Merry for the last ten years, pretended not to see the dowager Countess Millbank beckon to her, an imperious summons to attend whatever gossip she had to share. Never could one simply buss the dowager's cheek, exchange simple pleasantries, and move on. Especially not Merry, who, the countess always pointed out, had nothing better to do since she'd been foolish enough to reject the suit of the dowager's grandson. As far as the countess was concerned, Merry was firmly on the shelf and therefore ought not mind sitting on the sidelines with the chaperones, widows, and matrons.

As far as Merry was concerned, she was young enough, wealthy enough, and eccentric enough to do exactly as she pleased, when she pleased—within reason, of course. Thankfully, her formidable stature and gregarious nature afforded her the luxury of being indulged where others would not be. Never was there a hint of scandal because she moved about freely with only a maid as chaperone. Never was she openly criticized for the eccentricities she cultivated and unabashedly displayed. But then, neither was she considered a threat to the ingenues, or a predator to the bachelors. She was safe, friend to both men and women, who ironically found vicarious pleasure in her flaunting of the conventions to which they were forced to adhere. To a man—and woman—they assumed she accepted her unmarried state as a foregone conclusion and even enjoyed it.

She rather resented that. She had a mirror and was not blind to her attributes. Though her body was not willowy and delicate, it wore clothing well and moved with grace. Her face was not unattractive with its refined bone structure, large, expressive eyes, and pretty smile all set in a clear complexion. Her hair was long and thick and richly brown, streaked with tawny lights. None turned to stone upon regarding her, and there had been a few men over the years who had actually displayed a certain attraction to her physical presence or her sharp mind or her outgoing and congenial nature. Unfortunately, each had been attracted to one feature or the other and found it too daunting to take on the whole.

"I fancy having a wife who will look up to me rather than the other way around," one suitor had said.

"I quite admire your form," another said, "but . . . ah—"

"But you would prefer a wife who did not outweigh you," she'd supplied, saving the man who was a full head shorter—and as a result, proportionately lighter—than she from having to dance about another bush in an effort to spare her feelings. Grateful and touched by his attempt at sensitivity to her feelings, she had patted him on the head and quit his company with regal bearing.

Even her personality seemed to overwhelm many of the eligible men of the *ton*, though they enjoyed her wit and bold speech well enough when a possible match was taken out of the equation.

"Please do not take offense, Lady Lorelei, but I have in mind a wife who is malleable and bereft of opinions of her own," one forthright young man stated.

"Must you make light of your . . . condition?" another had groused after she'd made some quip about her height.

Her condition, indeed. He'd spoken as if she were either breeding or missing a limb.

And no matter what her mirror told her or what she knew to be good about herself, there was always doubt, always fear in the back of her mind that others saw through different eyes than she and perceived her differently than she perceived herself.

Merry had never abandoned her search for a husband, though she had become more circumspect and practical in both her requirements and expectations over the years. Where she had once dreamed of being swept off her feet by a dashing noble, she now methodically studied the circumstances of each man who crossed her path for just the right elements of a tolerable demeanor, lack of illusions, and need of a good connection. She'd had enough of dreams. It had taken only one experience with bell-ringing love for her to realize it was not at all what it was cracked up to be.

She hadn't coped well with a broken heart. And as an orphan, she'd had no one to comfort her, much less advise her on how to go about it. Even Harriet had been at a loss to understand. How could she, when Harriet was slim and beautiful and had snared the only man for whom she'd set her cap, never mind that her convenient husband had embarked on his quest to travel the world the moment the ink had dried on the marriage papers. Merry had listened in horror to Harriet's explanation, remembering that her own parents had left her in just the same way. But she'd been an infant and had not known to miss what she'd never had until she was old enough to also understand that she could have it—later and by her own efforts.

Yet Harriet knew what she'd had and did not seem to mind losing it. Merry would mind greatly. After a lifetime of loneliness, she would certainly expect her husband to provide her with companionship, if nothing else.

Somewhere, there existed a man who would have enough confidence not to feel inadequate to her proportions and enough character to appreciate her qualities. Sensible, rather than lofty, expectations were less likely to disappoint, and compatibility, rather than lust, was less likely to be rejected. Convenience, amiability, a tolerance for her foibles, and a lack of revulsion in the marriage bed were quite enough for her, thank you.

Of course, she wisely kept such conclusions to herself. Beau's ideals would have been offended beyond recall at what he termed "settling for less than she deserved." Far easier to allow him to continue his search for the perfect man for her. What harm could it do? Perfect men for her, or anyone else, did not exist, and it had kept Beau happily fulfilled for ten years.

"Merry," Harriet called breathlessly, as she approached with an absent smile and wave for any who greeted her along the way. "Is he here yet?"

"Who?" Merry asked, knowing full well to whom her friend referred. She had confided to Harriet her interest in a certain gentleman as a prospective husband—a widower ten years her senior who was too immersed in hunting and fishing to notice how Merry looked or what Merry did. He took only absentminded notice of her small gestures of affection, and once, when she'd initiated a lusty kiss to test his reaction, he'd blinked and stared and then gone about his preparations for a jaunt to hunt some poor beast or another. Sighing, Merry conceded that perhaps a man who barely noticed any kind of passion might indeed be as close to perfect as she could hope for.

Fortunately, he had three attributes which Merry considered essential: he was tall and clean, and he had no tendencies to nurture fanciful notions of love.

"Don't be coy," Harriet replied. "Has he come or no?"

"No, he hasn't arrived, and I daresay he won't. He is likely still tromping through the bush in search of quail. He may or may not remember to attend your house party, depending upon his luck in the hunt."

"Hmmm. Then I suggest you take the opportunity to feast your eyes on Viscount Dane before you settle for Earl Stick-in-the-Mud."

"I saw Dane in Hyde Park last week," Merry said lightly, "and I saw the way he stares at every woman as if he were trying to see into her. At that rate he will never settle on a wife. Everyone knows that the less one sees, the better."

"How cynical you are, Merry."

"Of a certainty," Merry said blandly. "How else should I be after a man like Dane paid notice to every female in the park, yet didn't spare me a glance until tonight, when I am standing straight in all my over-endowed glory?''

''Well, of course he didn't notice you. In the park, you were sitting down and likely wearing a large hat, depriving him of the sight of 'all your glory.' '' Harriet glanced at her slyly. ''Did you want him to notice you?''

''Don't be absurd. Dane has too much wealth to count and is quite the most handsome man I have ever seen, with or without his spectacles,'' Merry said peevishly as the memory of Dane standing tall and lean and powerful led her mind astray. Handsome seemed a tame word to describe a man with deep, dark eyes that seemed to smolder and burn though the thickest of artifice, with sharply defined cheekbones and fine, straight nose, with a wide, provocative mouth that tempted with every smile—

''Merry? If I did not know better, I would think you were daydreaming,'' Harriet said, interrupting her musings.

Merry blinked and focused on Harriet, disoriented by the strength of the image that tempted her to follow Dane, to discover if his stare of admiration had indeed been for her.

''You were saying?'' Harriet prompted.

Merry sighed in disgust and gathered her thoughts. ''I was saying,'' she said firmly, ignoring Harriet's smug smile, determined to ignore and banish her fascination for one Viscount Dane, a man like any other. ''I was saying,'' she repeated, ''that every single woman in England is fascinated by his reticence and aloof manner, not to mention his 'barbaric' beginnings in the colonies. If he so much as crooked a finger, he would be besieged by young misses eager to accept his suit . . . and their parents would hypocritically dance with glee at being connected to the Wyndham fortune, all disapproval of him forgotten.'' Merry didn't bother to remind Harriet that she refused to enter into competition for the interest of a man— especially a man who inspired raging desire at a glance. Physical interest was not a trustworthy emotion and certainly not one upon which to build a marriage. ''He is obviously not the type of man for whom I would set my cap.''

''Heaven forbid you should acknowledge attraction to a handsome man of wit and intelligence, particularly if he shows an interest in you.'' Harriet sighed. ''I liked it better when you were naive and given to daydreams.''

Merry winced and glanced away from her friend. She, too, had liked it better when she was naive. Life was easier when one approached it with blinders on. Unfortunately, once one had stumbled a few times, one realized that the blinders must be shed. ''Well, the handsome Viscount Dane is certainly the stuff of daydreams,'' she said, pursuing the safer subject. ''But I would rather fix my attention on a man who does more than lurk about the fringes waiting for a likely female to fall in front of him—'' She broke off at the awareness tingling at the back of her neck. ''How odd. I have the distinct feeling that I am being watched.''

''I'm certain you are, in *that* rig,'' Harriet said, with a sweeping glance at Merry's attire. ''How could one miss you?''

''Precisely,'' Merry said, as she struggled not to rub her neck. ''No one deliberately watches me. Why should they, when I am so difficult to miss?'' Unable to restrain the urge, she glanced around.

Her gaze collided with the most extraordinary eyes

she'd ever seen above a pair of spectacles perched on a fine, straight nose. Such dark gray-green eyes set deeply within a frame of thick, long lashes and beneath imposing yet beautifully shaped brows. Eyes that regarded her with neither amusement nor amazement, but with blatant interest. . . .

Blatant and quite indecent. She felt as if he were slowly peeling her clothes away, one garment at a time. Panic seized and shook her at the thought.

Surely she was mistaken.

Yet she had the distinct feeling that she might be on the receiving end of a lustful gaze. Everything in her responded at once to the man who was just tall enough to meet her eye-to-eye, his lithe, muscular body tensed as if he were ready to pounce on her.

She wished she'd worn a corset.

She quickly turned away, completely undone by such nonsensical thoughts. The gaze she'd exchanged with the very man she and Harriet had been discussing had lasted only the briefest of moments, yet it was long enough to restore the naïveté she had just claimed to have outgrown. She'd imagined admiration in that glance. Desire. And she'd felt it striking deeply and swiftly inside her, evoking a response she'd sworn never to feel again. Tingling breasts and quivering thighs meant trouble; they reduced a woman to fawning and stupidity.

"Oh, my," Harriet said. "I do believe he was going to ask you to dance, Merry."

"The man might be myopic but I doubt he is blind," Merry snapped, and abruptly walked away. Merry imagined Harriet standing where she had left her, mouth open in shock. Merry was shocked herself, not by the remark, but by her delivery. Never did she fall into self-pity, yet her voice had sounded quite full of that wretched emotion.

"Merry," Harriet called, as she rushed to catch up with her.

Closing her eyes for the space of a sigh, Merry halted as her friend reached her side.

"He *was* going to ask you to dance; I'm certain of it," Harriet said softly. "Why not give him a chance? You'll not regret it."

"Why does it matter to you?" Merry asked, as suspicion tickled the back of her mind.

"It doesn't," Harriet said quickly . . . too quickly.

Merry fixed her with a narrow-eyed stare and saw guilt written in every pretty feature.

"Well, it doesn't matter to *me*." Harriet met her gaze defiantly. "But I do believe—truly—that it might matter to you. Dane sees everything differently than the others. And he isn't dull," she rushed on, giving Merry no opportunity to speak. "He doesn't waste words on minutiae, like the rest of us. He's quite as brave and strong as you are. It takes a great deal of courage—as you are well aware—to set one's own rules rather than to blend in with the crowd. I think he would suit you better than—"

Suspicion became certainty. "You didn't," Merry said flatly. "Please tell me you didn't arrange for us to meet tonight." She could tolerate Beau's occasional foray into matchmaking, but she expected more sense from Harriet.

"I can't, Merry." Harriet swallowed and glanced away.

"You, of all people—"

"And who better?" Harriet interrupted, her gaze once more direct and defiant. "I watch you day after day and year after year being all things to all people—

friend, confidant, advisor. I watch the men—stupid, stupid men, I might add—running to you in droves for counsel on everything from their wardrobes to their romances, treating you as if you were neither female nor male, but some sexless creature put on earth for their convenience.'' She paused for a breath. ''And you—*you*—go along with them while convincing yourself that you enjoy helping them live their lives rather than living your own.'' Extending her forefinger, Harriet poked Merry in the shoulder with each subsequent word. ''I saw you flush when Dane looked at you. And I'll wager you experienced other responses as well.''

''You're mad,'' Merry choked out, as she reminded herself that it was those very responses she sought to avoid. Even now her blood was flowing hot, her nerves were vibrating with awareness, and her mind raced with fantasies of Viscount Dane— She shook her head, banishing the images. ''And I am equally mad to listen to this.''

''You'll be mad only if you turn your back on an opportunity you may never have again with a man you'll never find the likes of again. He noticed you the moment you entered the room, Merry. He saw you with the eyes of a man who appreciates the extraordinary.''

Sensation doubled at the implication that Viscount Dane might see her as more than a large frame and passably attractive face. That he might think her extraordinary . . . desirable.

With a quelling look, she shook off Harriet's grasp on her arm and stalked away, refusing to fall prey to foolish notions and false hope.

Sighing, she wandered toward the doors leading to the gardens, her embarrassment spiking as an image of those deep, dark eyes popped into her mind. Embarrassment, of all things. And for what? Because he might have heard her remarks about him? Or because she had been so foolish as to imagine that he had looked at her with desire . . . that she had actually entertained visions of sharing passion with him? Either way, it *was* foolish. Everyone knew that she always spoke her mind. They expected it. More likely he was aghast at her proportions and simply wanted to confirm that his eyes weren't deceiving him.

Those eyes again. They gleamed in her thoughts like beacons lighting the way into a dream she'd vowed never to entertain again.

Midway through her second Season, she'd fallen completely in love with a man of charm and good looks and sufficient height to look down at her rather than the other way around. He'd swept her into a courtship of compliments, devoted attentions, and an expressed impatience to meet her at the end of a church aisle. Every time his hand took hers, or he looked at her in a certain way, her heart melted into a pool of need in the pit of her belly. She lived for his affection, for his small caresses on her shoulder, for his whispers of love in her ear.

She'd been completely undone by him, allowing both her dreams and her theretofore unknown passionate nature to surface unchecked. She'd lain awake nights fantasizing about what it would be like when he finally kissed her, touched her. She'd wandered through each day in a haze of dreams—of life filled with affection and approval, of having someone to touch and hold and depend upon happily ever after.

Harriet had adored the man and began planning a wedding that she insisted should take place at the chapel on her estate. Beau, her friend and self-appointed brother, had approved of her choice, and offered broad hints about being chosen to walk her down the aisle. Lorelei had begun to choose names for their first five children.

Five months later, Harriet had ranted about the stupidity of men, and Beau had shaken his head and despaired at her reaction to being rejected by the man of her dreams. But then, Beau had been the victim of unrequited love for so long, he did not understand her determination to patch the cracks in her heart and move on. She thought it odd that women were criticized for being romantics when Beau was proof that men were tragically addicted to impossible ideals. The only difference as far as she could discern was that women openly spoke of and acted upon their feelings, while men hid theirs as if they were twisted fantasies too lurid for the light of day.

Still, the man she had loved hadn't had a jot of trouble expressing his feelings to her. Feelings of shock when he'd kissed her and she'd responded with great fervor. Feelings of disgust that she would not only accept his display of affection without a single coy protest, but incite him to more intimate caresses as well.

She'd pointed out that it had been entirely his idea to touch her breast; she had simply enjoyed the pleasure of it. He'd jerked away from her and expressed his disapproval of her lack of restraint that better suited a whore or gypsy than a virgin. "And how far would you have gone?" he'd asked coldly. "Would you have removed your clothing—whether I wished it or not—and welcomed the act itself?"

"I don't suppose you'll ever know," she'd said, deciding that if he wanted her to be coy, she would be so in her reply. "I am curious as to how you know of the nature of whores and gypsies," she'd added, praying she would get through this, praying she would not collapse into a heap of misery at his feet.

Never allow them to see you weep, she silently recited Beau's advice. *Never, ever allow them to know how weak and fragile you really are,* she added—a conclusion she'd reached shortly after her humiliating presentation at court.

Her fiancé had formally requested that their marriage plans be canceled, and gentleman that he fancied himself to be, offered to allow her to take credit for changing her mind. "After all, a gentleman would never speak publicly of a lady's lack of restraint."

Restraint—that word again. If love and the display thereof required restraint, then it certainly was not what she'd thought it to be. "Then I shall return the favor and refuse to speak of your lack of honor," she retorted.

"If I had no honor, I would have taken advantage of your behavior," he said.

"Really? Then one wonders why you *incited* it in the first place."

"I loved you," he gritted, "and thought to merely express my affection. It never occurred to me that *your* affection would be so . . . common."

Loved. He'd loved her. Could love disappear so quickly because of one mistake? Was love, in truth, riddled with conditions that must be met for it to survive? It would seem so. With that thought another illusion—perhaps her last—suffered a slow, tormented death.

"In other words," she said softly, to keep her voice from shattering, "you can love me only if I meet your conditions in expressing *my* love."

He'd stared at a point over her shoulder, silent.

"I see," she'd said, even more softly. "Then you are most certainly correct. It is best that we part ways, for any conditions that are placed on *my* marriage will not be those imposed upon me, but those to which I agree." It had been all she could do to turn and walk away, to hold her head high until she reached her carriage, and for the second time in her life, huddle in the corner with tears flowing down her cheeks.

For the first time in her life, she'd felt shame—in a passionate nature she hadn't known she possessed, in her body, which he'd implied he had no desire to see. Paralyzed by mortification and speechless with pain, she had seen it all as he described it—sordid and ugly, mocking what had touched her so profoundly.

She'd dashed away her tears and stiffened her spine, somehow knowing, even at nineteen, that she could not slink away in shame. That she had to fight back as she'd always fought against being a victim— of loneliness, of fear, of her own inadequacies. She'd never belonged. Nothing had changed except that she had been initiated to passion and exposed to the truth. She was a creature of strong needs and the even stronger urge to satisfy them, to share the love and affection that had apparently been awaiting the proper time to surface.

She, too, was strong. She'd had to be to grow up with only governesses and bankers and solicitors to guide her. She'd survived a lonely childhood and still had the ability to smile. She'd fallen in love and then plunged into disillusionment. She would survive that, too.

Somehow.

Sadly, survival always had a price. She'd paid for it with her ability to dream and to believe that beauty was in the eyes of the beholder, that it was seen as a whole rather than only the parts of a person that met with approval. And when two other men had shown interest in her and treated her with charm and consideration, thus encouraging that part of her that needed to touch and express what she felt, she'd been too wary to respond to them.

She shook her head and stalked past a statue of one Greek deity or another, immediately thinking that Dane put even those silent heroes to shame. How long had it been since she had felt such an overwhelming awareness of a man?

Not until Lord Dane had subjected her to a brief yet thorough scrutiny that had jolted all the old feelings she'd tucked away in her memories. They had merely stirred, she reminded herself, barely disturbing the dust they'd gathered over the years. Never again would she allow them to awaken to plague her and drive her to illusions, much less to thoughts of wearing corsets and worrying about how a man might see her. Never again would she allow physical responses to dictate her behavior. Never again would she believe that beauty was in the eyes of the beholder without condition. Everything had conditions attached, even love.

She was what she was and no corset in the world could disguise it.

Embarrassment swelled to a cold lump of humiliation. What had Harriet been thinking? More importantly, what must Viscount Dane think now that he'd seen—and heard—her?

She gave an inelegant snort as she passed another statue, this one a marble copy of the Venus de Milo in all her armless splendor. She really would have done well in ancient Greece, where statues were erected in homage to an amply endowed female form—

She frowned as she passed the figure. Venus couldn't possibly have moved. Shaking her head, she took another step and heard a rustle. She stopped short and whirled around.

A man with dark hair and deeply set eyes leaned against the hip of the marble goddess, his brow creased in concentration, his spectacles dangling precariously from his hand as he swung them back and forth.

For the first time in recent memory, Merry had an insistent urge to run the other way.

Chapter 3

Merry resented her cowardice. She resented Dane for causing it. Whether she wanted to leave or not, her pride stubbornly refused to allow her the choice. She was not and never had been a coward. She would not become one now because of the likes of Viscount Dane.

On the other hand, if she remained standing where she was or simply turned and casually strolled in another direction, it didn't appear that Dane would notice. She could be another statue for all the awareness he displayed.

Given her lack of desire to converse with him, she should be relieved. Contrarily, her dratted pride took umbrage that he was so oblivious to her presence when only moments ago she'd been ridiculously giddy with the idea that he found her desirable. After years of being an afterthought, a duty, and often completely overlooked, she had vowed that whatever else society chose to think or feel about her, indifference would not be a part of it.

She glared at Dane, at the spot on the ground at which he stared so intently, then back at Dane again.

He still hadn't moved, though the crease between his brows seemed to have deepened, giving every impression of his being altogether absent while his body held his place in the corporeal world.

So much for Harriet's theory that he'd been interested in having a dance with Merry.

So much for her own notion that he might have been interested in anything about her.

So much for her dratted, blasted pride.

She could walk away and he wouldn't even know she'd been there, she told herself, as she took one step and then another. She could continue on the path, walk right in front of him, and even sweep the hem of her tunic to keep it from touching him, and the rustle would not penetrate his thoughts—

Dane's gaze shot up and over to her as her tunic brushed his leg, proving her speculations wrong. He might be immersed in deep thought but he was completely alert and aware of what went on around him. If he had been absentminded or given to preoccupation, she might have been able to think kindly of him.

Instead, all she could think of was escape from the danger of his presence, his appeal, his hot, brooding gaze sliding over her. . . .

From the corner of her eye she saw that he still stared at her, studying her from the top of her head to the bottom of her hem . . . studying her without regard for her efforts to appear aloof, and without mercy for the secrets she strove to hide beneath artfully sewn fabrics. . . .

Wide hips and plump thighs and just a "bit of a belly," as Harriet said.

Just then it felt immense, like a lump of dough

rising with every moment he stared at her. Worse, she imagined that he still watched as she passed him by, giving him a view of her back and imagining that she waddled like a plump bird when the situation demanded that she glide with regal grace.

She quickly rounded a bend in the path. Knowing she was at last out of his sight, she picked up her skirts and hurried toward the door tucked beneath a cascade of ivy at the side of the manor. Thank heaven Harriet locked the inside door to the room she used as an office in which to conduct estate business. She groped behind a large urn for the key to the outside door Harriet had hidden for occasions when escape was needed. Here Merry would find privacy and peace.

Unlocking the door and slipping inside, Merry strode across the large room where her friend spent so much of her time balancing accounts, making decisions concerning the earl's holdings and settling the disputes of her tenants—all of which Harriet's husband should be doing, if they only knew where to find him. She paused at the marble fireplace and lit several candles, removed her gloves, then paced in the other direction, heaping invective on the head of the missing earl to keep from pondering the nature of her reactions to Dane. Halting to pour a glass of sherry, she stared blankly at the spill of wine on her hand. Her shaking hand.

She had not been this rattled over being rejected by the man she'd once loved. But then she hadn't stood naked in front of a looking glass to examine every detail of her body until his attitude had raised the fear that if she had been dainty and more gently shaped, he would not have viewed her response with distaste and disapproval. Not when gossip continually circulated about this couple or that falling prey to carnality, before marriage or outside of it. She was not so stupid as to believe others did not embrace passion. England had too many bastard children to think otherwise. Women might dutifully produce an heir, but to conceive children on the wrong side of the blankets could only be a result of unrestrained emotions and expressed need. Yet no man had ever made an improper suggestion to her, prompting her to conclude that she was not the sort of woman who could get away with it. And though she hated the notion that it might be because of her form, she had yet to find another reason.

Dane, blast him, had brought it all back to her with his penetrating stare that showed nothing of distaste and disapproval. With that stare, he'd made her feel . . . quite beautiful.

She bent over to sip from the overfull glass, then picked it up and began to pace again while reciting the truths she had memorized. Of course her belly was not a mound of dough, and years of training ensured that she most definitely did not waddle. She was properly shaped and proportioned—

Raising the glass to her lips, she drank half the contents. Oh, yes indeed, she was properly shaped and proportioned. She had everything she should in all the right places. She simply had more of "everything" than the average woman.

What she wouldn't give to be average, rather than ample.

She'd give even more to be restored to the complacency she'd enjoyed before she'd entered the ballroom and met Dane's gaze above the heads of Harriet's guests.

A chuckle broke past her lips at the absurdity of it.

Had it been only last week she'd heard some pretty young thing rhapsodizing about how she'd met the gaze of her "one true love" *across* a crowded room?

Other women were impressed by a handsome face or an generously filled wallet or a poetically glib tongue. Merry was impressed when she saw a man's face before she saw the top of his head.

A drift of night air chilled the back of her neck as she heard the outside door open, then shut again. She didn't turn to see who had intruded on her. Of course it had to be Harriet. This was her private domain, forbidden to all except during the hours Harriet set to hear disputes and settle accounts. Merry was the only other person allowed to come and go at will.

The chill in her neck warmed as awareness tingled over her skin. The silence she'd sought seemed suddenly alive with expectation.

It was those eyes staring at her; she just knew it. Dark eyes stripping her of control and reason. Deep eyes that seemed to see far too much.

She surreptitiously glanced at the mirror hanging above a chinoiserie table against the wall in front of her, seeing what she knew she would see, yet still surprised by the sight of him standing behind her, his gaze trained on her, his posture utterly still and alert. She, too, remained still and waited, reluctant to look directly at him, to see what could not possibly be present in those eyes.

Not ridicule, or disbelief, or even simple curiosity, but interest . . . admiration.

The silence lingered and seemed to vibrate over her, inside her. She had to say something, do something—anything to divert the gaze that felt as if it were boring right through her. "You are quite rude," she said, as she slowly turned, meaning to sound offhand and knowing she'd failed miserably. She sounded breathless, agitated.

His mouth quirked up at one end in an odd bemused expression, as if half smiled in discovery while the other half pondered the nature of that discovery. "So I've heard," he said softly. "If listing my faults will initiate conversation between us, please do so."

She opened her mouth and snapped it shut. Just then he had no faults that she could see. Unless it was that he was entirely too seductive—in his voice, his manner, his appearance. His eyes seemed liquid as he lifted his gaze to hers, his bold, sweeping brows arched in continual inquiry. His sculpted mouth appeared too wide on first sight, yet provoked carnal musings on second. The lean muscles of his long body seemed relaxed and fluid, lending an altogether too-sensuous quality to his every movement.

It was there now as he strolled toward her, slowly, as if he were approaching a skittish horse. "I have heard that I am a brash American upstart. That I am a dead bore, preoccupied with books rather than cultivating the social skills necessary to charm and impress the Upper Ten Thousand. It is said that in my preoccupation, I set out for an afternoon ride in the country and became lost for five years." He paused and held his arms away from his body. "Fortunately, I have one redeeming quality: I have chosen my tailor well."

She didn't think his tailor had anything to do with it as her gaze swept over wide shoulders, broad chest, flat stomach, and long, muscular legs—all of which would appear equally elegant clothed in rags. Or nothing at all.

She swallowed at the sudden vision in her imagination, of shadow and light playing over tanned skin—

everywhere—as he approached her with that slow, lazy swagger . . . in a bedchamber . . . or in a moonlit garden.

Silence fell again. Dane tore his gaze away from her and glanced over his shoulder at the door as if he were nervous.

But it was she who was nervous as he again regarded her with unsettling calm. Her palms were damp. Her heart lurched in her chest.

He cleared his throat, swiped at the back of his neck, and stared down at the floor as if something were written there. "This is mad," he said with a hint of amusement. "After losing the courage to ask you for a dance and not finding the fortitude to speak to you in the garden . . ." He shook his head, a boyish gesture that eased the tension surrounding her.

She leaned back against Harriet's desk and waited for him to continue, feeling both breathless and more in control than she had all evening.

He heaved a sigh. "Damn, it shouldn't be so difficult." Lifting his gaze to her, he reached for her hand, could not quite reach it, and awkwardly continued the motion to sweep his hand over the back of his neck again. "I am Adrian Rutland, and I am willing to grovel if you will make this easier for me."

"Viscount Dane, I know," she said mechanically, put out by the hoarseness of her voice. "I am Lorelei, Baroness Winters, and without a clue as to what it is you find so difficult."

His mouth quirked into that half smile of discovery, revealing engaging indentations on either side of his mouth. "As am I. I've not found it particularly difficult to speak with a woman before, though in this case I am intimidated by Lady Harriet's expectations of me."

Merry stiffened at the reminder of Harriet's machinations, at Dane's confirmation that he was a willing accomplice for reasons she couldn't begin to fathom. "To what expectations do you refer?"

He rolled his gaze to the ceiling, a mocking gesture that appeared directed at himself rather than at her. "I believe I have put my foot in it, and must apologize."

"It is I who must apologize, sir. I cannot think why Harriet would manipulate you in such a way."

"I make it a point never to allow myself to be manipulated," he interrupted, "and she made no secret of her intentions. The only thing I did not know was your name—"

"Nevertheless," Merry cut in abruptly, hoping to end the encounter as quickly and painlessly as possible. "Harriet is not here to see, so you are absolved of any duty—"

He shook his head. "My duty was to know—to *notice*—you immediately upon your entrance." He met her gaze over the rim of the spectacles that had slipped just below the bridge of his nose. "I performed my duty admirably and have not been able to stop noticing you since."

She swallowed against the sudden dryness in her mouth and willed her usual pragmatism to prevent her from wrongly interpreting such an intriguing statement. Surely he meant nothing more than the obvious. As she had reminded Harriet earlier, she was difficult to miss. Of course that's what he meant.

Of course, she repeated to herself, refusing to acknowledge the disappointment of it. "Well, then, since you have so admirably acquitted yourself, I will absolve you of any further responsibility."

"I think not." His mouth arched as if in challenge.

"I am determined that we will become acquainted."

Tilting her head she listened to his voice, to the deepness and softness of it, and stared at the long elegance of his body. "Acquainted?" The word seemed tame to her. Too tame to contemplate when coupled with the intent burn of his gaze. She cleared her throat and stiffened her spine. "Whatever for?"

His smile straightened, widened, then faded into sobriety. "Because we are each curious about the other," he replied. "Or because regardless of what transpires between us tonight, you will find me on your doorstep tomorrow."

Between us. It was the second time he'd used the phrase. The second time he'd said it as if it held more than two words . . . as if it held a promise. Standing as tall as she could, she raised her chin to give the impression of looking down at him, though he topped her six feet by a good two inches. "Then I shall take my leave of you now," Merry said, unable to bring herself to reject any promises he had the inclination to make. "I should hate to be caught out here—" Wincing, she broke off her sentence. How trite she sounded. How *coy.*

How dreadful. Never was she coy. Flirting or the desire to do so had never been one of her failings. She left such things to the young misses who were pretty enough to have their obvious posturings indulged. "If you will excuse me?"

"No, I will not," he said gravely, as he stepped nearer and slid his fingers under her palm, lowered his head, brushed his provocative lips over the back of her hand. "At least, not until I have the direction of your doorstep."

Excitement shivered up her spine at his insistence; a frisson of heat radiated up her arm at the brush of his lips. Her heart leapt in anticipation, as if it believed, as she would not, that he meant what he said—

No. Never again, she told herself. Never again would she succumb to witless attraction for a man. And certainly not this man, whose air of confidence belied his stated awkwardness with the moment, and whose calm manner unsettled her greatly.

Yet her mouth dried even more as he lingered over her hand. She swallowed as he began to straighten, his head tilting to look up at her. . . .

His spectacles slid off his nose, clung precariously by one earpiece, and fell to the floor at their feet.

A chuckle filled the room as he straightened and bent his head to stare down at the spectacles with a bleak sigh.

A sigh that felt as if it were sinking into her—a poignant sound that struck a familiar chord in her. A sound eloquent of his awareness of his shortcomings, his acceptance of them, even if they extended only to having a nose too straight to hold a pair of spectacles properly in place. In the few moments she'd had to observe him, she'd discerned no shortcomings of any substance. He was blunt rather than rude, engaging rather than boorish, interesting in his foibles—if they could be termed as such—rather than odd.

He shoved his hands in his pockets and nudged the spectacles with his impeccably shod foot. "Can I possibly make a bigger ass of myself?"

More sensation rippled through her at the low timbre of his voice, the heat of his nearness, the seduction of his mouth crooked by wry humor. Humor directed at himself, his expression offering no excuses and no apologies for what he was perceived to be. His brows arched in inquiry and his direct gaze offered her the opportunity to find out for herself what was true and what was not. His air of quiet confidence needed no blustering to prove he was worth the effort and his easy stance indicated that he knew it.

"Shall we find out over a glass of sherry?" she asked, with a sigh of her own and the nasty suspicion that she might regret making that effort to her dying day.

Chapter 4

Adrian hoped he wouldn't regret this. Not only was it highly improper to be alone in a private room with an unmarried woman, but he had no desire to discover just how easy it would be to truly make an ass of himself.

Under normal circumstances it wouldn't bother him. He'd never given a damn what others thought of him as long as his conscience was satisfied and he knew he'd done his best. But the circumstance was far from normal and had nothing to do with conscience. For the first time in his adult life he wanted more than his best. He wanted to be more than he was. For the first time in his life the opinion of another outside his family mattered to him. For the first time in his life he felt at a loss as to how to get what he wanted.

No longer was he satisfied with being a man of thought and ideas and methodical implementation of those ideas. He wanted the extraordinary woman before him to see him as an extraordinary man, a dashing figure who left a trail of wistful sighs and lustful thoughts in his wake. A fearless hero who captained his ship, *Bifrost*, vanquishing foes with one arm while sweeping this woman off her feet with the other. . . .

He was going to make an ass of himself.

No doubt he looked like one in this setting. He shifted uncomfortably and scouted out his surroundings for the chair most likely to support him. How Lady Harriet managed to conduct business here was beyond him. He couldn't imagine workmen or tenant farmers tracking up the Aubusson carpets patterned in shades of gold and green and lilac. Nor could he envision merchants, bankers, and solicitors finding ease on the delicate furniture upholstered in rich royal purple, moss green, and sunshine yellow. Only a fainting couch covered in a bright floral in the same three colors seemed large enough to accommodate a man's larger frame, yet no man of his acquaintance would feel comfortable among such a profusion of woven flowers.

As Lorelei poured glasses of sherry, he wandered about, studying the chintz fabric covering the couch, the baskets of dried flowers, the large desk that was the focal point of the room. The only windows were round affairs set in the wall well above eye level, denying its occupants—or visitors—the mental escape of staring out at the gardens. Everything in the large office was both feminine and aggressive.

"Intimidating," he muttered. "She is throwing her femininity in the face of every man who comes in here."

"Exactly," Lorelei said, a note of surprise in her voice. "How did you know?"

"Because I'm feeling very intimidated," he answered bluntly. "I'll wager Lady Harriet gets what she wants."

"Quite often," Lorelei said, as she handed him a glass of sherry, then sat on the fainting couch. "The decor is a shameless bid to arouse the protective, and indulgent, instincts of the males with whom she must conduct business. They are in her domain and are not allowed to overlook that for a moment." She sipped her wine. "I'm amazed that you understand that. Others are uncomfortable in here but they don't know why—other than the flowers and odd combination of colors, that is." Her mouth curved up in a Mona Lisa smile. "Is this where she persuaded you to fall in with her matchmaking plans?"

"She visited me at my uncle's house—and she did not persuade. She asked and I agreed."

"But you did not know who . . . a pity. You deserved some warning."

"I did," he said gravely.

Lorelei winced. "What, no gallant protest?"

Straightforward, he thought, as he regarded her grimace. No pouting, yet no stiff upper lip, either, over what could easily be taken as insult. Only honesty as she voiced her thoughts and expressed what she felt, the same honesty for which he was so often criticized. Perhaps that is what drew him to her. "Having no warning that the lady I was being set up to meet was an Original, I did not rehearse gallantry or charm. I wish I had. I would have liked to have made a better impression on you."

"I prefer your honesty to that drivel," she shot back. "An Original, indeed."

"Indeed," he said firmly, at a loss as to what to say that might convince her of his sincerity. Considering the way she visibly stiffened and set her glass on a table beside the couch as if she were about to rise and leave, he'd no doubt said enough. He'd never known a woman who became defensive at being paid a compliment. He lowered his head and rubbed the side of his nose with his forefinger. "If I cannot be honest, which I much prefer, and I cannot employ charm, which you obviously don't take seriously—" He angled a glance at her. "You leave me little with which to capture your interest."

"If I were not interested, I would not have invited you to remain here." She grabbed her glass and fidgeted with the stem. "Exactly what did Harriet say . . . about me, I mean?"

He frowned at the tentative quality in her voice. Uncertainty seemed at odds with his impressions of her. "Only what I've already told you. Lady Harriet said that if I lived up to her high opinion of me, I would immediately *notice* you. And then she said I would thank her. I have already done so."

"Of course you noticed me—"

"Of course," he agreed. "I noticed your smile first. I noticed your laughter and lack of affectation. I noticed how easily you move about in your skin, even though it is not the skin you would have chosen for yourself."

She sucked in a breath. "Well, that's certainly a unique way to bring up my . . . skin."

"You expected no less."

"On the contrary, I did not expect it at all." She leaned back and relaxed her hold on the wineglass. "I find it most entertaining to observe the extraordinary lengths to which people go *not* to notice or mention my appearance." She shrugged. "It takes them a while to recover from their shock, I suppose."

"I was stunned," he said conversationally.

"I beg your pardon?"

"Stunned, not shocked," he explained. "You are stunning, therefore I was stunned."

"And what am I to say to that?" she mused aloud, as she stared into the glass she clutched between both hands, uneasy again.

"If you took it as I intended it, you should say thank you very graciously and then change the subject."

"Are you so desperate for a wife that you would lie?"

He hadn't been until he'd seen her. But something in her manner warned him not to reveal that. Her challenging glare reinforced his impression that she had no experience with truth in the form of a compliment. That, for some reason, compliments hurt her. He managed to meet her glare with a bland gaze. "I am most definitely desperate for a friend . . . to begin with," he said softly, giving her what she could accept and what he could live with until he had the opportunity to more fully examine his reactions to her.

A hero he was not, but neither was he a bumbling idiot. At least, not usually.

She, too, appeared to be reacting, but not as he would have wished. She breathed deeply as if he'd surprised her, then exhaled as if relieved. He would have liked some sign of disappointment, some indication that she might be interested in more than friendship.

"Our society is not a kind one," she said on the last of her sigh.

He winced at the compassion in her voice, evidence that she did have experience with society's lack of kindness. For himself, he didn't give a damn if they were kind to him or not. He knew why he was here and what he wanted to do. Society would become used to it—and him—in time.

"Is it the same in your country?"

He shook his head. "England is my country, but if you refer to America, then no, it isn't quite the same." Distracted by the change in direction of the conversation, he stared down at the patterns woven into the carpet. "America was colonized and built by people who would not, or could not, conform. Ironically, the more civilized and structured the States become, the less tolerance the citizens have for the very qualities that made the country possible."

"I see you are a philosopher."

"A dreamer," he corrected, as he again searched for a place to sit and settled for leaning against the edge of the desk.

"No wonder you are so out of place here. England is not a land for dreamers."

"That depends on the dream, doesn't it?"

"I rather thought that most dreams were the same."

"How can they be, when dreamers are not the same?"

"I'm quite certain I can find an argument for that if I think about it," she retorted dryly, then took a sip of her wine. "Ah, I have it!" she exclaimed on a gulp. "If dreamers are different, there must be precious few of them, since most people of my acquaintance are frighteningly alike."

"Do you believe that?"

"No, not really." She smiled up at him, brightly, seductively if she but knew it. "But it sounded rather interesting and I am hopelessly out of practice in debates of this nature."

Engaging, he thought, as he studied her relaxed posture. *Charming, intelligent, and stimulating . . . in more ways than one.* He wondered if she was at all aware of herself in such terms. "It's quite possible that it is our dreams that determine whether we are misfits or not."

A shadow seemed to pass between them then, dulling her expression, the lively interest in her eyes. "Or our lack of them," she whispered, as if she were speaking only to herself, of herself. Her smile returned, yet it wasn't the same. It was brittle, fragile, forced. "At least you and I know what we are. There are those who have no such insight."

"We are misfits only because rather than hiding in shame for our deficiencies, we brazen it out by flaunting them."

"You mean that if we did try to hide our deficiencies, we would be like everyone else? How dreadfully maudlin." She rose to her full height. "And a moot point in my case, as it would be impossible for me to hide my peculiarities." She strode to a spot beside the desk and gracefully bent at the knees to retrieve something from the floor. "You, on the other hand, have hope. You could keep your politics to yourself, affect a proper English accent, and—" She straightened and held up her hand to display what she had picked up. "—replace these with a quizzing glass hung about your neck on a chain. Violà! You would no longer be *mal à propos.*"

He raised his hand, felt the bridge of his nose, his eyes. His spectacles. In his fascination for Lorelei, he'd forgotten them, forgotten even that he'd dropped them. He grinned sheepishly. "And now we know that I *can* make a bigger ass of myself."

"My gardener has a pet jackass of which I've grown quite fond," she quipped, as she slipped the spectacles on his nose, adjusted the earpieces over his ears, then straightened the set of the lenses. ''I could put a straw bonnet on you and feed you an apple every morning.''

''And scratch my ears?'' he asked, disarmed by her easy teasing and even easier manner of touching him, and unaccountably annoyed that she responded so easily to humor and lightness while distrusting anything of a serious nature. At that moment, with her body so close to his that he could see the golden lights in her brown eyes and the similar glints of gold in her deep brown hair, feel the bump of her hip against his, inhale the flowers and spice of her fragrance, he imagined her hands doing more to him than scratching behind his ears.

''Only if you behave,'' she retorted, then caught her breath as she met his gaze, her hand lingering on his cheek . . . trailing down his jaw . . . pausing on his shoulder and remaining there.

The last thing he wanted to do was to behave. Not here, where the air seemed to take on a sultry warmth scented by exotic flowers and a seductive woman. Not with her standing so close, her teasing smile softening to a wistful cupid's bow parted slightly, quivering slightly.

He stifled a groan at the immediate turn of his thoughts toward the erotic. It was only her hand gliding over his shoulder and down his arm, he told himself. But his imagination moved that long-fingered hand to other parts of his body. The couch behind her loomed in his view—inviting in its width and length. Wide enough for two to lie facing one another. . . .

His body reacted to the visions with enthusiasm.

He stepped back, dislodging her hand from his arm. She jerked it away as it brushed across his groin. Her breath caught.

So did his as he frantically sought a way to hide the growing evidence of his interest.

His first instinct was to turn away from her, but the desk was at his back, and she stood in front of him. In any event, curiosity held him rooted as her gaze dropped to below his waist.

He gave her a chagrined smile. "I don't suppose you could advise me on how to make a graceful exit? I believe I can find a bolt hole once out of your sight."

Her mouth twitched as she gave his arousal an arch look. "And I believe I have never met a man as desperate as you must be," she said with strained lightness. Turning, she snatched up her gloves from the desk and strode to the door, her easy glide a bit jerky just then. "I believe I shall return to the ballroom and brazenly flaunt my deficiencies." She kept her gaze away from him and spoke into the night beyond the door. "And . . . Lord Dane . . . thank you for the compliment."

He blinked as she stepped outside and closed the door behind her. And then he swallowed at the poignancy of her voice lingering in the air, hollow with loneliness and fragmented with something else. Like disbelief of what she'd heard and seen and even touched so briefly. Disbelief that his words and his physical response were meant for her alone.

Adrian sighed and pushed away from the desk, then took his time snuffing candles and setting their glasses on the sideboard. As he stepped out into the night air, he chuckled softly at the absurdity of what had taken place. He was an even thirty years old and Lorelei was not far behind him, yet they had just suffered all the awkward stumbling and embarrassment of adolescents groping for sophistication. He'd observed a young stableboy seduce a farmer's daughter with more finesse.

He strolled down the garden path toward the ballroom terrace, keeping a slow pace to allow his mind to recover control over his body. He wasn't likely to scale any towers, or slay any dragons, or carry Lorelei off on his ship and sail with her over the edge of the world without a great deal of subtle courting. He could only hope she would appreciate that his effort to face her again with any degree of charm, wit, and sophistication would require the steel balls of a hero.

What an extraordinary experience, Lorelei thought, as she pulled on her gloves and wandered through the gardens, reluctant to break the spell of feeling separated from the rest of the world, of feeling as if she stood on the edge of a precipice that might crumble at any moment and drop her back into reality.

But not yet.

The gardens were magically free of bored wanderers and reckless lovers seeking privacy. Doubtless it was Harriet's magic that kept everyone inside. Merry knew her friend well. Harriet never did things halfway, and if she set out to matchmake, she would be thorough about it, even to the extent of manipulating all her guests to unknowingly cooperate.

But it wasn't just Harriet's magic at work here; it was Dane's. Dane, who gave every appearance of being dark and brooding, his very silence promoting the impression that he was too cocksure for his own good. Dane, who appeared to be as comfortable in his skin as he perceived her to be in hers. Dane, with whom she felt comfortable regardless of his remarkable insight and equally remarkable arousal, considering he'd been with her at the time.

And in spite of her cynical pragmatism, she'd felt like a desirable woman as a result. She still felt like a desirable woman—light on her feet, as slender as a willow, as feminine as delicate lace and sleek satin.

She was smitten. Thoroughly. Surprisingly. Foolishly.

She knew it would pass. The sun would rise to cast unforgiving light on her looking glass and she would have to face the truth. His compliments had been prompted by his sense of obligation to Harriet—and perhaps pity for a woman whose popularity did not extend to the dance floor. Obviously he was that rarest form of humanity, a kind person. Tomorrow she would see him again and he would be polite and distracted as a dozen lovely and hopeful candidates for matrimony paraded their attributes before the most eligible man of the Season. Tomorrow she would accept what she already knew. His arousal hadn't been for her specifically. Tomorrow she would be certain of it.

Absolutely certain. Without a doubt.

But not tonight. Not when the moon sailed in a diamond-studded sky and she drifted on the memory of a man's admiration. It was too rare a feeling to waste on pragmatism.

Music wafted outside on the night breeze, dreamy and sensual. She glanced at the terrace at the edge of the gardens, at the light of a thousand candles reflecting off crystal chandeliers and the blur of couples pairing off for a dance.

Had Dane really been about to ask her to dance? she wondered. She loved to dance and did so regularly with the dance master she still employed. If not for Beau, who always claimed at least two dances with her at social functions, and her ability to pay for lessons she didn't need, she would never have the opportunity to dance. . . .

Humming along with the music, she winked at Venus and curtsied to an imaginary partner, then slid into the steps of a minuet, stepping forward . . . dipping slightly . . . turning and leaning her head back at the man who wasn't really standing back to back with her, his arms outstretched from his sides, his hands holding hers—

Heat radiated at her back as something solid took the place of fantasy. Strong hands replaced air, holding hers, guiding her in the steps of the dance, turning her, moving at her side now, then widening the distance between them, then drawing her close again.

Dane. Here. Dancing with her beneath the stars. . . .

She vaguely heard a clock chime twelve from the house that seemed so far away in another time and place. The witching hour. A time of enchantments and dreams and illusions. The moon had traveled on, leaving only starlight and the glow of the fairy lights Harriet had strung on a tree here and there. Dane was part man, part dream, an illusion that visited a woman when she had only a pillow to cling to. The perfect man. The only man. . . .

She glanced up at Dane, at his face that was a contradiction of itself—his eyes so dark and enigmatic, his expressions so vivid, so eloquent, even cast in starlight and shadow, his dark eyebrows sweeping across his forehead and arched precisely at their centers, his lashes incredibly long for a man.

He released one of her hands and held the other high to turn her around and around. She was giddy with the dance, with the scent of dew-glazed grass beneath their feet, with the man who seemed to envelop her with his strength, surround her with magic even though only their hands touched. Only their gazes embraced.

And one dance led to another and another, and she neither knew nor cared if the music paused in between.

His arm encircled her waist—just that—as he led her forward a few steps, then paused for a moment that seemed like forever, gazing down at her with a familiar glint in his eyes that told her he was again mocking himself.

Dane halted as the music faded away on a midnight breeze, bringing her up short when she would have danced on and on until morning. He stared down at her hand cradled in his, slowly slid her glove down her arm. She couldn't protest, couldn't look away from him as he eased it off her hand one finger at a time, caressing each in turn. She quivered inside as he stared at her hand. Her breath shuddered in anticipation as his brows drew together and he frowned at the glove as if he didn't know what to do with it.

His mouth slanted wryly as he draped it over his shoulder, then turned her hand over . . . bent at the waist in a courtly bow and kissed the center of her palm, breathing deeply as he skimmed his mouth up to kiss the sensitive flesh on the inside of her elbow, lingering longer than he should, yet not nearly long enough.

And then she watched him walk away with a swagger in his step, her glove still draped over his shoulder, forgotten.

She sighed as the clock chimed one in the distance. The hour of enchantment was over, the time for dreams and illusions gone. Yet as she walked—it felt like drifting—toward a side entrance that would take her to her bedchamber, she felt beautiful and graceful, feminine and . . . fragile.

Fragile.

She paused and shuddered and stared at the sky. And then she straightened her back and squared her shoulders and briskly paced back toward the ballroom, her feet touching the ground with every step.

Chapter 5

Adrian strode away quickly before he could say something that might destroy the moment . . . a moment every bit as stunning as the lady herself, he thought smugly. Given his practical nature and lack of experience in charming a woman who refused to be charmed, he thought he'd done rather well.

Seeing her alone, her eyes closed, her arms embracing only air, he'd reacted with outrage that she should have to dance in the arms of an imaginary partner. And then he'd acted on impulse to hold her and guide her steps beneath the shimmer of fairy lights, to kiss her hand in the shadow of an ancient goddess. As he'd walked toward her, he'd told himself that he did it because he knew that women enjoyed such things. That it was part of the ritual of courting a woman's favor. It hadn't occurred to him that men might enjoy it, too.

At first sight of him, had she felt as breathless as he? Had her heart thudded and raced and had her body heated as his had? He hadn't expected to feel such

66

things. Experience with tavern maids and mild flirtations with young debutantes had not prepared him for this awareness that encompassed more than his libido.

"Your taste in women is . . . interesting." A figure separated from behind a tree and ambled into his path.

Adrian focused on the man standing in his way and registered his comment. George "Beau" Brummell. *Wonderful.* "You were watching," he said flatly, as images of what Brummell had witnessed suddenly flashed through his mind. What a few moments ago had seemed like a profound moment took on all the aspects of a farce. His shoes were damp with dew. He'd almost stumbled more than once while performing the more intricate steps of the dance on uneven ground. He'd almost missed her palm while leaning over her hand to plant his kiss. Had his mouth been too wet? Too dry?

Oh, hell. He hadn't worried about such things since adolescence, and thus far no woman had ever complained.

"Seeing your performance was a rather entertaining accident. I am unforgivably late and hoped to sneak into Lady Harriet's ballroom by way of the terrace," Brummell replied, as he pretended to examine his nails in the dark. "Quite a performance. One would think the lady herself inspired you, rather than her fortune." He reached out and flipped the glove still hanging over Adrian's shoulder. "And will you continue to pursue her in secret to keep the snickers at bay?"

Sickened by the insinuation, Adrian snatched the glove and stuffed it in his pocket as he pushed past Brummell. "Good night, Brummell."

"Is that disgust I hear?" Brummell asked as he fell in step beside him. "Surely not because of something

I said? I am merely inquiring . . . as a friend who might advise you.''

Adrian snorted. ''By insulting a lady.''

''By attempting to discern your motives,'' Brummell said quietly. ''I don't often feel respect for anyone. When I do, I don't like to discover I'm wrong.''

''I don't give a damn what you like.'' Adrian walked faster, wanting nothing more than to escape Prinny's pet before he resorted to violence. The man offended him from the first moment they'd met by looking him over and then all but giving him a sweet as reward for his taste in clothing and fastidiousness in bathing regularly. Adrian had actually caught him sniffing—not quite discreetly enough—as if to discern his choice of soap, or more likely, whether he used it often enough. The worst offense had been Brummell's assertion that Adrian would be accepted by the *ton* not by virtue of his own qualities, but because Brummell approved the knot in his cravat. Adrian had met the offer by commenting that neckcloths were handy to have when the need arose to wipe horse droppings off one's boots. It had no doubt confirmed the popular belief that he was indeed a barbarian.

''Still disgustingly high-minded, I see. Not exactly in keeping with your methods in currying favor with the baroness.'' Brummell clicked his tongue and shook his head. ''Really . . . cornering her alone in Lady Harriet's office for over an hour, and then dancing with her in the garden . . . *if* you could call it dancing. Looked more like seduction.'' He sighed dramatically. ''Did you think she would be an easy mark, considering she is not only on the shelf, but society has never considered her a diamond of the first water?''

"Then society uses filthy water," Adrian snarled, "and wouldn't know a diamond from a ball of mud."

"It sounds as if you are defending the lady. Has no one told you that she can defend herself quite ably? Good God, man, she outweighs most of the bucks—"

Adrian whipped around and backed Brummell against a tree, his hand twisting Brummell's faultlessly arranged neckcloth. "One more word, Brummell—just one—and I'll—"

Brummell grinned up at him, saying nothing.

Adrian glared at him and twisted harder. "Share the joke."

Still grinning, Brummell spread his arms out at his sides. "You are besotted with her," he stated.

Adrian released Brummell as if he'd caught fire, and stood back, his gaze averted, his thoughts racing through a maze. Besotted. Very likely, and very startling. After meeting dozens of young ladies and feeling indifference at best for even the most appealing of them, he'd taken one look at an Amazonian spinster and gone headlong over the edge of reason.

"You are, aren't you?" Brummell pressed.

He'd swear Brummell sounded pleased, which was at odds with his earlier remarks. Adrian was in no mood to thrust and parry with anyone, let alone Beau Brummell. "Why don't you say what you mean?"

"I'd rather you tell me what your attentions to Merry mean," Brummell said, as he completely untied and unwound his neckcloth and fussed with his shirt points.

"Merry?" Adrian murmured, vaguely recalling the name being squealed and shouted earlier in the evening—when the baroness had arrived, to be exact.

"A pet name coined, I believe, by a certain thermometer of social acceptance.'' By touch alone, Brummell began to wrap his neckcloth around his neck, feeling each fold before proceeding. ''She quite lives up to it, don't you agree?''

Merry? Not really, Adrian thought. Not when her smile, though dazzling, had a wistful quality, and while she laughed and jested, her gaze darted about as if she were in the habit of searching . . . always searching. Adrian thought she better lived up to ''Original,'' but he wasn't willing to reveal that much of his feelings for her. Not when he'd just met her, and hadn't yet had time to analyze those feelings and put them in proper perspective. Besotted was too much like being drunk. Before he made any declarations to anyone, he wanted to be damn sure that his feelings survived the initial intoxication.

''High-minded, indeed,'' Brummell murmured. ''Few gentlemen are able to refrain from tossing a lady's name into a crowd like a coin to the poor.'' He patted his cravat and adjusted a fold. ''Is it any wonder that he is considered a queer card?'' he asked the sky. ''You affront society by not displaying the usual frailties. You don't seem to give a fig if you are included in one circle or another. You neither curry the favor of the prominent, nor ride the coattails of the powerful. Worse, you appear to have no need for the constant assurance of importance that the rest of humanity craves.'' He straightened his cuffs and brushed a minute speck of lint from his breeches. ''One wonders where such strength of character and confidence in oneself can be obtained. Such qualities certainly escape the majority of the population.''

With every word Brummell uttered, he reinforced Adrian's impression that he was a loyal friend to the baroness. Adrian could think of no other reason why

Brummell would seek him out and goad him in such a crass manner. "My taste in women is as interesting," he grumbled, "as your methods in seeking information are elaborate, Brummell."

"And if you would emerge from the labyrinth you call a mind more often, you would have realized what I was about much sooner." Brummell tugged on his coat and grimaced. "I really must have a looking glass, and there are some things you should know. Shall we repair to—"

Adrian stiffened. "I see you're not above tossing coins of gossip to the masses. I, however, have no wish to hear any more about Lady Winters except what she freely offers—"

"Admirable," Brummell sighed, "but I am not speaking of gossip. I speak of you, as well as myself, and activities which are deplorable, to say the least." He steered Adrian toward the arched ivy-shrouded door to Lady Saxon's office. "Now let us retire to a place where we can find privacy, sherry, and a looking glass. I presented the countess with a particularly fine cheval glass for her office a year past."

Adrian knew he should continue on to the suite Lady Saxon had assigned him and his uncle. He should, yet curiosity grew and multiplied as Brummell located the key Adrian had so recently dropped behind the clay urn, then unlocked the door he'd so recently secured. In light of her close friendship with the countess, he could understand how Lorelei would have access to the countess's office. That Beau Brummell also felt at ease invading Lady Harriet's domain with expensive gifts as well as his person implied an equally close friendship.

Upon first meeting, he'd judged Beau Brummell a dilettante and a parasite. But now, with his own sudden and acute awareness of how he might be wrongly judged by a lady he'd just met, he realized that fair play demanded closer inspection.

He stepped into the purple and green and yellow room resplendent with floral chintz and French lace and strode toward the fainting couch, reaching it before Brummell had finished lighting the candles. If he was going to be fair-minded and patient, he would damn well do it in comfort.

Brummell's expression showed obvious displeasure at his having been beaten to the only seat adequate to support a man's frame comfortably. He turned toward the sideboard holding refreshments and poured sherry into two glasses. "The palace has received a declaration of war from America," he said abruptly.

Emotion, swift and sharp, kicked in Adrian's chest at the news. He'd been expecting it, but having it confirmed so casually by a relative stranger felt like a headlong fall into a Connecticut snowdrift. War. Between the country of his birth and the country he'd adopted. A war that created a conflict within himself between loyalty for the land watered with the blood and tears of his grandparents and father, and the land of his ancestors. A conflict that could not be won. The only family he possessed, aside from his uncle, was in America. His convictions had been formed there. His spirit had been molded by the precepts of independence and rebellion that drove a nation of men to greatness.

Yet his dreams—his dreams—had been inspired by England, by her history and traditions that spoke so vividly of stalwart souls and enduring spirit, and by what he knew was possible for her to achieve. He'd arrived here wanting to show this country how to roll up her sleeves and march into a new era with grace and dignity and foresight rather than the bloodshed spawned by closed minds and stubborn hearts. Europe had endured enough carnage in the last quarter century. And America had barely recovered from its revolution against England.

A dream . . . a foolish and arrogant dream. He'd been so cocky with it that he'd neglected his lack of a practical plan. He'd studied instead. He'd watched and learned, and still he knew nothing except that bloodshed would once again rule. He would be torn between loyalties—gray rather than black or white, because even now he awaited word on the elder of his two cousins who had been taken off an American merchant vessel and impressed into service by the British Navy. And when word finally came, his loyalties would center only on the rescue of the man who was like a brother to him. He could not sacrifice one man for a country . . . any country.

Brummell turned back to him and pressed a brimming glass into his hand. "What path does your mind wander now?" Brummell asked. "Dreams or reality?"

Not dreams, Adrian silently replied. His dreams were of ships and vast oceans and the freedom to drift wherever the currents took him. His dreams were of being heroic and larger than life, of showering excitement and adventure and passion on the woman of his choice.

Lorelei—a woman he had immediately recognized as the right woman to give his dream a name.

He downed the sherry in one long gulp and wanted to howl at the futility of it all. There would not be time for dreams now. Only war. No matter who claimed victory in the end, the losses would never be justified.

"I was in the army, you know," Brummell mused as he stared into his glass. "The Prince's regiment. But my grandfather was a valet and my father a secretary. I am a gentleman by aspiration—and taste, of course—rather than temperament, and I have roused a good deal of rabble in the past." Carrying the decanter over to the fainting couch, he refilled Adrian's glass and set the cut crystal bottle on the table at Adrian's side. "And yet there is no greater strength than the collective heart of England. That a part of her heart is across the Atlantic is a tragedy that cannot be avoided so long as both halves are in conflict. It gives me an itch to revive my political ambitions."

Adrian stared at Brummell, following his languid pacing from one end of the room to the other. He'd thought Brummell a creature of the senses rather than the mind, a man whose visions were tuned to facades rather than foundations. He'd been wrong about that as well. Brummell, he realized, was aware of the dangers as well as the possible rewards of complete renovation and would have no patience for mere facades. But a man who dared to improve on an old foundation such as his was often long on concept and shy on any clear idea of how to shore up the old so that it might support the new. Ironic that he hadn't recognized in Brummell the same dissonance that was in himself.

It was quite possible that they were both idealistic fools.

"On which side of the pond does your heart reside, Lord Dane?"

"I am pledged to England," Adrian answered simply, knowing with a sick knot in his gut that it wasn't simple at all. A week ago he wouldn't have replied to any question posed by Beau Brummell. Now he suspected that if anyone might provide insight into the quandary of his thoughts, it would be this man who was as mad a dreamer as he was.

"A pat answer. Yet you have in Connecticut a family of cousins—Steven and Phillip, I believe. Steven has been impressed by the Royal Navy and Phillip is rebellious at best, which makes him a poor candidate to run the Rutland enterprises in America—namely a shipyard and a lucrative merchant fleet. And I understand the proceeds from your American interests exceed the marquess's income. You understand, of course, that *when* we win the war, your holdings will fall under English jurisdiction. How does all that fit in with your pledge?"

He regarded Brummell with narrowed eyes, immediately alert to possible ramifications if Brummell shared his information with any one of the powers in England, either at the palace or the war office. If it got out that his cousin was captive of the Royal Navy, his intention to rescue Steven would be dangerously compromised. "What concern is it of yours?"

"That brings us to my confession," Brummell said softly. "I have been making discreet inquiries about you since learning the countess's plan to bring you and Merry together. I should also mention that it would have happened much sooner if I had not secured her promise to wait until my investigation was complete." He met Adrian's gaze squarely. "I apologize, yet I am not sorry. I would go to greater lengths than that to protect Merry from further pain."

Digesting Brummell's revelation, Adrian tried to summon anger and found sympathy instead—for the act of simple loyalty to a friend, regardless of more complex loyalties and preexisting moral beliefs. "I am not the only Englishman who has interests in America," he replied carefully, not so sympathetic to

Brummell's actions that he forgot the man's closeness to the Prince Regent. Aside from the need to keep Steven's situation secret, suspicions concerning Adrian's loyalty were sure to gain momentum now that war had been declared.

"No, and because you are not, I must admit my question was not a fair one. I daresay your enterprises will suffer because of the war." He sipped his sherry. "But the war is still young and seems very far away at the moment. Here and now are a number of lovely ladies—not to mention their mamas and papas—who aspire to the Wyndham fortune and title even if it means suffering your barbaric ways and unnerving silences." He held up his glass in a sardonic salute. "For all their avowed fondness for Merry and her wisdom, they won't hesitate to discourage your interest in her. Their outrage alone at being slighted for a lady they consider to be flawed will ensure attacks on her character as well as her countenance." He sauntered to a chair and sat gingerly on the edge of the seat. "That I went to such lengths and expense to determine your character is a statement in itself that my concern lies with Merry—a woman I would have happily married myself had I not suffered an attack of conscience and admitted that she deserved better than a gambler for a husband."

"Am I to infer that you are satisfied that I am worthy of her?" Adrian asked, finding that subject a far safer one than that of war.

"I am satisfied that you are an honest man who will not callously hurt her. I am not, however, satisfied that you will not hurt her as a result of difficult choices."

"The last thing I would wish to do is hurt her. Unfortunately, we cannot guarantee such things,"

Adrian said, while wondering why he said anything at all. He'd spent a mere hour or so with the lady in question and another quarter hour observing her beforehand—hardly justification for making a declaration of any intent, much less a brash one.

Deciding he'd explained himself more in one evening than he had in the sum of his entire life, Adrian rose from the fainting couch, picked up the decanter, and carried it and his glass to the tray on the sideboard.

"Like you, she lost her parents, though at a much earlier age, and her only other relative passed on five years ago," Brummell said, as if to himself, his expression a cross between a small smile of commiseration and a slight frown of resignation. "She has no comprehension of love as it should be. She has not a whit of understanding of family. I would have her experience both. After what I witnessed tonight, I am certain you are the man to see it done."

"Why aren't *you* that man?" Adrian asked bluntly, more curious about Lorelei's affections toward Brummell than his toward her.

Brummell rose and rocked on his heels, his hands behind his back. "Alas, we cannot choose the path of our affections, and mine have long since gone astray. Believe me, at one time I tried very hard to be that man. And believe me when I say that if you ever have to *try* to love Merry, you had best withdraw immediately or face me at twenty paces."

Adrian bent his head and rubbed the side of his nose. "What am I doing here?" he muttered. Life had just become incredibly complicated and he was indulging in an often obscure conversation about a woman he barely knew with a man he could have sworn he didn't like.

Still, he couldn't take the necessary steps to leave. Whether or not he actually liked Brummell didn't seem to matter, since he'd grown a healthy respect for him in the last half hour. "You said that you would prevent Lady Winters from suffering further pain. She has been hurt before?"

"Haven't we all?" Brummell said, as he rose from the delicate chair. "Merry is the only one with the right to reveal the whys and wherefores." With that rather ominous sounding statement, Beau Brummell set down his glass and muttered something about going to his room to select another neckcloth, abruptly leaving Adrian standing alone once again among the flowers and lace designed to both intimidate and cajole a man into granting the wishes of a woman.

He wished he had a better idea of how to go about it. And he wished the endeavor wouldn't be further complicated by a war that divided his loyalties—not with a clean cut, but with a jagged tear into the fabric of his convictions.

Leaving the office, he darted his gaze right and left as he took a circuitous route back to the rooms Lady Saxon had assigned him and his uncle, hoping he wouldn't run into anyone else who might have witnessed his inept debut as a romantic hero.

Chapter 6

"We have an interesting view," Robert, the Marquess of Wyndham said as he stood with his back to the small sitting room connecting his bedchamber to Adrian's, his attention focused on what lay beyond the window.

Adrian pushed the door shut with his foot, and with a sinking feeling that he wouldn't like what he saw, snapped his gaze to the window and craned his neck to see the view over his uncle's shoulder. He bit back a groan at the sight of the gardens studded with fairy lights illuminating statues of Zeus and Apollo and . . . Venus. "You saw," he muttered, as he swiped his hand over the back of his neck. "I should have sent engraved invitations."

He cleared his throat and tried to change the subject. "I gather your luck was disappointing." After their conversation in the ballroom, his uncle had gone his own way to play cards in the game room. Adrian had expected him to remain there until the small hours of morning. He wished he had. Making a fool of himself was becoming appallingly close to becoming a public event.

"Talk of politics took the pleasure out of the game." The marquess gestured at the view below. "I found this far more interesting. Compounding my fascination was your confrontation with Mr. Brummell."

Something fell from Adrian's pocket to the floor. He scowled down at Lorelei's glove, annoyed to feel a flush of heat on his cheeks. He supposed he should be grateful that his trousers hadn't lost their moorings and fallen around his ankles. Someone should have warned him that being besotted with a woman could reduce a man's pride to whimpering humiliation.

Uncle Robert chuckled as he bent to pick up the glove. "You do the family proud, nephew. Our lineage is liberally dusted with the gallant and the romantic. Remind me to show you the manuscript our ancestor, the first marquess, compiled in honor of his lady. Troubadour's songs, his own poetry, and several love letters are faithfully copied into a leatherbound volume. He called it scraps of his heart." He arranged the glove over the foot of Adrian's bed. "I'm not certain, however, that the whimsical nature bred into every Rutland male for centuries will help you win the baroness."

"Have you decided that I am to win her?" Sprawling in a chair by the hearth, Adrian glared at the glove dangling languidly like a lady's hand over the edge of the bed.

"I wouldn't dream of making such a decision, but I daresay you have." Robert sat across from him in a matching chair. "The moment you told me you wanted her, I realized how perfect she is for you."

Yes, Adrian had decided without any clear comprehension of how or why one fell in love at first sight. The very thought of such a fantastical notion prompted a cringe. He waited for the onset of chest-tightening panic he'd observed in his cousin Steven when he'd realized he was in love with the woman who had later become his wife. Anger had followed as Steven had raged on about the injustice of having every lesson on the proper behavior and patterns of thought considered proper in males turned inside out by love, making buffoons of them all. In light of the complications inherent to the emotion as well as all the possible variables, Adrian was certain he *should* feel panic, yet it didn't happen. Instead he felt calm, almost detached, as if he'd suddenly become two people, one chasing dreams as if they were rainbows, and the other using logic to plot the course and speed of pursuit.

"I must caution you that Merry will be a challenge," Robert said. "But then I would have also cautioned that she might resist attentions embellished by moonlight and roses and candlelight if events hadn't proven how wrong I'd have been."

Upon reflection, Adrian, too, was surprised that Lorelei had responded to his act of whimsy. In the office, her attitude toward his attentions had been less than receptive, what with her self-mockery and her refusal to be charmed by compliments. Yet in the garden she'd seemed as caught up in the magic as he had been, her rejection as absent as his panic.

With Lorelei, it appeared that actions spoke louder than words.

He leaned his head back against the chair and closed his eyes to better savor the memory of how her hand had trembled in his, how her scent of carnations had wafted around him as they'd moved together, then glided apart, how his hand at her waist had slipped to brush against her hip, confirming that it was as full and womanly as he'd imagined. . . .

She'd been soft. So soft. And when she'd looked at him, he could have sworn he'd seen stars in her eyes. . . .

Wishful thinking. Male vanity. Poetic nonsense.

He snapped his eyes open and his stomach suddenly felt like lead. Of course he'd seen stars in her eyes. Or more accurately, fairy lights strung in the trees by Lady Harriet's gardeners. The light from them would have reflected—

"What I wouldn't give to have seen what went on between you in Harriet's office," Robert said.

"More like what you expected, I imagine," Adrian said on a sigh. "She did her best to convince me that I was not interested in her."

"Failing completely to scare you off, obviously."

"It would take far more than the baroness's candor to do that. She is apparently unaware that many American women are not as restrained by rules of behavior as are their English counterparts," Adrian said, keeping his eyes closed in hopes that his uncle would take the hint and leave him alone to ponder the evening's extraordinary events. "Steven's wife proposed marriage to him in a fit of pique because he was taking too long to get on with it."

"Doubtless, Merry met with you in that room without companion or chaperone in an attempt to put you off."

"Hmm. And she conducted herself as if none of the rules applied to her," Adrian added, realizing that her very lack of conformity was what had drawn him to her in the first place. He'd been too long exposed to the strength and independence of women such as his grandmother and mother and Steven's wife, Catherine, to appreciate meekness and unquestioning submission in a woman.

"The rules don't seem to apply to her, for the most part," Robert said. "Those charged with her care after her parents died didn't concern themselves with more than keeping her fed, clothed, and safe so as not to jeopardize their positions. Of course she was schooled in the proprieties, but discipline was nonexistent when she failed to observe them. After her swift disillusionment at the hands of the *ton,* she set about making her own rules and daring society to challenge them. Brummell's endorsement of her encouraged their indulgence. Her money and inherited title gave her the clout to ensure it." He gave a disgusted snort. "They all treat Merry like a pet and show nothing but utter delight in her, while in their minds they consider her their inferior."

"Merry," Adrian muttered. "A ridiculous name. . . ." His voice trailed off as he remembered her stating how desperate he must be for a wife to spend time with her, speaking matter-of-factly, as if she truly believed it, yet felt no self-pity or unhappiness over it. At the time her avowed undesirability had puzzled him. Now it irritated him. It was quite plain to him that the lady did everything in her power to convince others of her undesirability rather than the other way around. Could she, an intelligent woman, actually believe such nonsense, or did she merely wish others to believe it to protect herself? Did she perhaps initiate rejection out of fear that it was true, thus avoiding confirmation by *being* rejected? It made a skewed sort of sense—

"I believe the nickname is derived from her second name of Meredith," Robert intoned, as if giving a lesson in Latin. "Though she lives up to it in company, few realize there is more to her than a dazzling smile and genial nature.''

''Brummell gave her the name,'' Adrian said. ''I wonder why.'' It did seem strange, since Brummell had made his respect for the baroness quite clear. From what he could determine, Brummell was one of the few who saw beyond Lorelei's height and well-endowed frame to the beauty of *her*.

''Perhaps to render her harmless in the eyes of the *ton*,'' Robert replied. ''If anyone is aware of just how vulnerable Merry is, it is Brummell.'' He chuckled and stuck a cigar in his mouth. ''Come to think of it, Brummell seems to be her self-appointed brother . . . and a right good job he's done of it in the last . . . why, it must be ten years now.''

Adrian digested the information as his uncle's voice trailed off. Ten years since her first Season would make her approximately eight-and-twenty—a good age for marriage, in his opinion. An age well suited to his own thirty years. An age impatient with silly posturings, bored with coy games, and tempered by experience. He frowned at a grim recollection. ''From what you implied and what Brummell said, I gather that she has a past,'' he said offhandedly. ''It must be a colorful one for Brummell to be so discreet as to advise me that I would have to hear about it from her.''

''You'll not hear it from anyone else if he is about . . . or not, for that matter. To protect Merry, I do believe Brummell would take advantage of having the Regent's ear to have anyone with a loose tongue tossed into the tower.'' Picking up a taper from the table next to his chair, he touched the flame to the tip of his cigar and puffed until clouds of smoke drifted around him. ''I have always failed to see what was so terrible about it other than Merry's hurt, which was considerable. It is the only time I can remember when the *ton* stifled gossip rather than embellished it, thanks to Brummell.''

Adrian sighed as he stifled his curiosity. He hadn't expected she could reach her age without one or two unfortunate incidents, and he wouldn't care if it weren't for his suspicion that it was responsible for her refusal to accept, much less believe, a compliment. ''Brummell said he might have loved her if his affections had not already gone astray,'' he mused aloud.

The marquess raised his brows as he regarded Adrian with a wry half-smile that Adrian had concluded was a family trait. ''I daresay you've made quite an impression on our Mr. Brummell if he told you that much. For all his outspokenness, he reveals little of a personal nature.''

''Hmmm.'' Adrian turned his head to stare at the fire, unable to forget what else Brummell had said. He'd been trying to avoid thinking about it, much less mentioning it, until he had the opportunity to sort through his feelings on the matter. But his thoughts were disorganized at best and he had little hope that they would become less unruly anytime soon. Like it or not, he had to face it. ''He revealed a good bit more, Uncle Robert . . . America has officially declared war,'' Adrian said baldly, as he clenched his hands in frustration. He'd been comfortable with his choice to return to and become a part of the country of his ancestors. In truth, he'd known it was where he belonged from the first time he'd visited over fifteen years past, after his parents as well as his aunt and uncle had been taken. Yet Brummell's news of war had finished the job Lorelei had begun, separating the parts of himself even more until another war raged between his heart and his mind.

Robert's shoulders sagged. "I am sorry, Adrian. I had hoped . . ." He shook his head and stared down at his hands, then pounded the arms of his chair. "Blast it! This is insane. America is scarcely recovered from the revolution against England and we are at war with Boney. Why couldn't we honor America's sovereignty and leave her ships alone? Why couldn't President Madison have been more reasonable in his demands? Are there no sane men left in government?"

"There is little point in debating the issue now," Adrian said. "All we can do is be grateful Madison and Congress discarded their thoughts of also declaring war on France, and hope that hostilities with England will end soon."

"You will find it difficult to return to Connecticut now."

"If you'll recall, I did not plan on returning to Connecticut in the foreseeable future. With Steven running the shipyards and activities of the merchant fleet suspended until an accord could be reached between America and England, there was no reason to return unless an emergency arose." Ironic, he thought, that the Rutland merchant vessel Steven had been taken from was undertaking the last—and presumably safe—voyage until hostilities ceased.

"But with Steven missing, you will have to return to see to his affairs if he is not found," Robert said quietly, voicing their worst fears. "Yet now there will be a blockade off the American coast, and if you are caught anywhere near, you will be immediately suspected of spying by whichever side happens to find you. And after the war you will again have a merchant fleet to contend with." Grimacing, Robert seemed to sag even more in a posture of defeat. "If only Phillip would climb out of his cups and help."

"Phillip is gone again," Adrian said flatly, hating to tell his uncle what Steven's wife had related in the letter he'd received only last week. "He took a newly built ship and a large sum of money and sailed four months ago."

"Ah, damn." Robert averted his gaze to blindly stare out the window. "I keep praying. . . ." He shook his head. "Phillip is so bright, so full of potential. If he could only divert his thoughts from himself . . . damn!"

"According to Catherine's letter, Phillip hasn't had a drink since hearing about Steven. Apparently he tired of trying to bribe my agents for information and decided to take to sea."

Robert's gaze skated to Adrian, full of both hope and dread.

"He's been looking for a fight a long time now, Uncle Robert, and for all his recklessness, his loyalty to family is as strong as ours. I cannot fault him for wanting to save his brother."

"He must be stopped. He is too hotheaded. If he finds Steven first, God knows what might happen. It would be like Phillip to start a fight and end up on one of His Majesty's ships himself . . . and Steven could be hurt."

"I'll get to him first," Adrian said, hoping he could. "I'll be happy to have Phillip's aid in freeing Steven once we find him."

"Then I pray that you find Phillip before he finds Steven. Otherwise we might lose them both."

"As do I, Uncle Robert. I chafe at the waiting, and a hundred times a day I want to send every ship we own out to search. But the ocean is too vast and the British Navy too powerful.'' He chafed with impatience at the necessity for caution and logic. If he had no one but himself and Steven to worry about, he would have taken more immediate action and damn the consequences. But Steven had a wife and three children, and Uncle Robert stood to lose everything as well if the situation were handled badly. "I've sent word to the American privateers to check the crew of every ship they take for Steven as well as to notify me of any sightings of Phillip. The frigate he took is quite distinctive.''

"One of the new slender-hulled warships?'' Robert asked as he leaned forward.

"Yes, we built it for the American Navy.''

Robert pursed his lips in a silent whistle. "With the speed of that design and sixty guns, Phillip could do some damage.''

"I also have *Bifrost* searching under Captain Mathers. He is supposed to rendezvous with Blackwell and deliver whatever information my agents have gathered. The moment I receive word on either Steven or Phillip, I will sail.''

"And where will Mathers put in?'' Robert asked. *"Bifrost* is far from usual and with an American crew will be hard put to sail up the Thames.''

"Mathers knows how to navigate the cove near Spindrift. He will put in there with no one the wiser.''

Robert's eyes gleamed in excitement. "The *Bifrost*, in our waters? I must see it again . . . a fast ship built of lighter woods and a design far ahead of its time. . . .''

Adrian rubbed the side of his nose as he regarded his uncle with affection and gratitude. From the day Robert had found him burying his father's body beside those of his mother and aunt and uncle—all taken by influenza within a few weeks of one another—he'd treated Adrian as an adult, giving him choices and respecting his decisions. And now, even when Adrian's choices might damage the Wyndham name beyond repair, he said and did nothing to influence him. Instead he expressed excitement over a ship that had been first conceived by Adrian's father and then had become Adrian's dream.

Adrian didn't want to think about what would happen if *Bifrost* were discovered, though he'd altered the surface of the ship to resemble that of a very elaborate yacht. He'd made certain that his love of the sea was well known and hoped that if the ship were seen, it would be attributed to an eccentric man with enough wealth to indulge his interests in equally eccentric ways. He could almost hear them now, tittering about Viscount Dane having a large ship built and fitted out just so he could play captain when the whim took him.

Still, the sooner he could remove the need to have his ship harbored in English waters, the better he would like it. The entire situation was rife with hazards, not the least of which was Phillip, who had all the characteristics of a loose cannon on the deck, capable of creating havoc within the family and without. "I should have remained in England with you when I was ten," he said, as he massaged the tension from the back of his neck. "I was impressionable then. I would have been formed by this country. I wouldn't have had divided loyalties. I would barely remember my cousins and—" He broke off and pressed his lips together, containing his fury and grief, as well as a good bit of guilt. Fury that the British would impress a partner in a prominent business that had—until the Orders of Council and resultant embargo—traded reg-

ularly with England. Grief because the longer Steven
went missing, the worse their chances became of finding and recovering him. Anything could have happened to Steven, from being killed by pirates to
drowning while trapped below decks on a ship sunk
by the French.

The worst was his guilt over Phillip. Adrian knew
that as eldest and head of the family, he had failed
his cousin in some way, yet he didn't know how, and
Phillip wasn't forthcoming on the reasons for his anger and resentment. Adrian and his cousins had lost
their parents so unexpectedly, and though Uncle Robert had arrived from England to take them into his
custody, they had all asked to remain in Connecticut.
Since they had loving guardians in the manager of
Rutland shipyards and his wife, Uncle Robert had
honored their wishes to spend the rest of their youth
in the home in which they'd been born, and continue
to work in and learn about the legacy their pioneer
grandparents had left—

Robert shook his head sharply, cutting off Adrian's
thoughts. "Nothing would have changed except that
you would not have such a broad education and such
a unique understanding of both countries. You would
never have forgotten your cousins or your origins.
You would still search for Steven, and upon finding
him, move heaven and earth to return him to his home
and family, regardless of your patriotic allegiance."
He slid forward and placed his hand on Adrian's arm.
"You cannot change what you are, Adrian. Family
has always, and will always, take precedence in your
loyalties."

"Yes, and that is why I shouldn't be thinking of
beginning a family of my own right now. Not when
the one into which I was born is in chaos."

Robert rose and stood facing the fire, his hands behind his back. "War does not negate the choices you've made. Wars come and go with annoying regularity, and people continue on with their lives in spite of it. Phillip is three-and-twenty—a man who must make his own choices and mistakes and take the responsibility for learning from them. Steven is a shrewd and strong man who will go beyond his limits to survive for the sake of his own family." He turned and softened his voice. "You've found a woman who inspires interest rather than yawns. A fine woman, who I believe is the ideal mate for you. Will you toss that away because of the folly of nations?" As if he had no need of an answer, Robert strode toward the door to his bedchamber, then turned back, his hand on the latch. "Or are you simply looking for an excuse not to pursue her because you haven't a clue how to go about it?"

Adrian stretched out his legs in front of him and pretended a preoccupation with the toes of his shoes until he heard the door swish open, then click shut a moment later. His uncle knew him too well. It was one thing to indulge in flirtation or dally with a courtesan and quite another to "pursue" a woman in earnest, to care what she thought of him to the point of making awkward attempts to impress her.

And where Baroness Winters was concerned, he had the feeling that she might see his heart dangling on his sleeve and still not recognize it for what it was.

"What?" Harriet said, her eyes wide and innocent, though she didn't quite meet Merry's gaze as she curled her legs beneath her on the sofa and arranged her skirts in a pretty sweep.

"You know very well what," Merry said, as she

completed another turn about Harriet's private sitting room. Her patience had frayed as the last of the guests had either departed for their nearby homes or wandered off to rooms Harriet had provided. It had snapped by the time she and Harriet had retired upstairs. ''What on earth were you thinking to do such a thing?''

''Such a thing?'' Harriet said, with a click of her tongue. ''You make it sound as if I'd tossed a kitten in with a pack of dogs . . . which, upon reflection, might be somewhat apt, since Dane is so calm and watchful and you chase and bark at anyone who wants to pet you.''

''Pet me, indeed,'' Merry muttered. Yes, Dane appeared calm, and he certainly was watchful, like a pedator rather than a house pet. A predator intelligent enough to study and outsmart his prey. Nothing escaped those sharp eyes. Pewter eyes, darkly tarnished by what they'd seen, yet wide open and frank and thoughtful rather than cynical. . . . Could Harriet be right? Was Dane a kitten, unaware of how easily he could be either frozen out by the *ton* or left to flounder in the acid of their cruelty for the sheer amusement of it? The thought appalled her. Cynical men she could handle in droves. But one sincere man with a reckless trust in humanity was a different matter altogether.

She had all the female instincts to protect and nurture and teach. And as one who understood how ice could freeze the heart and acid could corrode the spirit, she would be particularly susceptible to a man like Dane, whether he was afflicted with reckless trust or a reckless tendency to invite mockery and not give a hang if he got it. At least it seemed reasonable that she would. Since she'd never known a man like Dane, she couldn't be certain.

That Dane was a sincere man, she had no doubt. She'd felt it in the firmness of his hands as he'd held hers, lifted it for his kiss. She'd sensed it as his lips had touched her palm, then pressed against it, caressing . . . lingering. And then he'd breathed deeply as if her scent provided the only fresh air he could find. And later, she'd known it as he'd appeared like a ghost to dance with her, not for a single dance or a single moment, but until the music stopped and the moon disappeared over the edge of the world. A man who did such things was either an accomplished seducer of heiresses . . . or he was genuinely interested.

She knew for a fact that he hadn't seduced a single heiress since taking up residence in England.

Oh, Lord have mercy. Every stray dog and cat in England knew she was good for a warm bed, a hearty meal, and a warm cuddle. She'd had new stables built on her estate so her strays could have the old one. But she knew that if she stopped feeding them, they would be gone in an instant, searching for greener pastures without looking back. And so she refused to name the animals and made it a point to find homes for them once they were healthy again.

"Dane is healthy, whole, and appealing," she blurted, as she whirled to face Harriet. "He has more wealth than the government. Why me? What does he want? He must want something." She waved her arms in agitation. "I wouldn't trust him at all if he didn't."

"And if he does, would you be willing to provide it?"

Her heart danced a jig in her chest at the memory of how he'd looked leaning against Venus's hip, absently twirling his spectacles, how he'd followed her into Harriet's office and looked so utterly lost among the fripperies, how he'd dropped his blasted spectacles and called himself an ass . . . how he'd given her that endearing quirk of a smile after stating—not asking—that he would be on her doorstep tomorrow regardless of her attempts to put him off.

No, he was not a pet, not with his determination and courage. Not a single man of her acquaintance had the confidence and strength to forsake his vanity and ask if she would scratch behind his ears if he behaved.

A man who had enough confidence and arrogance to challenge the Upper Ten Thousand to accept him, or not, as they wished, and then to shrug off their rejection. A man completely without affectation. A man who knew he was eccentric and didn't care.

She understood eccentricity. Yet while hers was cultivated, she suspected that his was natural, rather than an act of defiance or a bid not to be overlooked.

"Well, would you be willing to provide what he wants?" Beau Brummell asked, as he sauntered into the room.

"How should I know?" Merry said in exasperation, then turned an accusing glare on Harriet. "Is your little plot a matter of public record?"

"I beg your pardon, Merry, but I take great exception to being regarded as 'the public.' Lady Harriet and I have been conspiring together all along," Beau drawled, as he swept aside Harriet's skirts and sat in an elegant sprawl on the opposite end of the sofa. "And if your tête-à-tête with Dane in the garden is any indication, you know very well what you would like to provide for him."

"I daresay you're correct, Beau," Harriet said, as she fussed with her shawl. "I was having palpitations just watching them from the ballroom." Sitting back, she gave him an arch look. "Did I do well?"

Beau slid his hand under Harriet's and raised it to his lips. "You did indeed, Countess. I have always said you have an extraordinary talent for putting things together."

"I am not a thing," Merry gritted, as she stood in front of them, her hands on her hips.

"You will be if you marry stick-in-the-mud. He'll dust you off when he remembers you're around, or heaven forbid, he'll mistake you for a trophy and mount you above the mantel."

Merry opened her mouth to argue, then shut it again as she realized that Harriet was right.

"Quickly, Beau," Harriet said, "say something wise and irrefutable before she finds her tongue."

"At this hour?" Beau stifled a yawn. "Oh, very well." He met Merry's gaze. "You, Merry, are likely the only woman who can save Dane from himself. And I daresay you would be vastly entertained while doing so. He is an idealist, you know."

"I don't require an idealist; I have you to entertain me."

"But that's the beauty of it, darling." Beau rose from the sofa and bussed her cheek. "Each of us has his own vision of what is ideal. We're an unpredictable lot at best, and therefore incapable of inspiring boredom. We are also quite rare. And since I am not on the marriage block, you'd do well to take Harriet's advice and get one of your own before we're all gone." He sauntered toward the door. "Most of my gender lack the imagination to see beyond your belief that you cannot possibly hold a man and therefore believe it themselves—" He abruptly closed his mouth as his gaze skated to Harriet.

Merry's eyes narrowed as Harriet gave Beau a brief warning shake of her head. She needn't have bothered. Merry wasn't about to remind her friends that it had been a man who had convinced her that she was better off—and far safer—being a friend, advisor, and comforter. It would lead to an old argument which Dane had unwittingly resurrected in her own mind.

Beau shrugged and sighed dramatically. "In any case, you're quite taken with Dane. Can you say the same for the earl? If you wish to marry, then why not to someone you like?" Before she could reply, he stepped out into the hall and shut the door firmly behind him.

"I wouldn't at all mind having one like Dane for my own," Harriet said on a sigh. "I'm quite weary of pretending contentment at having all the advantages of marriage without the burden of having the company of my husband."

"Matchmaking is not the way to relieve your malady." Taking Beau's place on the sofa, Merry fixed her friend with a warning glare. "I will not have it, Harriet."

"I'm afraid you will have to, Merry, for I am quite determined that if you will not show sense, then I must do it for you." She leaned over and covered Merry's hand with hers. "Don't, please don't, marry for the sake of marrying. You would be better off a spinster. There is nothing worse than conducting a marriage by oneself."

"Can it be any worse than conducting a life by oneself?" Merry asked.

"Oh, yes." Harriet stood abruptly and pulled her shawl closer about her shoulders, as if she were cold. "At least your life is your own. Mine belongs to a man who I doubtless would not recognize if he stood nose to nose with me.'' She shrugged in a sad small way that tightened Merry's throat. ''And it belongs to a pile of stones and a hundred people who depend upon me—none of whom are my children. I have these wretched visions of you and me growing obscenely old together and having nothing to talk about but the weather, nothing to remember but our regrets.'' Smiling brightly, she bent down and pressed her cheek to Merry's. ''It is up to you, my very dear friend, to make enough memories for both of us to enjoy in our dotage. I beg you not to settle for anything less than very, very good ones created with someone you like.''

Merry watched her walk toward her room, acutely aware that she would walk to the other side of the sitting room and enter the second bedchamber in the master suite—the bedchamber that the Earl of Saxon should be occupying. The irony of it was that even the servants no longer thought it odd that their countess had redecorated the room for her friend to inhabit when she visited. But then, why should they when it had become obvious in the past ten years that the earl had neither the interest nor the intent to use it himself?

She blinked back tears, unsure if they were for Harriet's loneliness or for her own fear of learning what it would be like not to be alone only to be forced to adjust to it again.

In some ways, perhaps she and Harriet had already become old and resigned to what life doled out to them.

Resigned. Merry closed her eyes and found the image of Viscount Dane waiting for her. A memory . . .

exciting, provocative...tempting her to reach for more.

And if she did reach out—if she dared—she wondered if he would step toward her or back away. She wondered if she had the courage to find out.

Chapter 7

North Atlantic
Late July, 1812

Phillip stood high in the crow's nest of the newly built ship he'd commandeered from the Rutland shipyards, a spyglass to his eye as he searched for sign of the British ship *Falcon* in the waters of the Atlantic. He'd finally received word that his brother, Steven, was on the *Falcon.*

Phillip had set sail immediately upon receiving the report from Blackwell, Adrian's chief agent, over four months ago, carrying as little weight as possible and keeping his ship, which he'd aptly, if unimaginatively, named *Reckoner,* at full sail. It was a sign, he thought, that the wind had been steady and the narrow-hulled frigate fleet and solid, her sixty guns concealed behind hinged ports. And though he'd been furious at the time, he had to admit that Adrian's decision to suspend operations of their merchant fleet after Steven's impressment had served him well. It had been no problem at all to take seamen Adrian continued to pay even though they weren't working and use them as crew in his search for Steven. He'd be quite cocky over his ingenuity if Adrian hadn't done it first, selecting the best of their merchant navy to man his own ship.

He frowned as he again thought of the ship Adrian had designed and ordered built in secrecy—going so far as to have a building erected around the structure—and then sailed it down the river and to the Atlantic under cover of night. He did know that the ship was commanded by the most seasoned and trusted of Rutland Shipping captains and that Adrian himself was in England waiting for word on Steven's whereabouts. More than that he had not been able to discover.

But no matter, Phillip thought. He would find his brother and he would get him back. He had to—for himself and for Catherine and the children. He stared at the horizon, haunted by the memories of the day after they'd learned of Steven's abduction, of Catherine's anguish and his own sudden feeling of humiliation and shame. Catherine had remained so silent after she'd explained to the children about their father, watching young John sweep his gaze from his mother to his uncle, then silently leave the kitchen to do his chores, his breakfast uneaten. His twin, Robbie, had followed, tugging little Caro behind him.

As the door shut behind the children, Catherine had set a bowl of porridge down in front of him and gripped sides of the table, trembling so hard his coffee sloshed over the rim of the cup.

"You should have been the one on that ship!" she had shouted, then pressed her hands over her mouth, her eyes wide in horror at her outburst. Stiffly she turned back to the iron stove to stir the porridge she had just stirred a moment before.

He watched his sister-in-law begin cleaning up after the meal that had gone untouched, shooing the kitchen maid away in a voice thickened by tears. Catherine insisted on serving her husband and children every morning, refusing to allow the cook into the kitchen until after the family had eaten. Except that her husband was gone and all she had now was a brother-in-law barely able to keep his seat in the chair after another night of hard drinking. Drowning his problems in a bottle of rum had had been his answer to everything for years.

Catherine, he knew, regretted her words as soon as she'd said them. But she wouldn't apologize. Catherine never apologized for telling the truth. Nor should she.

Phillip *should* have been on that ship instead of Steven. But he had resented Adrian's order for him to act as purser on the voyage that would carry trade goods to France. It was time for him to do his share in the business that made it possible for him to live so well, Adrian had said. It was time for him to be a man rather than an overgrown boy throwing one tantrum after another and pickling his brains in cheap rum. Adrian had been right, as always.

And Phillip should have been the one to hire men to search for Steven. But as always, Adrian had put the wheels in motion without saying a word, accepting responsibility because he always had and knew better than to expect Phillip to do it. He'd been right then, too.

Phillip had pushed away from the table and stood at the window, not wanting to leave Catherine alone with her tears, even though he had no idea how to

soothe her. Catherine rarely cried and hated to be
caught at it when she did.

He'd watched his two nephews perform the chores
Catherine and Steven insisted upon in spite of the servants employed to handle them. The boys reminded
him of two others a long time ago. One was quietly
serious, approaching every task with as little fuss as
possible, yet he played every game with laughter and
an annoying habit of not caring if he won or lost.
Balanced, like Steven, Phillip thought of his eight-
year-old nephew. Never confused, never distracted,
John approached every thought as he would a straight
road, always knowing where it began and where it
would end, and more important, seeing the potholes
and obstructions long before he reached them. He
continually followed behind his two siblings, picking
up after them while instructing them on the natural
order of things.

On the other hand, his twin brother Robert peeled
back the layers of a thought, then turned it inside out,
looking for what was beyond the vision of others. In-
satiable curiosity and wonder accompanied him as he
wandered through the landscapes of his mind, his
mouth slanted in a familiar half smile. Adrian's smile.
And like Adrian, Robbie was always accepting blame
for his baby sister's transgressions, of which there
were many, always excusing her small rebellions in
such a way that no one could fault his logic—though
they rarely comprehended it—always fair-minded to
a fault. Like Adrian, damn him.

Six-year-old Caroline tried so hard to be good, but
she was in too much of a rush to do everything and
tried too hard to perform tasks that were beyond her
with chaotic results. And every time John picked up
after her, or Robbie offered incomprehensible expla-

nations for her behavior, Caro vehemently protested being protected, whether she liked it or not. Like yesterday, as she'd glared at Robbie while clutching the fragments of a clay pot she'd broken in her headlong rush to finish a chore, warning him to leave her be. Like now, as she made mud and used it to glue the last piece in place, insisting on repairing her mistake herself, and making a bigger mess in the process. At least she had tried.

At six, Caro had already gone farther in accepting responsibility and gaining her independence than Phillip ever had.

But that would soon change, Phillip had decided that morning, after Catherine had left him to stew in his hangover. He'd taken matters into his own hands once before and botched it. But, even he eventually learned from his mistakes. Steven and Adrian had taken care of him, because unlike his diminutive niece, he had allowed it, always following them, always too much in awe of them to defy them. And the one time he had, he'd gone off half-cocked to join a band of pirates and then refused to admit he was wrong, instead standing by while Adrian paid for his error. Just as he'd allowed Steven and Adrian to share in the blame for all his mistakes, always taking it for granted that his older brother and his cousin would tolerate, excuse, and forgive his actions.

It couldn't go on. He no longer had anyone to rely on but himself. Adrian was in England—one of the enemy now. He was an English lord, and by association, as guilty of Steven's abduction as the Regent himself.

And Steven was lost, perhaps never to be found, leaving a wife and three children to go on in the anguish of not knowing whether he was alive or dead.

Phillip had done his best for them, but an army of employees and the Rutland wealth protected them more than he ever could. Hell, even the shipyards and merchant fleet didn't need Phillip, thanks to the excellent managers, staff, and lawyers Steven and Adrian and Uncle Robert had employed and trained.

Catherine and the children needed a husband and father, respectively. Adrian needed to live his own life after spending his adolescence and most of his adult life torn between what he had to do and what he wanted to do. If they found that Steven was dead, Adrian would give up his own life in England to care for the rest of the family. It shouldn't matter to Phillip, but it did, regardless of his anger and resentment for Adrian.

Sighing, Phillip greeted the seaman who climbed into the crow's nest to take over the watch, grateful to leave the solitary post in favor of the company of his men below.

The confusion of both loving and hating Adrian gave Phillip a headache. If he could get drunk, he'd feel nothing but anger at Adrian for abandoning his country and his family, for being a part of the system responsible for the cessation of trade between America and Europe and forcing President Madison to declare war. He could blame him for Steven.

Yet sober since that morning in the kitchen with Catherine, Phillip's mind cleared more with every day, seeing what he'd tried so hard to drown. He had to acknowledge that family came first with Adrian, even his drunken younger cousin. That whether Steven was found or not, Adrian would pick up the pieces and hold them together by sheer force of will, no matter what it cost him.

Phillip couldn't allow that. He couldn't bear the

guilt of it. Not anymore. He couldn't imagine Adrian undertaking what amounted to high adventure and succeeding. A man who fervently believed in peace, he was too likely to try to talk the British into letting Steven go, and Phillip knew that it would take a battle to pry an able seaman such as Steven from the British.

He told himself that Adrian would never spontaneously enter into a battle without first taking the time to examine his weapons curiously and explain their efficiency to friend and foe alike. Enough time for a fighting man to run him through. He knew it wasn't true. Adrian could and would fight, if it became necessary. But Adrian would be risking everything to rescue Steven even if he could manage it, and resentment aside, Phillip didn't want that, so he preferred to believe that Adrian would botch it. This was his chance to prove to his family that he was no longer a hotheaded sot. To finally prove to himself that he deserved their respect. To prove, rather than simply tell them, how much they meant to him. Once his conscience was clear, he could determine how to manage his own life.

As he descended the rigging to the deck, he smiled. For the first time in twenty years he'd taken decisive action. Prompted by Catherine's accusation and driven by the memory of her tears, he'd found one of Adrian's agents willing to report to him first for a considerable sum of money. Phillip had gladly paid for the news that Steven was on the *Falcon*. In the past he'd spent more than that on whiskey in a single month.

And as he'd told Catherine of the news and his plans to sail immediately, his sister-in-law had turned to him, her eyes bright with tears, staring at him as if she wanted to say something and couldn't find the words. Instead, she shook her head and bustled from the room to rap out orders to the housekeeper. His sister-in-law had once accused him of being a muscle-bound child, too indulged and too spoiled to accept responsibility, and now she regretted her loss of control. He couldn't stand that. Catherine had no reason to blame herself for anything, just as Steven and Adrian had had no reason to accept responsibility for Phillip's many failures. Why couldn't they have just shouted at him and maybe beat him senseless for it? Why did they have to be so damn reasonable and kind, leaving him to ferment in his own culpability all these years?

One way or another, Phillip was determined to make it right. He would get Steven back. He would keep Adrian from getting killed. He would take his place as a partner in Rutland Shipping, perhaps captain his own ship for the company after the war was over and Adrian resumed the trade side of the Rutland enterprises.

And then he could tell Adrian to go hang.

Chapter 8

"**M**erry is hiding," the countess said, as she approached the sideboard.

"We laid it on a bit thick and frightened her," Brummell said, and spooned eggs onto his plate.

"So is my nephew," the Marquess said as he joined them, a cup of coffee in his hand. "Hiding, that is . . . or more accurately, running. He is an early riser and left for a day in London the moment the sun appeared . . . according to my valet."

"Merry is not an early riser, nor a particularly pleasant one, yet she was up at dawn, singing and puttering around the dressing room in her chamber," Harriet lamented. "Thank heavens no one else is about yet. I am not up to playing the gracious hostess just now."

"Merry singing? God help us all," Beau said, with a roll of his eyes. "A melodic voice is not one of her endowments."

"She *was* singing," Harriet corrected. "After an hour, she became silent except to mumble something about remaining in bed to nurse a slight fever.''

Beau smirked. ''A fever named Dane, perchance?''

The marquess arched his brows.

A grin tipped up the corners of Harriet's cupid's bow mouth. ''I suspect so, since I am quite certain she was trying on gowns all morning.''

''Apparently none pleased her.'' Heaping berries on his plate, Beau moved on to the toast. ''Will she hibernate for the duration, then?''

''Merry is not one to choose solitude when there is company about,'' Harriet said. ''She may last a day before she talks herself into disliking Dane and decides to prove it by making an appearance for the express purpose of ignoring him.''

''She has a regrettable talent for ignoring all manner of things,'' Beau said. ''Such as what is good for her . . . what she feels . . . what she wants.''

''Except when she first awakens and has not yet begun to think of all the reasons why she shouldn't ignore what she feels and what she wants.'' Harriet signaled a footman to fetch coffee and chocolate to the table.

The marquess selected toast and honey. ''A pity we cannot induce a near dream state in her to last until after the wedding.''

''The wedding?'' Beau said with an amused lift of his brows. ''Has something taken place of which we are ignorant?''

''Wedding . . .'' Harriet mused. ''All I wanted was to keep Merry from marrying Earl Dunworth. Of course, after last night I had hoped . . .'' She shook her head as she sank into a chair at the head of the table. ''Still, I wouldn't want her to act impulsively.''

Chuckling, the marquess sat next to her. ''Have no

fear, Lady Harriet. I am indulging in little more than wishful thinking at this point."

"Little more?" Beau asked as he sat across from the marquess. "Has Dane given you cause to do more than wish?"

"I have not asked my nephew's intentions. No doubt we shall all find more gratification if we allow ourselves to be surprised."

"That will occur only if Merry leaves her room and Dane does not ride to London every day," Beau said. "I find it amazing that two such intelligent people can be so undone by a simple meeting."

"Somehow, I doubt it was simple." The marquess waited for the footman to refill his cup, then added cream to his coffee. "You know, it never occurred to me—Merry and my nephew. Yet now, I can't fathom why. I watched them dancing, and I must say, was quite touched by how *right* they looked together. In the last few hours it has become my wish to see your scheme succeed."

Harriet met his gaze. "Am I to infer, sir, that you have no objection to Merry becoming the wife of your heir?"

"I would think," Beau added, "that you would have reservations. Everyone else is only too happy to take advantage of Merry's good nature, yet would balk at bringing her into their family. She is considered, after all, too eccentric and outspoken for marriage to a prime catch such as your nephew."

The marquess smiled slightly and sighed. "My father migrated to the Colonies as a penniless third son with no hope for fortune or consequence. He married an indentured servant and together they built an empire in shipbuilding and trade. Adrian's father—my brother—and I, and our younger brother, grew up in a cabin and began sweeping floors at the shipyard office at six, then graduated to each level of employment within the company as we learned and matured." He shuffled crumbs of toast around his plate with his forefinger. "When, by some quirk of fate, my father's family here in England dwindled until I became heir to the titles and estates, I came here on a lark." Pushing his plate away, he waited until a footman whisked it off before continuing. "It remained a novelty only until I became acquainted with the fine traditions upheld by Rutlands for generations. I remained here by choice, knowing that my two younger brothers would continue to establish new traditions in a new country. So, you see, I—the son of an indentured servant with family engaged in trade in America—am hardly in a position to regard a lovely young woman unsuitable simply because she is independent and forthright." He stirred his coffee absently, then glanced at Harriet and Beau. "And if we are very quick and very sly, we can perhaps bring Merry and Dane out of hiding and arrange for a . . . collision of sorts between them."

Beau glanced from the marquess's deadpan expression to Harriet's surprised one. "It appears we have an ally, my lady." He held up his cup as if to offer a toast. "Perhaps between the three of us we can make your wish come true, sir."

Merry heartily wished she had remained home at Winterhaven rather than promising Harriet to attend the Little Season. Of course she could always return home before the Season began. She never missed Harriet's late summer house party but that didn't mean she had to go on to London with the rest of the guests in a fortnight's time.

All she had to do was avoid Dane for those two weeks. *Easier said than done*, she thought, as she stared glumly at the pile of gowns on the dressing room floor. She'd lain awake for what was left of the night, seeing him and feeling him in her memory, wanting to see him again. She'd been afraid to sleep, afraid that if she did, she would dream impossible, foolish dreams. She'd never much cared for dreams. They made everything seem possible, only to abandon her to the light of day, where every flaw of illusion stood out in sharp relief.

Yet Dane hadn't been an illusion. She'd seen his flaws, though they hadn't seemed like flaws when he made no effort to hide them. Instead they'd seemed like natural charm and strength of character. They'd been endearing . . . refreshing . . . fascinating. A man who thought deeply, then acted upon his conclusions rather than merely reacting to what went on about him was refreshing . . . fascinating.

His interest in her had not been a figment of her imagination. Last night she'd accepted it, reveled in it. She'd lingered on the fringes of her enchantment with him into the morning, trying on gowns to find just the right one to please his eye while singing like a naive little miss entertaining thoughts of a blissful happily-ever-after.

She'd finally remembered that she'd rather look to a certain today rather than to an unlikely ever-after.

She'd finally come to her senses. Dane needed a wife and appeared interested in her. But she was far too interested in him and far too susceptible to the illusions he inspired. She wanted to marry a man who did not have the power to make her forget herself, to prompt her to make a fool of herself, to devastate her with his criticisms. She wanted to marry a man she liked and with whom she felt comfortable but who could not shatter her with his rejection.

Liking was real and honest. To love was to drift among the clouds, oblivious to what waited below until the inevitable fall to earth.

The problem was that she very much liked Dane. Worse, she was afraid that one more of his crooked smiles would convince her that she was also more than half in love with him.

Love that happened so quickly could not be, in actuality, any more than lust. And lust was the last reason for marriage she would ever entertain. She nodded sharply in affirmation and began to pick up her gowns from the floor, one by one, careful to smooth out every fold and wrinkle and hang them up again.

The modiste caressed the full-bodied silk and handed it to Merry. "My lady, this would suit you very well. The shade of violet has a touch of smoke with reflected light shading it to rose to blue and gray and the barest hint of green."

"How soon can you have it ready for me?" Merry asked, as she wondered why she had wandered into the shop in the first place. She'd driven her curricle the seven miles into London from Saxon Hill with the idea of avoiding Dane for the day. That she'd planned to search for some candlesticks and other whatnots for a bare room at Winterhaven had provided the perfect excuse. She'd left a note and slipped away to the stables before Harriet returned from breakfast.

But instead of acquiring candlesticks, she'd wandered from shop to shop looking at fabrics and trying out various scents. She carried a box with several cakes of fine soap and a bottle of her favorite carnation scent, disgusted that she'd lacked the small spirit of adventure required to try something different. She'd left Saxon Hill a coward; she refused to return as one.

Leaning over the counter, she picked up a quill and dipped it in ink, then made a quick sketch of a gown. "I would like it made up like this, if you please, Mrs. Powell. How soon?" she repeated.

"If I put all my girls on it, I can have it by—"

"Tomorrow afternoon would be fine," Merry interrupted, in no mood for the usual protests and cajolery. "Naturally, your promptness will be suitably rewarded." She swept out of the shop before she could change her mind about the design that would be sure to raise eyebrows as well as a buzz of derogatory remarks. It should adequately demonstrate to Dane the reasons why he should turn his attentions elsewhere.

The next hour passed in a flurry of selecting just the right undergarments to go with the new gown and then two hours flew by at the jewelers. Jewels were her weakness. Any jewels. She'd even been known to mix paste beads that caught her eye with the Winters collection of diamonds to which she'd just added amethysts and emeralds.

With the seat next to her piled with packages, she turned the horses toward the road leading out of the city. If fortune was with her, she would arrive while everyone was dressing for dinner, yet before the sun set.

Three miles outside the city, the curricle lurched and wobbled and nearly toppled her out as one side collapsed and came to rest drunkenly on the surface of the road.

*   *   *

Adrian reined in his horse as a wheel rolled toward him and clattered into a ditch. Alert for highwaymen setting a trap, he swept his gaze over the road ahead as he urged his mount into a stand of trees. He could hold off one or two men, but a contrived accident on the road to a prosperous estate suggested a pack of miscreants at work.

A curse delivered in a feminine voice reached him, amplified by the evening silence as his mind registered the skill with which the driver of the curricle calmed the team and left her perch in the precariously leaning vehicle.

Her? He squinted into the gathering darkness, his breath whooshing out with the slam of recognition.

Lorelei. It had to be. Yet it couldn't be. Even she would not venture out alone without so much as a footman to accompany her.

All day he'd imagined seeing her in one place or another—at the docks, where he'd met with his agent stationed there to search for information on Steven; outside the tavern, where he'd taken a meal; on a fashionable street, where he'd visited his tailor—each time the figure too far away or too shadowed for him to discern details. All it took was an intricate coil of brown hair, or a proud gliding walk, or a costume that deviated from the current fashion for him to imagine she was nearby. More likely the woman on the road was the accomplice of a thief, playing lady in distress to lure victims into a trap.

Except that she didn't appear at all distressed as she retrieved her wheel and rolled it back to her curricle, examined it for damage, then dropped to her hands and knees to search for something on the ground as if she knew exactly what she was doing.

"Oh, blast and botheration!"

Certainty kicked in his chest at her exclamation. It *was* Lorelei.

Before he could signal his horse to move forward, he saw her pick up a large stone from the side of the road and place it beside the curricle, then ease the body up while pushing the stone beneath the undercarriage to hold it up. Pulling something from her hat—a viciously long pin, he thought—she positioned the wheel over the axle. He remained still, dumbfounded that she was not only attempting to repair the wheel, but that she actually appeared to understand the mechanics of it.

She showed not a sign of panic, not a hint of helplessness. Not once had he seen her glance around as if searching for aid.

He really should reveal his presence and help her, yet curiosity held him rooted as she worked with the wheel and its moorings. Fascinated, he watched her rummage through her reticule and retrieve several objects too small to be identified and what appeared to be a ball of string. He'd always thought that women carried delicate handkerchiefs, a scent bottle, and a few coins in their bags.

Adrian held his breath as she sat back on her heels and stared at the mounted wheel, then with both hands, tested the strength of her repairs. He winced as a loud crack split the air.

The wheel broke free in Lorelei's hands and toppled her onto her backside.

"Damn," he muttered, inexplicably disappointed that her efforts had failed. Before he could again become preoccupied by her ingenuity, he dismounted and stepped out of the trees.

"Oh, blast and drat," she said in an oddly choked voice as she glanced at the road back toward London, then forward toward Saxon Hill, too far yet to be seen. Undaunted, she rose, brushed off her skirts, and began to unhitch her team.

His step faltered at the sight of her shoulders shaking. He paused as something glittered in her eyes and trickled down her cheeks, shaken at the sight of her tears. A woman who did not so much as flinch at being stranded on a quiet road and having to repair a broken wheel would not be one to weep easily. Yet she continued to work, threading her parcels onto the string and lengths of the reins she cut with a small dagger—also from her reticule—and draped the burden over the back of one of the horses. And all the while she worked, she impatiently swiped at her cheeks and swallowed her sobs and berated herself for her weakness.

She wasn't angry at her situation; she was angry at her tears.

The realization reminded him of how Steven's wife had thrown eggs at him, then hidden her face when he'd come upon her sobbing into her apron over a series of kitchen disasters.

Instinct warned that he should retreat, yet he was too close to do so without being seen. He quickly turned his back on her and stood quietly in the center of the road, battling the frustration of wanting to soothe her, yet sensing that she would not appreciate his comfort. And since there were no eggs about, he didn't want to take the chance that Lorelei might throw her dagger instead.

Her sobs stopped except for a single wrenching gulp. Silence expanded. Adrian felt an itch between his shoulder blades and knew she had seen him.

"What are you doing here?" she asked.

He had to smile at her apparent recognition of him

in the uncertain light. "I am on my way back from—"

"I mean why are you standing in the middle of the road with your back to me?" she said impatiently.

"I was afraid you'd throw your knife at me if I watched you cry." He heard her inhale sharply and then clear her throat as if he'd caught her by surprise, though he couldn't imagine how.

"Oh . . . did you just arrive?"

"No."

"And you didn't offer to help? Why?"

He shrugged. "Would you believe that my male instinct was distracted by your female resourcefulness?" He heard a strangled sound that might have been a burst of laughter, but decided to remain where he was until he identified the mood behind it.

"And did you find it amusing? Or perhaps shocking?"

"I found it admirable," he said with a slow shake of his head as he faced her. Her expression was blank, yet he caught the hint of a smile tipping the corners of her mouth.

She turned her profile to him and dashed away the last of her tears. "It would be admirable if I hadn't failed."

He approached her and leaned over to examine the wheel. "You could not have succeeded. The fittings are worn smooth and the wood is cracked." He lifted the wheel into the curricle, then dragged the whole into the ditch. "I don't recommend that you attempt to ride one of the team."

"I don't intend to. I am going to release the one to find his way home with a message tied to his harness, and lead the other with my packages."

Straightening, he stood deliberately close to her.

"You will ride with me and I will lead the pack horse."

"I think not, sir." She lifted her nose in the haughty way she had the night before to stare down at him. "My weight, coupled with yours, would surely strain his back, and I am not in the habit of misusing an animal."

His mouth tightened in annoyance at her reference to her size; he no longer admired her brutal candor. Without a word, he bent, hooked an arm behind her knees, lifted her over his shoulder, then her atop the large gelding before she could gasp in outrage. "If I can lift you, my horse can certainly bear our combined weight. However, I will walk to spare you cause for worry." He stepped back to survey her form seated sideways in the saddle. "Since that is not a sidesaddle, I suggest you hitch up your skirts and ride astride," he said bluntly, then strode to the front of the animal and picked up the reins, wishing that she would berate him for making such an improper suggestion, or squeal in protest that he would even think of it, or giggle nervously as she recognized the sense of it. Anything to make her seem more like the other females he knew.

But then, she was unlike any other female he knew, taking his suggestion with sensible calm as she swung her leg over the saddle to sit astride regardless of the impropriety. It would have been absurd for her to affect reluctance in any case after she'd driven herself into town with scandalous independence, then attempted to repair her wheel rather than submit to vapors over her plight—

"Lord Dane . . ."

Determined not to listen to any protest or self-directed insults from her, he began to lead the mount toward Saxon Hill.

"You forgot Harriet's team . . . and my parcels."

Oh, hell. Gritting his teeth more at her bland tone than at the reminder, he halted, turned, and strode back to the team. At least she'd already unhitched the team, saving him possible embarrassment if he should bungle the job in his present state of idiocy. "Have you a calling card in your reticule?" he asked evenly, as he pulled one of his own cards from the pocket of his riding coat.

Silence.

Judging it sufficiently dark to conceal any signs of his humiliation, he dared a glance at her, his mouth tightening even more at the sight of her straddling his horse, her silk-stocking legs bared, the flesh luminous as a creamy pearl in the soft glow of twilight.

His mouth felt suddenly filled with cotton as he stared at those legs, the thighs plump and fair and incredibly inviting above her garters. His gaze skimmed past her knees to sleekly curved calves and ankles that were small in proportion to the rest of her, and kidskin shod feet that seemed too dainty to support her height. He groaned at the thought of those feet locked together around his waist, those thighs open around him, cradling his hips as he plunged into her—

He jerked his gaze up to her face, the beginnings of yet another unexpected arousal sagging at her expression.

Her lower lip was caught between her teeth, obviously biting back laughter as she held up a small rectangle of stiff paper.

He snatched the card from her hand.

"I believe the best way to do it is to cut a piece

off of the end of the string tying the parcels, poke a hole in the cards, and run an end of the string through—''

Already in the process of doing just that, he lowered his hands from the harness of the unburdened horse, bent his head, and inhaled slowly, deeply. "If you please, my lady," he said, carefully enunciating each word to keep from shouting them, "show enough compassion to allow me the delusion that I am rescuing and taking care of you." He peered up at her from the corner of his eye, saw her open her mouth. "Keeping silent would likely be the best way for you to accomplish it," he continued, as he finished securing the cards to the bridle and slapped the horse's rump to send him home. Picking up the lead of the second horse, he quickly returned to the head of his mount, anxious to return to Saxon Hill before he completely lost his composure.

Never in his adult life had a woman tempted him to kiss her in one moment and throttle her in the next. As he led his gelding down the road, he wondered if she had enough string in her reticule to tie together the scattered bits of his pride.

Chapter 9

She'd hurt his pride. Merry stared at Dane, walking with ground-eating strides, as if he couldn't be rid of her soon enough. It stung that he was so vexed he didn't even want to speak to her, let alone slow down and walk beside the horse rather than as far ahead as the length of the reins allowed.

Yet she couldn't seem to summon any contrition. She'd never rattled a man's pride before. All the men she knew considered her one of them, like a tomboyish sister or worse, a woman they couldn't bring themselves to acknowledge as such. She was accepted into their groups at social occasions and was expected to find amusement in the bawdy jokes they told in her presence. She often thought she could walk right into Tatt's to bet on a horse race, or into White's for a game of billiards without causing a stir. She even addressed them by their last names, as only men were allowed to do. No doubt if she ever grievously insulted one of them, he would expect her to meet him at dawn on Primrose Hill with her choice of weapons.

It felt rather nice to sting a man's pride ... to know that she could.

Twilight gave way to the star-studded indigo of night, so silent that every hoofbeat of Dane's horse seemed to echo all around them. She glanced around at the landscape, a collection of shadows only slightly darker than the night sky, but always her gaze wandered back to Dane, to his broad back wedging down to narrow waist and hips as her mind wandered through visions of sun-darkened flesh stretched over tensile strength, of long fingers reaching out for her, caressing her.

She wanted to hear his voice again, to laugh at something he said. But he was angry with her, and she should be angry, too. Why did a man always have to be the strong one? Why couldn't he acknowledge that she not only might be able to repair a broken wheel, but think of more than the design of her next fan?

He'd said he found her efforts admirable.

She'd been difficult ... and rather silly. How could she have made that absurd statement about straining his horse's back? Why had she felt compelled to advise him on what to do rather than graciously thanking him for his aid?

Because, she reminded herself, she needed to convince him that he couldn't possibly be interested in her. And after the hungry way he'd stared at her legs, she'd panicked and said the first thing that had come to mind. But, why a suggestion that he had already thought of? She'd sounded patronizing, condescending. There were better ways to discourage his interest in her than trying to convince him that she was one of the fellows.

She rather liked the way Dane made her feel like a

woman. In fact, beginning tomorrow night, she planned to discourage his attentions by overwhelming him with just how *much* of a woman she was.

But, right now, she had to make amends.

"Da—" Merry bit back the improper form of address and cleared her throat. "Lord Dane," she said quietly.

He neither turned nor spoke.

She sighed and tried again. "I am grateful that you came along when you did." She grimaced at how difficult it was to admit even that much. It had been so long since she'd had the luxury of relying on someone else to solve a problem for her . . . to take care of her. Except for Beau stepping in to ensure her acceptance into society, it had been forever.

She rather liked being taken care of, though she would never admit it. Beau had once counseled her never to show weakness, never to admit fear. Now, more than ever, it seemed important to remember his advice. Perhaps it would be better to say nothing more and allow Dane to remain angry. Except that it was night and they were again alone and she *had* been frightened at the prospect of walking to Harriet's in the dark. She wanted to discourage Dane, not repel him, though she couldn't fathom why it mattered.

All she knew was that she wouldn't like it at all if he frowned upon her. Not after the way he'd talked to her the night before, looked at her, smiled at her. She had to make amends and told herself it was because there were better ways to show how weak she wasn't than slapping down his helping hand. Except that he continued to stride down the road, saying nothing, as if he hadn't heard her. As if he didn't want to hear her.

"Please stop," she called, amazed that she sounded genuinely distressed.

He halted abruptly and turned on his heel, his gaze sweeping over her as if to check for trouble or injury, then sliding away from her bared legs to focus on the ground.

She swung her leg over the saddle and balanced with only one foot in the stirrup. "Will you help me dismount, please?"

"I think you can manage nicely without me," he said, his mouth slanted in a mocking smile, "given your size."

She deserved that; she knew she did, yet it inspired regret rather than a droll quip. "I believe we are both behaving in a ridiculous manner, sir . . . and I grant that I am responsible." Her mouth was open, yet nothing else came out. Her pride seemed to be in revolt, screaming for her to resume her seat in the saddle—without Dane's help—and take the reins in her hands. It was beyond her experience to feel defensive and apologetic. At least since she'd been a child and tried so hard to please her nanny or governess or even the butler and said she was sorry every time she'd not lived up to her own expectations.

Adjusting her grip on the saddle before she lost her hold altogether and landed in a heap at Dane's feet, she began to swing her leg back over to the other side.

Strong hands grasped her waist. A warm, hard body pressed against her back as she slid to the ground. She turned around with a quick jerk and came face to face and chest to chest with Dane, his hands still around her waist. She didn't dare move. She didn't want to move.

Nor did he move as his mouth slanted in a smile that seemed half cynical, half expectant . . . of what?

Every time he breathed, his chest moved ever so slightly against her breasts, the air he expelled caressing her mouth as his hands tightened at her waist, then eased and glided partway up her ribcage.

Her breath snagged as her body began to develop some expectations of its own.

"It wasn't delusion," she said in a rush, her voice a high squeak lowering to a husky whisper. "You *did* help me and you *are* taking care of me."

"Not yet, but I do have aspirations," he said gravely.

Her gaze flew back to his face, finding gravity rather than humor. She moistened her suddenly dry lips, swallowed against the excitement beating in her throat as she searched for the humor that must be lurking in his expression, praying she would find it. She knew he couldn't possibly be serious . . . could he? Failing to find a suitably clever reply, she resorted to sincerity. "I . . . I am grateful."

He tilted his head to the side and again gave her that odd half smile. "It's difficult for you—" He raised his hand to her cheek, to beneath her eye, then down, so slowly, so gently, as if tracing the trail of the tears she'd shed earlier. "—To need help, to admit it. Why?"

Fire spread through her at his touch, warm and comforting, then hot and seductive as it settled in the pit of her belly. She knew she trembled yet couldn't stop it, didn't want to stop it. She felt small and weak and minded neither with him so near. As he turned his hand and stroked her cheek with the backs of his fingers, his body still pressing against hers, strong and solid and steady, she felt safe, believing in that moment that he would never turn away from her, never mock her, never hurt her.

"Why?" he asked again.

A thousand memories rose like restless spirits to remind her why she didn't dare believe in anything but herself.

She stiffened and straightened and shrugged her shoulders, shrugging off his hands at the same time. "I have never felt the need."

His brows, perfect arches raising expressively, spoke of speculation, of questions, of some understanding that couldn't be explained, nor its source identified. "You've never felt the need, or you've never admitted to it?"

Oh, mercy, but he was too close to what she had learned to keep hidden, too aware of secrets she'd kept for too long. She forced herself to remain where she was, to not run or turn away from the probe of his dark, dark gaze. "I've never felt the need, sir. I said I am grateful for your aid. I did not relish walking back to Saxon Hill with only a horse for company." Some impulse prompted her to raise her hands to his shoulders and lean forward and press her lips to his cheek, right at the top of the crease that bracketed his mouth, then stand back again, as far as the animal behind her would allow. She meant to lower her hands, casually, as if it was the most impersonal of touches, yet the strength and hardness of his shoulders, the heat she felt through the fabric of his coat, invited her to lower her hands slowly down his arms, smoothing over the muscles that suddenly tensed under her touch, leaving him—so surprisingly hard to do—only when she could linger no longer. "But being grateful for company means only that, Lord Dane. With or without you, I would have managed to return to Saxon Hill, none the worse for it."

His quirky smile spread to both sides of his wide,

handsome mouth. "Of that I have no doubt," he said. "Now, shall we continue?"

Continue what? she wanted to ask, then sighed as he explained by the simple act of turning back to the road ahead.

"Can you mount, or do you want my help?" he asked over his shoulder.

Merry stepped up beside him and gave him an arch look as she took the reins of the horse bearing her packages from him and began walking at a sprightly pace, feeling quite smug at having made her point.

He said nothing as they fell into a rhythmic, easy walk, whistling softly, tunelessly, as if something had pleased him.

When had he ever felt so smug? Adrian wondered. Or so encouraged? The harder Lorelei tried to prove how unaffected she was, the more she betrayed herself. That she had to try at all was proof enough that he did affect her.

Thank God. He'd hate to think he was going through the rather debasing business of attraction—perhaps love—for nothing. Yet as he glanced at Lorelei's silhouette against the evening sky, at her straight nose raised proudly in the air, her gaze unwavering on the road ahead, her lower lip caught at the corner between her teeth, he knew without a doubt that she would be worth the price.

He had always known what he wanted very quickly upon seeing it or imagining it. This was no different. And he'd always known that nothing came easily. Lorelei was no exception. He had to be careful not to frighten her off, which would be surprisingly easy to do. She'd given him enough clues—in the panicked flutter of her eyes when he came too close and became too intimate, and in the way she employed words and attitude to put distance between them. Brummell, too, had hinted at the reasons with his cryptic references to her past and his warning not to hurt her. Even his uncle had mentioned it. Adrian wanted details, wanted to know what ghosts haunted her, yet as Brummell and Robert had said: it would have to come from Lorelei.

It gave him precious little to work with except the present. An uncomfortably silent present growing more unwieldy by the moment with her wariness of him and their shared physical awareness battling like tomcats in a bag. He groped in his mind for something to say that would, he hoped, place the burden of conversation on Lorelei, distracting them both from the lingering effects of standing too close in the dark. Far too close. Had she felt just how much he desired her? How urgently? Did she know how difficult it was for him to put a damper on his lust for her? Just thinking of her carnation scent and her soft contours enveloping him like a sultry breeze was enough to tempt him to spirit her off into the trees, to . . .

". . . Scare her off completely," he said under his breath as he willed his body to respect the need for caution.

"What?" she said, her voice a little high and breathless.

"Hmm?" he said, preoccupied over the struggle between mind and matter. "Did you say something?"

"I believe you said something first."

His step faltered as he realized that he must have voiced his warning to himself. "Did I?" He smiled and shrugged. "I have a habit of woolgathering—hadn't you heard?"

"I've heard," she said dryly. "But while others

believe you are easily distracted, I suspect it is just the opposite and you are not diverted. One would think you are hatching plots.''

''You are very perceptive, Lady Winters.'' He grimaced. ''That makes you sound like a dowager.''

''As are you, I think—perceptive, that is.'' Her voice faded, leaving only the *clip-clop* of the horses behind them.

''Then we will have to be especially careful to hide our secrets.'' He sensed rather than saw her cast him a sharp look. Damn. He hadn't wanted to alarm her, yet now that he'd chewed on his foot, he'd might as well swallow it. ''Or we could tell all and save ourselves the trouble.'' Deliberately he resumed his tuneless whistle to hide the seriousness of his suggestion. He'd meant it to sound like a jest, yet as soon as he'd said it, he'd been struck by how badly he wanted to know her secrets—all of them, including the tantalizing ones she so skillfully hid beneath layers of exotic cloth—

''My friends call me Merry,'' she said tentatively after a lengthy pause, then inhaled deeply. ''You may also, if you like.''

He chuckled at how quickly she shifted to arrogance from one sentence to the next. ''A sprightly name,'' he mused, ''yet I find that Lorelei suits you far better.''

''No one calls me that.''

Did he hear confusion in her voice? He hoped so. ''I shouldn't wonder. A sprite is not as threatening as a siren.''

Again, she inhaled deeply, opened her mouth and shut it again, apparently rendered speechless. Unfortunately, she also widened the space between them, as if he was the one suddenly posing a threat.

His brow creased as he rubbed the side of his nose, dismayed that he couldn't seem to avoid trying to compliment her when she so obviously distrusted flattery of any kind.

The lights of Saxon Hill appeared in the distance as they topped a hill, an ethereal glow cast by the chandeliers inside and the fairy lights strung in the gardens, all merging into an aura reflecting off the night sky. And then it disappeared again like a chimera bobbing up and down in the imagination as they descended the rise, isolated from the world once more. Soon they would be there, surrounded by people, separated by the restrictions of good manners and social chitchat. Suddenly it seemed of vital importance to put her at ease before then, to relax her guard against him before she felt the need to hide from him in the crowd.

"Tell me, Lorelei," he said, before he could think better of it, "who is Earl Stick-in-the-Mud?"

Chapter 10

Frowning, Merry tried to concentrate on the words he spoke as she gathered her thoughts from other, more enthralling topics. Her mind trailed at least a mile behind her—at the place where she'd slipped from the horse and stood so close to Dane, giving in to the temptation to touch his wonderful, expressive face, fighting the impulse to burrow into his strong arms and allow herself to feel safe and secure just once. Just for a moment or two. Odd how Dane's presence alone comforted as well as excited her.

Closer still was the memory of him referring to her as a siren. Even her long ago love had never paid her such a compliment, and certainly not in a way that suggested sincerity rather than gratuitous flattery. Yet she knew she couldn't trust such things, sincere or not. All one had to do was behave against expectations, or change one's appearance, or say the wrong thing, and compliments became insults, disapproval, rejection.

Sincerity, like love, was perishable.

That sobering reminder was enough to urge her back to the here and now, to drop frivolous thoughts in favor of—what? She blinked and frowned harder at the realization that she'd forgotten what he'd said. "I beg your pardon?" She gave him a brief sheepish smile. "I . . . didn't quite hear you."

He tossed her a disbelieving glance, equally brief. "Who is Earl Stick-in-the-Mud?"

"Exactly as Harriet's name for him implies," Merry replied candidly, thankful for any subject other than the ones that insisted on lurking in the shadows behind her. Still, she had the unsettling sense that even this was a topic best left alone. She had no business in the company of a man who so unnerved her. She should have walked away from him in a fit of suitable outrage upon discovering that he'd stood out of sight watching her struggle with the broken wheel without offering aid. Yet he was quite the most interesting man she'd met in years, and awkwardness and blatant physical responses aside, she had to admit that she liked his company and was having too much fun to dismiss him.

Fun—walking at least four miles in the dark while leading a horse laden with packages with a man who continually threw her off balance. A man who called her by her given name in a low, husky voice, as if it tasted too sweet on his tongue to release all at once. A man who called her a siren, who made her feel like one.

A siren. A blatant lie! She really ought to know better than to be taken in by such an absurdity. She ought to, except that she seemed to possess her full portion of female vanity. A vanity that rose quickly at a word or a look or a touch from Dane, as if it had been lying in wait all this time, waiting for him.

Light-headed from thoughts that raced without reaching any sane destination, she gave a little cough and forced her attention back to the subject. Earl Stick-in-the-Mud. That was it. The man she had almost decided to marry. She spoke quickly before she could wonder when she had decided *not* to marry him. ''Earl Dunworth is also a good and kind man whose most endearing trait is his failure to notice anything other than creatures that can either be consumed or stuffed and mounted to decorate his trophy room.'' *A nice, safe man,* she added silently, a man who never became aroused at a simple touch from her.

For the first time in her relationship with the earl, she wondered what it would take to arouse him. What would she do if he never became aroused? She'd counted on some male need from him.

She halted abruptly and stared blindly into the darkness. When had it begun to matter whether Earl Dunworth wanted her or not? The earl had fit her requirements exactly. A lifetime of benign neglect would be nothing new to her. She could certainly handle it, and in fact, had thought it was what she wanted. But suddenly the concept took on a dismal cast. What would be the point of marrying the earl if nothing in her life would change? More to the point: did she want anything to change? It occurred to her that she should perhaps find out before she proceeded with her plan to marry a stick-in-the-mud.

Merry blinked several times and refused to acknowledge the sudden burn behind her eyes . . . the despair that had been hovering over her since meeting Dane beneath the statue of a headless and armless Venus. A body without a mind. No one seemed to care what the head held. All that mattered was the body, for good or ill.

Dane shifted beside her, as if he, too, had been lost in thought. "You are weary. Come sit at the side of the road with me. There is a soft patch." He grasped her hand and tugged her, unresisting, to the carpet of grass and wildflowers, then shrugged out of his coat and spread it out for her to sit upon.

Still, she didn't protest but sat down with her legs to the side, thinking silly thoughts about Sir Walter Raleigh laying his coat across the mud for his queen—

Dane folded his long frame to sit beside her, his legs bent in front of him, his arms on his knees. She shouldn't be doing this. Allowing him to escort her safely back to Saxon Hill was one thing as long as they kept moving, but to linger by the side of the road with him for all the world as if they were enjoying a moonlight picnic was quite another—

"I won't tell if you won't," he said from the side of his mouth, as if he'd heard her thoughts.

"I won't tell," she vowed with a nervous smile. *I won't tell you that it is not the opinions of others I fret over but yours,* her mind added. How could she tell him that she feared what interpretation he would put on her behavior when even she didn't know what construction to put on it? All she knew was that disappointment had stabbed her sharply at the brief glimpse of Saxon Hill. She wasn't ready to step back into her life yet. She wanted to remain a siren named Lorelei for a little while longer.

Ruffling her hand over the lush grass at her side, she listened to the hush of night, to the lightest of breezes brushing through the trees across the road and the rustle of nocturnal creatures in the branches. The moon hung full, a round silver brooch against velvet sky, its surface etched with what appeared to be a face looking down on them with a smug grin—

"You are fond of this man who notices nothing about you?" Dane asked beside her, seemingly determined to remind her of the life she sought to avoid.

Try as she might, she couldn't find an answer for that. "We get along well enough," she finally said. "On rainy days we even manage to converse on subjects of mutual interest. . . ." Her voice trailed off at how pitiful that sounded. And the more they discussed her absent suitor, the more unnerved she became. Seeing him through Dane's eyes presented a very different picture of what life with the earl would be than the one she'd imagined. "But enough of that," she said, desperate to find another topic, another thought. "Do you miss America?"

Dane glanced at her again as if he knew she was grasping at straws. "I miss my cousins."

"Cousins? Have you no other family there?"

"Just Steven and Phillip. Steven was handling our enterprises there, and Phillip—" He shook his head. "Phillip is always searching for enterprises of his own."

"Was?" she asked. "Where is Steven now?"

He hesitated and plucked at a spear of grass. "He is on a British ship—one of the few who were actually impressed by His Majesty's navy."

"Oh," she murmured, not knowing what else to say. She knew the practice existed and had heard much on the subject, yet how much was exaggerated on the part of the Americans and how much was diminished by the British, she didn't know. Sadly, she doubted anyone knew for certain. "I'm sorry." Her hands fluttered up and down. "I don't know why things like that have to happen."

"I have agents searching for him."

She ached at the hopeless note in his voice. "You are very close."

"We are more like brothers."

"And Phillip, too?"

"I would like to think so, but Phillip is remote at best. We try to leave him alone as much as we can in hopes he will find what he is searching for."

"You try but you don't always succeed," she guessed.

"No," he said. "It's difficult. Just after I completed my tour of England three years ago, I received word that Phillip had taken one of our schooners and joined Jean Lafitte and his pirates at Barataria. I sailed for New Orleans immediately and spent another year trying to pry him away."

"And did you?"

"After I presented Lafitte with a brand new ship, he agreed to expel Phillip from the community. Now Phillip is more angry than ever." A wealth of pain throbbed in Dane's voice as he clasped and unclasped his hands. "He is the youngest of us, and carries his anger around like a loaded musket. . . ."

Merry sensed a story in his last statement, one that caused Dane as much anguish as his cousin. It was a story she very much wanted to hear. For all his candor, abstractions, and the confidence she'd seen in him, Dane became more an enigma to her with every passing moment.

But then, she'd known there was more to him than met the eye. Beau liked and respected him and did not suffer fools of any sort. Yet how could she approach what sounded like yet another painful subject?

"You cannot make such a statement, then expect me not to ask what happened," she said, careful to keep her voice low and even, careful to keep her gaze from him, careful not to make him feel as if she were pouncing on him in her curiosity.

"I have no idea," he said bleakly. "Phillip just began to change and refused to discuss why."

Dane remained silent so long, she became resigned that he would not answer. "I'm sorry, Lord Dane. Until now, I've not had the need for subtlety and therefore never perfected the art." She shifted her legs out in front of her in preparation of rising . . . and moaned.

Dane's head snapped around. "Have they gone to sleep?"

She bit her lip and shook her head. "A cramp."

"Right or left?"

"Both," she gasped, and leaned over to massage her calf.

Before she knew what he was about, he slid his hands under her legs and eased them around to rest across his lap. "Three years in the saddle jaunting around England and Scotland taught me how to relieve such things—" He grinned boyishly. "Even in my . . . hindquarters." He spoke softly, soothingly, continually, giving her no opportunity to protest. "This is no time for modesty. These cramps can be the very devil if not attended to." His grin slanted as he met her gaze with a wry expression. "In any case, I know what flesh feels like and I've already seen your le—your limbs." His hands dipped beneath her skirts and began to knead her calves.

"It sounds perfectly reasonable to me," she said on a gasp, as he found a knot and rolled it between his fingers. It felt so good, so much of a relief, that

she discarded all thoughts of protest. It felt so right
that he should take such an improper liberty with her,
as if it was meant to be, and not improper at all. "I
had a governess once who was a confirmed bluestock-
ing. She said that limbs grew on trees and the image
of sprigs and leaves protruding from our legs was far
more obscene than calling a leg a leg."

"That is what I like about you, my Lady Lorelei,"
he commented, still in that low, soothing voice. "No
pretense. No posturing and suffering for the sake of
propriety. No bluff and bluster."

"Odd. That's what I like about you," she said
breathlessly, as he coaxed each spasm to relax and
went on to another. His ministrations hurt dreadfully,
even as the warmth and strength of his hands felt so
very, very good.

"Is it?" His hands paused as he tilted his head and
regarded her with a tender, quizzical look that robbed
her of breath altogether. He had so many expressions—each so eloquent, each seeming to speak only
to her, for her.

"So we like one another," he said, as he resumed
massaging her calves, releasing each knot and moving
on to another with a glide of his fingers. "I'm glad
to know I didn't make a fool of myself for nothing."

"A jackass," she reminded him.

"Hmm."

She leaned back on her elbows and arched her neck
to stare at the stars, enjoying the feel of his rough
fingertips on her flesh, wallowing in the pleasure of
having someone take care of her, absorbing the same
magic that had so enthralled her the night before,
wishing it would last. How peculiar that his touch last
night and again this evening had stirred such turbulent
responses in her, yet now only comforted her, calmed

her. Odd that though she'd never been one to remain still for long, always needing to keep her mind and hands active, she now wanted nothing but stillness, nothing but to savor the contentment she felt.

Stillness was not a state she cultivated. It was too much like being alone in an empty room. Contentment was not a concept she'd ever entertained.

But this was different, like having the whole world spread at her feet, the entire universe revolving around this one tiny spot—all of it hers. Never had she known that such gentle moments existed. Even with Harriet, who always had a faraway look in her eyes as if her heart dwelled in another place, or with Beau who filled his moments with quips and observations and arrogant pronouncements about what was good for everyone about him.

And Dane liked her. He'd as much as said so. Many people "liked" her, yet never had it felt so special, so profound, so vitally important.

"When I was ten," he said suddenly, "influenza struck my family. It killed Steven's and Phillip's parents as well as my mother." The words came in a ragged whisper, haltingly, wrenchingly, as if he'd never spoken them before. As if he forced himself to speak them now.

As if he was illustrating his liking for her by sharing with her a past that had so disturbed him only a few moments ago.

She remained still, all but holding her breath, waiting for him to continue, needing him to continue.

"My father had promised to take Steven, Phillip, and me on a hunting trip as soon as the snow melted. Phillip had nagged and nagged—as only a child can do—to learn how to shoot. We didn't know Father was ill, and he was not one to break a promise. He became delirious and we had to drag him home in a litter. He died along the way.'' Dane recited the events now, his voice flat, emotionless, as his hands stroked her calves, then the backs of her knees, then the exposed flesh above her garters.

She felt nothing just then but stark terror at what she might hear.

''We each felt guilty for being the cause. If we had stayed at home, perhaps he wouldn't have taken a turn for the worse. If we had not gone hunting, we could have summoned the physician right away. Phillip insisted it was all his fault for demanding that Father honor his promise. I knew I should have refused to go. Steven thought he should have refused and explained to his younger brother why we shouldn't go. It all seemed to begin then.''

His hands stilled as he stared at the sky, relating in a flat voice how he'd held his father, feeling the life draining from him, hearing his father's last words, absolving him and his cousins of blame.

Carefully she eased her legs off his lap, wrapped her arms around them, and rested her cheek on her knees, watching him.

He didn't seem to notice her movement as he plucked at the ground and continued to stare into the darkness, continued to tell his story as if it were a simple observance and had nothing to do with him. But she heard the slightest fracture in his voice as he spoke of Phillip's hysteria and Steven's assumption of the blame. She saw the agitation with which he pulled stems from the ground, scattering uprooted wildflowers all about as he told how he'd claimed the fault was his and demanded that it not be spoken of again.

''We never have discussed it,'' he said. ''I've never

been able to speak of it . . . until now. It hurt too much. I don't suppose I need to tell you that.'' He turned to look at her.

Suddenly a chill seemed to freeze all that lived within her. He needed someone to understand, and he had chosen her. How could she have just sat there and listened? Why hadn't she stopped him? Her throat felt as if it were closing up and her stomach seemed to be tying itself in a knot. ''Yes,'' she said flatly, spacing her words to keep from choking on them. ''You do need to tell me if you expect me to understand how it feels to lose parents or family of any sort. I was an infant when my mother and father left me with nursemaids while they took a jaunt to Egypt. They remained there for three years, mucking about in old tombs without once returning to England or writing to me, or to the nursemaid, for that matter. My life didn't change after I was told they had died. Why should it have? I have no memories of them, beyond a portrait on the wall to prove they were real. One would think I simply sprang up in a patch of weeds.'' She pressed her lips together at the realization that she felt shame, not because she didn't understand Dane's anguish, but because at twenty-eight she had expended more energy and time learning how to jest about herself and bluff her way through each day than she had over the holes in her emotions. It hadn't occurred to her until now that the holes existed.

''I'm sorry, Dane,'' she said, forcing herself to go on. ''I have no concept of family or of the grief of losing a loved one. I wasn't particularly aware of families until I was old enough to pay attention to the villagers.'' She propped her chin on her knees, averting her gaze. ''All I do know of it is that people come and go in one's life, often without warning or comment. I have learned to expect it."

"What of Harriet and Beau?" he asked, so softly that she barely heard him. "You care for them . . . very much if I'm any judge."

"Yes, I care very much for them," she said as she straightened, feeling brittle, yet needing to stand and resume walking down the road with as much dignity as she could.

"And I expect I will continue to care for them long after they have gone on to other interests."

"I see," he murmured, giving her the terrifying sense that he did indeed see . . . that he understood a great deal more than she ever would.

"I truly am sorry," she said crisply. "I wish I knew how to sympathize—to comfort you over the loss of your family. I wish I had the wisdom to offer counsel about Phillip. I—I hear the pain in your voice and I know I should feel it, too. I wish I knew why I should feel it. I wish I did understand . . . for your sake. I wish I knew how. . . ." The emptiness yawned wider inside her, smothering any further words. She'd always known it was there, yet never had it felt so cold and barren. Never had she felt so lacking, so hollow. Managing to rise without shattering into a thousand pieces, she stood with her back to him, afraid to leave him, and equally afraid to turn back to him.

Afraid as she had never been to do the wrong thing. "I can't imagine why I've told you this as if it were some remarkable tale of woe. I'm not the only one to reach adulthood without knowing her parents. Our society is not noted for lavishing personal attention on its children."

"Hush," he said. "Don't spoil it."

Don't spoil what? she wondered a bit hysterically, and stiffened at the feel of his hands on her shoulders, at the caress of his breath on her ear, warming her in spite of her need just then to remain cold and empty until she was alone.

"We become acquainted with our emotions through experience, Lorelei," he said, in a voice that lulled and soothed her. "Experiences that have eluded you. But not for long, I promise you."

She trembled at the promise felt more than heard—in the gentleness of his hands on her shoulders, in the way he stood so close, almost surrounding her with his warmth, yet not overwhelming her, not forcing her to face him in a shame she'd never recognized before.

More warmth—heat, really—touched her cheek, penetrated her skin, permeated her blood. Dane's lips, kissing her gently, lingering, then moving to her jaw, drawing away slowly, as if he didn't want to draw away at all. She caught a faint drift of fragrance, like earth and leaves and flowers, absorbing it as if it were life itself, beginning to soften the hard shell of her, beginning to fill the emptiness.

His hands left her, yet she didn't feel abandoned. He stepped back from her, yet she still felt his warmth. She saw him gather up the leads of the horses and step back onto the road, his shirt sleeves stark white against the night shadows, and realized that he'd draped his coat over her to ward off the chill. The fertile scent of summer earth clinging to the fabric wafted around her as she joined him, softening even more as the inside edges of his eyebrows quirked upward and his mouth curved in a smile.

"Here," he said, as he held out one hand while rubbing the side of his nose with the other. "I've never bared my soul before," he said with a silent laugh. "It rattled me so much that I seem to have uprooted some flowers. I'd hate to think they died in vain."

She glanced down at the blooms hanging limply from his hand. He'd gathered them up and bunched them into a nosegay, rather than leaving them scattered in the grass. For some peculiar reason, the gesture touched her, reassured her that he would not do the same with her confidences.

Don't spoil it. She thought then that she knew what he'd meant. He'd shared with her a confidence that he had never shared before, had not spoken of before, even with his cousins. She had done the same. Somewhere in the past day they had each come to trust the other, and that was more magical than a midnight dance beneath the stars.

The cold left her completely as she walked beside him, keeping her gaze on the road ahead, saying nothing, feeling both pleasure and comfort in the silence between them.

He reached over to her, enfolded her hand in his, holding it as they strolled toward the lights of Saxon Hill, making her feel as if she were a pool of melted chocolate, ready to be molded into something new and infinitely special.

Chocolate! Merry rolled her eyes and punched her pillow with her fist later that night. What kind of corkbrain was she becoming? How could she have walked beside Dane for that last mile, so completely besotted that her mind rambled with lines for bad poetry?

She needed to remember that regardless of how fine or rare the confection, it inevitably was consumed and forgotten. Just as Dane was consuming her, one piece of resistance at a time.

Melted and ready to be molded, indeed! She was molded quite enough, thank you. More than enough. And tomorrow night she would make absolutely certain that he knew she was a great deal more than he would care to handle.

Chapter 11

Adrian knew the moment Lorelei entered the room, not by the sudden stir followed by a general hush, but because she was impossible to miss. Particularly in a gown of some iridescent silk that changed hues with every movement, every change in shadow and light, every breath. And most particularly when that gown followed every line and curve from neck to hem of her magnificent body, like water clinging to her flesh in the moonlight, yet revealing nothing but line and curve and dimension. Over the gown a tunic of a similar but more diaphanous fabric drifted around her as she walked, a misty waterfall shimmering in prisms of color, casting a shade of intrigue over the vision of her.

Magnificent . . . beautiful . . . proud and elegant . . . a woman in every sense of the word.

Of course, he doubted very much that she would appreciate his reaction. Her smugness increased visibly with every snatch of criticism and every loudly whispered expression of outrage, indicating that she fully expected him to be as shocked and repelled as the rest of the guests. He didn't doubt for a moment that her performance was for his benefit. Her studied avoidance of him while managing to parade in his line of vision confirmed his theory—at least to his satisfaction.

It disturbed him that she would go to such lengths to warn him off, even as it pleased him that she felt the need. That perhaps he had touched her as deeply as she had touched him. "You appear inordinately pleased with yourself," Brummell commented, as he sauntered into Adrian's line of vision.

"What?" Adrian murmured absently, as he tried to see around him.

"Ease up, old man." Brummell stood fully in front of him, his eyebrows cocked. "It's bad enough your chin dropped to the floor when Merry made her entrance. You wouldn't want to add to the gossip by tripping over your tongue."

"Oh . . . I might," Adrian said, resigned to allowing Brummell to have his say. "If it would divert the talk from Lorelei."

"Lorelei is it? Most people found it too absurd to call her by such a name. The Baroness Winters, a siren," he said, mimicking a well-known gossip. "What were her parents thinking?" Brummell smiled fondly in Lorelei's direction. "Merry overheard that and remarked that it was wishful thinking on her parents' part to name her after a siren. She went on to say that all anyone really cares about is a provocatively aristocratic name and a desirable fortune, both of which she possessed. That caused more than a ripple in the *ton*'s complacency. It might be true, but it is bad form to voice such things."

"Is that when you stepped in with a more palatable name for her?"

Inhaling deeply, Brummell swept his gaze over the assemblage and changed the subject. "Lady Harriet sent me into town to find Merry last evening."

Not liking Brummell's too-casual manner, Adrian had to work hard to affect nonchalance. "Oh? Did you find her?"

"First I found her curricle in a ditch." Brummell spoke with alacrity, seeming all too eager to tell his tale. "I dismounted and searched for what I feared would be her broken body. I walked for a distance before I found her, quite whole—thank heaven—and half reclining in a rather interesting position." He smoothed an artfully arranged curl of his hair. "You appeared quite intent on—what was it you were doing? Examining her for injuries, I trust? When I heard Merry instruct you rather tartly on the difference between limbs and legs, I was assured that she was in top form."

Adrian said nothing as bile rose in his throat at the thought of what else Brummell might have heard. Last night with Lorelei had been, to Adrian, a deeply personal intimacy and something not to be shared with anyone.

"Good fellow that I am, I retreated to a safe distance to wait, hoping fervently that you would not linger overlong and force me to announce my presence. I have an aversion to messy situations. I would deny myself the pleasure of hearing a juicy bit of information to avoid having to defend a lady's honor, which she would not appreciate and one of us would no doubt regret. I understand you are a crack shot and quite proficient with foils."

Hearing the subtle threat embedded in Brummell's words, Adrian continued to hold his tongue. It appeared that he was stuck with the man's company and opinionated soliloquies until he knew exactly what Brummell knew and what Brummell wanted.

"In any event, Merry demonstrated no signs of distress, absolving me of any duty beyond seeing that she arrived back at Saxon Hill safely. And, chivalrous—and discreet—fellow that I am, I made certain I was just out of earshot." He arranged himself in an elegant lean against a pillar in front of and to the side of Adrian's position and contrived a dramatic yawn. "Have you any idea what a dead bore chivalry can be? I was practically frothing at the mouth in curiosity ... particularly over Merry's seeming contentment. Never have I seen her so still for so long. Usually I am exhausted within an hour of watching her flit about."

Absorbing the information Brummell had just—unwittingly, or purposely?—provided, Adrian crossed his arms and regarded him blandly, still suspicious that he and Lorelei had been overheard, and hoping he was wrong. "She is an energetic woman," he said carefully. "We had to walk a good four miles back to Saxon Hill, yet she wasn't winded in the least."

"How fortunate that you happened along in time to escort her." Narrowing his eyes, Brummell fixed him with a deceptively lazy stare. "That *is* what happened, isn't it?"

Adrian smiled. "I came upon her attempting to repair a wheel."

"Attempting? I'm alarmed that she didn't succeed. She usually does. Resourceful is our Merry."

"She would have succeeded admirably if the axle had not been split."

"Then I daresay Dame Fortune was with you. Otherwise, Merry would have raised a cloud of dust behind her before you could have regained a seat in the saddle. I have, once or twice, been compelled to suffer the grit of her wake so as not to offend her sense of self-sufficiency." Holding up his hand, he examined his nails. "It's all a ruse, you know."

"Her self-sufficiency seems quite genuine to me," Adrian said.

"It is," Brummell agreed, "as far as it goes. She has worked so hard to convince us all that she almost believes it herself. If allowed to continue in her delusion, Merry will never learn what is good for her. Already she avoids society more than she joins it."

Adrian had been wondering why he had not seen Lorelei during the last Season, or at any function since. Something very close to anger began to simmer at the accompanying realization that not once during the Season past had he heard her name mentioned by any one of the persons who'd surrounded her that first night begging for advice, reassurance, comfort. It seemed apparent that out of sight, Lorelei did not exist for those who were so ready to take advantage of her when she was present.

"I see your mind is working, no doubt drawing the appropriate conclusions," Brummell said. "Merry is aware that her popularity—or anyone's, for that matter—is fleeting and that the interest shown in her is shallow at best. So she withdraws a bit more each year, doing first what she expects others to do to her. If it continues, others will begin to take as little notice of her as she does of herself."

"Why don't you call a leg a leg?" Adrian said, impatient with Brummell's rambling. "If you have a point, make it. If not, go sharpen your wits on someone else.''

Sighing, Brummell met his gaze. ''My point is that Merry has many reasons to disbelieve a man's genuine regard for her, both affectionate and lustful, as well as a great deal of experience in turning disbelief into fact. More than once she has chased away suitors who found her attractive and entertained aspirations of marriage.''

''If they were frightened off,'' Adrian said, as he nodded toward Lorelei, still strutting about the ballroom, ''by displays such as this, then their 'regard' had the depth of a sheet of parchment.''

''Agreed, but as words add character and importance to parchment, so does time and familiarity add depth to emotion. They were, for the most part, good men who found her attractive in spite of—or perhaps because of—her height and well-rounded proportions. After all, there was once a woman who found our Regent quite attractive, and he goes rather beyond mere plumpness. Merry might have been happy with either of her suitors, perhaps found love. . . .'' Brummell returned a man's wave, then abruptly turned to face Adrian, effectively discouraging the man from approaching. ''Instead, she decides to court marriage with a man who hasn't the wit to see beyond the barrel of his musket or the shaft of his arrow. A man who will notice her needs as little as she does. A man,'' he paused dramatically, ''from whom she expects nothing and who therefore will not have the power to hurt her with his rejection.''

Brummell had the grace to look chagrined at his continued verbosity and held up his hands in surrender. ''Yes, I know I digress, and you have already surmised much of what I tell you.'' He grinned mockingly. "Hope for Merry lends my tongue wings with which to pursue it."

Adrian rolled his eyes. "You hang about with Lord Byron too much."

"Only because I allowed the woman I love to slip through my fingers."

Adrian ignored the immediate curiosity the statement raised, sensing Brummell used it to illustrate rather than to confide. "Finally I sense that Brummell is prodding me with a point," he mumbled to the elaborately frescoed ceiling.

"My name is George. I give you leave to use it."

Feeling a curious pleasure at the privilege granted him, Adrian pushed away from the wall. "All right, *George,* you have one minute to drive your point home."

"Put on your damned spectacles, Lord Dane, and you might see desperation in Merry's actions tonight. She always follows desperation with full retreat. One way or another, she will remove herself as the object of your interest. I suggest you make a decisive move."

Absently, Adrian patted his coat until he felt the familiar shape of his spectacles, then pulled them out and slipped them on as his gaze again tracked Lorelei. Her step seemed to be dragging and her nose was not quite so high in the air. Her eyes were glazed as if she were focused on anything beyond the room, hearing anything but the chatter making the rounds in overloud whispers.

". . . Displaying her shape with such a design, as if she were *proud* of her size . . . beyond decency . . . they must have sewed it right on her . . . a waste of such beautiful cloth to drape it over so much . . .

plump as a Christmas goose and decorated like one. . . ."

"For Merry's sake," Brummell added, "I suggest you do it quickly and firmly." He half turned as if to walk away, then seemed to think better of it. "And if you don't do it in such a way that will make everyone choke on their damned superiority, I will—"

Adrian strode away without hearing more. Impatient as he'd been with Brummell's—George's—lecture, he had been interested enough not to realize how quickly Harriet's guests had turned ugly, or how loudly. Action was definitely called for. And after hearing what George had to say, Adrian felt a definite urgency to suspend the game of courtship barely begun and abandon subtlety altogether. Lorelei had set the *ton* on its collective ear tonight. He might as well finish the job. He knew what he wanted, and though she hadn't admitted it in so many words, her actions spoke well enough of what she wanted. It was, he knew, an arrogant assumption, but one upon which he was willing to gamble.

Lorelei stood in the center of the room, alone and surrounded only by space, as if she were an island unto herself, passed by and deserted.

An island upon which he would like to be stranded.

Yet her nose regained its former lofty position and her shoulders straightened as she saw him approach. Her eyes narrowed, as if she anticipated and prepared for a final blow.

He reached for her hand, bowed, lifted it to his lips, lingered over the kiss, hiding his grimace at the texture of her gloves and wishing it were her skin instead.

"Lord Dane," she said, with a brittle smile that barely cracked her features.

"Lorelei," he said, as he slowly straightened, chiding her in a clear voice for all to hear, blindly following an instinct that did not share its intent until each word was delivered and each action performed. "We have gone beyond such formality, I think." Placing her hand in the crook of his elbow and covering it firmly with his own, he led her to the terrace doors and turned her to face the assemblage. "Be still, my love," he said as she tried to pry her hand from his grasp. "I find I cannot wait as you wished. I trust you will forgive me . . . eventually."

She stilled instantly and so completely he wondered if she breathed. "What are you doing?" she asked, without moving her lips.

Ignoring her, he watched Brummell edge his way around the room to take a position nearby—within strangling distance, Adrian thought with some amusement.

Lady Harriet raised her hands to her mouth as if she either contained a shriek or was trying not to faint.

Uncle Robert continued to sit in his chair in the nearby corner, his mouth quirked. It occurred to Adrian that his uncle had heard every word he and Brummell had passed between them.

Rubbing the side of his nose, Adrian glanced down at his feet to conceal his struggle to swallow the lump that had suddenly risen from his chest. "Countess Saxon, ladies and gentlemen," he said firmly. "Lorelei—*Lady Lorelei*—" He tossed out a sheepish smile. "—asked me to wait until the banns were posted, but in light of her recent choice of attire, I find I cannot. If she must flaunt her beauty before society, then I must insist that she do so before me first, and in private, so I may have time to collect myself.'' He hoped the grin he lavished on the company was suitably bemused.

Brummell quickly lowered the glass he'd just raised to his lips and coughed.

Lady Harriet's eyes widened above her hands, still covering her mouth.

Uncle Robert chuckled with glee.

Lorelei stood as stiff and still as Venus in the garden.

''To that end, I must deny Lorelei's wish that we wait and announce that we will be wed, here at Saxon Hill, in ten days' time. Of course, we would like for Lorelei's *dearest* friends to witness our marriage and therefore request that you all attend the ceremony.'' He squeezed Lorelei's suddenly clammy hand and shot her a hard look, warning her to keep silent.

A collective gasp whooshed through the room and no doubt the halls beyond.

Brummell, apparently recovered from his shock, saluted him with his glass, then drained it in one gulp.

Lady Harriet stifled a shriek.

Uncle Robert nodded in approval.

Lorelei began to tremble and her fingers dug painfully into his arm. From the corner of his eye, he saw the color drain from her face, then reappear as red flags of outrage on her cheeks. ''You're insane,'' she said from the corner of her mouth. ''Take it back. Now . . . Dane, I'll sit on you if you don't take it back.''

Knowing he had to do something before she recovered enough to shout at him, he turned, pulled her into his arms, bent her backward, leaned over her, and smothered her continued mutterings with a deep, thrusting kiss.

He knew Lorelei's hands were fluttering in the air

as he caught her off balance, as he tasted her lips and
then beyond, coaxing her to respond with a thorough
exploration of her mouth. Her tongue retreated, then
thrust to repel his. He felt her shift as if she were
regaining her footing and preparing to kick him. He
bent her lower, enfolding her in a firm embrace that
allowed her little room to maneuver. Sound roared in
his ears. Fever swiftly raced through his blood. His
body responded predictably, swiftly, pressing against
her.

It *was* insane, what she did to him.

She stilled, rested her hands on his shoulders, became limp in his arms, a dead weight he was hard
pressed to keep from dropping. Tightening his grasp
at her waist, he straightened and withdrew from the
kiss, allowing the barest space to come between their
mouths, as he reluctantly lowered his arms to his
sides. Aware that he was in a blatantly embarrassing
state, he continued to face her, allowing the gossamer
folds of her tunic to shield him.

''Do not move,'' he muttered.

Lorelei stared at him blankly, her lips parted and
moist, her chest heaving with short, rapid breaths.

Smiling, he cradled the sides of her face with his
hands, he stroked her cheeks with his thumbs, unable
to stop touching her. ''It's done, Lorelei,'' he whispered against her mouth and tasted her once more.

It's done. A whimper escaped her as Dane brushed
his lips—so gently, so slowly—from one corner of
her mouth to the center to the other corner and then
back again, barely touching her, yet touching her
more deeply than had his passion a moment past.
More completely than she'd ever been touched before.
Her fingers dug into his shoulders. Her mind screamed

"*No!*" as every vein in her body seemed to vibrate with a low thrum at the feel of his arousal pressed against her. Her heart warmed and rolled over in pleasure even as she refused to give in to the beauty of his tenderness and the need to encourage him to go on and on until his kisses turned to passion once more and she felt him inside her, filling her. . . .

He lifted his mouth, then lowered it again, a last light kiss that lingered and stole a nibble, then two.

Her lips and jaw ached with her effort not to respond. Her eyes burned with her refusal to acknowledge her sudden urge to cry at the sweetness of it. Such sweetness that it felt as if he were nurturing her, and the promises she'd heard in his voice more than once. Promises he was determined to keep. Promises she wanted very badly to believe.

It's done. And she had done it—with her efforts to scare him off before he could touch her, before she could foolishly believe. "Please stop," she whispered into his mouth. "Please."

He raised his head and stepped back, turning his head toward their rapt audience and clearing his throat. "As you can see, ten days will be quite long enough for me to wait," he said, with an endearing grin that widened as more than one woman sighed and more than one gentleman chuckled.

He arranged Lorelei's hands—one on his shoulder, the other in his hand—and grasped her waist. "Lady Harriet, if you will be so kind as to have the musicians play, I fancy a dance with my fiancée."

Before Lorelei could become alarmed at the implications of their positions and the music that began to drift from the quartet of musicians on a balcony overlooking the ballroom, Dane swept her into the scandalous glide of the waltz.

As scandalous as her gown. As scandalous as his proposal and his kisses. As scandalous as the heat gathering inside her. Yet she pliantly followed his lead as he whirled her into a turn around the ballroom as guests moved out of their way . . . back to the doors leading out onto the terrace . . . into the enchantment of a balmy night lit by a silver brooch of a moon against an indigo velvet sky.

The outrageousness of it appealed to her. The beauty of the moment held her in Dane's arms as surely as his strength.

She brazenly tossed a bright smile at the guests still staring at them, boldly stepped closer to Dane, too close, yet not close enough, allowing herself—for now, for tonight—to be enchanted by the magic that was Dane.

For now, for tonight, it was done.

Chapter 12

How did he do it? Merry wondered for the hundredth time since Dane had left her at the door to her bedchamber the night before, still moon-eyed, still in the grip of a spell that wouldn't allow her to voice the protests churning in her mind. Those same protests were joined by others as the night wore on and finally gave way to dawn. She'd sat in a chair all night, trying to think logically, yet succeeding only in reliving every moment she'd spent in his company. She hadn't even removed her gown—reluctant, she admitted, to disturb the magic that lingered even now in the light of day.

How did Dane render her so helpless against her own good sense? She'd been kissed before, but never with such urgency, as if he'd waited too long and couldn't get enough. The tenderness that followed had been so exquisite that she'd nearly wept with it. She'd never become so completely lost in a kiss before . . . not even with her long ago betrothed. The kiss that had ended her hopes of marriage for the sake of love had indeed paled in comparison to Dane's assertive passion and his persuasive tenderness.

Horrified by her thoughts, she firmly told herself that she hadn't become lost in Dane's kiss. *She hadn't.* Somehow she'd managed to keep her wits about her, not responding when she'd wanted to—so much. She'd had to struggle with her more primitive instincts to keep from melting into a puddle at his feet, but she'd managed it, somehow. And she would manage, somehow, to face Dane and graciously thank him for his attempt to save her from her self-inflicted disgrace and then firmly say good-bye to him.

As soon as she found him. As soon as she found the resolve to end the fairy tale.

She shook her head against the doubts parading through her mind and glanced out the window of the sitting room adjoining her bedchamber. Thankfully, Harriet was playing hostess and Beau was no doubt rescuing her "good name" by rhapsodizing over the romance of it all. Beau seemed to think it was his life quest to convince the *ton* that whatever she did was "the very thing."

Why, she wondered, did it feel so different, so unbelievably special, when Dane rescued her? Why had she not immediately protested at his shocking announcement when she'd suffered no such reluctance to spurn the ardent attentions of other suitors? Their charm had certainly been more polished than Dane's candor and, yes, arrogance. They certainly had been more vocal and socially active than Dane, whose mind often wandered so deeply into a thought that one wondered if he would ever emerge.

Yet his body had become quite alert every time they'd touched since meeting—only two days ago? She wished she had the courage to accept the obvious reasons why. If she gave it serious thought, she would also have to entertain the reasons why she completely forgot herself in his company. Thank heavens a woman's body was not so obvious in its needs. And that was all it was, all it could be. Needs, nothing more. Everyone had them, though she had always had more than was seemly.

But Dane's kisses had been strong and sure and convincing in the way he seemed to lose control. He had danced with her that first night when no one was watching, when he could have just as easily ducked behind a bush rather than again seek her company. He had executed the waltz with grace and no small measure of sensuality, staring at her with smoldering eyes, seducing her with a touch, a look, a breath.

She gave an inelegant snort of disgust and focused on the moments when she'd entered the ballroom to a buzz of shocked comments and unkind remarks. She'd anticipated an unfavorable reaction and had not been disappointed. After all, she'd been counting on those reactions to show Dane the truth. She hadn't anticipated how much it would hurt to be so criticized by people who were supposed to be her friends after years of having their acceptance and affection. She hadn't anticipated the look of horror that Harriet had so quickly concealed as she'd greeted Merry's entrance with warmth and dignity, nor the way she had snapped at several of her guests and attempted to remain close to Merry, to protect her. Ordering the gown had been a whim. Wearing it in public had been a tantrum that had hurt her friends as well as herself.

And Dane, damn him, with his ability to see beneath the surface, to think and act rather than mindlessly react, had known exactly why she'd done it. Dane, damn him, had taken extreme measures to show her that it hadn't worked. Heaven help her, she'd never known a man such as him. A man who looked and behaved like a hero. A man who never did anything halfway.

Merry sank onto the cushioned seat built into the outward bow of the window and blindly stared at the dark clouds lumbering in from the coast. She was eight-and-twenty years old—too old to be behaving as she had last night without considering how it might affect her friends, and taking it for granted that they would contrive to smooth it over—

Movement outside caught her eye. She leaned nearer the window and squinted as the sun peeked out from behind a cloud, brightening the landscape until another gray cloud overtook it. A man strolled along the bank of a pretty little pond, an aimless drift to his steps as he tossed something to the ducks in the water, then reached into another pocket and scattered something else over the ground for the squirrels foraging around the nearby trees.

Dane. He was alone. The time was perfect for her to seek him out, to end this absurd situation before it went on and he ended it instead. She frowned as she tried to decipher the thought. Regardless, it would be easier this way. Easier to wonder forever if he would have ended it than to know for certain after it was too late.

She wasn't altogether certain that it wasn't already too late. But just in case it wasn't, she had to do something . . . now.

Yet she continued to stare at Dane, imagining the inside corners of his brows curving upward as he crouched and held perfectly still, watching the ducks, studying them as if he were a small boy who had never seen such creatures before . . . just as he had watched and studied her as if he had never seen a woman before.

Abruptly she rose from the window seat and strode to the door. She was eight-and-twenty years old. Too old to put off facing the consequences of what she had wrought. Too old to believe in heroes and fairy tales.

The house was silent, deserted but for the maids and footmen going about daily tasks and the butler who opened the front door for her without so much as raising a hair of his brows at her appearance.

"Saunders, why is the house deserted?"

"My lady and her guests are on a picnic," he replied. "You will find them in the parkland. Since rain seemed a possibility," he added, as Merry cast a dubious glance at the sky, "a tent has been erected. My lady said that we should not expect them back until evening. She instructed me to tell you that you should have sufficient time and privacy to sort yourself out."

Gaping at Saunders over her shoulder as she wandered out the door and across the broad portico, Merry nearly stumbled and toppled down the steps. She sighed at Harriet's continued manipulations, descended the steps, and headed for the pond. In light of all that had transpired, she supposed that gossip about her and Dane being alone would be redundant.

She, on the other hand, would prefer to have her conversation with Dane in public, and privacy could go hang. For the last ten years, precious little about her life had been private.

Thoroughly annoyed at her cowardice, she walked faster, more determined than ever to extricate herself and Dane from the untenable situation that she'd created and he'd carried to an illogical conclusion. He really didn't deserve such consideration. She certainly hadn't asked or expected him to play the hero. She'd expected him to run in the other direction. Women such as she weren't supposed to get heroes of their own. Dane should have realized that.

Halfway to the pond, she halted and surveyed the banks, the meadow on one side and the copse of trees on the other. Nothing was there but the pond. No ducks. No squirrels. No Dane.

Thunder rumbled in the still air.

She looked up at the clouds hanging heavy in the sky and felt a sprinkle of moisture. Rain. She'd seen the clouds roll in. She'd heard Saunders mention rain—

It hit her before she could lower her gaze and turn back toward the house—sheets of rain, drenching her within seconds. Her feet squished in her kid slippers as she walked back to the house. Her hair, weighted by moisture, toppled from its coil and straggled over her shoulders, down her back, in her face. She would have to go straight to her room to dry off and change before cornering Dane.

She had been given a reprieve.

Her steps slowed, and she raised her face to the rain, feeling light and carefree even as she told herself she was annoyed at the delay in seeing Dane, in cutting him from her life. A life that had seemed to begin only two nights ago, as if she'd been sleeping until then, waiting for Dane. . . .

Another fairy tale. Another illusion.

She tasted salt and began to run toward the nearest door—the entrance to the library—running faster than she had in years. Running away from the sudden realization that she was dangerously close to believing in fairy tales. To believing that she could have one all to herself.

Gasping, she pushed open the double doors leading into the library and ran inside, straight to the slate floor laid in front of the fireplace to keep from dripping on the carpet. Bending her head, she gathered her mass of hair over her shoulder, twisted it, and wrung it out. A puddle grew at her feet and began to steam from the heat of a freshly lit blaze. Her sodden gown clung to her body and made flapping noises as she kicked off her slippers, pulled her bodice away from her breasts, and turned her back to the fire. . . .

And saw Dane sitting in a chair, his spectacles perched halfway down his nose, a book dangling from his hand. His eyes had that distant quality she'd seen before, as if his thoughts had been far away and hadn't yet caught up with what he saw and heard.

Swallowing down a scream of frustration, she measured the distance to the door, wondering if she could disappear before he became oriented to her intrusion. She looked down at her hands still holding soaked cloth away from her breasts and abruptly lowered her arms. Her bodice remained as she left it—jutting out in twin peaks. Quickly she yanked on the skirt, the fabric immediately becoming plastered to her chest again.

He tilted his head, regarding her from head to foot and back again. "I hope you're not still wearing that gown for my benefit," he said softly. "I saw your dimensions quite well last night."

Not now, she wanted to shout. Not when she was so bedraggled and her face was wet with more than rain. Not when she was struggling so hard to maintain her determination. Not when she suddenly, inexplicably, felt so fragile at having him see the flaws she'd so defiantly displayed the night before. But it had to be now, she realized a little hysterically. It had to be now because she didn't really want to convince him that he didn't want her. Because it would be incredibly easy to put it off again and again until they were actually wed. Because with every moment she spent with him, hope expanded inside her, and today, or next week, or ten years from now, he ultimately *would* be convinced.

"I must apologize to you as well as to Harriet. Ordering this gown was a whim. Wearing it in public was a tantrum." She shoved a wet strand of hair from her face and met his gaze. "But since it is done, I urge you to take another good look, Dane," she said, as she held her arms out at her sides. "There is no tunic now to soften the truth."

He looked her up and down, studied her legs and thighs and hips, clearly outlined by the clinging silk, stared at her breasts, her nipples hard nubs beneath the fabric.

"What is your point, Lorelei?" he asked with a hint of impatience.

Lorelei. Why couldn't he call her Merry, like everyone else? Why couldn't he treat her as others did? "You can't possibly want to marry me."

"Yes, I can." He gave her a small smile, tender, whimsical.

"Why?" She quickly turned her back to him, wanting to run, yet knowing there was nowhere to hide from his answer. There were so many reasons why: money, connections, convenience, children. From Dane there was only one reason she wanted to hear. Conversely, it was the only one she wouldn't believe.

"Wel-l-l-l," he said, drawing the word out, driving her mad with his delay. "I don't suppose you believe in love at first sight?"

"At first sight," she said with a humorless laugh.

"Love at first sight is no more than fascination for a beautiful face, or an appealing form, which can't possibly last if the person does not live up to the image. Therefore it cannot possibly be love." She turned back to face him. "In any case, I do not present the sort of image that captures a man's fascination."

He sighed. "Because you are tall."

"Very tall," she agreed, careful to keep her voice even, her tone casual, though she felt quite breathless at his failure to mention that she was plump as well, almost as if he didn't think she was. "And not in the least delicate or dainty."

"No, you're not," he said with a cheerful note. "Though to be fair, I would point out that delicate and dainty can be tedious. I somehow doubt that you are given to swooning, or that your health is fragile. You can repair a broken wheel and walk four miles and more without complaint. I also doubt that you are preoccupied with vanity and therefore spend your time more productively. And since you are wrongly convinced that you do not have beauty to cultivate and lean upon, you cultivate your mind and rely on your wits."

"I am outspoken and brazen and unconventional," she shot back, not wanting to think about what he'd said for fear she'd take his statements as compliments, and perhaps truth.

"Yes, you are—shockingly so, at times." He removed his spectacles and tucked them in a pocket. "As you said: beauty can sustain interest only for so long if there is nothing beneath the surface. I prefer attributes that will not fade with age, such as humor and intelligence. I am also curious by nature and therefore appreciate an unpredictable disposition such as yours."

"I am intolerably independent, as you discovered when you tried to rescue me," she said desperately, confused by the turn of conversation.

"That is frustrating, I admit. A man likes to think he is useful from time to time." He continued to watch her, to hold her gaze, a silent command for her to carefully attend what he said. "On the other hand, your independence and self-sufficiency will save me from feeling as if I have a millstone around my neck rather than a wife by my side."

"I am not submissive," she said. "I never will be."

"Good. I abhor slavery in any form."

"I'm very wealthy, you know," she said, trying another tack. "And I refuse to allow anyone to manage my fortune for me, much less take possession of it."

"If I'm not mistaken, an agreement can be signed which will leave your inheritance in your control. Besides," he added with an amused smile, "I have more wealth than you and don't know what to do with it. Having more would strain my imagination."

Merry closed her eyes for a moment and wondered why she felt as if they were engaged in a wager with marriage as the stakes. If she had the final word, Dane would bow out. If he had the final word, they would marry. And just then she had the bizarre notion that the only way she would win was if he did.

Bizarre indeed, and altogether unsettling, given the risk. Dane always did this to her—confusing her as he reduced her convictions to uncertainties and her pragmatism to whimsy. She'd always known what she wanted, yet thanks to Dane, she no longer knew why she'd made certain choices. If she didn't stop him, she would likely forget that she preferred Merry to

Lorelei and wouldn't know by which name to call herself.

"I don't know if I want children," she blurted, unearthing a fear she had never voiced except in the privacy of her mind. "I know nothing about them, you see, and am quite terrified by the prospect of having one depend upon me. You need an heir."

He flinched at that, then shook his head. "I don't need an heir. Steven has two sons. I would like to have children, but it is not a requirement for happiness."

Taking a deep breath, she glared at him, preferring anger to thinking about his implication that she was a requirement for his happiness. "I have a passionate nature that is unseemly," she said, determined to end this nonsense once and for all, no matter what.

"We would be tragically mismatched if you didn't." He stepped closer to her, his eyelids lowered a bit to give him a lazy, seductive look. "And passion is only unseemly when misused." He took another step. "Did you misuse it?"

"My former fiancé thought so," she said flatly. "He likened me to courtesans and gypsies and found the prospect of enduring my demonstrative nature in marriage distasteful." She paced the square of slate, then expanded her range to the carpets as she hurled the words at him as fast as she could. "You think I am intelligent? Think again. I convinced myself that I loved him because I was fascinated with a handsome face and loved his charming words and pretty compliments. I believed it all without once giving thought to the man who uttered them. I threw myself at him." She paused, suddenly unable to draw enough breath, to calm the erratic beat of her heart. Her throat seemed to close, denying escape for confessions she'd made to no one but herself, denying her shame a voice. But she had opened that dark closet in which she'd hidden the memory from the world and it would not be pushed back inside. In spite of her fear of what Dane would think of her, of how he would look at her, the words continued to tumble out, burying her in panic, reminding her of why she'd been willing to settle for marriage with Dunworth rather than take a chance on watching a man she cared for turn away from her in disgust. "Blast it, Dane, I enjoyed every bit of it. I felt no shyness or shame. And then I wanted to beg him not to leave me. I had to run away before I promised him that I would be anything he wanted."

Dane stared straight ahead as she paced around the room. "And you are afraid that I might put you in a similar situation."

"Not at all," she said with a mocking look. "For the question will never arise. I will not marry you, Dane." She leaned against the wall by the window, staring blindly at the rain running down the glass in sheets, blurring her view of the outside world. She'd broken rules and society indulged her small rebellions, yet those were actions resulting from choice. They didn't have to be repeated. She had listened to other women and she'd read whatever books she could find. Sex was a pleasure for men and a duty to women. Ladies did not enjoy it. They certainly didn't participate enthusiastically. Even Harriet, who admitted to being in love with her husband when she married him, had not disrobed for him. She had lain still and accepted his lust, her nightrail pushed up just enough to allow him entry. She had not arched beneath him, touched him, begged for more. Yet Merry would. She knew she would. Since meeting Dane, she'd imagined it in lurid detail. And if Dane were to reject her, she feared she would do what pride had not allowed her to do with her first love. She would beg. She would chase him to the ends of the earth to be near him because a man like Dane was worth the sacrifice of pride. She knew that, too.

She glanced over her shoulder at Dane, watching her, waiting, saying nothing.

She walked silently across the room toward the door, knowing there was no reason to remain, no reason to exchange another word with Dane. She should be pleased at her success. She'd had the last word. She had won.

Yet as she reached for the latch, she wondered why she felt as if she had lost.

"You think too much, Lorelei," Dane said angrily, as he flattened his palm against the door, preventing her from pulling it open, "and render me speechless with your conclusions."

Startled that he had come up behind her so silently, she pressed her hand to her chest, sagged against the door, and looked up at him from beneath her lashes, then wished she had not. His gaze burned into her with not a hint of distaste or coldness or disappointment. It simply burned with the emotions chasing across his face—anger certainly, impatience definitely, desire . . . shockingly.

"It's quite simple, Dane," she said wearily. "I was unbelievably stupid. I mistook the opportunity to fit in—to be accepted—for love. If he wanted me, then everyone else would like me. I wanted so very badly to fit in, you see . . . and I wanted him because he was handsome and well liked and he told me what I wanted to hear. I have not been certain since that I would not be driven to accept a man such as you for the same reasons. Passion aside, you deserve to be loved. I do not know the difference between love and my own need. I need to be loved, yet I am not certain how to love in return. You are a highly principled man who values sincerity. I fear I am sincere only in my selfishness.''

"You wanted to give yourself to a man because you believed you loved him and because you wanted to fit in. And I, like other boys, visited my first brothel when I was fourteen because it was the thing to do . . . and I wanted to fit in. Because it's a rule or some such idiocy. I didn't enjoy it and I cast up my accounts all over the woman's bed afterward.''

"Dane," she said forgetting wretchedness in favor of exasperation. "It is not the same."

"Why isn't it? Who made the decision that a boy can rut with a whore with the blessing of society, yet a woman cannot make love out of love—misguided or otherwise? Who proclaimed that a husband can feel pleasure in the act, but if a woman enjoys it, then she is not decent?''

All Merry could do was shrug helplessly. It made sense, and it appealed to her own peculiar notions of what was right and what was not. Still, she could not give up. "He—my fiancé—was my first memory of love, you see," she said, each word like shattered glass in her throat. "A bad memory, which I am determined not to repeat.''

"And I am determined not to be a memory at all," he said firmly, "but a reality in your life every day . . . for as long as we both shall live.''

It was a promise she heard and felt with every sense she possessed. A promise that touched her so deeply it planted hope in the darkest parts of her mind. A promise she'd dared to wish for only in her dreams.

Dreams she'd successfully denied having until now . . . until Dane.

Apparently done with patience and logic, he lowered his head and took her mouth in a wild, primitive kiss that shot sensation through her, eliciting a response before she knew what had happened. Gasping, she met his tongue with hers, dancing, dueling, seeking.

"Like passion, love comes naturally. It is not learned or acquired. It simply is," he said against her mouth, then jerked his head up to pin her with his gaze—prey caught in the light of a torch. "You give, Lorelei, not with the desperation of one who takes, but with the open spirit of one who wants and needs to share your gifts as well as those offered to you."

"Dane, you are making me dizzy with your arguments," she said, as she massaged her temples.

"Shall I demonstrate in a more straightforward manner?" he asked harshly. "Shall I show you here and now how eloquently passion expresses what we are afraid to say in words . . . what you are so damned afraid of admitting?" His expression became as hard as his voice, determined and uncompromising. "Your choice, Lorelei. Now or after we are married. But make no mistake, we will be married, and what we do in the marriage bed will be the least of our conflicts."

"You call that a choice?" she asked defiantly, even as she gasped inside at his insistence, at his certainty.

He swooped down on her again, taking her mouth without quarter, his arms gathering her close, holding her tightly against him as he crushed her lips and drank deeply of her. She gasped and clung to him, not fighting him, not passive, but with the understanding that she gave as much as she took, knowing that she wanted to give everything to him.

"You will marry me because you want to," he said, as he angled his head back. "Deceive yourself as to the reasons why you wish it. In the end, there will be only truth between us. You know it as well as I."

He strode to the middle of the library and stood without turning to her, silent and waiting.

This was her chance. She could run now and she did not think he would follow her. If she ran now, he would know that he was wrong, that she did not want to marry him, that his persuasions were for nothing. He would know what a coward she was.

"I know it as well as you," she said softly, admitting it in spite of her fear, unable to allow him to think her so craven as to run from him. "But—"

"I do not want to hear your 'buts,' Lorelei. I want to marry you. You want to marry me. It is settled."

"Then know," she said flatly, feeling wretched, feeling as if she pronounced doom for them both, "that it will be for better or worse. That once I give them I keep my promises, and will expect you to keep yours." It sounded insane to her own ears. "I am truly stupid to think such a pronouncement can be enforced. Of course it cannot be."

"No, it cannot be enforced by only one person," he replied, as he turned back to her. "Only time will prove to you that our marriage will involve two people . . . for better or worse." He regarded her with his head cocked to the side, his mouth slanted in the half smile that was his alone, a glow in his eyes that seemed very much like tenderness. "Lorelei," he said in a near whisper as he walked slowly toward her. "I am relieved that you are passionate. I would not like to feel as if I were rutting with my wife.'' He lifted a strand of her hair from her shoulder and rubbed it between his fingers, staring at it, examining its texture.

She licked her suddenly dry lips, pressed her hand to her belly to still the quickening Dane inspired with his talk of making love with shared intimacy rather than the mere tolerance Harriet had spoken of. ''It's not the same.''

''Why? Who made that decree?''

''I don't know.'' She raised her arms in exasperation at the convoluted workings of Dane's mind. ''It's the way things are. We are to accept it.''

''So we can fit in?'' He asked quietly. ''Lorelei, neither of us fits in. We never have. I doubt we ever shall.''

All she could do was blink. She had no rebuttal for the truth.

''I submit that perhaps so many women 'suffer their husband's attentions' ''—he held up his hands to count off points as he made them—''either because they are afraid to be criticized for their natural inclinations, or because they have no feeling for their husbands and have no such natural inclinations toward them. Why else do so many women take lovers?''

''Dane, stop!'' she cried, completely overwhelmed by the points he raised and afraid—so horribly afraid—to consider them, to become further mired in his persuasions, rather than take shelter in her own resolve. ''If I did choose to test your assertions—right here and now—would that make you go away?''

He crooked his forefinger under her chin and lifted her face to meet his gaze. ''Lorelei, does the thought of making love with me . . . do you like the idea?''

She blinked again, knowing that to answer truthfully was to trap herself. "Yes." The word escaped without her permission. She closed her eyes, not wanting to face him after such a shameless admission. Yet Dane didn't think it was shameless, not if she'd interpreted his ramblings correctly.

"And I want you to enjoy it, to share and to participate in the pleasure." His mouth touched hers, gently, tentatively, sweetly. Her lips parted on a gasp as his hand covered her breast, his fingers tracing her nipple, bringing it to a firm, expectant peak. His tongue dipped into her mouth, exploring slowly, leading hers in a seductive dance. Instinctively, she followed where he led, sighing as he deepened the kiss, gentleness and sweetness transforming into demand and urgency. His fingers played upon her breasts until her body thrummed a tune of its own, reducing her to warm, flowing liquid. She should push him away, argue with him, but he would win again. He already had.

He tore his mouth from hers, his chest heaving against hers. She opened her eyes, rested her forehead against his shoulder and abruptly jerked her gaze upward again. His breeches left nothing to her imagination.

"I will not go away, Lorelei. And I will not accept your choice in the form of a test." His breath came hard and deep. His face was tight, controlled; his eyes were dark and turbulent. "It should be obvious to you that duty will be the last thing on my mind when we meet in our marriage bed." He glanced down at himself. "Tall and ample, outspoken and maddening, your mere presence robs me of control."

He again turned away from her and stared up at the ceiling. "The marriage has been announced. Uncle Robert is in London, begging the archbishop for a special license. Beau is with him, to enlist the Regent's aid, if necessary. Since the dowager Countess Millbank was present last night, the word has no doubt spread to all of England by now.''

''Regardless of your allies, you still require my agreement,'' she said, despairing over the lack of defiance in her voice. ''You did not ask.''

''To ask would have inspired another round of your skewed arguments. And I already have your agreement in your actions,'' he said, as he faced her and slanted a smile with a cocky lift of his brows. ''You may succeed in wounding my pride by not allowing me to rescue you on a dark road''—his mouth spread in a purely male grin of triumph—''but I am consoled that you can resist me as little as I can resist you.'' He reached out to smooth her cheek, to brush his hand over her breasts in a feather touch. ''You made a mistake, you know. If you had told me that you were frigid, I might have had second thoughts about marrying you. It takes only one to rut, but it takes two to make love . . . and I have no taste for rutting.''

She backed away before he could demonstrate again, before she dragged him down to the carpet and gave him no choice but to demonstrate, which she was perilously close to doing. ''Very well, Lord Dane, I will marry you.'' The agreement slipped away from her too easily for her comfort, as if the eagerness of her heart overruled the fears in her mind.

As he'd so arrogantly proclaimed, she did want to marry him. She wanted the excitement of him, and the tenderness of him. She even wanted the challenge of discovering just how far his most amazing attitudes toward women and marriage went. She could admit that much to herself. She could almost admit to herself that she felt as if he were rescuing her now.

She whirled and walked swiftly toward the door, yanked it open, and all but ran into the hall, up the grand staircase, and into her room, trying desperately to outrun another admission that would not be silenced in her thoughts.

Against all reason and argument, against every belief and vow she had made, she had contrarily fallen in love with Dane. Worse, she had fallen in love with him at first sight, or near enough to convince her that once a fool, she would always be a fool.

Yet she had the feeling that if she did not see this through, if she did not take what she'd thought never to have, she would be a lonely fool with nothing but regrets for company.

Chapter 13

〰〰

"I hope Dane won't regret his action—"

"All because he felt sorry for Merry—"

"He has condemned himself to marry her out of some outmoded sense of chivalry—"

"I think it very sweet—"

"Really, Lizzie, how can you say so when his fortune and title will be lost to you? I had hoped that he might find an interest in you—"

"He isn't lost yet. Not until the wedding is over—"

"No one would blame him if he had second thoughts—"

"Of course he'll have second thoughts. Any decent man would—"

"But not a barbarian from America," Adrian said, as he approached the knot of women standing near the sideboard, then glanced at the men clustered at the opposite end of the large room as if they, by some silent agreement, had separated themselves en masse from the gossip. "And definitely not a barbarian who happens to be very much in love with his betrothed."

With an elegant bow, he picked up a plate and moved from one serving dish to another, selecting a bit of everything for his breakfast.

Hands fluttered and more than one head turned to hide an embarrassed flush. Suddenly he was the only one who appeared interested in food.

His plate full, he faced the dining room. "I am touched by your concern, ladies," he said dryly, "but I assure you I will not regret my action. I could never pity Lady Lorelei when she is so clearly a most superior woman. I know little of chivalry and must confess that I acted solely out of selfishness—" he winked at the ladies "—though I would not mind if my lady believed me to be chivalrous. I would like it very much if she thought me sweet." Bestowing a smile on the young lady who had made that remark, he chose a seat at the table and calmly began to break his fast. He'd hoped that the guests would have talked and gossiped themselves hoarse the day before at Lady Harriet's hastily contrived picnic. He should have known better.

"Well, Lord Dane, it would seem that you are quite happy with the opportunity Merry presented you by wearing that ridiculous gown," the dowager Countess Millbank said as she sat across from him.

"Indeed," Dane agreed.

"The gel has frightened off more than one worthy fellow, you know, including my grandson. I told him that he should not have allowed her the opportunity to protest, for I swear she was born with a seemingly sensible argument on her lips. You have proved me right. You have excellent instincts."

Adrian glanced up to favor the countess with a bland expression and one raised brow. "Then I can only offer my sympathies for your grandson's short-sightedness. Lady Lorelei would be an asset to any family."

"Quite right," the dowager said. "Though I had despaired that any man would have the fortitude to take her on."

"I believe, ma'am, that the desire to take her on is more important than fortitude."

"I take it, then, that you have no intention of changing your mind?"

"None whatsoever."

The dowager swept her gaze from one rapt on-looker to another, fixing each in turn with a glacial stare. "Well, I trust that will end speculation on the matter. Now we can all enjoy the house party and look forward to the wedding of the year at the end of it. It will be quite the thing, I daresay."

"To what do you refer, ma'am?" Brummell asked, as he strolled in with Lorelei on one arm and Lady Harriet on the other.

Adrian saw only Lorelei, her face pale and pinched, her posture stiff as Brummell seated her at Adrian's side and immediately escorted Lady Harriet to the sideboard.

"You heard them," he said, softly enough for only her to hear.

Staring straight ahead, she didn't reply.

"I'm sorry, Lorelei."

"Why?" she said flatly. "You did nothing wrong."

"I'm sorry that you are hurt."

Her sudden smile was brittle. "I am not hurt. Why should I be? I've always known that they are my friends only when it is convenient for them."

"They are afraid of you," the dowager said from

across the table. "And they are quite envious."

Lorelei stared at her, her eyes wide in disbelief.

"You needn't look at me like that," Lady Millbank snapped. "You are not like the rest of them, which in their eyes renders you inferior as well as a threat."

Lorelei flinched and clenched her fist in her lap.

"You flaunt your differences and become stronger for it," Lady Millbank continued, allowing her voice to carry. "Of course they envy you, the weak-minded twits. And in turn, they resent you for your strength. Now you've not only snared the most eligible bachelor in our midst, but he publicly declares his love and admiration for you when the most they can hope for from their husbands is tolerance." She patted her turban. "I, on the other hand, enjoyed a great passion with my late husband in spite of my horse-face and flat chest, so I do not feel at all threatened by you."

For the second time in as many days, a collective gasp rose in the air.

Adrian spooned fruit into his mouth to keep from laughing, then grasped Lorelei's hand beneath the table.

"Therefore"—Lady Millbank cast a challenging glare on each of the assemblage in turn—"I wish you happy." She rose from her seat. "Now, come along, all of you," she ordered, opening her arms wide to sweep everyone from the room as if they were no more than clutter on a desk. "I'm quite certain Merry has had quite enough of you for one day and would prefer to enjoy her meal without the taint of sour grapes to spoil her appetite."

Brummell chuckled as he seated Lady Harriet on the other side of Lorelei, then took the seat Lady Millbank had vacated across from her. "If only our Regent could enlist the dowager's aid against the Prime

Minister . . ." he said to no one in particular, as a footman placed a plate of fruit and toast in front of Lorelei.

"Well," Lady Harriet said, as another footman arranged silver pots of chocolate and coffee before her, "I do believe we have a wedding to plan."

"I am determined that it will be the best the *ton* has ever seen," Brummell said, "and that I get credit for it, of course."

Lorelei sagged as the last of the guests left the dining room, though her hand clutched Adrian's as if it were a lifeline.

With a burst of purely male satisfaction, he sat back and stretched his legs out beneath the table, allowing the plans to drift around him as he savored even that small sign of dependence from Lorelei. He doubted she realized what she did, or that it required trust to hold onto another for stability. And he had no doubt that she would rally from the shock of hearing her so-called friends speak against her and again assert her lack of need for anyone or anything.

As if his thought prompted her, she snatched her hand from his and set her nose at a familiar lofty angle. "I had thought to have a simple ceremony, but you are right, Beau. It really must be the grandest affair in all of England."

"I said the best," Brummell corrected. "Not the grandest. For some odd reason our society considers a grand wedding to be vulgar."

"Exactly what they will expect," Lorelei said. "I wouldn't want to disappoint them."

"Come to think of it, I haven't set any trends lately. Might as well proclaim a grand wedding as quite the thing," Brummell declared, and launched into a suggestion for Lorelei's gown, which she immediately

altered to suit herself. Lady Harriet spoke of flowers—
veritable acres of them—to which Lorelei responded
with a pronouncement that the marriage would take
place in the gardens so that "no flower should have
to give up its life on my account."

Bemused, Adrian tilted his head at the shy smile
she gave him. "You remembered," he said, referring
to the nosegay of wildflowers he'd plucked by the side
of the road.

"It was only two days ago," she chided, then
jerked her attention back to the discussion as if embarrassed by her sentimentality.

Uncle Robert strolled in with an offer to act as her
father in the ceremony, which Lorelei followed with
the gentle suggestion that Adrian might wish for his
uncle to stand with him. George would escort her to
the altar and Harriet would stand with her. Adrian
considered each suggestion, opened his mouth to add
his tuppence worth, then swallowed his opinions as
debates volleyed from one person to another over
plates of forgotten food, somehow missing him altogether.

Unable to slide a word in edgewise and hopelessly
behind in the conversation, Adrian propped his elbows on the table and entertained his own thoughts
as the tide of details rolled over him. His stomach
churned at the idea of being at the center of "the
grandest affair in all England." It hadn't occurred to
him that Lorelei would wish her marriage to be a
spectacle. He supposed it would serve him right since
he'd begun the whole thing by making a spectacle of
her. He'd made a spectacle of them both.

Lorelei had apparently decided that one good spectacle deserved another.

Panic bolted through him and came to an abrupt

halt in the center of his chest. He'd really done it. He'd fallen in love with Lorelei at first sight, without thought, much less reason. He'd engineered their engagement on an impulse. He'd met her protests the day before with logic to which he had given not a single thought beforehand. He'd set the course for the rest of his life on instinct alone.

An insane thing to do.

He covered his face with his hands. It was real. Lorelei would be his wife.

Silence fell. He raised his head and met three expectant gazes and one of challenge—Lorelei's, of course. "I have a feeling that I am supposed to reply to something I confess I did not hear." His mind separated and placed bits of information. The ceremony would take place in Lady Harriet's garden. Lorelei's gown would be made by a Mrs. Powell according to Lorelei's specifications—watered silk, and had she said embroidered satin? Ah yes, he thought, Lady Harriet had announced that no wedding was complete without satin—

"I asked," Lorelei said with exaggerated patience, "if you have anything to add. If not, I will proceed with the arrangements as I see fit."

"As long as your arrangements include you and me, a member of the clergy, and vows before God—as well as enough satin to make it binding—I am quite certain I will be happy with whatever else you decide," he replied, as he met her challenging glare with a smile of utter contentment, feeling it in the deepest part of himself.

For with every decision she made, Lorelei backed herself farther and farther into a corner. And his panic and insanity aside, all he could do was hope that her

pride would keep her cornered until the vows had
been spoken.

"I vow this is my best work," Mrs. Powell stated,
as she stood back to view Merry from head to foot
the day of her wedding. Behind her stood women
trained to coax hair and complexion into submission,
and yet more women who had fashioned everything
from a corset to gloves—each item *au courant* and a
confection in itself.

"You look beautiful, Merry," Harriet whispered.

Beautiful. Merry broke out in a cold sweat as she
turned toward the looking glass. She saw nothing but
six feet of womanly frame upholstered in a Grecian
styled gown of tea-dyed watered silk and a sleeveless
tunic of pure white satin embroidered with tea-dyed
silk thread and drawn through circlets of pearls at her
shoulders.

Her wedding gown, stained white, somehow sym-
bolic of her jaded expectations for the future. *Her*
wedding, to a man who didn't care about stains and
imperfections. *Her* future, forever bound to Dane's.
How could she have agreed to marry a man she
loved?

Yet she had agreed and sailed through the past ten
days, kept too busy to think by Harriet and Beau during the day, and too enchanted by Dane during the
evenings. Too busy to think of why it shouldn't be
so. Not wanting to think at all.

But suddenly the spell had been broken by the image of what she saw in the looking glass. Fragments
of a woman, who had no experience with family or
love or faith, and no real belief that she could have
what eluded even the most beautiful woman she
knew.

"Have you your slippers?" Harriet asked.

Merry wiggled her toes and nodded as her stomach seemed to turn inside out. She'd ordered the slippers with heels on purpose, refusing to give Dane or anyone else quarter by wearing flat-heeled shoes. Adding even more to her height, her hair was gathered at the crown of her head in an intricate braided coil twined with pearls. Dane had said he wanted her; he could have her in all her Junoesque glory.

Juno . . . a goddess. . . .

Merry . . . a caricature of herself, flaunting everything that made her different, everything she hated.

Suddenly she couldn't breathe for the constriction of the corset nipping in her waist to accommodate her girdle of gold kidskin embellished with embroidery and pearls. She'd worn the corset out of vanity, a silly impulse, really. No man would ever span her waist with his hands regardless of how tightly she was laced. No man would ever lift her in his arms and carry her up a staircase. No man would ever make her feel small and delicate. But she had a waist and she would display it.

She swayed as she remembered how Dane had swept her off her feet a fortnight ago, holding her weight as he kissed her to within an inch of her sanity, then straightened with stiff movements, as if he'd strained a muscle. Sound roared in her ears as she thought of the night to come. She stared at her reflection again, seeing only the imperfections, knowing she would always see them no matter what Harriet or Beau or Dane said.

"I cannot do this," she said, unaware that she'd spoken aloud, hearing only the buzz of voices drifting through the window from the gardens below.

*   *   *

Dane shifted and again glanced up at Lorelei's chamber window. The vicar cleared his throat and looked longingly at the tables on the terrace, groaning with food. The guests tittered and cackled with glee as the hour set for the ceremony passed and another approached.

Apparently Lorelei had decided to leave her corner. To leave him.

He would not—could not—let her go.

Anger outpaced his control, driving him from the garden, into the house, to ascend the grand staircase and stride down the hall to the master suite.

He halted abruptly and stared at the door, waiting for reason, needing it to keep his balance.

The door flew open. Lady Harriet collided with him. "Lord Dane, thank heaven," she said breathlessly, as she grasped his forearms. "I don't know what to do. I've never seen her like this. She was fine and then she became white as a ghost and . . . Dane she just stands there, staring—"

"See to the guests. I will bring Lorelei down." He set her aside in the hall, entered the room, kicked the door shut, and again abruptly halted.

Lorelei stood in front of the cheval glass, her face as white as the satin falling from her shoulders, her stare fixed on her reflection, her body still and stiff.

He approached her slowly, stood behind her, his reflection joining hers.

She blinked. "I can't, Dane," she said in a monotone. "I thought I could but I can't . . . not ever."

"You damn well can, and you damn well will," he said tightly.

"How can I?" she said with a shudder, seemingly unaware of his anger, "when I know that you will tire of this"—she waved her hand at the looking glass—

"and will not know how to tell me? You're a kind man. It will hurt you to tell me."

He grasped her shoulders and pulled her back, one step, two. "The only thing I won't tell you is good-bye."

"Everyone says good-bye." She shrugged. "Some simply disappear without a word."

"Lorelei, the only way I can convince you otherwise is to show you, day by day, year by year. Will you deny me, and yourself, that opportunity?"

"You are very good, Dane."

"Good at what?" he said with a mirthless laugh. "Good at convincing you of what I see when you take every compliment as a lie? Good at making you believe that I know my own mind and am not at all mad to want you? Shall we see how good I am?" He pointed at the glass. "I see a magnificent woman, almost as tall as I, with proportions that are in perfect accord with her height. I see softness rather than skin over bone." He flattened his hand over her hipbone, over her belly, then around to the side of her thigh. "I look forward to your softness, Lorelei."

Encouraged by the tremble that rippled through her body, he pressed a kiss to the hollow beneath her ear. "I will not tell you how beautiful you are, for it would not be the truth. You're unique and stunning—a quality that pleases me more than simple beauty."

His mouth missed her cheek as she shook her head. "Nothing can be this right, Dane. Nothing. You can't be everything that I see. No man is as kind and broad of mind as you are. No man is so gentle and tender. It frightens me."

He stood back as anger once again grabbed him by the throat. "I see. Baroness Winters, free-thinker and independent woman, is frightened of a man because he does not demean her.''

"You don't understand.''

"No, I do not. But since you have promised to marry me, you will have a lifetime to make me understand.'' He turned her and lifted her over his shoulder·as he had the night her wheel had broken. It had worked once. . . .

"Dane, don't.''

"Why ever not?'' he asked harshly. "Tenderness frightens you, and you are suspicious of compliments, so I will refrain from gentle persuasion.'' He strode to the door, yanked it open, and carried her into the hall and down the stairs, ignoring Lorelei's protests, ignoring the startled glances of the servants as they opened doors for him and stood aside to let him pass. It was more difficult, however, to ignore how Lorelei became limp, a dead weight in his arms that threatened his balance and tested his strength. He stumbled and righted himself with sheer force of will, refusing to land himself and his bride in a heap at the doors leading outside.

Just inside them he halted, lowered her to her feet, and tried to stretch his back without her noticing his discomfort.

She sighed and stepped behind him, her hand delving beneath his coat to rub his back, as if noticing and ministering to his discomforts was completely natural to her. "You should have left me upstairs, Dane.''

"I should have asked two footmen to carry you,'' he muttered. "My fantasies appear to be beyond my abilities.'' He plowed his hand through his hair. "Perhaps you shouldn't marry me.''

"What fantasies?'' she asked offhandedly.

"Of being a hero,'' he said around a moan, as she

found the center of a particularly nasty spasm. "I don't think I should have admitted that."

"Why not?"

"I think there is an unwritten law somewhere that a man is supposed to give every impression of being a hero regardless of his blunders. I should have kept my tongue behind my teeth and glowered at you ... or something."

She chuckled. "I have never thought glowering to be heroic."

He sighed as she eased the spasm with her fine, strong hands. "That's better, thank you. In fact I may just be able to redeem myself by carrying you the rest of the way."

"Dane ..."

Heartened by her warning tone, he wrapped his fingers around her arms and forced her to look outside the glass-paned doors. "Look at all your friends assembled to witness your marriage. Will you have them witness your cowardice instead?" He reached behind her to straighten the train that fell from the shoulders of her tunic and spread it wide behind her. "Lorelei, the formidable Baroness Winters, afraid and defeated by the prospect of happiness. After all it was denied you once and you slunk away in shame."

She shook her head and murmured too low for him to hear.

"What did you say? Tell me, Lorelei."

"I said,"—she seemed to strain the words through her clenched teeth—"that I didn't slink away until I raised my knee into his—" Shuddering, she continued to stare at the crowd watching them. "He ... said he had a reputation to maintain, and it did not include a wife who might stray because her appetites were too strong for any one man to satisfy ... so I raised my knee and said that I also had a reputation to maintain.''

Adrian couldn't help but laugh, a deep sound from his gut that carried through the doors and startled the onlookers.

It appeared to startle Lorelei as well. For the first time since he'd barged into her room, she directly met his gaze, her cheeks sucked in as if she held back her own laughter. ''I had to summon footmen to carry him out.''

''As I will carry you to the vicar, if need be,'' he said soberly.

''You would be better off if I wielded my knee against you,'' she said tartly. ''Next time you might cripple yourself.''

''You will not leave me standing at the altar without a bride, Lorelei,'' he said firmly. ''You want to marry me. Deny it.''

''Why me, Dane?''

He frowned and bit back a dozen ready answers, none of which she would trust, settling for the only one she might accept. ''Why not you?'' Again he plowed his hand through his hair, distracted by a sudden thought. ''Because no matter how difficult the circumstances or how delicate the subject, we get on as if we had known one another for years.'' He grinned triumphantly. ''Nor will my patience be strained by boredom. It will likely take me a lifetime to find a way just to charm you.''

She closed her eyes for a moment, then met his gaze with a softness in her expression he had never seen before. ''You already have,'' she said quietly.

He crooked his forefinger under her chin. ''Are you ready to plight your troth to me now?''

She gave the barest of nods. "But I won't vow to obey you."

"Heaven forbid you should lie," he said as he held out his arm, waiting for what seemed forever for her to take it. "You won't make me carry you?"

Her mouth curved upward as she hesitantly placed her hand atop the back of his and stepped through the doorway. "I should not like to risk crippling you."

"Thank God," he said, as he took the first step toward the arbor of roses at the end of the stone path swept clean for the occasion. As he focused on the faces raptly observing their progress, the path suddenly seemed a mile long. Faces hungry for a *faux pas* to provide them with enough scandal to carry their conversations through the Little Season and beyond. Eyes watching every step, minds hoping for disaster. Yet at the end of the path, Lady Harriet stood with love for her friend clearly shining in her eyes. In the first row, Brummell watched, his gaze inspecting the cut of Adrian's coat and the flow of Lorelei's gown, then gave a slight nod of approval. Stationed across from Lady Harriet, Uncle Robert beamed at them as if every wish he'd ever had was about to come true. And in the center of it all, the vicar waited with ill-concealed impatience.

Lorelei faltered.

"I'm terrified," he said from the side of his mouth, hoping to distract her.

She turned her head sharply toward him, her eyes wide.

He halted right in the middle of the path to the vicar and kissed the tip of her nose. "I *am* terrified, my lady Lorelei. But I am consoled by the knowledge that I will not be alone—a situation that has grown tediously familiar to me over the years."

She blinked up at him. "*Not* alone," she whispered, as if it were a discovery, then turned and smiled and resumed walking down the cobblestone path by his side.

Adrian reached over in a seemingly affectionate gesture to coax her fingers to relax before she crushed every bone in his hand.

Chapter 14

The Bahama Islands

"I'll crush Blackwell's head with my bare hands," Phillip roared, as he threw his glass across the cabin. Water splashed back at him in the small space. *Water*, he thought in disgust. He needed rum.

After months of scouring the wrong end of the Atlantic for the *Falcon* and having to put into a secluded cove to make repairs, he damn well deserved a drink. He never should have gotten Letters of Marque, authorizing him to act as a privateer in the service of the American government. It hadn't occurred to him that his men would expect to take British ships. As a result of their successful confrontations with the enemy, *Reckoner* was fast becoming notorious, and the islands were crawling with British searching for her.

Damn it! He paid his men well and had told them that their primary mission was to find the *Falcon*. As former seamen on Rutland merchant ships, they knew Steven and liked him. He'd made it a point to hire loyal, patriotic men.

But loyalty and patriotism did not preclude greed. Opportunities to trounce the British as well as to collect prize money was impossible for them to resist, especially when *Reckoner* could outrun and outmaneuver lumbering warships. Ironically, they were all going to come out of this as rich men.

Phillip might appreciate having money of his own if his brother weren't on a ship that had just sailed from England, while he'd been stagnating in the West Indies.

He balled his fist and slammed it against the bulkhead. Adrian's agent had given him the name of the right ship, but he had given him the wrong location. The scrawny scavenger had feathered his own nest at Phillip's expense.

Time . . . too much time lost. By now Blackwell would be in England, giving Adrian the right information. Hell, by now Adrian could be on his way to rendezvous with the *Falcon*. He should have had his men in Connecticut hold Blackwell until the end of the war, but he'd wanted Adrian to know where Steven was. He'd wanted to save Steven from the British and keep Adrian from getting killed. He'd wanted Adrian to know what he'd done—perhaps even witness it.

It would have settled things between them once and for all.

But Steven's ship was within Adrian's reach, rather than his.

He needed a drink.

"Sir," Morton, his first mate, called through the cabin door.

"Enter," Phillip said, as he unearthed a bottle of rum from his locker and popped the cork.

Morton peered around the door. "We'll be ready to sail within three days, sir."

Phillip gave him a feral grin. Three days. His men had outdone themselves. "Then we sail toward England to intercept the *Falcon* . . . and Morton," he added firmly, "there will be no more taking of prizes until Steven is safe."

Phillip glared at the door after the mate closed it without comment. The men would grumble, but he could handle that. They had enough booty to set themselves up nicely after the war. He had enough to go his own way if he wished, never again dependent on the Rutland fortune.

And if Fate was kind, he still had a chance to get to Steven before Adrian. *Falcon* had sailed from England over a month ago. If fair winds pushed her south, he could still get to her first.

Smiling, Phillip opened the porthole and tossed the bottle of rum into the ocean. Only three days more. It was nothing. Nothing at all.

Chapter 15

Cornwall
August, 1812

Three days. They had gone by so quickly, Merry could scarcely credit they had happened at all. Three days since her marriage to Dane, who'd stood with her beneath the rose arbor, his hair spiked from the impatient rake of his fingers at her last minute rebellion, and his stock off center from his tug—in defiance, she suspected, of Beau's careful scrutiny and nod of approval of his attire. Never, she thought, had she seen a man so handsome, especially when he'd given her his slanted grin after she'd twice "neglected" to repeat the word "obey" during the ceremony.

As handsome as Dane was now, sprawled across from her in the large traveling coach, his long legs stretched over the space between the seats, his stockinged feet resting on the cushions next to her. Rather large feet, she observed, as she traced her finger along the length of the one pressing against her hip.

They had left Saxon Hill shortly after the ceremony, Dane muttering that Lady Harriet's guests had had their entertainment, and he'd be damned if he would spend his honeymoon in a house where they were likely to listen through doors and watch through keyholes. Merry had almost argued with him, but thought better of it. He'd appeared at the end of his tether, and she'd reached the end of hers when everyone had rushed up to her the moment the last "Amen" had been said, gushing over everything from her gown to their best wishes for her happiness.

Beau and the marquess had extricated her and Dane from the mob and rushed them to the front of the house. Harriet had been waiting there with tears in her eyes and a basket of food in her hands, allowing no time for lengthy farewells as she shooed them into a waiting coach the marquess had brought to Saxon Hill from his estate.

The moment they were alone and on their way, the rapport they had shared from those first few moments in Harriet's office had begun to take on a more intimate texture as Dane removed his shoes and urged her to do the same. As both of them rested their feet on the opposite seat, often nudging a hip or a thigh. As they slipped into easy conversation while the coach rolled through the varied landscapes of England.

"Already, marriage has its advantages," she'd sighed, as she tugged off her gloves after the coach had rolled through the gates of Saxon Hill. "I needn't suffer these any longer when I am in your company."

He'd leaned forward to help her, plucking the soft silk casings from one finger at a time and tossing the gloves out the window of the coach. She'd laughed, drawing his stare, his expression arrested as he raised her bared hand and kissed each fingertip, then the insides of her wrists.

"I neglected to kiss my bride," he'd said in a low voice.

"No," she contradicted softly, "you didn't."

"That was not a kiss, but a sop to the masses," he murmured, as he shifted to sit beside her and angled her across his lap. "This," he said against her mouth, "is a kiss." His mouth took hers, his tongue slipping inside, advancing, retreating, seducing, taking. It had gone on and on—kisses that deepened with urgency, then gentled with tenderness . . . such tenderness as she hadn't known existed.

She received equal pleasure from watching him now as he slept, his arms crossed, his head cocked at an unnatural angle. He was her husband—difficult to believe. But then they had yet to share a bed. At each inn where they'd stopped along the way, he'd taken two rooms, spending his waking hours in hers, sharing a meal, or conversation, or simply a few quiet moments with her before retiring.

Their first night alone together, she had felt wilted with fatigue and strained with apprehension. She'd jumped at the squeak and groan of the bed in her room as Dane had sat on it.

"You're nervous," he'd said, with a smile in his voice. "Who would have thought it from a woman of passion?"

"You will not let me forget that, will you?" she'd asked, peeved that he would tease her at such an awkward moment. The bed squeaked, for heaven's sake, and this was her wedding night.

"I can but hope that you will not allow *me* to forget it in the years to come," he replied.

"It would have been nice if you had revealed your

beastly nature to me before the wedding,'' she said with a glare at him. ''I thought you were a gentleman with great sensitivity.''

''I have no intention of being a gentleman in our bed, Lorelei,'' he warned, as he slowly stalked her around the small and sparely furnished bedchamber. ''And I will not tolerate your being a lady during our intimate moments together.''

She whirled on him and forgot whatever biting reply she'd been ready to make. He was standing so close and the visions he conjured with his statements turned her knees to porridge and her blood to hot, flowing honey. ''I am not without restraint,'' she said, dismayed that it was a trembling whisper rather than a firm assertion. How did he do such things to her? How did he manage to drive her memories from her mind and make life seem new and fresh? What was it about him that made her feel new and innocent and free of disillusionment?

''You will be,'' he promised, as he plucked the hat from her head and tossed it onto the bed.

''You are disgustingly sure of yourself,'' she said, as she groped behind her for one of the two chairs flanking the hearth and holding onto the arm as she sank into the seat. A chair was safe. . . .

''I'm pleased you think so,'' he said with a chuckle, as he leaned over her to pick the pins from her hair and drop them wherever. Her breath stalled at the feel of his strong hands combing through the strands, freeing them to fall around her shoulders. ''I cannot imagine that you would be happy with a milksop.''

''Do you imply that you are deceiving me and you are, in truth, a milksop?'' she asked around a sigh as his fingers massaged her scalp, lifted her abundance of hair as if it were strands of fine gold, then let it sift through his fingers as if he reveled in the wealth he found there.

"Not at all. In truth, I am stubborn and accustomed to getting what I want. I am also possessive and willing to fight to keep what I have, though I would prefer to use reason rather than force. Both can be either good or bad traits, depending on how you view them." He kneeled before her and cupped the back of her head, drawing her face close to his, using a thumb to coax her lips to part, taking advantage of her acquiescence with his mouth, devouring her, carnality in every thrust and withdrawal of his tongue.

He ended the assault slowly, provocatively, his lips exploring the shape of hers, his tongue tracing them, his breath hot and short, bathing her with his need, seducing her with it.

One of his hands lowered, skimming her neck and shoulder and settling on her breast through her bodice, exploring the curve of it, circling the center, driving her to gasp with the arrows of desire that penetrated the deepest part of her.

"Dane, please," she whispered, stifling a whimper of need, and of fear for the strength of her need. "Make the fear go away. Show me—somehow—that I am foolish to cling to it."

He sighed and sat on the floor at her feet, his arm over her leg in a casual, intimate way. "I will order our evening meal served in here," he said, his expression tender, patient, though his voice was measured, controlled. "And until we reach my home, I will show you how foolish you are. If you are not convinced by then, you will have to abide with me as your husband within the bedchamber as well as without and come to terms with your fear without my patience"—he rose and strode to the bellpull, giving it a sharp yank—"for I vow I will have none left for such groundless apprehension."

She stared at him, oddly comforted in spite of his threat—by his willingness to indulge her uncertainties, and by the small seedling of trust his speech had planted in her wary heart.

Since that night, they had had many such encounters, each unraveling her avowed restraint a little more. Without warning, he would settle her on his lap as he had that first time and kiss her and pet her, encouraging her to do the same to him. His hand would cover her breasts, one then the other, caressing her nipples through layers of silk, coaxing her to lose her breath and turn to liquid in his arms. Over and over again, his lips and his tongue tasted her, plundered her mouth, explored languidly as his hand left her breasts to stroke her rib cage and her waist and hips, never once touching bare flesh below her neck, as if he knew she could not bare more to him than her hands and feet. She'd done the same, exploring his mouth with her tongue while her hands roamed over his broad shoulders, his chest—so hard and planed with muscle—his flat stomach and narrow hips, his desire for her rising beneath his breeches.

So many times she'd wanted to free him, to explore that part of him that would soon join them together, yet she hadn't wanted to disturb the beauty and the safety of what was happening between them. She hadn't been ready to open herself to Dane after so many years of keeping her passion imprisoned within a bad memory. She hadn't been ready to sacrifice the tenderness and languid discovery for more primitive urges. She had been afraid to believe he could be more—so much more—to her than another bad memory.

She didn't understand the play between them—if it could be called play when Dane accompanied every touch with an intent steady gaze, his mouth in that odd half smile, a crease deepening between his brows that tipped up at the inside corners as if he were asking a question or perhaps examining an answer for truth. She didn't understand why his touches, from the most fleeting casual brush of a knee to the lingering caress on her breast, seemed to gather and remain inside her like living memories. Why she hungered for more and more, every moment filled with need until the next wisp of a touch or the next caress, either deliberate or accidental. It never mattered which, as long as it happened.

Just as it didn't matter that he slept now, leaving her to her own thoughts. The quiet and muted light inside the coach was a welcome sanctuary to Merry; the privacy after constantly being under the scrutiny of a hundred curious souls at Saxon Hill was heaven itself. Dane had been right about how well they got on together, as if they'd known one another forever. She kept forgetting that they hadn't. She'd forgotten a lot of things in Dane's company—forgotten everything, in fact, but Dane.

Dane immediately awakened as the coach slowed, then halted in front of yet another inn. Dusk gathered on the horizon, startling her. Each day passed too quickly when she would have them last forever.

"Can't we stay in the coach?" she asked, as Dane stepped down and extended his hand to help her alight.

"We must eat," he said, capturing her lips as she descended and spilling the words into her mouth.

"Why?" she breathed into his.

He nibbled his way up her neck to her ear. "Because, we will need our strength when we reach Spindrift.''

"I need strength now," she sighed, forcing down the excitement his reminder brought. Spindrift . . . his home and now hers. Spindrift . . . where their marriage would become more than a slow seduction and building frustration. "I vow I cannot walk from here into the inn after sitting for so long."

"I was hoping," he said into her ear, "that you would carry me inside. . . ."

Eventually they had walked arm in arm from the coach to the inn, and up to their rooms. He lingered with her in the hall, pressing her back against the door, his hands propped on the wood on either side of her shoulders, his head lowered, his mouth taking hers in a last hungry kiss.

"Eat well and sleep soundly," he said, "for tomorrow we will be too busy consummating our marriage to either sleep or eat."

"Why wait?" she asked, as she sought his mouth with hers. "Why not tonight?"

Straightening away from her, he held her gaze and cocked his head. "Not until tomorrow at Spindrift. Not until everything is perfect." He gave her a slow, lazy smile and strolled down the hall to his room, whistling a jaunty tune.

As they rolled through Cornwall the next day—Dane again napping across from her—she wondered if anything could be more perfect than being in this small world moving within the larger one. A world in which she was beginning to understand closeness and intimacy in a completely different way than she'd known before. Closeness was conversing on serious topics as well as silly ones and not having to watch every word, control every tone, stifle unladylike snorts of laughter. It had nothing to do with bodies pressed together in a bed. Intimacy was bare feet and mussed hair, accidental brushes of one body part against another and deliberate caresses with eyes wide open. It was touching just for the sake of touching and had little to do with carnality.

She'd never known what contentment was until the past three days with Dane, never known that she hadn't experienced it before. Contentment was Dane treating her as a friend, giving her time to become accustomed to marriage before expecting more of her.

A good thing, she thought with wry humor, since Dane had not given her any time at all to become accustomed to being in love. She was still trying to understand how she'd fallen in love after avoiding it so successfully for ten years.

She puzzled over why she didn't resent him for manipulating her into marriage, but then, she couldn't be entirely certain he had manipulated her. Still she had her suspicions. At the very least he had knocked her off balance at first sight and kept her teetering ever since with his logic that mixed truth with confusion and sounded too reasonable to be right, and with his hot, lazy looks that melted her on the spot.

She really ought to care whether he'd bamboozled her or not, but she couldn't seem to manage it. And she couldn't stop thinking about what would happen after they arrived at Spindrift House—a retreat built by a Wyndham ancestor that Dane had taken as his home. He'd said that she would never want to leave. Since she'd been reluctant to leave the confines of the coach each night in favor of an inn, she didn't doubt him. But it was the man rather than the place. It was the atmosphere he created with his candor and thoughtful silences, with his frequent displays of affection that always turned into a slow seduction that had her both anticipating and fearing the first night they would spend together in the same bed. Anticipating the feel of Dane inside her, knowing that, for her, it would be as perfect as every moment she'd spent in his embrace had been.

Tonight.

"You look sad," he said, breaking the silence.

Startled, she met his gaze, then quickly glanced away. When had he awakened? It wasn't the first time she had wondered how long he had been watching her from beneath half-lowered lids.

She shrugged. "I don't think I'm ready for the journey to end," she replied honestly, not wanting to corrupt the sense of connection—of belonging—that she felt with her husband, a connection she'd not experienced before. A belonging she'd never expected to experience.

She knew it couldn't possibly last—this new and magical feeling of being cherished. She told herself it wouldn't, determined to accept that fact, to be ready to accept its absence when the time came.

"Why?" he asked evenly.

Because I would rather you anticipate perfection than realize it can't exist, she thought. *Because in this small moving world I can almost believe it does exist.* Averting her gaze to the window, she shrugged, knowing he suspected that she feared the night to come. She did, but she didn't want him to know that. She didn't want him to be angry or impatient with her after their idyllic journey. "Because this journey is as close to perfection as I have ever been," she said, hoping he would understand her warning, her entreaty for him not to expect the impossible.

"Oh . . . I don't think our journey will ever end,"

he said, with the barest hint of a smile at one corner of his mouth and his eyes steady and full of promises.

She'd never known a person so eloquent in his expressions and wondered if his face would be as articulate in disappointment.

Merry caught her breath and leaned forward to better see the ''house'' that seemed to rise from the ocean in a cloud of sea spray and prisms of color shimmering in the refracted sunlight, giving it the appearance of drifting and bobbing on the waves.

Having passed the marquess's seat of Wyndham Hall earlier that morning, she'd been watching for Dane's home, expecting a manor perched on a cliff above the sea, but the coach had rumbled along the cliffs, then descended a pitted road to a cove below.

A narrow spit of land ran from a rocky beach to a high mound of an island a respectable distance from shore, connected to the mainland only at low tide. And in the center of it, stone ramparts glistening with a ghostly frosting of spindrift rose and dipped in round towers and crenellated walls. It wasn't a house at all, but an old castle, scaled down to fit the foundation of land, its crumbling ruins restored and altered with mullioned glass, solid chimneys, and what appeared to be a domed conservatory shining like a diamond in the center of it. Somehow, she knew that it had been Dane who had rescued the place from ruin. Only Dane would build a glass-encased garden in a place of rock and salted soil where little could grow without protection from the salt.

''I should have known you would find a way to be at sea even in a house,'' she said. He'd told her of his love for the sea, of how he felt most at home when surrounded by water.

"I couldn't believe my good fortune when I saw this place," he said, as he slipped his spectacles on and craned his neck to peer out the window, "though Uncle Robert thought me mad to want it."

"How long did it take you to restore it?"

"I was seventeen and visiting Uncle Robert before beginning university when I drew up the plans for restoring the structure. I spent holidays riding between Wyndham Manor and here and did much of the work myself in between my Grand Tour of Europe and then England, Scotland, and Ireland. It was completed a year ago."

Seventeen! No wonder he'd spoken of Spindrift House with all the animation of an excited boy. He'd been one when he'd first seen the place, though she couldn't imagine him as being anything but a man. "Were you never a child?" she mused.

"Uncle Robert says that I was born half child and half man and would always be so." He cocked his head, his eyes sparkling with a mischievous light as he cleared his throat and gave a little cough. "I'm still a child when it comes to ships"—he gestured toward the small island—"even ones that only give the illusion of dancing on the waves."

"It is a perfect home for you," she said wistfully.

"Perfect?" He shook his head slowly. "Perfection is a moment, when you feel happy, or when those you care for are in harmony, or when you first see what you have been looking for. It isn't a lack of flaws, but your pleasure in the flaws that make something unique. Like your first sight of my little islet and the castle that seems like a dream until you arrive there." He sat back and gravely regarded her. "You arrive and see that there are still signs of decay. The castle is small by most standards, and it's drafty and damp.

It costs a fortune to maintain and might crumble if the right storm blows in."

"Then why go to so much trouble and expense? Surely you could find something less burdensome that suited you almost as well." Her mouth dried as she held her breath, waiting to hear the rest of it.

"Because thirteen years of work is worth that first glance. Because I love it and find pleasure there. Because perfection is in the eyes of the beholder." He pushed his spectacles up his nose and grinned. "And as everyone will agree, I do not see things as others do." Sitting forward, he grasped her hands, smoothing his thumbs over the backs, then turning them over to stroke her palms. "I will *never* see things as others do, my Lady Lorelei."

Merry swallowed and blinked back the sudden urge to cry, forced back the sudden need to believe he meant her, pinched off the sudden bloom of hope that she would never prove him wrong.

Chapter 16

Adrian had a bad feeling that Lorelei had been adding one and one and coming up with three. He'd tried to keep her too busy to think on the journey, though trying was not the right word. Touching her had been a pleasure of which he could not get enough. Kissing her had been a torture he gladly endured, though it gave such rise to his need for her that he prayed she would accept without fear pleasures and rightness of passion between them. He wanted to nurture her responses, to take the moment as far as it would go. He wanted to give her what she had been taught never to expect. To make her question her belief that no one could possibly love *her*, much less her body.

He thought he'd succeeded until he'd awakened in the coach to find her staring at him, her eyes too wide, as if she were fighting tears. He hated seeing her like that, vulnerable and trying so hard to be strong. He'd rather deal with her tears.

He glanced out the window again and rapped on

the roof of the coach, ordering the coachman to stop.

The door opened and one of the footmen riding outside positioned the steps leading down from the high carriage.

Adrian stepped out and rolled his cramped shoulders. "Leave our baggage here and I will have someone from Spindrift retrieve it," he said to the driver, and pressed a pouch full of coins into the man's hand. "You should be able to reach Wyndham Hall and your own bed by nightfall. Lady Dane and I will walk the rest of the way." Holding out his hand, he smiled as Lorelei took it and descended from the coach, her bearing regal if one did not see her gaze darting all about, full of wonder rather than distaste. She'd enjoyed the journey. She'd relished his attentions in the coach. She liked his home.

He rather thought she liked him as well. He was certain she loved him, though he wondered what it would take to get her to admit it. Or how long. He wanted to hear the words from her, needed to hear them. But he understood that she expected the worst, and why. That she had married him at all and accepted his affection so readily encouraged him to be patient, even as the resignation implied by her acceptance chafed his restraint.

He guided Lorelei to sure footing on the sandbar and casually draped his arm over her shoulder. "Just right," he murmured.

"What is just right?" she asked.

"You. If you were taller, I would dislocate my shoulder to hold you. If you were shorter, my arm would no doubt cramp. As you are, you support it nicely."

Her lips curved upward as she nestled close to his side, her hip rubbing his as she walked, not looking down to watch her footing, not mincing carefully, but matching his stride, unconcerned that she might stumble in the rocky sand—another small sign of trust.

Keeping silent to allow Lorelei to appreciate the view that seemed to change with every inch gained, he whistled tunelessly and kept his gait to a casual stroll. Water lapped at the edges of the sandbar, the rumble of the waves as they rushed toward land magnified by the craggy cliffs surrounding the bight on three sides. He glanced over Lorelei's head to a forbidding cliff jutting out into the water on the right. On the other side were yet more granite ramparts towering from the sea—a maze that frightened most worthy seaman even in boats with a shallow draft. But if one knew the waters and swirling currents, one could navigate a warship through the labyrinth and conceal it in a high, deep cave carved from the land by centuries of pounding waves.

His curiosity had served him well the first year he'd come to Spindrift, leading him to explore the cliffs and caves and currents. He'd found the cave by accident and spent many a summer day studying the debris left behind by smugglers, or pirates, or whatever adventurers his imagination conjured. Every time he'd visited his uncle since, he'd gone back to the coastal labyrinth, measuring the varying depths of water at different points, taking notes on the currents during different stages of the tide. Little had he known then that the cave and cliffs would serve a more vital purpose than his curiosity.

He'd known exactly what to do after Steven had been impressed, exactly where to conceal a ship when the need arose. The *Bifrost* had already once been anchored in the surprisingly deep water of the deceptively narrow maze of rocks and cliffs. She would be again. Until now, he'd been anxious to again sail his sleek ship, to stand at the bow as she cut through the waves with unheard of speed and maneuverability. Now he prayed for a little more time even as guilt stabbed him for his selfish disregard of Steven's plight. For the first time in his memory, he yearned for something other than a fair wind and a solid deck beneath his feet.

"Dane? We have arrived."

He stumbled as Lorelei's voice reached through his preoccupation. A little behind him, she reached around his waist, hauling him back before he sprawled face down on the stone steps leading up to the house.

He cursed vehemently at his uncharacteristic clumnsiness, hating that Lorelei had witnessed it.

"It is heartening to witness proof that you are not always surefooted in the steps you take through life," Lorelei said with a chuckle. "Your confidence and self-assurance can be quite intimidating."

"Then I will refrain from trying to convince you that I contrived the stumble to put you at ease," he said, and glanced away to hide the embarrassment he was certain stained his face.

She gave him an arch, disbelieving glance that immediately alerted him to the possibility that she would exploit his lapse into awkwardness. "What is it you think about when you venture away from the world at hand?" She took the first step, then held out her hand. "Don't worry, I'll make sure you don't fall," she added, tongue-in-cheek.

"I want a wife, not a keeper," he grumbled under his breath.

She snapped her arms down to her sides, turned, picked up her skirts, and ascended the steps at a brisk pace, muttering something about the last thing she wanted to do.

His hands on his hips, he frowned up at her, wondering at her swift change in mood. His comment had been innocent enough and said to himself rather than to her. Sighing, he took the uneven steps two at a time to catch up with her.

"Blast it, Lorelei," he said as she reached the entrance gate to the house, "if you are going to eavesdrop on conversations I conduct with myself, you ought to know you will hear things you might not want . . . to . . . hear. . . ." His voice trailed off as she stopped, her back to him as stiff and straight as he'd ever seen it. He almost fell backward as she turned to face him.

"You're quite right, Dane. It was exceedingly rude of me to listen just because your mouth was moving."

He lowered his head and rubbed the side of his nose. "I suppose I should mumble more quietly."

She laughed, that deep, throaty sound that had reached out to him from across the room the night they'd met. "Did we just have a quarrel and resolve it?"

"Don't you know?"

"I . . . no, I don't," she replied with a defensive upward tilt of her chin. "I have never had anyone to quarrel with."

"Not even Lady Harriet, or Brummell?"

"I would never—" She shook her head and bit her lip, looking more uncertain than he'd ever seen her. "There has never been any cause."

And perhaps you were afraid to, he supplied silently. Afraid they would abandon her if she were not agreeable. It pleased him that she'd gone into a snit so spontaneously, displaying her reaction to his bad humor—another measure, he hoped, of how relaxed she felt in his company. It was almost worth the ignominy of nearly landing in a less than manly sprawl at her feet. Almost.

Taking the last step to her level, he pulled her against him and lowered his mouth to within a breath of hers. "We had a very trivial quarrel, which cannot be truly resolved until we observe a certain ritual." He cut off her retort with his lips, taking his time as he had every day they'd spent in the coach, kissing her thoroughly, deeply, hungrily.

Her arms fluttered at her sides, then her hands pressed against his chest, moving restlessly, urgently, as if she were frustrated by his coat and waistcoat and shirt, her fingers curled as if she might try to shred them.

He knew exactly how she felt.

Tearing his mouth from hers, he willed his passion for her to heel—just for a while longer. "Now we are at peace with one another."

"I warned you that I have little experience with such things," she said breathlessly.

"Well, now you have more experience than a few moments ago." Cradling her cheek with one hand, he traced the shape of her lips with his thumb. "I love your passion, my Lady Lorelei."

She gave him an arch look that he was beginning to recognize as a mask for uncertainty, fear. "If I had known that such . . . stimulating rituals existed, I might have been peevish sooner."

"The ritual is acceptable upon a whim, Lorelei, for any reason, or for no reason at all," he said gruffly, as he pushed open the gate and ushered her into the courtyard.

"Oh, my," she breathed as she tried to look everywhere at once—at the clutter of lush plants and potted trees, the bright profusion of flowers, also in clay pots and wooden boxes and stone urns, at the diamond panes of the domed glass ceiling that covered it all. "How do you do it? I have heard of greenhouses, but this, surrounded by water . . ."

He stood back and stared at her as she wandered from one thing to another, the wonder of a child on her face. "I enjoy puttering around and I have a gardener who is experienced with cultivating growth out of season."

"My peonies have long since bloomed and shed their petals. It's like a dream . . . everything . . . like a wonderful dream."

"It is my belief," he said, as he walked slowly toward her, "that one should give as many of one's dreams as possible a prominent place in reality." Leading her to a secluded corner shielded by fragrant orange trees and a ladder holding layers of peonies, he backed her against the stone wall and ran his forefinger from the hollow at the base of her neck down between her breasts, down her middle and her belly, then up again. "I look forward to an especially vivid dream becoming reality many times over the course of our life together." He covered her breasts with his hands, caressing, teasing, rotating his palms over her swelling nipples.

"Tonight?"

"If I can last that long," he said against her mouth, then nipped at her lower lip.

"Then why not here?"

"Because . . . the servants are waiting inside to greet their new mistress," he said, containing his smile at her boldness. "It would not be seemly—"

"Of course," she said, and dipped beneath his arm

and out of his embrace, smoothing her gown and looking as if she had stays in her posture, then meeting his gaze with a blank expression. "But, I also warned you that . . . in certain situations, *I* am not seemly."

"And I told you," he said, chagrined at his poor choice of words, "that I love your passion." Wincing at the frustration in his voice, he reached for her hand, placed it on top of the back of his, and assumed a very proper pose. "But servants, I have discovered, are snobs, and expect us to live up to their conceits. As a 'barbaric American,' I have disappointed them quite enough."

Merry knew him for a liar as he escorted her through the double doors arched to a point in the center and introduced her to each of the servants by name, receiving everything from disconcertion to blushes in response to the respect with which he treated them. She was rather disconcerted herself as he caressed the nape of her neck while listening to brief reports from the house steward and housekeeper.

"They are not disappointed in you," she said, as he led her from room to room, driving her mad along the way by backing her into a corner in the drawing room to kiss her, leaning her back against the table in the dining room to stroke her breasts, the press of his hips leaving her in no doubt as to his mounting desire. She tried to maintain her composure, reminding herself of all she'd been taught about ladylike behavior and proper comportment with one's husband, but then she would feel his hand stroking—always stroking— some part of her through her clothing, taste his kisses in her memory and then on her tongue when he'd suddenly pull her into his arms and steal her breath away. She would remember his words and experience his passion and feel the rise of his need and abruptly stop caring about anything but the moment.

It occurred to her that caring would not save her in any event. She could bluff her way through society, might even manage to bluff her way through marriage with any other man. But not with Dane, who constantly took her by surprise with his affection, kept her off guard with his candor, nurtured the hope she struggled to suppress with his encouragement for her to respond openly to his every word, his every touch. A response so natural she couldn't help but give it.

She strolled with him through the gallery, uneasy with the portraits of his family on the walls, yet drawn to them with a morbid fascination. It had been a simple matter to avoid the framed miniatures in the drawing room and in his study, yet even those had led her into unfamiliar realms. Everywhere in the house were objects for which Dane had a story—of a childhood friend or a family member. He'd collected memories and mementos all his life. He'd grown up with approval and affection and more freedom than she could imagine, choosing the manner and locations of his education, traveling across the ocean at will, then touring whichever countries in Europe were not at war with England. Yet always, he had family waiting for him to return. Always he was met with love and a place to which he belonged.

All she had was a portrait of a man and woman she'd never known, memories of a great empty house save servants who addressed her in formal terms, and solicitors and trustees who had been interested only in their fees and her school reports.

She hated the gallery, hated how incomplete she felt among the reminders of his past, hated that she couldn't comprehend sentimentality. Her memories of feeling a connection with another human being began with her first meeting with Harriet at school. They were confined to Harriet, and later, to Beau as well.

She walked briskly to the end of the gallery and through another arched doorway, possessed by an odd restlessness, driven again by the need to reach out to him, to burrow in his arms and believe once more that nothing existed beyond the world created by his embrace. The insistence of it terrified her, as if she had become dependent on Dane and could not survive without him. As if only Dane could keep her world in the right position. Rubbing her arms against a sudden chill that came from within, she wished he would take her in his arms, giving her no chance to think, robbing her of the desire to protest. Yet she quickened her pace, putting distance between them to prove that it wasn't so, that she could do very well without his touch, his affection, his very presence. That she didn't need him and never would and could manage quite well without him.

Blinking, she halted and glanced around, her gaze colliding with Dane's right behind her. "Where am I going?" she asked stiffly, the irony of being lost and having to ask Dane for direction a thorn in her side.

Her heart leapt into her throat at the feel of his hand on her arm, the warmth of his body at her back, the drift of his breath on her neck as he kissed her there. "Where do you wish to go?"

"I have no idea," she retorted. *Away,* her mind cried.

"Do you care?" He turned her, held her loosely at her waist.

Anywhere far from here. She chased the thought away—a coward's thought.

"We will fill this, or any home we occupy, with new memories, Lorelei."

Her gaze jerked to his, then skipped away like a flat stone tossed on a pond. She wanted to lash out at him for so easily discerning her uneasiness among the portraits and mementos of his past. She wanted to escape the trap into which she'd so blindly walked. Except she hadn't been blind, not really. She'd known it would be a mistake to marry Dane and had chosen to take the chance. She'd chosen not to fight his determination, his gentle persuasions and sometimes slow, sometimes demanding, seductions. Just as she'd chosen other courses in her life, like her small rebellions against current fashion and conventionality, even as she cultivated grace and accomplishment and an aristocratic manner for balance. Like her insistence upon reaching the end of every road she took.

She had married Dane, taking the most perilous road of all. She would see it through to the end.

"This is the master suite," Dane said.

"Not a moment too soon," she said brightly, and reached for the latch. "I am weary."

Her hand collided with his. Suddenly feeling awkward, she snatched it away.

Dane took a deep breath as if he, too, were nervous, then turned the latch and pushed the door open.

Striding into a small sitting room, she whirled to face him, determined to face him and speak of her fear. "What is it you do to me, Dane? I do not quail at a show of irritability, yet several times since we left the coach, I have taken umbrage at a simple remark from you. I am very good at controlling my baser instincts, yet since we left Harriet's I have encouraged your"—she raised her hands in a gesture of exasperation, as if she couldn't find the right words—

"*your* baser instincts." She backed up as he took a step toward her. "There are times I fancy that you are some sort of sorcerer who turns me into someone other than myself."

"A sorcerer," he mused, then regarded her gravely. "Lorelei—"

"Don't you dare tell me that it is because I am weary from the journey, or that it is my having to adjust to a hasty marriage. And don't, under any circumstance, suggest it is a state peculiar to women once a month."

"All right," he said, visibly quelling his amusement.

She presented her back to him and shook her head. "I cannot believe I said that."

"I know about such things, Lorelei," he said around smothered laughter.

"Then you should know that it is not a laughing matter."

"That is why I have nearly bitten my cheek clear through in an effort not to laugh."

She pivoted and glared at him, at the arch of his brows, and the way he held his cheeks sucked in. "That makes absolutely no sense at all. I want to know why I behaved so shamelessly since the moment I met you and why now of a sudden I feel . . ."

"As terrified as I?" he said.

"Do not jest at a time like this," she warned, and stared at the window as the sun slid over the edge of the world, painting the air with vivid hues of pink and gold.

"I assure you I am not jesting, though it occurs to me that it is the perfect time—"

"Perfect! That is exactly what is wrong. You have played the perfect, ardent, and gallant lover without taking it to the imperfect stage of awkward maneuvering of arms and legs, and the rather messy business of . . . of . . .'' She waved her arms again. ''And now here we are . . . and all I can feel is out of sorts—''

''Yes, I see what you mean,'' he drawled as he advanced toward her, the look in his eyes holding her in place, fascinated.

''You're glowering,'' she accused. ''You said you don't glower.''

''I never said that. And I am glowering because I spent three days seducing you so that you would feel at ease with me, and then bungled it by taking you on a tour of the damned house. I bored you with reminiscences about people you don't know, and with my conceit over a house that would convince the *ton* once and for all that I belong in bedlam''—he paused for breath—''which left you completely unimpressed. And you wonder what I have done to you?''

He took the last step possible without knocking her down and studied her, his hands on his hips, his eyes narrowed. ''It appears that I have not done enough— my fault entirely. You are my first attempt at seduction.''

She snorted in disbelief. ''Not likely.''

''I have experience with women, Lorelei, but none required deliberate seduction . . . and none where success meant so much—'' He broke off his sentence and cocked his head. ''You know, there is something I have always wanted to do.'' Without warning he slid one arm under her knees and the other around her waist and picked her up, not to heave her over his shoulder, but to cradle her against his chest. ''Do not spoil this by moving and throwing me off balance,'' he said with a grunt, as he strode toward an open door at one end of the sitting room. "One humiliating incident is quite enough for a lifetime."

Too startled by his action, too stunned that he had managed it at all, and too afraid his staggering steps might tumble them both, she wrapped her arms around his neck and held still.

"You inquired earlier as to where my thoughts wander, and I didn't answer," he said in a strained voice as he shoved the door farther open with his foot, swayed, then proceeded into a bedchamber. "Since seeing you that first night, I have spent a great deal of time dreaming about sweeping you off your feet, carrying you to my lair, and keeping you there until you were resigned to keeping me." He dropped her onto the center of a huge bed and again propped his hands on his hips. "But since I am feeling less heroic than unbearably aroused, you will have to settle for a great deal of urgency and flailing limbs . . . as soon as I catch my breath."

"Dane—"

"You would do well to remain stupified at my absurd behavior until after I have ravished you," he said with mock severity as he shrugged out of his coat and then his waistcoat. "Your arguments now would likely unman me completely, and that would cause me to display a rare fit of temper." He kicked off his shoes.

She struggled to get her elbows to support her and half sat, half reclined, absently noting that the sky was quickly fading to twilight silver. "Dane?"

He glared up at the ceiling. "Damn it . . . what?"

"Please do be quiet, close the window hangings, and ravish me before I lose interest in being at your mercy and put you at mine instead."

His hand paused in the act of releasing the buttons

of his shirt. He raised his brows, then covered her body and took her mouth all in one overwhelming motion.

She met his kiss with parted lips and demanding tongue as her hands worked at the rest of his shirt buttons. He searched for the fastenings of her bodice, then groaned and parted it with a rip. She fumbled with his breeches, opening them, finding him, releasing him, stroking him.

He broke the kiss to take one nipple in his mouth while his fingers teased the other. She stroked his hardness, cradled the softness below, then stroked again as she tasted his chest, trying to nibble and kiss him everywhere at once. He groped for her hem, pulled it up, caressed the inside of her thighs.

Heat flared between them, misting their bodies as urgency doubled and redoubled. Sensations piled up on one another so quickly, she didn't know one from another, knowing only the heat and moisture, the building ache in her belly, the need that became a world in itself. Dane's body was heavy upon her, a welcome seductive weight. His hands were everywhere—on her bared breasts, then her still clothed midriff, on her bared thighs, then inside her, probing, driving her beyond need to madness.

His mouth returned to hers, devouring her. She raised her knees and opened for him, wanting to consume him. He plunged into her, withdrew, and plunged again. Ignoring the burning stab of pain, she met each thrust with the arch of her hips, faster and faster until it became a different kind of pain, a pain of needing. Such desperate needing. She wrapped her legs around his waist, taking all of him, holding him as flame ignited inside her and bloomed, shattering her into a thousand sparks flying upward.

And still she arched and rotated her hips as Dane drove into the very heart of her and stiffened, thrust again, and shuddered with his own release.

She held him inside her, gasping as her spasms matched the ferocity of his, hearing his heartbeat thunder in tune with hers, feeling as if they were nothing but ash drifting through the air.

Twilight silver had darkened to black. Dane raised up above her, still a part of her, a shadow in the darkness. "My Lady Lorelei," he said, as if he were in awe as his hand stroked her cheek and his mouth covered hers in a kiss so tender she trembled with it, feeling beautiful and cherished and infinitely feminine in his embrace.

"You ravish very well," she said softly.

"So do you," he murmured.

She framed his strong face with her hands, stroking the texture of his evening beard, smiling at the feel of his hands still stroking her, as her lips reached for his again and again, wanting that most perfect of moments to last forever. . . .

Dane shifted and eased away from her, sitting up on the edge of the bed and reaching for a candle.

A candle. Light. She didn't want the light, didn't want Dane to see her as she must look now, her hair a tangled mass, her gown ripped and bunched up, exposing what she did not want him to see. What even she hated to see. Her body, too tall and too round, everything an exaggeration of what it should be.

Swallowing a sob, she pulled the edges of her bodice together and smoothed down the hem of her skirt and turned to curl up on her side, knowing that the moment was gone. . . .

That nothing lasted forever.

Chapter 17

"Lorelei . . . I meant for it to last longer . . . to be slow . . . to not hurt you," Adrian said, at a loss for the proper words. Their quips aside, he hated his loss of control, his roughness and urgency. "I wanted candlelight and dinner and to make love to you with holding and little bits of conversation." He raked his hand through his hair.

"It was perfect," she said in a choked voice.

He glanced at her over his shoulder, frowned at the way she had covered herself, and rolled to her side away from him, as if she were hiding. Suddenly he felt an urgent need to don the breeches he'd kicked off and reached for them, cursing under his breath as they tangled and resisted his efforts.

"Did I hear you ask the housekeeper to send up water for a bath?" she asked.

"Yes . . . the door over there"—he pointed across the room, though she couldn't see him—"leads to an alcove. The door in the middle is the bathing chamber. The one to the right is your dressing room."

She sat up on the opposite edge of the bed, still facing away from him. "Where is my bedchamber?"

"Here."

"Where is yours?"

"Here. There is only one, Lorelei. That is why the bed is so large."

"But—"

"My parents shared a bed for their entire marriage." He saw her tremble. "Lorelei? Do you not wish to share a room with me?" He had to push the question out, then held his breath, waiting for her reply.

"I have my own dressing room?" she asked instead.

"Yes."

"You want me to sleep with you?"

"I cannot imagine having you in another room where I cannot hold you in the night."

She turned and met his gaze. "It . . . will take some getting used to," she said, again choked. "Being held through the night . . . sharing."

He barely heard the last but it was enough. Securing his breeches, he cautiously rolled across the bed and sat beside her, wanting to hold her now, yet afraid with her seeming so fragile just then. "Would you rather I have a separate room made up for you?" He nearly gagged on the offer and reminded himself that it all was strange and overwhelming to her.

She shuddered and leaned her head on his shoulder, then jerked it up again. "No . . . no," she repeated, then clenched one hand in her lap, the other clutching the edges of her bodice together.

Adrian wrapped his arm around her and pressed her head down to his shoulder. "Do not feel awkward, Lorelei," he said harshly, unaccustomed to the strain of thinking of another before himself. Of trying to comprehend her feelings when his experiences lacked any clear reference to them.

"It's a new experience . . . feeling awkward."

"I am sorry, Lorelei. You deserved better than that your first time."

"Please," she cried and jerked away from him to stand and stumble toward the door. "Please don't apologize. It was my fault and I enjoyed it and I don't care what you think." She rushed into the alcove and slammed the door behind her.

He heard another door slam, and for the third time that day, reacted with temper rather than an effort to understand. Striding to the door, he yanked it open, listened for sound coming from each of the three doors, then yanked open the one leading to the bathing chamber.

Lorelei stood in the center of the large room, frozen in the act of removing her gown, staring at him in horror. "No!" She quickly pulled the garment up again, hugging it to her with a desperation that stupified him, mixed with a lingering stare at his bare torso that prompted a swell of pride. And then she lowered her gaze to the floor, as if she were ashamed. "Please do not look at me now."

He pivoted sharply as a deep chill invaded him at the realization that she was ashamed. Ashamed of her body. Ashamed of herself. He should have realized it sooner. How could she not want to hide herself when everywhere she went, everyone she met made jests or cruel remarks or criticized as if it was her fault alone for the way she was made? He should have known the moment she'd told him of the humiliation and heartbreak she'd suffered at eighteen.

He didn't know what to say beyond platitudes she

would never accept as sincere. Anger magnified at his inability to say the right thing to gentle the fear he saw in her eyes. Anger, too, that there should be a need, that she thought so little of him as to expect him to look upon her with disgust. Had she paid so little attention that she'd learned nothing of him? Was she so steeped in conviction that she had nothing to offer, that she would never learn?

He inhaled, striving for a control that did not come. "I will not look at you, Lorelei, but neither will I have you run from me. We are husband and wife. We will share a bed even if you come to it swaddled in heavy wool from neck to feet. And you might remember that you are eight-and-twenty years old—too old to continue hiding from yourself. You might open your eyes, and your mind, and see what *is*, rather than what you dread might be." Unable to say more without giving in to the urge to shake her, he strode from the chamber and felt an irrational pleasure in slamming the door so hard it rebounded and then banged shut.

Abruptly he swung around and pushed it open again, his mouth slanting in derision as she again clutched her gown to her body. "I have seen you clothed, Lorelei, and have touched your flesh. You think I do not know you are tall and well rounded? You think that the images in my fantasies of you would be so different from the reality? Do you—" he said, then lowered his head and gave a mirthless laugh. "To hell with it. You will believe what you wish." Once again, he stalked from the bathing chamber, this time closing the door very softly, very firmly.

Merry soaked in a porcelain tub of luxuriously hot water and fragrant oil. Carnation-scented oil. Dane had noticed her preference and provided it, going so far as to have the maid add it to her bathwater.

She had snuffed the candles in the chamber after Dane had left, not wanting to glimpse her reflection in the cheval glass standing in a corner. Yet it was not the looking glass that drew her gaze, but the outline of what she had briefly seen upon first entering the room. A nightrail and robe hung on pegs—not something she had brought, but something Dane had apparently purchased for her. Though nothing had been said, the robe fashioned in her favorite tunic style, and the fresh peony sticking up from the pocket left little doubt that it was a gift from her husband. The fabric of the gown shimmered in the shaft of moonlight that streamed through the single window and fell on the folds of what had to be rose silk embellished with rich ecru lace. She favored silk and suspected he had noticed that, too.

She closed her eyes against the sight and laid her head back on the edge of the tub. Her mind would not close, no matter how strongly she willed it. She had behaved like a child, just as Dane had implied. A terrified child—not her way at all. Even in her youth, she'd dealt with her fears and her nightmares with determination and reason, refusing to be at their mercy. As a young woman, she had not cowered in the face of a man's scorn. Yet now, with a man who had never once criticized her appearance or her manner, never once shown disgust for her, she had surrendered to her own vulnerabilities without a struggle, then stood behind them as if they could shield her from being hurt. As if they could drive Dane away before he tired of the novelty of her and walked away on his own, or worse, became bored and indifferent.

Childish. Stupid. Had she learned nothing in all

those years? Had she not learned to acknowledge—
and flaunt—her peculiarities before others had the opportunity to deride them, thus robbing them of the
pleasure? Had she not learned to ferret out her admirable qualities, not only for her own benefit, but to
promote them, forcing others to recognize and appreciate what they would otherwise have missed if she'd
cowered before their ridicule? Had she not, over the
course of time, realized that those qualities were far
more worthy of self-confidence than a beautiful face
and lithe body?

Dane thought so. Everything he said and did proved
it. He was a man of honor and truth. Perhaps more
important, he was, like her, not cut from cloth cur-
rently in fashion. Any one of the young ladies on the
marriage block would have wed him for his wealth
and title. Many would have wed him because he was
not ugly or riddled with gout or old and sour. None
of them would have found his silences, or his forthright manner, or the way his spectacles sat askew and
slipped down his nose endearing, much less fascinating. None of them would have loved him for his oddities as she did.

She rolled her eyes at that rather pompous thought
as another came forward. Could it be that she and
Dane were really well matched? That perhaps he
cared for her for the same reasons that she loved him?

She sank deeper in the tub and stared wide-eyed at
the gown and robe as her mind asked a final, stunning
question: why didn't she employ all the strength she'd
acquired over the years and do all in her power to
keep him interested?

Even novelties could become treasures.

She thought of Dane's many gestures of consideration and many expressions of admiration, Dane's ur-

gency to have her after days of careful, gentle seduction. A seduction that had caused him no small amount of discomfort while giving her nothing but pleasure. A seduction that hadn't been necessary. She'd married him. She'd had few expectations—none that would try him. Surely he knew that.

The cooling water seemed to sizzle against her flesh at the memory of what had passed between them—every touch, every kiss, every thrust and slide of their bodies. An odd restless energy charged her limbs as she touched her breasts, felt them swell and peak. Pleasure shot from her nipples to her belly as she pressed her hands against them.

Water cascaded down her body as she rose quickly and lurched from the tub. She moaned at the gentle abrasion of the heated linen towel. Dropping it, she reached for the gown and slipped it over her head, sighing at the slide of cool silk that ironically covered most of her but for the squared neckline that bared her upper chest and the length of her arms. The bodice was intricately smocked and embroidered with deep rose threads that matched exactly the color of the robe and flowed into a skirt from the line created by a tie in the back that drew the gown to a flattering fit over her breasts and midriff. Small carved ivory buttons marched down the front to below her waist, one on top of the other. Deep lace that was indeed ecru flounced the hem.

Sighing again in pleasure at the gown that was so well matched to her taste and preferences, she lit the tapers in a branched candelabra and donned the velvet robe, then turned this way and that before standing in front of the cheval glass to admire the way it remained open like a deep vee almost to her waist, a broad band inset fitting closely in front while the velvet flared out loosely in back.

She felt positively fetching . . . alluring . . . beautiful.

She rushed out of the bathing chamber and into her dressing room, finding her hairbrush and toiletries already arranged on an elegant dressing table topped by a simple looking glass. Dropping her hairpins onto the table, she swept her long mane over her shoulder and brushed, wincing at the pull of tangles. Finished, she tossed her head, her hair falling down her back in soft, thick waves of chestnut brown.

Setting the brush down, she wondered where Dane might be. She'd heard enough grousing from other wives to know that when things became disagreeable, husbands usually found somewhere else to be. No matter. She would wait, regardless of how long it took.

She'd be a fool to allow her appearance, and her resolve, to go to waste.

Merry swept into the sitting room and halted in the center of the room, completely undone by what she saw.

Dane sat by the fire, one leg hooked over the arm of his chair, his attention buried in a book. He wore a dressing gown loosely belted at his waist, and a gilding of firelight on his bared chest. His hair was damp, his face shiny from a recent shave, as if he had bathed elsewhere. A round table draped in fine damask and decorated with a bowl of flowers was set with covered silver serving dishes and fine china and crystal. Her mouth watered at the fragrance of well-prepared food.

Dane snapped his book shut, startling her. "Our

meal grows cold,'' he said, as he rose to seat her.

Dazed, she sat where he placed her and stared down at her plate as he served her, politely asking her preferences.

She nodded at everything, the colors and textures of the food blurring into an indistinguishable mass. Eating mechanically, she drank frequently from her wineglass, not once wondering why it always seemed to be full. She knew why and didn't object that Dane was obviously plying her with spirits. The moment she'd seen him, her nerve had wavered. Perhaps the wine would fortify it.

"I rarely become tanglefooted," she commented, refraining from mentioning that she felt nicely euphoric and uncommonly bold, even for her.

He said nothing.

"I rarely wallow in my own stupidity for long," she added.

He placed his fork on his plate and sat back, silent, his gaze steady on her.

She took another bite and chewed slowly, determined to appear casual and sophisticated as she discussed the deficiencies in her repertoire of experiences. The quail or fish or whatever it was stuck in her throat, threatening to choke her. She grabbed her wineglass and gulped half the contents, then slapped it back down on the table. Opening her mouth, she shut it again to swallow a burp, appalled that her body would choose such a moment to embarrass her. She smiled triumphantly as the bubble of air decided not to surface.

"Though I'm fairly certain I am not tanglefooted, I must admit to the possibility of my being a bit tipsy." She held her thumb and forefinger apart an inch to demonstrate. "Therefore, I believe it prudent to get on with my attempt at humility." Expanding her chest and squaring her shoulders, she focused to the best of her ability on Dane, still silent, still staring at her. "I do not understand affection. I did not know it existed until I met Harriet. I do believe I was never hugged until she introduced me to the practice, which I might add, discomfited me greatly. In fact I still don't know what to do with myself in such moments . . . except with you."

A crease formed between his brows, tipped up at the inside edges.

"Nor do I understand why your touches—from the casual brush of a knee to a lingering caress here"—she pressed her hand to her breast—"seem to gather and remain here"—she flattened her hand over her heart—"like living memories—" She broke off as his brows arched and his mouth quirked up slightly at the corners. "Pardon my bluntness, but delicacy eludes me." Stifling a hiccup, she forged ahead. "Never before have I been so aware of my hunger for affection." She raised her hands and shrugged at the same time. "Deliberate or accidental, it never matters as long as it happens. And I don't care why or how this aberration has taken root in my nature. Just as I don't particularly care that I behave in a primitive way with you. Since you don't appear to object there seems little point, in any case."

She waited for him to give confirmation, then nodded before he had the chance. "You don't object. A definite advantage given my whorish nature."

"Lusty," he corrected, his mouth angled upward at one corner.

"You have quite a wonderful mouth, you know—beautifully shaped and very masculine," she said, after another swallow of wine. "But I digress." The room spun around her. She widened her eyes on Dane, the nearest fixed object upon which to focus, and blotted her forehead with her napkin. ''I have resolved to keep you, oddities and all, and direct my energies to convincing you that you are quite pleased about it.''

''All right,'' he said reasonably.

Again she blotted her forehead and beneath her nose. It was becoming increasingly warm in the room, though the fire was low in the hearth. ''You must realize that we are wed because I wished it. I like being touched and I like conversing with you and I like kissing . . . very, very much.'' Frowning, she narrowed her eyes. ''I cannot recall what I meant to say.''

''What you like,'' he prompted.

''Oh, yes. Thank you.'' Rising, she stood rigidly, her hands clenching the back of her chair. ''I do not, however, like to be seen unclothed; I believe the reasons are obvious. I do not know if I ever will be agreeable to displaying my abundance. I expect you to understand that.'' With a nod of satisfaction that she had presented her point unsheathed, she turned and walked very carefully into the bedchamber, deliberately leaving the door opened wide.

Adrian stared at the open door, aware that he was grinning ear to ear. Would Lorelei never stop surprising him with her resilience and great spirit? She had more reasons than most to indulge her fears and cower from life, yet she always rallied, stronger and wiser than before. But, as he had observed over the past fortnight, only when it mattered to her. When it didn't, she simply walked away, refusing to wage a battle that in her eyes was not worth fighting.

He could only surmise that he mattered to her. But

then he'd known that when she'd said the vows that bound them together.

They had met three weeks ago, yet it felt to him as if they'd always been together. They knew so little about one another, yet seemed to understand so much about one another. As he understood that the greater her fear of something, the more she defied it and exposed it, like the emperor without clothes, refusing to acknowledge his nakedness.

He suspected that she'd become cross so easily earlier in the day for the same reasons he had. It had been so simple to play at making love in the coach because it wouldn't go beyond play. But the closer they'd come to Spindrift, the more aware he had been that it was no longer a game. The more important it had become to him not to disappoint her. It had rattled him to realize how important. There was so much he wanted her to know: how truly, deeply beautiful she was; how completely special she was; how he loved her smile and her laugh and then her wit, and by the end of that first night, how he loved her. How could he possibly tell her so that she would believe it? How could he show her?

The suddenness with which he'd fallen in love with her, wanted her, needed her, had concerned him most after they'd reached Spindrift. He'd panicked. What had he done? Why? How had it happened? He could almost have read the same questions running through her mind. Questions that came too late with answers that were a feeling, or a sense, and for which no words existed to voice them. Blind faith in an inexplicable feeling or sense of rightness was a frightening thing for a woman, or a man. But a woman had the advantage. She was allowed to give vent to her emotions.

A man was expected to be strong and bear his uncertainties in silence.

He finished his wine and rose from the table. He should be saying these things to her, explaining to her that he felt the same as she, that he was as vulnerable as she. But he was a man and it was not allowed. A man had to hope that the woman he loved would have blind faith in an inexplicable feeling or sense of rightness within herself.

He strolled toward the door she'd left open for him, discarding his maudlin philosophies. Perhaps Phillip had been right to accuse him of thinking too much. Tonight, with Lorelei waiting for him in his bed while he pondered the mysteries of men and women, he was inclined to believe it.

Pausing on the threshold, he smiled ruefully as he rubbed the side of his nose. Lorelei had fallen asleep sitting up, waiting for him. Her head lolled to the side and her hands lay on the mattress at her sides palms up, her fingers curled slightly, her wealth of hair drawn over her shoulder and fanned over her breast.

He walked toward her, taking his time, enjoying the sight of her, finding pleasure in knowing she had arranged her hair that way deliberately, to entice him, apparently believing it might be possible. Once upon a time not so long ago, she hadn't believed it. She'd been so sure of it that she'd been willing to settle for a man who would barely notice her presence in his life.

Instead she had married him.

It was a good beginning.

Adrian slid into bed beside her, eased her off the pillows behind her back, and arranged her head on his shoulder, her body against his. She sighed and moved her leg over his as he pulled a quilt over them both. He clasped her hand, kissed the backs of her fingers, and held it on his chest, smiling as his eyes closed and contentment led him into sleep.

Chapter 18

◡◠◯◯◠◡

How lovely she felt—all warm and safe and comfortable with Dane's heartbeat beneath her ear and his body next to her, his hand clasping hers even in sleep. Sharing a bed was nice, she thought drowsily. Very nice.

Her eyes snapped open. Dane. Beside her. Holding her. She must have fallen asleep waiting for him. He must have decided not to disturb her and taken her in his arms. Her leg was over one of his, her knee nestled against his passion that was even now rising beneath the sheets. . . .

Oh, dear heaven. His passion, so blatant, so provocative. Warily, she moved her head a bit and peered up at him. He met her gaze with a seductive, drowsy look in his eyes and a faint smile on his lips. He'd been watching her. He wanted her.

She glanced at the window, at the pitch darkness outside with only pinpricks of sparkle winking at them from far away in the ether. She felt the weight of a quilt over her shoulders and smiled at her husband lying so silent beside her. "I've never been tucked in before. I'm sorry I missed it," she said softly.

Saying nothing, he rolled to his side and urged her to her back, angling across her, covering her mouth with his, taking it in a slow, lazy exploration. Nothing else—just a long, tempting kiss. The sound of her breathing mingled with his as she returned each slide of his tongue, each nibble of his lips. His hand skated over her breasts and back again, a wisp of a touch. His mouth left hers and lowered to her nipples, taking one into his mouth through her gown, drawing on it, then doing the same to the other, over and over, so slowly she felt languid and weak with the desire that bloomed like a night flower, one petal at a time.

His fingers released the ivory buttons one at a time with agonizing care, his mouth tasting each bit of bared flesh as his other hand found her and stroked her through the gown, sliding silk over her, creating a slow, delicious friction between her legs. She twisted restlessly, wanting more.

"Shh," he whispered and slowly—unbearably slowly—drew her gown up her legs. "Shh," he whispered, as he caressed her breasts and rolled the centers between his fingers and tasted them, drawing them deeply into his mouth, one, then the other.

She sobbed in pleasure as he trailed his tongue down to the end of the opening of her gown.

"Shh," he whispered as he moved lower, kissing her belly through the silk, then lower still to the bared flesh below.

She arched her hips at the stroke of his tongue, the slide of his mouth, and then the stroke of his tongue again. She felt bathed in dew and felt it on his body as well. She thought it would go on forever, that he would consume her with hands and mouth alone. Needing to touch him, to taste him, she reached for him and whimpered as he deepened his caress inside her. Frustrated and filled with pleasure, she reached above her head, wrapped her hands around the headboard, and arched her hips higher, closer to Dane, letting him have his way as her breath became shorter and heat surrounded and filled her. And then she cried out as wave after wave of ecstasy washed over her, rolled through her, swept her away.

She sobbed with it as Dane slid up her body and plunged into her, drowning her in more sensation than she could bear. She cried out in protest as he withdrew and sobbed again as thrust again, harder, deeper. It would never end—his filling of her, his withdrawal, like the ebb and flow of the tide, making her a part of it.

Holding tightly to the headboard, she moved with him, forcing herself to match his slow rhythm, to torment herself as much as he tormented her. And all the while, she stared up at him, at his male beauty silhouetted shadow against the night, at his eyes watching her with an intensity that was as seductive and stirring as the stroke of him inside her.

She barely noticed when his movements quickened, drove more deeply, faster—waves crashing inside her as she thrust upward to meet him hard and frantic, flooding her with a rush of pleasure, of need, of drowning in pure sensation, of dying and becoming a part of the tide, liquid and flowing around him.

Dane's mouth crashed down over hers, taking her cries of completion into himself as she took his release into her, becoming more whole than she had ever felt in her life.

He lay above her for what could have been a moment or eternity, and then he rolled to his side, taking her with him, remaining a part of her as his hands gently fastened the buttons of her gown again, his gaze on her face, only her face, as he shielded her body from his gaze.

Nothing had ever touched her so deeply as that last, simple gesture.

Merry stood at the window, listening to Dane's breathing as he slept, staring at the ocean, watching dawn brush the horizon with a subtle, sheer light soaked in hues of pink and rose and gold and blue splashed across the sky. A ship sliced through the water, trailing luminous froth in its wake. A beautiful ship, long and lean and full of grace, its sails taut in the wind, harnessing its power, matching its speed. She could see Dane at the helm of such an extraordinary ship, guiding rather than controlling, seducing rather than forcing her response. Dane, who could charm the wind itself with his skewed smile.

The ship approached so closely she could see two men in the crow's nest, one intent on what he saw through his spyglass, the other leaning over from time to time as if he were shouting instructions. She frowned at the shape of the vessel, unique, unfamiliar. At the way it hugged the coast, then quickly glided out of sight behind the craggy cliff jutting out into the water almost even with Dane's island domain.

Where had it gone? There were no safe harbors nearby, only cliffs and rocks that would devour the mightiest ship like a dragon devouring its prey.

Adrian felt cloth beneath his hand and only coldness in the space next to him. He opened his eyes and saw only an expanse of bed. He raised up and glanced around the room, his gaze racing past then returning to Lorelei standing in front of the window, her nose pressed to the glass, her hands flat against it, her bottom sticking out.

He kicked the covers away and left the bed, silently approaching her and slipping his hands around her waist. "You cannot fly out the window," he whispered in her ear, nibbling her lobe between words, his body becoming alert as she started, her bottom pushing against him in the process. "You can, however, fly with me if you return to bed."

Straightening, she leaned her head back, presenting her neck for his attentions. "I could swear I just saw a ship fly," she said on a sigh. "It was quite incredible."

A chilling dread settling in the pit of his stomach, and a thrilling sense of anticipation batted its wings in his chest, as he stilled and raised his head to stare at the ocean beyond the window. "Where did you see such a phenomenon?" he asked with studied nonchalance and tightened his arms around her, not wanting to let her go. Not wanting her to escape him. Not when he had just found her.

"It was the most peculiar thing," she said, as she placed her hands over his on her waist. "A ship like I have never seen before, sailing so close and then disappearing around that cliff. I'm not entirely certain I saw it at all, it was so fast, like a dream."

Yes, a dream, he thought, as the chill froze inside him. *His* dream—of a new kind of vessel, one that could achieve enough speed and carry enough cargo to make long voyages economical. One that would fly on water. His dream, now a harbinger of both hope and disaster. Hope for Steven. Disaster for his marriage to Lorelei, for what they had begun only four short days ago.

He couldn't tell her of the ship, of why it was here. She was born and bred British. He could not expose her to knowledge that would test her loyalties, compromise her safety in a time of war. Yet she had seen it. He'd been right the night he'd told Uncle Robert that he had no business marrying just now, that he had no right to begin a family until Steven was returned to his own family. Adrian had known the risks. He'd known he could be captured or killed in the act of trying to rescue Steven. He'd known that his loyalty to family would be considered a treasonous act by his adopted country.

He'd thoughtlessly exposed Lorelei to the dangers as well, all because he'd wanted her, loved her with a blindness to everything but her. Even now, he didn't want to leave her. Even now, for the space of a thought, he contemplated allowing Captain Mathers to undertake the task.

But he couldn't. Steven was not Mathers's cousin, closer than a brother. If Mathers and the rest of the crew were to stake their futures to recover Steven's, then Adrian could do no less.

He turned Lorelei in his arms, his breath stumbling as she arched her brows at his nudity. Wondering if she found him pleasing, he didn't move, groaning as his arousal became limp in a rather pathetic show of shyness.

"It's quite all right, Dane. I have seen you clothed and I have touched your flesh," she said with a mischievous lilt in her voice, repeating what he had said to her the night before. "Do you think I am not aware that you are tall and well made and quite up to scratch at the required moment?"

Pleased at her boldness and the compliment itself, and chagrined at his body's refusal to flex its muscles in pride, he took her mouth, holding her tightly, as if he could absorb her into himself, taking every part of her kiss with the desperation of fearing it might be the last.

Raising his head, he framed her face with his hands, absorbing the image of her. "Smile for me, my Lady Lorelei. Let me see what captured my heart."

Her remarkable eyes widened; her lips parted. A slight frown creased her brow.

He knew why. He'd all but told her he loved her, avoiding the actual words because she would distrust them. She'd been abandoned by her parents—people who should have loved her enough to remain with her, to nurture the emotions she feared, to hug her and tuck her in at night and tell her she was beautiful. He would not say the words and expect her to accept them when he, too, was about to abandon her, even if—God willing—it was for only a short time.

She gave him his smile—a brilliant thing that rivaled dawn. A beautiful thing that enriched him more than she had in the night with her body.

"I fancy a brisk walk," he said gruffly, as his thumbs traced the shape of her smile, imprinting it on his memory.

She trembled. "I fancy food," she said with a grimace. "And a powder for my head. False courage in the form of wine exacts a price."

He couldn't help but smile. "Most would not be able to bear the thought of food."

"I can always bear the thought of food," she replied. "Especially this morning, after having been so depleted through the night. In fact, I have a definite craving for chocolate this morning."

"My pride winces that you did not say 'repleted.' "

"That, too. But in this case I believe one goes with the other." She turned her head to kiss his hand. "I will leave you to your walk while I seek a meal."

"And a powder for your head," he added, hoping with cowardly fervor that she might fall asleep, that he might leave her with a note. He was not certain he had the fortitude to face her with a good-bye. "All you need do is use the bellpull in your dressing room to ring for your abigail."

"I never require aid in dressing, though I might ring for a bath and eat while I soak in that lovely oil you provided." She gave him another smile and ducked out of his embrace, flinching at the movement.

"Lorelei," he said, needing to say many things, yet not knowing how. "I am sorry I drove you to drink," he said instead, hating himself for his weakness.

She met his gaze and sighed. "It was worth it to discover that in future I need not go to such lengths to share myself with you." As if discomfited by such an admission, she abruptly strode to the alcove and her dressing room beyond.

As the first door clicked shut and he heard the second close also, he trudged back to the bed and sat on the edge, stared blindly at the wall. His shoulders heaved and he covered his face with his hands to muffle his grief.

Chapter 19

A drian halted at the entrance to the cave that, even now, his men were draping with heavy canvas dyed to blend in with the cliffs. Inside, lit by lanterns and torches, the *Bifrost* looked like the apparition Lorelei had thought it. He'd had the hull painted a blue-gray with new pigments Steven had been experimenting with—an attempt to make *Bifrost* less conspicuous by blending it with the color of the sea. Even the copper sheathing the planks of the hull seemed to blend with the glints of sunlight reflecting off the water.

Bifrost—his dream for so many years, named for the Norse bridge to Valhalla. It had been so for him as he'd sailed her from Connecticut to England, testing her strength and endurance and speed, feeling as if she were *his* bridge to Valhalla, for the sea had always been his paradise.

Until Lorelei.

Forcing the thought to lie still and silent, he examined the ship for signs of stress and wear. But she stood proud and regal with her three masts and streamlined sails, lunging against her anchor and moorings as if she could not wait to dance again on the waves.

He'd imagined such a ship for years and finally, he'd put the design on paper, calculating dimensions and sail. He'd ordered her built after he'd completed his Grand Tour, remaining in Connecticut to supervise every detail until the structure was finished. Then he'd returned to England, trusting Steven to see to the rest of it—the fittings and interiors, knowing Steven would keep it secret, trusting the men he'd chosen to build it to keep silent as well. He hadn't wanted attention on what might or might not work. He'd even admitted to Steven that he could not have dealt with public ridicule of his dream. He would see it a reality first, completed and tested on the waters of the Atlantic before he exposed it to the world.

He'd gone back to Connecticut only last year to captain her himself on her maiden voyage while Steven took Phillip's place on a run to the West Indies. Always, since their fathers had begun the Rutland Merchant fleet, members of the family took turns to sail on one voyage a year.

Adrian clenched his hands at the memory of returning from his run down the coast of America to discover Steven's ship had been stopped by the British, her cargo seized and Steven and several others impressed. Ironic that of the three cousins, only Steven had completely mimicked the British accent of their fathers, while he and Phillip had an odd mixture of that and the more relaxed drawl distinctive to Americans—

"Lord Dane," a man called from the rear of the cave.

Adrian watched his agent approach, knowing what his presence meant. If there had been any doubt before as to *Bifrost*'s appearance, none existed now at the sight of Blackwell. He'd hired the agent out of Jamaica—an expatriated Englishman with strong opinions in politics. He'd left England under a cloud because of his outspoken beliefs that England and America should become allies, and that England's policies restricting American trade in Europe would prove disastrous. Adrian's plight had appealed to his righteous belief that impressment of men was tantamount to slavery, and the man had proven a loyal ally.

"Sir," Blackwell said as he approached. "I have news."

"You've found Steven?"

"Aye, that I have. He is on the frigate *Falcon*, which was scheduled to sail from England to Port Royal a month past." He shifted uncomfortably. "Your cousin—the other one—also knows his brother is on the *Falcon*."

"You told Phillip?" Adrian said in a low voice, his eyes narrowed, his hands itching to connect with Blackwell's face.

"He found me and was most insistent. With him being the brother and all, I felt he had a right to know, but I was a bit uneasy about him—he's a temperamental sort and a bit too driven for my ease."

"Go on," Adrian said, his temper mounting.

To his credit Blackwell faced him squarely, neither voicing nor displaying apology for his actions. "I knew the *Falcon* had returned to England for new orders and would sail for Port Royal after. I told him the name of the ship, but that *Falcon* was taking the northern route to Canada to throw him off. Far as I know, he's been searching there all this time." He grimaced. "I did expect to get here sooner but was held up in the Indies." Reaching into the pocket of his heavy woolen coat, he pulled out a pouch bulging with coins. "I took young Phillip's money for the information. He wouldn't have believed me if I hadn't." He held it out to Adrian. "Mayhap you'll return it to him when this is over."

Adrian barked with laughter as tension and anger deserted him. "I don't know why I am always surprised when a man proves to be both wise and loyal." He briefly clasped Blackwell's shoulder. "Thank you, my friend, for protecting Phillip from himself."

"I have lost much for my convictions," Blackwell said soberly. "I would not compromise them for a pouch of gold."

"I wish my choices were as clear," Adrian said, more to himself than to his agent.

"Is there a problem, my lord?"

Adrian glanced away. "I was married but four days ago."

"You like to cast dares at fate, sir?" Blackwell asked with a roll of his eyes.

"It would seem so." Adrian stared at *Bifrost.* "You say *Falcon* left England a month past?" A month . . . before he'd met Lorelei . . . before he'd involved her in the chaos of his life.

"Aye, sir, but there is more."

Captain Mathers strode forward and extended his hand. "Adrian, boy," he boomed. "Damned good to see you."

Adrian took the captain's hand and grinned. He'd learned everything he knew about sailing from Mathers, a short man as trim as the ships he commanded. The captain's sister had been the Rutlands' housekeeper since he was a boy and her husband the man-

ager of the Rutland enterprises. They had taken care
of him and his cousins after the deaths of their parents, Bea mothering them at home and Ben acting as
their mentor in business. Several of the sons and
nephews of the large family worked in the shipyards.
Two of Mathers's nephews were members of *Bifrost's*
crew. "It's damned good to see you, too, sir. I could
use some of your wisdom."

Mathers peered up at him with one squinted eye.
"What have you done now?"

"He married four days ago," Blackwell said.

Mathers grinned broadly, then sobered. "You don't
believe in making things easy on yourself do you,
boy?"

"A failing of mine," Adrian said.

"Did you tell him?" Mathers asked Blackwell.

"I was about to," the agent replied.

"Hmph," Mathers snorted. "We found the *Falcon*.
Put into the Azores for water and the captain got himself beaten senseless by a husband who took exception to finding him in bed with his wife. It appears
the officers decided to wait until he regained con-
sciousness to continue on. For all we know, they
might still be there."

"You didn't engage them?"

"Your orders were specific, boy. Do nothing without you, so we didn't." He cleared his throat. "I'm
not pleased about it. We could have taken Steven and
got him home without involving you."

"And if you had been caught or killed, I would
have had neither ship nor crew and Steven would still
be a prisoner," Adrian said, repeating an old argument. "I still believe it best to go in alone. I'll not
risk my men, and I'll not compromise the Wyndham
name more than necessary by initiating a battle. If I

fail, you'll have your chance to go in with guns blazing," he added, knowing Mathers would do just that out of loyalty to the Rutland family.

"Stubborn son-of-a-bitch," Mathers muttered.

Blackwell coughed as if in warning.

"I learned from the best," Adrian shot back, not the least offended, either by his friend's remark or his familiar form of address. It felt good to fall into old patterns, comforting to know that some things in life remained constant, like old friends and candid honesty.

"If *Falcon* has taken to sea again," Mathers said, "she won't be too far. It should be easier to catch up with her. She's an old ship, and sitting heavy in the water with a cargo of cannons and ammunition."

"We sail out with the tide tonight." Adrian said. "Have you any special needs?"

"The usual," Mathers replied. "Fruit, fresh meat. I'd give a year's pay for fresh bread."

Blackwell loudly cleared his throat as his gaze fixed on a point behind Adrian.

The hair on the back of Adrian's neck prickled as one by one the men stopped what they were doing to stare. A sick feeling in his gut, he turned slowly.

Lorelei stood at the mouth of the cave, her face pale, her eyes wide, unblinking. A basket lay at her feet, a loaf of bread and pot of honey spilled onto the stone floor.

"Continue loading, Captain." Without another word, Adrian strode toward his wife, grasped her arm, and pulled her outside. "I expected you to be asleep from your headache powder," he said evenly.

"And were you going to sail while I was asleep, without saying a word?"

He swiped his hand over the back of his neck and

glared over his shoulder at the men staring at them. "What are you doing here?" he asked as he led her farther away and backed her into a depression in the cliff out of sight of the men. He didn't like the way she allowed him, without protest, to pull her about.

"I felt so much better after eating that I thought to find you and walk with you," she said flatly. "I brought some bread and. . . ." She waved her hand in the direction of the cave, swallowed, and looked away.

"Lorelei," he said, standing in front of her, trapping her. "We sail tonight."

"All right, Dane."

He removed his hands from her, hating the way she cringed at his touch, hating the cold, hard feel of the stone as he flattened his palms on the cliff face on either side of her. "No, it is not all right. Not with you and not with me. But it is necessary." He swallowed down the harshness of his voice. "Lorelei, Steven has been found. He has a wife and three children. I love him. I have to go."

Her gaze jerked up to his as his voice cracked, with anger, with regret. "He is alive?"

Adrian nodded.

"Then you will have to take him off an enemy, ship—a British ship."

"Not an enemy, Lorelei. Not *my* enemy beyond that they abducted my cousin."

She gave a short strangled laugh. "I never asked how you felt about the war—odd, don't you think?"

"Does it matter?"

"No, not really. I think I know in any case. You must be terribly torn about it all. And I suspect that, being a man of peace, you see both sides and are frustrated that no one else does."

"Thank you for that," he said, wishing she would shout at him, throw a rock at him—anything but engage in calm conversation as if nothing was wrong.

"You are the soul of reason, Dane. I admire that in you."

"Lorelei—"

"I suppose I should pack simple clothing," she interrupted quickly, giving him a bright smile tarnished by apprehension. "Will I need woolens, or something lighter? Where are we going? Somewhere—"

"*I'm* going," he said as he stepped closer, curled his fingers over her shoulders. "You must remain here."

"No," she said in a high voice and shook her head fiercely, her hair falling on one side from its upswept style. "No," she said more firmly. "I'll not be left behind. Not after—" she swallowed again. "You can't make me stay behind," she said, as if she were a child.

She looked like a child with her eyes bright and glazed with terror, panic.

"Lorelei, this is not a pleasure jaunt," he said gently, as he tucked a strand of hair behind her ear. "I'm going after Steven. My ship is fitted with cannon and small arms. If I do not succeed in getting Steven out on my own, there will most certainly be a fight. I may not be able to return . . . ever."

She jerked her head away from him, averting her gaze, blinking her eyes. "All the more reason for me to go with you. I won't allow you to leave me. I'll not be left behind. Not ever again."

He didn't like the way she looked, the way she trembled, the way her skin felt cold and clammy, as if she were dying. "Lorelei, we may be caught. I would be considered a traitor, a spy. If you were with me, you would be tarred with the same brush.''

''No risk could be greater that the one I took by marrying you, Dane. No other could terrify me as much as that.''

He grasped her upper arms, gave her a little shake, denying the sudden emotion that rocked him to his core. ''Damn it, I'm not offering you a choice,'' he said, his voice harsh.

She straightened and met his gaze, as haughty and proud as he'd ever seen her. ''I do not wait to be offered choices. I make my own decisions . . . just as I made the decision to marry you.'' Her eyes hardened with challenge. ''You went to great lengths to convince me how right it would be. You also went to great lengths to convince me that you respected my independence and intelligence and strength. Shall I now assume that you are a liar?''

''I didn't lie,'' he said gruffly.

''Then prove it, Dane. Don't rob me of choice.'' Her voice broke on a sob. She pressed her lips together tightly.

''Don't,'' he countered angrily, ''make me regret that I married you so impulsively.''

He heard her intake of breath, heard it catch in her throat.

''I wouldn't dream of it,'' she said stiffly, coldly. ''I would, after all, be a fool to do so, wouldn't I?'' Her features smoothed to a blank expression, her stare seeming to look through him as if she had just awakened from a dream and realized that nothing was there. ''Please let me pass, Dane,'' she said with perfect calm.

He didn't know what to say, what to do to negate his harsh words, spoken in frustration and anger, spoken before he could stop them. He knew how they'd sounded to her—not how he'd meant them at all. But she would never believe that, not now. Not when all her life experience had taught her to believe actions rather than words. Actions like abandonment.

"I have a great deal to do," she said patiently, barely moving, staring through him as if she were already alone. "I'll dismiss the servants who have their own homes and suggest the others attend the fair in the village we passed yesterday. If I can manage to blush, they will assume that you and I wish to be alone, although they'll no doubt wonder why you would want to be alone with one such as I—"

"Self-pity doesn't become you, Lorelei," he said, again without thinking.

"I am entitled to a bit of wallowing, don't you think?" she said with the falsely bright smile he hated. "But don't get into a stew over it. I always manage to overcome such lapses fairly quickly. In any case, you have more important things to concern you." She spoke quickly, flatly. "As I said, I'll get the servants away for the day so you can have some of your men come to the house for supplies; I noticed that you have barrels of flour and such, but you will need fresh food as well. Cook was baking bread for the week; your captain should be happy about that. I don't know much about ships. Do you carry things like chickens and pigs for fresh meat? If so, you'll be able to take some without anyone questioning you. I'll think of something to tell your steward; would he believe that I gave it all to a starving band of gypsies? And then I must pack. I'll return to Winterhaven—" She shook her head as if she realized she was babbling. "Please step aside, Dane."

Stunned by her rational organization of tasks, all to aid him, he stepped aside, telling himself that it was best, that he would return and sort it all out with her, that if Lorelei, who had no real interest in saving Steven, could focus on what was important, then so could he. So *must* he.

Lorelei walked away, and then stopped, not turning, not looking at him. "I wish you had simply seduced me, Dane. You could have, you know, and it would have been far kinder in the end." She walked away from him, and disappeared around the edge of the cliff.

Adrian squeezed his eyes shut against the temptation to give in, to take her with him, to keep her with him no matter what. Numbly, he turned away from paradise to return to his ship, walking past the cave entrance at the last minute to walk to the opposite cliff and back again. For the first time in his life he hated the thought of a steady wind and a solid deck beneath his feet. Hated the thought that he might never see Lorelei again.

He stood on the deck, surveying the preparations, amazed at how quickly the men worked. Amazed that Lorelei bustled about in the cave, directing the men and even boarding *Bifrost* to suggest better ways of arranging the supplies and storing them so they would keep longer.

He'd returned to the cave to find her there, imperiously directing several men to come to the house in an hour's time dressed as poorly as possible. The men in question had looked at him for confirmation. Mathers had stood by, his expression hopeful. Apparently she had mentioned the fresh bread to him.

"What are you doing?" he'd asked curiously, completely bemused by her behavior.

"It occurred to me how difficult it might be to get

rid of all the servants. I deduced that some of your men could appear at Spindrift to beg for food. It's quite in keeping with my reputation that I would simply give them what they need. If your steward objects, I'll inform him that I will pay for the food out of my own money.''

"Lord Dane's steward will not object, my lady.'' A man stepped forward from a stack of barrels containing foodstuffs—one of many Adrian had been collecting and storing for this day. "I am Jeffrey Mathers, ma'am, both secretary and steward to Lord Dane, at your service.'' He sketched a smart bow.

Lorelei glanced in confusion from the small man who appeared dapper even in rough working clothes to the captain. "Mathers? But your accent . . .''

"I am Captain Mathers's son and was schooled in England with Lord Dane.''

"How fortuitous,'' she commented. "Well, then, I should say that between us, we can manage the servants nicely. If they grouse about my actions, you can act aggrieved while informing them that I am reputed for my oddities and well known for taking in strays.''

"Your reputation precedes you, ma'am,'' Jeffrey said, "though it only extends to four-legged unfortunates.''

"All right, Mr. Mathers, you should return to the house first, then instruct several men to follow in a quarter hour. I will putter about the solarium so that I will be on hand to keep the butler from turning them away.'' She turned without a word or glance at Adrian and left the cave.

Adrian fumbled for his spectacles and slipped them on, as if they could heighten his comprehension as well as his sight. "What reputation?'' he asked. "What four-legged creatures?''

Jeffrey grinned at him. "You didn't know? Your wife is known for taking in stray dogs and cats, then foisting them off on aristocrat and commoner alike with warnings to care for them well."

"Oh," Adrian said with a sigh. He should have known she would have a soft spot for other abandoned souls, no matter how many legs they were born with.

He hadn't been able to stay away and had returned to the house with Jeffrey to observe his wife's masterful handling of the servants. He'd barely had to say a word in support of her.

And ever since, he'd been telling himself that she didn't need him, that she would be fine without him for however long he was away. So damned fine that he wondered if she would take him back if—*when!*— he returned.

That thought had put him in a sour mood which drove him to speak as little as possible to his men. He'd been lurking on *Bifrost* ever since to keep from taking his frustration and confusion out on the innocent.

Why was she helping him? He told himself that he didn't like it; he wanted her safely in her room, completely uninvolved. He'd really like it if she would cast acerbic remarks his way, or screech at him like a shrew. Instead, she was proving quite brilliantly that *he* needed *her.*

As if he required proof.

He didn't dare think about why she'd so quickly and decisively insisted on going with him. He didn't dare consider the reasons why she was going to so much trouble now to see to the comfort of him and his men after he'd spoken to her so harshly.

He darted a frantic glance at the edge of the canvas covering the mouth of the cave, measuring the sliver of light leaking through. It was getting late. Another four hours at best before they had to catch the tide.

How was he going to leave her?

"I'm going now."

He pivoted around to find Lorelei standing more than an arm's length away near the bow of the ship, like a proud figurehead ready to be mounted on the prow.

"Be safe, Dane," she said, her gaze as soft as her voice.

"Can you not call me Adrian?" he asked, tilting his head, absorbing the flush on her cheeks, and the way her gown clung to her body with perspiration, drinking in the sight of her hair hanging down her back, tendrils on either side escaping the leather thong she'd purloined from one of his men to tie it at her neck. She'd worked as hard as the men today. For him.

"I see little point in calling you something different when you will be gone before I can become accustomed to it." She took a deep breath. "It isn't too late to change your mind and consent to take me with you."

"No!" he said firmly, as he took the necessary steps to reach her. He eyed her suddenly defiant posture, the mutinous set of her chin, the lofty elevation of her nose. "You wouldn't dress in trousers and stow away, would you?" he asked suspiciously.

"Don't be absurd, Dane." She thrust out her chest and planted her hands on her wide, womanly hips. "Whatever my deficiencies, there are none that would allow me to disguise this figure as anything but female."

He angled a small smile at her. "You have a point. You are most definitely a woman," he said, as he reached out for her. "The most beautiful woman I have ever seen, my Lady Lorelei."

She stepped back quickly, avoiding him, her eyes cold with warning. "No longer," she said without inflection. "No longer will I allow you to touch me, Dane." Her voice broke as it had earlier, ending with a desperate sound trapped in her throat. "Not anywhere," she choked, then pushed past him toward the gangplank.

A memory twisted in his mind—of Lorelei telling him how his touch affected her body and her heart, of Lorelei admitting that she hungered for his affection. Of Lorelei admitting that she didn't care how or why, just so he continued to touch her and hold her.

He whipped around and reached for her arm, grasping it without gentleness, tugging her toward him, imprisoning her in his arms. "Don't mistake me for your parents, Lorelei. I am not deserting you. And I intend to participate fully in our marriage when this is over. If circumstances prevent me from coming back to England, I will expect you to join me in America."

"You forget that I do as I please," she said. "It does not please me to sit about waiting for your summons. I cannot think of one good reason why I should."

"Because you cannot hide in ignorance any longer," he said gruffly. "Because you now know something of love and affection and sharing. You've displayed it admirably today and will no longer be satisfied with less." He pressed his hips against hers, wanting her to feel what only she could do to him anytime, anywhere, and with little provocation. "Because I have touched you"—he thrust against her once—"there . . . and I have touched you here." He opened his hand over the center of her chest. "Because you know that you don't have to be alone any longer. That you will never again choose to be alone.''

''Perhaps not, but why should I choose to be with you?''

He grasped the hair tied at the nape of her neck, pulled her head back, forced her to look at him. He lowered his head, his mouth a scant breath away from hers. ''For the same reason that you have helped me today. For the same reason that you want to go with me.''

His lips took hers before she could scoff at his conceit, plundering her mouth, claiming it, claiming her.

She held still, denying him a response, giving him nothing but rejection.

''Don't lie to me, Lorelei,'' he said against her lips, then waited, doing nothing as she closed her eyes, shutting him out.

He continued to hold her, refusing to back away from her, refusing to leave her with a memory of him standing apart from her. And then he felt her tremble, felt her lips open to receive him, felt her arms wind around his neck and hold tightly, so tightly, as she kissed him good-bye, saying with her actions what she could not put into words.

''Can you not tell me that you love me?'' he said, needing to hear it said, needing to know that she could admit it, to him as well as to herself.

She broke away, stumbling backward, glaring at him. ''I already have . . . more than you realize,'' she choked out, then whirled and ran away from him, slowing to a walk at the gangplank and leaving the cave with a quiet dignity. Yet all he really knew was the anguish he heard—a small sound trapped in her throat, strangling her voice.

It tore into him—that small sob that sounded like the whimper of a heart dying.

Chapter 20

Merry ripped off the gown she'd ruined with seawater and mud and perspiration, dropped it on the floor, and sank onto the bed in her shift and petticoat. Reaching for Dane's pillow, she hugged it close, inhaling his scent as she stared out the window at the beginnings of dusk, at the end of experiencing the state of being *not* alone. She felt the tears and allowed them to flow. Sobs wrenched her from the inside out, ripping her apart. She heard the sound and allowed it to build, hoping it would drown out the thoughts that kept her from hating Dane.

She wanted to hate him. She wanted fury and bitterness, but it didn't exist. Not for Dane, who she knew was only trying to do what was right, to protect her. No one had ever tried to protect her. She'd done all he would allow her to do to protect him as well, to make certain he and his men would have decent food—such a paltry thing when he was sailing into the middle of a war. She'd wanted to go with him thinking that if she were there, nothing could hurt him, that she could somehow prevent it by sheer will alone.

How foolish really. She would have been in the way, a burden to distract him. Knowing that she had the power to distract him was little comfort.

Knowing that she could not help him more than she had was her only source of anger—not enough for a satisfying tantrum. Enough, though, to terrify her. She had no power to control the most important thing in her life. She could not manipulate Dane's fate as she did that of her stray animals. She could not keep him safe.

She could not even tell him that she loved him, not in so many words. For that, too, terrified her—that final commitment brought out into the open, exposed to ridicule and rejection. Reason told her that Dane would never hurt her in such a way. He would never have married her if he did not at least care for her. *Care* . . . it was all she dared trust him to do. She could not bring herself to trust that anyone would love her.

That, too, was foolish. She was not the first woman to be hurt by a man. She was not the only child to be abandoned by parents. It happened every day—parents leaving their children in the care of servants while they pursued their own pleasures. It was exceedingly selfish of her to indulge that particular hurt, to allow it to command her behavior, to tolerate it in the form of fear and give it power over her.

She sobbed harder, making up for years of not crying for her parents who walked away from her so easily, for her fear that she would discover that most of her friends were not friends at all. For her inability to believe that Dane would return. Once gone, always gone. No one had ever returned to her.

She curled around Dane's pillow, her hair plastered by tears to her cheek and getting in her mouth as time passed and she blinked in an effort to see out the window, to see Dane's magnificent ship carried away by the tide.

Dimly, she heard sounds in the dressing room and didn't care. It was only her maid taking care of her clothing. The poor woman had little else to do, since Merry would not accept her aid in dressing and undressing. Another foolish thing. What did it matter if the abigail helped her? Fabric and fripperies could not conceal her size and shape.

Dane had said that he thought her beautiful. She had believed him. When Dane looked at her, she felt beautiful. She felt like Lorelei, a siren, rather than Merry, a good-natured and passably attractive "character."

Sobs turned to wails of irrational self-pity. The only man to think her beautiful was about to sail to the other side of the world. She sucked in her lower lip, willing herself to stop such pathetic carrying on. Dane said self-pity did not become her. He thought her strong enough to bear anything.

"He is an ass," she said derisively. She was not strong at all; she was merely clever enough to make others think she was.

"I believe we established that some time ago," a deep voice said.

And now she was having hallucinations. "He did this to me," she cried.

"I am about to do a great deal more to you," the voice said.

Her heart seemed to stop. Her lungs felt as if they had collapsed. She was not hallucinating. She sat up in the middle of the bed, saw Dane standing at the foot, his grim face underlit by the candle he held. He looked huge and dangerous to her until she saw the spectacles perched on his nose, reminding her that he was thoughtful and gentle—a thinker rather than a warrior.

"Get dressed," he ordered. "I've packed for you."

She blinked up at him and wiped her eyes with his pillow.

"Now, damn it!"

"What should I wear?" she asked with a squeak, too shocked by his anger to think what he was about . . . or to care. He was here and she had little energy for arguments.

"The servants think we are going to travel around a bit. Dress accordingly."

We . . . He'd come back for her. Scrambling off the bed, she ran into her dressing room, fueled by a hope so strong she couldn't breathe, didn't need to breathe as she tossed a traveling dress over her head, grabbed a woolen cape, and slapped a bonnet on her disheveled hair, then ran back into the bedchamber while fastening the front of her gown.

She glanced around. "Where are my clothes?"

"Jeffrey has already had them taken to the ship." He strode out the door.

She hurried to catch up with him, but was too breathless to manage it until she collided with him halfway across the sandbar.

He caught her before she fell and steadied her then released her quickly. "You will have to keep up," he said with ill-concealed impatience.

She'd never seen him so angry. This was not the time to tell him she had forgotten her shoes.

Dane stopped at a coach waiting at the end of the bridge of land and opened the door. "Get in."

She stepped up into the coach, wondering how it could take them to the ship. She turned ready to land him a facer if he thought he would send her off to who-knew-where alone after giving her so much hope.

"Get out the other side," he barked behind her.

Her legs threatened to collapse with her relief as she scrambled out the opposite door.

Jeffrey caught her and staggered back, saved from falling by Dane's steadying hand as he emerged from the coach. "Easy, my lady. You would not fare well aboard ship with a broken leg."

She stilled and swayed at the confirmation that Dane was taking her with him.

"Jeff, take the coach to Uncle Robert's cottage in Scotland, then return here. You have the letters?"

"Yes." Jeffrey waved a sheaf of folded and sealed papers. "I'll see they are sent at intervals so the servants will think I am receiving instructions from you on a regular basis. Later I will tell them you and your lady have taken sail on your new yacht."

"Thank you, my friend," Dane said, and embraced the smaller man.

Merry blinked at such blatant affection between men, wanting to weep at the sweetness of it.

Jeffrey stepped in front of her. "May I?"

She nodded, not knowing what request she was granting. The next thing she knew, Jeffrey had embraced her as well and planted a fleeting kiss on her cheek. "Take care, my lady, of him and of yourself." He leapt up into the driver's box.

Dane clasped her hand and dragged her toward the narrow, rocky beach that bordered the base of the cliffs.

She stumbled and hopped over pebbles and rocks,

pressing her lips together to keep from crying out. They had to hurry; she knew that. She would worry about her feet later.

She lurched into Dane's back as he abruptly halted. Taking the opportunity, she surreptitiously raised her left foot beneath her skirt and rubbed it through the fabric of her gown.

"What is wrong with you?" he asked tersely as he circled to her other side and lifted her skirts. He muttered a half dozen curses in the space of a few seconds. "Blast it all. I cannot carry you everywhere."

"I'm fine, Dane. You needn't carry me."

Cursing again, he hefted her over his shoulder. "Your foot is bleeding," he said, and continued around the cliff, his gait stiff-kneed and slower than before.

"Dane, please put me down. This is ridiculous. I can walk if you will give me the chance to dodge the rocks rather than having to run over them."

"Be quiet."

Hanging upside down over his back, she kept her silence.

Dizzy from being unceremoniously plunked onto her feet the moment they reached the deck, she clutched at the rail behind her.

"Don't move," Dane ordered, then fumbled in his pocket and produced a handkerchief. "Press this to your foot until I can bandage it properly."

"I can bandage it myself," she said. "Just point at the direction of your cabin."

He tossed her a cold glance, then turned back to the helm.

Deciding that perhaps she should obey him for a little while longer, she slid down to sit on the deck and examined her foot. The moment she saw the blood streaming from a cut, she realized that it hurt. The handkerchief was not going to do the job. Sighing, she pulled up her skirt and ripped the ruffle from the hem of her petticoat, then sat cross-legged, placing her injured foot atop the opposite leg.

As she folded the petticoat ruffle into a thick pad, the ship lurched forward, and Dane ordered the lanterns extinguished until they were well out to sea. Immediately the men adjusted their movements to caution, though they were already walking about without shoes. Understanding that sound carried at night and Dane wanted no attention drawn to *Bifrost*, she moved cautiously as well, tying her makeshift bandage to the bottom of her foot, not wanting even the whisper of cloth to distract her husband as he steered them out of the cave. He had the most uncanny knack for noticing the most subtle things about her.

The starlit night bled into the utter blackness of the cave as *Bifrost* began to ride the outgoing tide. Tension seemed to charge the air as a maze of rocks and pillars of stone rose from the sea ahead of them. She wanted to ask Dane if he had ever negotiated the twisted cove at night, or if he had ever done it all, but prudence kept her silent.

He stood at the helm, his body—only a silhouette against the night—straight, his shoulders broad, his stance wide as he turned the wheel a bit this way, then a bit that way. Monoliths rose in front of them, looming like demons of the sea, then seeming to stand aside in deference to his skill, some so close she thought surely they would tear into the hull. Her ears roared and her heart beat the tempo of a heavy dirge, each time seeming to rise a little higher in her chest.

Yet Dane moved with the wheel so naturally it seemed like a dance between them. Even his hands were relaxed rather than tight around the protruding spokes. As they had been when he'd led her through a maze of statues and trees and bushes, dancing with her in a garden beneath a midnight moon.

The cliffs themselves lurked just ahead, one on either side of the cove, gnarled like gargoyles ready to lunge for them, claws unsheathed and wings ready to open.

Bifrost groaned as if afraid, yet she valiantly rode the tide, her three masts swaying overhead like lances at the ready.

Merry stared at the cliffs in horrified fascination as *Bifrost* drifted past, slowly, so slowly. Then she heard a snap and whoosh as the ship sprang free of the crosswinds and treacherous eddys of the labyrinth, her sails unfurling to catch the night wind.

Merry's jaws ached from being clenched. Her hands were curled around her foot, her knuckles white. Her mouth felt full of sand, and her heart thudded so heavily she was certain it had grown to thrice its size. Dane's figure blurred as he moved aside, relinquishing the helm to Captain Mathers. She barely realized he stood before her now, reaching for her arm, pulling her to her feet, steadying her, sighing heavily when her legs turned to mush, unable suddenly to support her.

"Once more," he said under his breath as he again lifted her over his shoulder. "Only once more," he said as if it were a litany.

Giddy and limp with relief from the apprehension she hadn't known she'd felt, she closed her eyes as her stomach bounced around inside her with the dip and rise of the ship, then the sudden descent of her body unsupported by Dane.

She snapped her eyes open as she tumbled onto something soft that leaned one way and then another while rising and plunging. Always rising and plunging. . . .

It was rather fun.

She released a giggle as her gaze found Dane, sprawled in a chair, his legs outstretched with his heels on the floor and his toes pointing straight up, his body more reclining than sitting, his head erect, his eyes closed. For some reason his posture struck her as funny.

A burst of laughter escaped her, then another and another. "I feel as if I have been dropped into the middle of a Gothick," she sputtered. "Carried off by a man in black clothing, to a ship in a cave that sailed through an army of demons and gargoyles."

He raised his eyelids halfway to regard her coldly.

That, too, seemed funny. "Oh, my. Now my abductor stares at me with a sinister glower. What is his purpose? What will he do to me?" She pressed the back of one hand on her forehead, feigning a swoon as she scrambled to cower against the bulkhead. "What will I do?"

Dane sat so still he could have been carved from the same granite as the cliffs. "I suggest you restrain your mirth, or I will be tempted to gag you." He closed his eyes again.

She sobered and bit her lip at the tightness in his voice, the strain in his expression.

He peered at her out of one eye as if he didn't trust her sudden silence.

Frowning, she sagged back and watched his chest rise and fall, the lines gradually smooth from his face,

the rigid tension of his body give way to a more relaxed posture.

Just like that he had fallen asleep, leaving her to
wonder why he was so harsh and angry, why he
would not speak to her after going to so much trouble
to bring her here . . . and most of all, why he had not
left her behind.

Adrian concentrated on regulating his breathing, on
relaxing the muscles that felt more like knotted ropes
in his back, on forgetting for just a little while that
Lorelei had laughed in the aftermath of clearing the
narrow, twisted channel—a task he and his men considered to be deadly serious. Laughing, when at any
given moment they could have been smashed against
the rocks. Laughing at his anger.

He was more than angry; he was bloody furious.

And all she could do was sit in a most provocative
manner on his bunk, her back against the bulkhead,
her knees upraised and slightly spread. At least her
skirts covered her legs—her legs . . . her foot. He sat
up straight and groaned, unable to move farther, afraid
to try to move his arms, which were bent back with
his hands clutched over the arms of the chair, supporting him.

He gritted his teeth and tried to find a way to either
slide back in the chair or ease up out of it. Pain paralyzed him.

He smelled carnations and knew Lorelei was near.
And then he felt her closeness like the sizzle in the
air during a storm. "Get off that foot," he said,
breathless from the effort.

"Dane, what is it?"

Nothing except his idiocy in bringing her here
when all he'd intended was a last good-bye, and an

attempt to reassure her. Nothing except a woman who rendered him a dupe with her damned logic and her damned tears. Nothing except that he was in agony.

"Dane, what is it?" she repeated, with an edge to her voice that cut into what was left of his pride.

"Nothing, except that you are here," he said, with a sharper edge as he glared up at her.

She straightened and crossed her arms over her chest, defensive rather than defiant. "Well, since I did not get here under my own power, I really have no answer to that. If you wish contrition, you will have to get it from the reflection in your looking glass." She continued to watch him, her arms still crossed over her chest, pushing her breasts out until he could reach them if he raised his head a bit more.

He averted his gaze, disgusted that even now he thought of making love to her. "Now that would be a neat trick," he mumbled.

"You are obviously in pain and unable to move," Lorelei said reasonably. "I can either leave you there to shore up your pride with martyrdom, or I can help you. However," she added, "I can help you only if you tell me what is wrong."

"Stop badgering me and get off that foot," he gasped. "I will manage."

"*Pax*, Dane. If you wish to be angry with me, do it some other time." She paused and hugged her arms tighter around her. "I really can't bear to see you like this, and I have a wretched feeling that I am responsible."

He said nothing. It was her fault, and it wasn't. He was so damned confused about what he'd done tonight that he'd might as well blame the full moon.

Sighing, she backed away and sat on the edge of the bed, glaring at him.

His arms trembled and were about to give way. If they did, he would slide to the floor in a pathetic mass of misery. He glanced at her quickly, then away. "I have strained my back," he said testily. "If you will call one of my men—"

Her brows arched. "Shall I tell your men that you injured your back carrying your wife to your ship like some demented hero?"

He winced as everything seemed to hurt, even the flush rising in his face. He wanted very much to crawl away.

Lorelei stood and approached him, then crouched down to meet his gaze. "Dane, I am going to stand in front of you, and you are going to hold my forearms and ease your backside forward. Use your knees and thighs to stand, not your back. And do not let go of me—I am quite sturdy, in case you hadn't noticed, and will not allow you to fall."

Desperate to do anything before his arms collapsed, he nodded and followed her instructions, wondering how she knew what to do, or if she was just guessing. "God, please don't let her be guessing," he gasped as he gained his feet and almost fell trying to straighten to a normal position.

"I am not guessing. Beau hurt his back while bestowing a lovely bow to a pretty young lady one day. This was the only way he could move . . . no, don't straighten . . . keep your hips thrust out . . . that's it . . . now, take small steps . . . pretend you are holding something between your—"

"I get the idea," he gritted out, as she walked slowly backward, holding his arms and leading him to the bunk.

"Now lower yourself the same way you stood,"

she instructed, as she gently wrapped her arms around his waist to turn him.

Sweat beaded his forehead as he managed—barely—then wondered how he would lie down.

"Take a very deep breath," Lorelei said, then stooped over, slid her arm under his knees, and lifted them to the bunk, swiveling him on his backside at the same time.

He fell back and moaned at a renewed burst of pain immediately followed by relief.

"I warned you, did I not?" she asked conversationally as she released the fastenings on his breeches and peeled them down his legs with his stockings. "Foolish man to think you can go about carrying me and not suffer the consequences." She eased his coat and waistcoat and shirt off one arm all at once, then leaned across him to do the same with the other side, her breasts brushing across his face.

He groaned.

"Now, I am going to roll you to one side, then the other, to remove these—" She broke off and stared at his groin, grinning at the part of him that seemed to act independently of the rest of him when Lorelei was near, regardless of the situation. "Is that for me?"

He turned his head toward the wall, wishing he could reach the blanket and cover his head with it.

"I'm flattered, but perhaps you should stick it in a vase until you are able to put it to use." She whipped his clothing away. "Really, Dane, pretending to be Sir Galahad is for little boys and their imaginations. You are a grown man and must be more prudent." She raised his knees and pushed a folded blanket beneath them.

He groaned again and squeezed his eyes shut. It

was too much. For a woman who had so little experience with human emotion, she was remarkably astute at the most inopportune times. "If you have any compassion in your soul," he said in a strangled tone, "you will have mercy on me and not say another damned word."

"All right, Dane." Extinguishing the lantern, she climbed carefully over his feet.

"What are you doing now?"

"If you think I am going to sleep on the floor, or in a chair, you are mistaken. I will leave acts of misguided nobility to you," she snapped, as she crawled up to her pillow and turned on her side away from him.

Adrian stared into the darkness, resigned that his intrepid and stubborn wife would always manage to have the last word.

Chapter 21

The most personal thing Dane said to Lorelei during the next fortnight was to accuse her of being a tyrant followed by the observation that she would look quite natural—as well as magnificent—wearing the metal breastplate and horned helmet of a warrior queen.

In retaliation, she had commented, in what she thought to be admirable good humor under the circumstances, that he was petulant, fractious, and too proud by half. Even then she thought she had understated the case.

Fortunately, Dane recovered sufficiently to walk about unaided after three days of enforced rest flat on his back and frequent soaks in hot water. Beau had told her that he was most comfortable in his bath, the hotter the water, the better. And though Dane had grumbled through her massages while he was immersed in heated seawater, his voice had inevitably trailed off into the snores of a relaxed and contented man. It had been a trial to wake him long enough to get him dried off and back into bed.

By the end of the first week, her husband had insisted he was quite fit and she'd been more than happy to take his word for it.

Since then, they had barely spoken beyond ritual politeness and comments about the ship, the crew, and the weather. It gave Lorelei the peculiar notion that they were behaving like a couple just introduced, rather than one that had been married for three weeks.

It didn't seem possible, she thought, as she puttered about the cabin, wishing Dane weren't quite so neat so she would have more to do. Nor did it seem normal for her to feel comfortable with their rather distant relationship. It was beyond her ken how she could feel so at ease with a man she'd known for such a short time, particularly with his present preoccupations as he appeared to focus all his thoughts on his ship, his crew, and the smallest aberration he saw on the horizon. Strangely, she regarded his remoteness as a reprieve of sorts, after the whirlwind of his so-called courtship and subsequent assault on her senses followed by the appearance of *Bifrost*. She was beginning to feel quite comfortable with her world turned topsy-turvy. There would be time enough later to sort everything out.

Dane, on the other hand, made up for his three days abed with restlessness and a plethora of tasks. If he wasn't making notes and quick sketches for adjustments in hull design, he was pacing the deck in frustration over the westerlies that hampered their speed, or the weather, which seemed perfectly lovely to her, or the angle of the stem of his ship that was not pointed enough.

She couldn't imagine how they could go any faster. Granted, she had never been on a ship, but she had seen them and knew none could match the speed of

Bifrost. It occurred to her that her husband had at an early age passed from intelligent to brilliant—a true visionary. He'd told her how his father had begun thinking about a ship like *Bifrost* during America's revolution. Dane had kept the dream alive, building and rebuilding it in his mind over and over again until he was ready to make it a reality.

It was an extraordinary vessel with its sleek lines and billows of sail and arrowed prow. Dane had built it with traditional hardwoods, but he eventually intended to build a fleet of them in more economical lighter woods common in the forests of America. What amazed her was the small crew required to sail her. The ships she had seen had crews numbered in the hundreds, yet *Bifrost* functioned well with only fifty men.

That pleased Dane, and he was obviously proud of his one-of-a-kind ship, though he unreasonably continued to grouse over her speed. She'd never seen him so reticent and brooding and giving every indication of being in a pout.

Of course she couldn't be certain. Not when his behavior was peppered with small acts of consideration for her, not to mention his spontaneous physical reactions to her nearness. She had to admit that she'd deliberately tested those reactions and gloried in the proof that she could indeed inspire them. It appeared that her husband not only cared for her, but that he really did lust after her as well. Unfortunately, he had not made love to her once since they'd boarded ship.

In a way, she felt as if it were a reprieve. Dane had overwhelmed her from the moment they'd met, prompting her to react in desperation rather than respond with control. She'd felt as if she were in a flood, bailing water only to take on more. She'd told him things she would never have spoken of if she'd been in her right mind. She'd responded to his lovemaking with complete abandon. The opportunity to step back from the events of the last month gave her a much needed sense of being in control and allowed her to more logically assess the life into which Dane had swept her. She missed his lovemaking, craved it constantly, yet was reluctant to do anything to initiate it.

She could wait. He had enough on his mind and she had no need to know anything beyond that she was with him. That it had been his decision to make it so. Later, she would ask him why. At the moment, with *Bifrost* cutting through the waves and the concerns of the world conveniently somewhere behind her, she was quite happy to take each day as it occurred, observing Dane as she'd had no opportunity to do before their marriage. Knowing what lay ahead of them, she refused to entertain a thought heavier than her next meal.

Oddly enough, she did not fear that Dane had lost interest. She felt no panic that her heart might once again be in the hands of a man who would take what he wanted from it, then toss the remains onto a pile of refuse. Not when Dane had risked missing the tide to fetch her to the ship. Not when he'd been concerned about her foot while negotiating the treacherous waters of the labyrinth. Not when she'd awakened in the night to find Dane curled around her holding her, his legs entwined with hers. Often he touched her in some small way, giving her the impression that it was done absently, as if it were the most normal of practices. It still startled her when he tucked a stray tendril of hair behind her ear, or absently placed his hand at the back of her neck while they stood on deck, his thumb tracing small circling caresses on her flesh, or trailed his hand across her shoulders after seating her for a meal. It didn't seem to matter to him that Captain Mathers and the other men witnessed his affection.

If he continued, she would most certainly become accustomed to it. She would have no choice.

But then—though she would never admit it—Dane had never given her much choice in anything, and she had done little beyond vocally asserting herself to set him straight. Why should she, when she loved the way he treated her? She especially loved the way he said her name, and no longer cared why he refused to call her "Merry." His men, too, called her "Lady Lorelei," and she was beginning to think she would be hard pressed to respond to any other name. Even in her own mind, she was now Lorelei, somehow vastly different from Merry.

She paused at the porthole as she did many times a day, pushing aside the heavy black drapes Dane had ordered to cover all the portholes, to search for sight of a ship. They had stopped briefly in the Azores, though no one had gone ashore, save Mr. Blackwell and a few men, for water and whatever fresh fruit and vegetables they could purchase. While the men transferred supplies to *Bifrost* anchored in a secluded inlet, Mr. Blackwell ferreted out information.

Dane had become even more restless and taciturn after hearing that they had missed *Falcon* by a mere week. In the two days since then, no one took more than a few steps without searching the horizon, and Dane and his crew constantly cleaned and checked weapons and practiced their marksmanship. Several were on deck now, engaged in fencing matches while *Bifrost* cut through the water at an even faster clip, now that they had harnessed the northeast trade winds.

A roar of approval followed by cheers and prompts drowned out the normal shipboard sounds. Smiling, she snatched a shawl from a chair and swung it over her shoulders as she left the cabin and made her way to the deck. As she'd suspected, Dane was engaged in a match with Captain Mathers—an odd combination given the disparity in their height and muscularity, but an ideal one in terms of skill. They would go on and on, neither besting the other as they thrusted and parried and whatever else it was that men did with swords.

Though such activities had never held much interest for her, she'd developed an immediate fascination for fencing the moment she'd first seen Dane shirtless. After observing him, she'd realized that though her husband was by nature a thinker and man of peace, he had all the instincts and skills of a warrior, and kept them honed in case they were needed.

Both brawn and brains, she thought, awed by the sight of him. *Both strength and gentleness. . . . Utterly and overwhelmingly magnificent.*

As he was now, his chest and shoulders glistening with perspiration in the sun, his muscles alternately smooth and supple, then hard and plated as he moved with masculine grace and power in a dance of strength and agility and endurance.

One of his long legs thrust out as he advanced on his opponent, not in a polite contest to demonstrate technique, but in the kind of extemporaneous offense and defense of a real battle. Mathers ducked and thrust. Dane whirled and backed up a stair leading to the quarterdeck. Mathers advanced and Dane leapt over the rail behind him.

Feeling warm, Lorelei pulled her shawl off her

shoulders and trailed it from her hand as she watched the play of muscle in the wedge of Dane's back, the dance of light and shadow and moisture glistening on his bronzed flesh. Her blood seemed to flow faster as she stared at the way his buttocks tightened with every move, how his narrow hips arched back to avoid the prick of Mathers's tipped foil, how his thighs seemed to swell as he dipped into a sudden crouch, then sprang forward to press an advantage.

She might not be disturbed that she and Dane hadn't made love, but her body complained continually.

How badly she wanted Dane's body against hers, moving with hers, sharing passion. . . .

She shifted restlessly and turned away to stare out to sea, to let the breeze cool her flushed skin, fighting images of bare flesh meeting bare flesh, wishing she could display her naked body as casually as Dane, without inhibition. She would like to feel the length of him without fabric bunching between them, separating them. She wanted the courage to trust him with that part of herself that still cowered at the thought of being exposed and vulnerable.

"You are chilled," Dane said from behind her as he draped the shawl over her shoulders, then silently stood beside her, leaning on the rail.

"Not really," she replied.

"Regrets, Lorelei?"

"Good heavens, no. I'm having an immensely good time," she said, shocked that he should think otherwise. "I do believe I am the adventurous sort."

"Adventure," Dane said tersely, "is visiting new lands, or taking a different path, or trying something new." He plowed his hand through his hair. "What we are about is—"

"Call it by any name you like," she interrupted, as she turned, leaning her back against the rail. "I have no regrets, and refuse to entertain yours. I am here. It was your decision to take me along, and that is that."

Adding depth to his scowl, he stared out to sea, his mouth tight. "We could sight *Falcon* at any time," he said grimly. "And *here* could very quickly become a very unhealthy place to be."

She'd said the wrong thing; she'd known it the moment the words were out of her mouth. Yet suddenly, she was tired of playing cat and mouse with her husband, tolerating his moody silences and glowering impatience. In one short month he'd gone from one extreme to the other—from congenial, thoughtful, and endearing, to grim, restless, and driven. It had not occurred to her that he could be dangerous until she'd witnessed how he turned his ability to concentrate into a weapon more effective than any sword. It occurred to her now that such an ability could blind him to the possibility that a sword might not be necessary. Until recently she never would have thought that Dane would actually be spoiling for a fight. It frightened her, compelled her to neutralize his anger with her before they encountered the *Falcon*.

"Dane," she said softly, "would you be less angry if I had dressed in trousers and stowed away?"

His scowl was enough to send the faint of heart scurrying over the side with the lemmings. "Yes, damn it, I would," he snarled, and stalked away.

Well, that explained his anger, she thought, with an amusement contrary to what she probably ought to feel. He was angry with her for compromising his determination to protect her. And women were thought to be illogical. Yet as she turned to lean back against the rail, she realized that she understood. She, like any other woman, wanted to feel feminine and enjoyed being taken care of. Dane, like any man, wanted to feel like a man, to protect his woman and preserve his pride. Men were not supposed to give in to unreasonable demands from their wives, or weaken their resolve, or make exceptions to their sense of honor. It was all very complicated and ridiculous.

It seemed to her that both men and women ought to remember that they were only human and had to live with that.

Straightening, she followed Dane to the cabin Captain Mathers had relinquished to them. Halting outside the door, she waited until she heard water splash. As the cabin boy left, giving her a bob of his head in greeting, she slipped inside and firmly shut the door.

Dane sat in the copper tub soaping his body, ignoring her presence.

She pulled a chair to the foot of the tub, unmindful of the scrape of wood against wood, and sat down, taking her time in arranging her skirts, then leaned forward, her elbows on her knees, her chin propped on one fist. "So, you are angry with me because *you* hauled me out of Spindrift and carried me to your ship. Is that correct?"

He said nothing.

"Am I to infer that by asking to accompany you, I somehow robbed you of choice in the matter?'

"You didn't ask," he said.

"All right . . . I didn't ask. I expressed my wish to accompany you."

"You expressed a *wish?*"

"A bit more than that, if you insist on splitting hairs. I arrived at the wrong conclusions and nearly became hysterical, and then I tried to manipulate you by demonstrating how useful I could be . . . how much you needed me.'' She widened her eyes artfully and leaned farther forward, keeping her balance by holding onto the end of the tub. ''Don't tell me that I succeeded. And here I've been deluding myself that you realized that you couldn't bear to be without me.''

He drew up his knees close to his chest, as if he had suddenly become shy.

''Apparently not,'' she mused, then met his gaze and held it. ''Then why, Dane? Why am I here?'' She held her breath, waiting for his answer, suddenly aware that it was important, that it had always been important. That she hadn't asked before because she'd been afraid the answer would not be one she wanted to hear.

He threw the soap down. Water splashed up over his face. Gasping, he rubbed his eyes.

Lorelei rose, grabbed a linen towel, and soaked a corner of it with drinking water from a pitcher on his desk. ''Be still,'' she ordered, as she slapped his hands away from his eyes and dabbed them with the towel.

He wrapped his fingers around her wrist, holding her bent over him, her face only inches from his. ''You are *not* here because I honored your right to make the choice. You are *not* here because you overwhelmed me with your manipulations, or because you appealed to my conscience.'' He released her wrist and rose from the tub, snatching the towel from her and wrapping it around his waist. ''You *are* here because I was afraid that if I left you behind, you would abandon me,'' he said in a monotone, his back to her.

Stunned, she stared at him as he swiped another towel over his chest and shoulders and arms. Memory of what she had said that day in her panic and fear returned to her with vivid clarity. ''You're right,'' she whispered. "I said I would go to Winterhaven. I implied that I would not choose to wait for you or go to you. . . ." Covering her mouth with one hand, she closed her eyes, unable to face him. "I threatened you, didn't I?"

He said nothing as he donned trousers, then a simple white shirt and black coat, without the added layers of a waistcoat. He sat on the edge of the desk to pull on knee high boots, completing a costume that made him look quite dashing . . . and frighteningly reckless.

"One would think you cared for me very much to worry about such a thing and take such drastic steps to avoid it."

"I don't believe I have made a secret of that. It is you who trivialize it," he said, in that same monotone that chilled her.

Again he was right. And at his declaration and accusation, she felt small and churlish. He did care. She knew it. When, she wondered, had she accepted it?

"I didn't behave very well, did I? I'm so sorry, Dane. Of course you are angry." Stricken, she dared to look at him. "I don't suppose you would believe that I didn't know what I was saying? That I didn't purposely manipulate you?" Her heart sank as she recalled something else he'd said to her. "Dane, I wasn't testing you. Please believe that I would not play such games with your feelings."

"Of course," he said, averting his gaze.

"Of course," she repeated dully, then whirled, yanked open the door, and ran out into the companionway. Dear heaven, how long would she continue to live her life as if nothing ever changed, as if everyone was like her parents and the young man she had loved with youthful naïveté? How long before she didn't react with terror to the vagaries of normal existence? How long before she accepted the truth as it was rather than what she dreaded it might be?

Entering the saloon where they took meals, she stared in horror at Captain Mathers, the officers and mates at one table, the other men not on watch at several other long tables as they all stood waiting for her to be seated. Nothing could be done but to walk to the captain's table and allow him to hold her chair as she took her place to his right.

She hadn't meant to enter the saloon. But then there were precious few places on *Bifrost* to hide. She shook her head, immediately discarding the thought that she wanted to hide. It would serve no purpose. It certainly wouldn't change what was already done. She'd behaved badly. She'd inadvertently pushed Dane too far, taking advantage of his compassionate nature. That she hadn't done it with forethought and calculation was beside the point.

She should have known better. She should have learned by now that she could not live in the shadow of childish fears. She'd known why Dane had to leave. She'd understood. She should have trusted him. Yet the only time she had trusted, it had turned on her. . . .

She'd reacted as if Dane were like the man who had hurt her ten years ago, never once considering that she might be hurting Dane—

Could she hurt him? It was a heady thought. And a distressing one. It occurred to her that she didn't know how to manage that kind of power. That her ineptitude in matters of the heart could cause pain, no matter how innocent her intent.

She didn't want that kind of power.

*   *   *

The woman would have his sanity yet, Adrian thought, as he searched *Bifrost* from stem to stern for her. Where the hell had she run to? And why the hell wasn't he in the saloon, eating with his crew? They wouldn't begin the meal until he arrived—a courtesy that still discomfited him. Nevertheless, why should his men starve because he and his wife couldn't seem to sort themselves out?

Determined to leave Lorelei to lick her wounds in private—her choice, he told himself—he approached the entrance to the saloon and paused at the sight of Lorelei sitting in her usual place, her head lowered as she stared at the table as if she wanted to crawl under it and curl into a ball. He'd never seen anyone look so miserable as Lorelei did then.

Except Lorelei looking miserable in their cabin half an hour past.

He'd hurt her. All because of his blasted pride. He'd done it on purpose, lashing out for no good reason that he could see, other than to prove he wore the breeches in their marriage. Because of pride.

It had to stop. He'd once chastised Lorelei by reminding her of her age, and he was two years older than she. How could he expect her to behave in keeping with her years when he could not manage it?

Love was a most effective equalizer in the differences between men and women.

He strode into the saloon, ignoring his usual chair across from Lorelei in favor of the one beside her, imagining that he heard a collective sigh of relief mingled with the sound of forty grumbling stomachs. Examining the serving dishes laid down the center of each table, he was reassured by the steam rising from the mounds of food. At least the men wouldn't have to endure a cold meal on his account.

Dishes and bowls were passed to the head of the table. Frowning with obvious concern that Lorelei showed no interest in food, Mathers chose a serving of fish and placed it on Lorelei's plate.

"She doesn't care for too much sauce," Adrian said automatically.

Her gaze flew up to his, remaining there as he took each dish and served her first. "An extra serving of pineapple," he whispered conspiratorially, piling the slices of the fruit they'd acquired in the Azores on her plate. "And the heel of the bread with honey."

She appeared surprised that he'd noticed her preferences.

From the corner of his eye, he saw Mathers's mouth twitch.

"Any sightings?" he asked the captain, as he did every evening.

"A squall," Mathers replied. "We'll have fresh rainwater for Lady Lorelei's bath tomorrow."

"Thank you, Captain," she said, subdued. "I am constantly moved by your consideration, but what I would use in the bath would be enough to provide a comfortable shave for every member of the crew."

"The crew is accustomed to saltwater, ma'am. You are not. And if I may say so, the sight of your lovely complexion provides more pleasure than a shave in rainwater."

"Oh!" She flushed pink, but recovered quickly. "I don't believe I've ever received such a nice compliment. Thank you."

"*I* told you I thought you beautiful," Adrian said in her ear.

She gave him a weak smile, then turned to address the captain, speaking quickly, as she did when distressed. "It's a pity Dane's uncle was unable to negotiate for Steven's release."

"The British government denies the practice of impressment, so how can they negotiate for the release of an impressed man?" Dane said, with a trace of bitterness.

"Then it's a pity it could not have been done on the sly with bribes offered or favors exchanged. I know such things are done every day."

"The navy," Captain Mathers replied, "is engaged on too many fronts—with Boney, as well as in Canada and America. No one was willing to institute a search for one man when they are occupied with war."

"No, I suppose not," she sighed. "What will you do when we overtake *Falcon?*"

"We will negotiate with the captain," Dane said wryly. "Perhaps offer a bribe or exchange a favor."

Mr. Blackwell entered, frowned to find his seat taken by his employer, and then calmly skirted the table to take Adrian's place on the captain's left. "Well, the captain of *Falcon* does enjoy his pleasures. It might work, and it would prevent a fight."

Adrian fixed Blackwell with a warning look. This wasn't the first time Blackwell or Mathers had alluded to avoiding a fight, and rightly so. Yet lately their remarks seemed purposely directed at him, as if they expected him to jump his traces the moment *Falcon* was sighted.

"And if the captain of *Falcon* will not negotiate, how do you plan to extricate Steven from a warship in the middle of the ocean without a fight?" Lorelei asked quietly.

Adrian opened his mouth and shut it again. Mathers stared down at his plate. Blackwell pursed his lips.

Lorelei cleared her throat as if she were uneasy, but not enough to allow conversation to lag. "I can see how it might be accomplished if we found *Falcon* in port. Then you could get aboard, free Steven, and sneak off again. But what if we find *Falcon* before we reach the West Indies?"

"Then we will have no choice but to fight," Adrian replied, hating to put his certainty into words, yet not wanting to mislead Lorelei either.

"I see," she said and placed her napkin alongside her plate. "If you will excuse me, I would like to take a walk."

Adrian rose and helped her from her chair. "I'll accompany you," he said, taking the opportunity she presented. He wanted to talk with her, to make things right with her, even if it meant having, once more, to admit to being an ass. And he'd rather do it on deck than in their cabin. It had become increasingly difficult to keep from tumbling her on the bunk and making love to her until neither one of them could walk. For two weeks, his pride had kept him from doing just that. He'd be damned if he knew why and his pride hadn't bothered to explain it to him.

Lorelei placed her hand on his arm and shook her head, not quite meeting his gaze. "I'd rather you remained here. I know you have things to discuss with Captain Mathers and Mr. Blackwell."

He cast a frustrated glance at the ship's company so studiously eating and avoiding looking at him and his wife. Of course they had noticed her unusual subdued behavior. Of course they recognized that something was wrong. And of course, damn it, this was not the time to pursue it. He knew that just by Lorelei's troubled yet thoughtful expression. He didn't know what was going through her mind and would give *Bifrost* to find out, but something told him that she would go to great lengths to keep from discussing it with him until she had reconciled it within herself. He wouldn't put it past her to take a lifeboat out to avoid talking about it. And he knew Lorelei well enough to know that with or without the fortification of wine, she would most certainly discuss it with him when she was ready and not before.

In the meantime, he would have to honor her request for privacy and solitude whether he liked it or not.

He hated it.

Chapter 22

Phillip continued to look through his spyglass, afraid that if he didn't keep *Falcon* in his sight, she would disappear. His men had sighted her on the far horizon at dusk. By dawn, he will have overtaken her.

Steven was almost within reach, and *Falcon* was loaded with guns and cannon and rockets—a nice prize which the United States would put to good use.

Soon his brother would be home with his family.

"Sir," a seaman called from the crow's nest. "Another ship over the port bow."

Phillip swung his spyglass to the right, swept it slowly over the horizon. "Look again, Hastings. I see nothing."

"It's there, sir. She's like a ghost on the water, sir, and running without lights. It took me awhile to make her out. It's like she's painted the color of the sea."

A cold finger of dread scraped up Phillip's back as he made out a blur in the distance. Only one man would paint his ship the color of the sea. Only one ship could be so swift.

Too damned swift.

Adrian had found them. Blackwell, the son-of-a-bitch, had no doubt reached him with the right information.

He swung around again, focusing on the *Falcon*, calculating distance and speed.

He might make it. Speed notwithstanding, a squall was threatening to break loose, which might slow Adrian down or even throw him off course. Adrian's ship was close to twice the distance from *Falcon* than the *Reckoner* and would lose speed if the squall forced Adrian to take in sail. If Phillip put every man on sail, and watch, and clawed his way across the distance one knot at a time to keep a steady course, he might reach *Falcon* in time to take her before Adrian's blasted odd ship caught up. He wouldn't think about the wind or the approaching squall. He wouldn't think about the speed of Adrian's ship. *Reckoner*, too, had been designed by Adrian. She was fleet and carrying little weight.

Luck had been with Phillip thus far. He refused to believe it would desert him now.

Lowering his spyglass, he smiled into the darkness. Surely it was luck that brought Adrian close enough to witness his triumph.

Chapter 23

Adrian stood at the helm, keeping Lorelei in sight from the corner of his eye. She stood on the forecastle, releasing the pins from her hair, letting it flow around her in the rapidly cooling wind, her gaze fixed on the water turning to creamy froth against the hull as the bow sliced through the waves.

He studied the clouds gathering overhead, eerily backlit by the silver glow of the moon. Soon it would rain. Enough for Lorelei to have a proper bath in the tub he'd insisted be a part of the ship—a circumstance that had attracted more than one sidelong glance. He thought with some amusement that Brummell would be pleased to know Adrian practiced cleanliness even aboard ship.

Lorelei had not complained about having to wash in seawater, or having to care for her clothing herself, except for the day she had washed a velvet gown in seawater, failed to rinse it, and wailed in dismay when it dried, standing by itself like a headless and armless Venus, fully clothed.

Her dismay had turned to panic as he'd picked up the thing and carried it on deck.

"You cannot toss it overboard," she'd wailed, clutching his arm to prevent such an action. "It is one of my favorites."

"Lorelei," he'd said, enjoying her purely feminine reaction to a ruined frock, "you cannot wash velvet, and you cannot leave the soap in it, in any case. The gown is done for."

"How would you know about the care of fabric?" she'd demanded, stung by his chiding—another purely female reaction. "And I forbid you to bury it at sea."

"Credit me with more reverence than that for such a beautiful thing," he'd said, casting a long-suffering look at the seamen gathered around them, gaping at the gown and chuckling at the sight of Dane holding it. He set the gown on the deck against the foremast and arranged the sleeves to cross over the bodice in a posture very like the one Lorelei adopted, her arms crossed over her chest. "Such magnificence should surely be a memorial, don't you think?" He stood back and eyed it over the thumb he held up as he'd seen an artist do. "It will do nicely until I can have a masthead carved in your image."

She'd blinked as her glance skittered from the gown to him to the men and back again. "Oh, aye, Dane, it is a marvelous memorial," she'd gasped around laughter, holding her sides as she bent over double with mirth.

He'd never heard a sound so rich and wonderful as her laughter, unrestrained, and coming from deep inside her. But then she'd abruptly stopped, her expression becoming somber as she straightened and met his gaze, tears of mirth sparkling in her eyes. She'd stared at him so long and so hard that the men had shifted uncomfortably and drifted away.

"Dane, do you really want to put my image on the prow of your ship?"

In answer, he'd smiled at her and patted the back of the gown standing so stately against the mast.

And it continued to hold that place of honor, a shrine of sorts that the men lovingly patted in various places as they passed—for luck, they said. Instead of being horrified, as most women would be, she swallowed and blinked very hard every time she witnessed the homage paid to it by his men as if that peculiar expression of affection and acceptance touched her in a profound way.

She hadn't complained about eating with the men either. In fact, after her initial uneasiness with the camaraderie between everyone aboard and which included her, she had asked wistfully if the sense of extended family was common to life in "the Colonies."

He'd told her how, by necessity, Americans held fast to the concept of community, helping one another and working closely together. He'd explained that families such as his and Mathers's tended to become a larger family of many individual parts through the generations. That it was common for every family in a given area to become intertwined in work, in play, and in worship.

"So this is what family is," she'd said, "helping as your men are helping you to save Steven, love as you and Captain Mathers share in friendship and respect, ease with one another that permits sharing of meals and open discussion and teasing regardless of rank."

It had struck him again how strange it was to hear

her speak of things such as family and sharing as if they were foreign words for which she had no translation. "Family is not defined solely by blood, Lorelei, but by love—for friends, and for relatives. People come together and unite by choice and out of affection as well as need."

"They accepted me immediately, Dane," she'd said, "as if I belonged without question."

"Do you feel as if you belong?"

"Not quite yet. But I've adjusted and am certain I will." She'd smiled then. "I'm becoming fond of democratic concepts. It makes the world seem both larger with more possibilities, and smaller with its blurred lines of social division."

It occurred to Adrian that perhaps bringing Lorelei along had been good for her, illustrating to her what he could only make an attempt to explain. Family—as he and Mathers and some of the convoluted relationships among the men aboard illustrated. Community—as the men demonstrated while working toward a common goal formed by loyalty and support. Affection—as Jeffrey had so adroitly shown her the night they had departed Spindrift. Continuity—in all those things as they regaled Lorelei with stories of their families back home and how they'd worked together for more than one generation, how they gathered to share in tragedies as well as good fortune.

Though he doubted that Lorelei had realized it yet, she had taken to being "not alone" with all the enthusiasm and curiosity of a child discovering the world beyond the nursery, even to the extent of playing a few pranks of her own. It had been wrenching to watch her the first time, so seriously devising and carrying out her prank—a simple one of stuffing a handkerchief into the toes of his boots, then standing back, biting her lip in apprehension of the reaction she would receive. Though he'd wanted to take her in his arms and soothe her, he'd given her a mock look of disgust, then chased her around the deck, threatening to dunk her in the rain barrel for her mischief.

He couldn't begin to imagine what it had been like for her to spend her childhood with no laughter, no affection, no sense of connection to anything but a house and a name. She'd have been better off in a nunnery, where she might have at least been held from time to time.

But she was infinitely adaptable, learning fast and working hard to adjust even to those experiences that rattled her. He loved watching her listen to the men, expressions from wistful to rapt chasing across her face. He loved the way she met compliments first with suspicion, and then with blushes as she realized they were sincere. He especially loved the way she no longer frowned at being addressed as Lorelei.

So why in hell had he been behaving as if her presence was a trial to be endured? Why in hell had he been so blasted angry at her for a decision he had made? He'd been so bullheaded as to convince himself that he'd brought her aboard because of her distress when the truth was that he'd literally leapt off *Bifrost*, rapping out orders as he'd hurried back to Spindrift, unable to bear the thought of being without her.

Without Lorelei, he felt completely alone, and it rankled. In a manner of speaking, he'd been on his own since the year his parents had died, making his own decisions, traveling back and forth to England, and as the eldest, looking after his cousins. He didn't like the feeling of being dependent on Lorelei—or anyone else—for anything. It hadn't been something he'd anticipated from marriage.

He'd often wondered how she had borne her cloistered existence all the years of her life when he couldn't seem to stand the thought of being without her for a few months. Because she knew nothing else, was the obvious answer. In his own way, he, too, had felt separated from society and even from his cousins—by his own traits that made him an oddity, and by his own choices to follow his own path, no matter the opinions of others. Steven and Phillip had had one another. He'd grown up with dreams for company, never realizing they weren't enough until he'd met Lorelei. And she, too, had become a dream—one that thought and reasoned and made decisions on her own. One that refused to behave like a dream, refusing to fade into the back of his mind when he willed it.

His other dreams waited for him to fashion and mold them and make them reality. He'd had no experience with a stubborn living dream. It chafed that for all Lorelei had to learn, she adjusted far better and far faster than he. And she could tolerate her own company far better than he could tolerate his.

She was doing it now—being alone by choice. Alone and drawing God knew what conclusions. He hoped that it wouldn't take her too long to realize that it was no longer necessary. That a problem shared was a problem halved. That a husband and wife could also be friends, as his parents had been.

He hoped it wouldn't take too long for her to come to him once again as a wife. She struck him as being entirely too contented with celibacy after the night they'd shared in passion, and the more time that passed without making love, the more difficult it became for him to approach her. In truth, he wanted—

needed—her to approach him. He'd been incapacitated for only a few days, yet still she climbed into their bunk at night, gave a him a quick peck, and turned onto her side away from him.

Had he failed her that first night at Spindrift? He didn't think so, but what did he know about the intricacies of women? Perhaps he'd frightened her. Heaven knew he'd frightened himself with the intensity of his need and his appalling lack of control. He'd been so damned cocky, thinking she desired him, if nothing else. He'd used it against her arguments and protests. He could hear Steven's wife now, mocking his conceit and saying, "Isn't that just like a man?"

What if Lorelei had been swept away—and perhaps curious—and now that her curiosity and the passion he'd so deliberately stoked had been quenched, he'd lost his appeal in that way? What if all she wanted from him now was friendship—a nice, comfortable arrangement where she went her way and he went his and only occasionally would they meet? It was what she had expected from marriage to Earl Stick-in-the-Mud.

How would he find out? Simply asking seemed fraught with peril. Waiting seemed safer, even as it drove him over the edge of patience.

Oh, hell.

Mechanically he scanned the horizon because it was what everyone did these days in the hope of spotting *Falcon,* though they all knew it was a large ocean and they might not find her until they reached the Indies. Lorelei had been right in her assessment that if Falcon was docked it would be easier to slip aboard and free Steven without a fight. But a thousand reasons why it wouldn't work plagued him. Jamaica was a British holding, full of British soldiers and seamen and settlers. It would be risky to walk among them without being recognized by someone, and that would raise immediate suspicions. It would also place him at the same location and time that a British ship was raided. Uncle Robert would be dragged into it and also suspected. The *ton* might have overlooked his uncle's American affiliations because he'd been in England so long and he was a jolly good fellow, but they would never forget. What was the sacrifice of a reputation or even a peer when there was scandal to be had?

Adrian knew their best chance for success lay in the element of surprise, either on land or at sea. The drapes and covers were closed on all the portholes to keep light from leaking through at night. No lanterns were lit on deck. The voices of the crew naturally lowered to whispers as the sun dipped into the sea. At night, *Bifrost* became as much a phantom as it was possible to be and still be solid and dimensional. Too, there were the natural superstitions of sailors the world over. A strange and ghostly ship would certainly hamper an enemy with his own fear. And by day, her unusual coloring would blend with the water, giving her an advantage of approaching nearer before she was spotted . . . or so went his theory.

His gaze skipped between two points without really seeing what was there as he hatched and discarded a dozen plots to get to Steven, none of which offered a clean escape, much less anonymity. He could disguise himself as a pirate, complete with mask, and go in with swords drawn, muskets primed and cannons roaring. He could dress as a poor man and bluff his way onto *Falcon* while she was in port. He could spirit away the captain of *Falcon* and negotiate a trade—the captain for Steven. . . .

With every plan he became more thoroughly convinced that his imagination was more absurd than logical, more fanciful than practical. Pirates were hanged when caught; aristocrats disguised as poor men were taken as spies; kidnapping a captain of the Royal Navy would leave a witness, unless he killed the man—not a desirable option. Adrian was a pacifist and honed his fighting skills only for survival. He'd rather live in exile than kill a man—

Adrian concentrated harder on the view through the glass as energy suddenly pumped through his veins. He reached for his spectacles and slipped them on with clammy hands. Squinting at a distant point to port, then at another to starboard, he still wasn't certain what he was seeing.

Raising the spyglass, Adrian focused on the horizon to port, adjusting to the reality that he *was* seeing something: a ship with the lines of a frigate riding low and lumbering through the water like a warship loaded with ordinance and men. He swung the glass to starboard convinced now that he had seen a ship there as well. That, too, had the lines of a frigate, yet there were differences in the hull and speed. Though he did not know the identity of the first ship, he had no doubt as to the origin of the second. It was a Rutland ship, a new design, more streamlined and as a result a good deal faster than an ordinary frigate.

Phillip. He was as certain of it as he was of his own name.

Collapsing the spyglass, he strode toward Lorelei. She glanced up at him. "Am I seeing things?"

"No."

"Two ships, one converging on the other?"

Three ships, including Bifrost, he corrected silently—three points of a triangle collapsing on itself.

He nodded. "One of them is a Rutland frigate, meaning Phillip. I must assume the other is *Falcon.*"

"When—"

"Too soon," he said grimly. "But we'll hang back until dawn."

"What will you do?"

He slanted his mouth in a grim smile. "The only sane thing I can do—approach the captain of *Falcon* and ask. If that doesn't work I'll try bribery or blackmail." He shrugged. "And if that fails, cannon. We can outmaneuver and outrun *Falcon.* . . ." Abruptly he reached for her, held her as closely and as tightly as he could without crushing her. "This is madness, you know. I have no idea what I'm doing and have little chance of accomplishing it in any case. Damn it, this situation is impossible."

She clutched his arm. "Dane, you cannot be the one to initiate any sort of action to free Steven. In fact, it would be best if the captain of the *Falcon* did not know of your relation to him."

He snapped off his spectacles and frowned at her.

"Dane, listen to me. Steven is an American citizen, and though you have become a British citizen and peer of the realm, any step you take off the straight and narrow path will be suspect. Isn't that why you are not sitting in the Lords with your uncle? Because if you take any stand not firmly in keeping with public sentiment, you and Lord Robert will be viewed in a dangerous light?"

He nodded, unsure as to where she was aiming her point. He had been cautious, keeping his opinions to himself—and to Uncle Robert—and had planned to remain in England until the issues between the two countries had been settled. Knowing war would likely come, he'd planned for three years, rushing projects, giving over his active role in Rutland enterprises to Steven. He'd pushed Phillip too hard, hoping he would take over his share and free Adrian altogether. But it hadn't worked out the way he'd planned, none of it.

"All I've wanted to do since I was very young was to live in England, to be a part of her," he said, more to himself than to Lorelei. "But I am learning that I cannot make every dream bend to my will." He cupped the side of her face, smoothed her eyebrow with his thumb. "I never should have brought you along—"

"Bringing me along may have been the best thing you could have done." She stepped back and held his arms as if she were afraid he would walk away. That was his whole problem—he couldn't seem to walk away from her when he should.

"Dane," she said urgently, "I have an idea."

"I'm glad to hear it," Captain Mathers said, as he approached with Blackwell at his side. "God knows none of us has been able to hatch a decent plot."

"I have learned never to ignore a woman's insight into a problem," Blackwell said as if he were speaking directly to Adrian. "They are not so quick to light fuses, or to burn bridges."

"I don't want my wife involved any more than she is," Adrian said, then met Lorelei's gaze. "I want you in our cabin."

"I am involved, and rightly so," she shot back. "And I can be of use."

"Pray continue, ma'am," Mathers said.

The sky rumbled and rain began to fall in torrents as if a giant bucket had been upended directly over them. Maybe it would shock some sense into Lorelei.

"In the damned cabin, Lorelei," Adrian barked. "Now!"

"Come along, gentlemen," she said, as if he hadn't said a word. "We shall discuss this in the saloon."

Outnumbered as the men fell in on either side of Lorelei, rushing her into the saloon that also served as a charting and meeting room, Adrian stared after them, wondering how and when he had become redundant. Reluctant to join the others, he slicked the rain from his face only to have it replaced by more. Damn it! He was supposed to be the protector, the hero . . . the man. He didn't like Lorelei protecting him, coming up with ideas that escaped him, adapting to marriage and everything else faster and better than he. He didn't want her in danger.

Cursing the thoughts that squirmed like restless children in his mind, he followed, determined to remind them all of the dangers to which *Bifrost* raced. Issuing orders lacked something when water streamed down one's face and one's lips were trembling from cold, though Lorelei had been quite adroit at commanding everyone's attention with her hair soaked and plastered down her face. Pushing aside the thought that he was yet again not living up to his years, he sloshed into the saloon, determined to gain the upper hand before Lorelei went completely out of control.

"It can work," Blackwell said with glee. "Lord Dane, your wife is brilliant."

"Really," Dane said, as he poured coffee from a server on the table. "Whatever her plan, if it requires her involvement, I have no wish to hear it. If it does not, then I will be relieved to consider it while she returns to our cabin and gets into dry clothing . . . and remains there.'' He regarded Lorelei with narrowed eyes, daring her to defy him. "I'll not repeat myself, madam. This is beyond your experience and is not your concern.''

Her face paled. Her chin quivered as she stared at him, her eyes wide and stricken. Rising so quickly that her chair toppled backward, she held her hands clutched together at her waist. "Of course, Dane. You're right, of course. I know nothing of such things and should not have interfered. If you will excuse me?'' Without waiting for him to respond, she left the saloon.

"Well, that was the finest bit of chest beating I ever witnessed.'' Mathers regarded him gravely. "I'll be at the helm, awaiting your orders.''

Blackwell snorted in disgust and turned away. "It was a good plan,'' he muttered as he stomped from the saloon. "Might've saved all our arses.''

Adrian stared blankly at the places where Mathers and Blackwell used to be a few moments ago, resenting his sudden demotion to villain. When had it become wrong to wish to protect one's wife? What happened to the men fighting the war and the women running the household?

Lorelei happened. Lorelei, who had always relied on herself because there had never been anyone else. Lorelei, who had learned to fight battles in her own way and on her own terms. He tasted bile as his behavior returned to haunt him. He lowered his head as he realized that she most always won. . . .

But she was not on her own any longer, and she'd damn well better learn to trust him.

They were winning the race to avert disaster. At least Adrian hoped so as he kept a careful eye on the two ships, one gaining on the other. Sweeping his glass over Phillip's frigate, he was relieved to see that Phillip had the sense to fly Portuguese colors—a good choice this close to the Azores. To his credit, the captain of *Falcon* appeared to be employing caution and was actually attempting to evade Phillip's ship.

Knowing caution was no longer necessary now that they had been spotted, Adrian had allowed lanterns to be lit on *Bifrost* and had given orders to pursue Phillip rather than *Falcon* in the hope of stopping his reckless cousin. He glanced upward at the Union Jack as well as the Dane and Wyndham pennants he'd ordered unfurled as soon as the squall had passed an hour ago. He could imagine the consternation of the *Falcon*'s crew as they wondered what sort of situation was brewing. *Bifrost,* with all her elaborate fittings and odd color, gave every appearance of being the private yacht of a frivolous and self-indulgent aristocrat. Given *Falcon*'s course, which avoided coming within cannon range of Phillip's ship, yet circled rather than escaped, the captain of the British ship apparently had decided to lurk on the fringes in case said aristocrat required assistance.

And apparently Lorelei had given in to the temptation of a proper bath, Adrian decided, as he again glanced over his shoulder and saw two men hauling buckets of rainwater down to the captain's cabin. He fervently hoped that she would take to the bunk and fall asleep afterward, though such meek capitulation was definitely not in her nature.

If they could get through this, he knew he had another battle waiting for him below. He knew she was hurt. He also knew that it wouldn't last. Sooner or later, Lorelei would rally and he would have to defend his actions toward her. Unfortunately, he couldn't imagine how to accomplish it. There was no defense for his heavy-handed behavior. An apology wouldn't be enough . . . at least, not for his peace of mind. Somehow, he had to explain to her what he barely understood.

At the moment, he felt every inch the husband in disgrace.

And all he could do at the moment was stop Phillip and pry Steven off a British ship.

Dawn poured a misty pastel light over the seascape. The two ships he watched seemed not to be moving at all, as if they were part of a pretty tableau painted on canvas.

He raised his glass, his mouth twisting as he read the name painted on the bow of the Rutland frigate: *Reckoner.* Phillip would choose something dramatic and sinister.

Through the lens he found Phillip and held the glass steady as his younger cousin stood with feet braced apart, hands on hips, glaring at him across the rapidly narrowing distance.

"What do you want to do?" Captain Mathers asked.

"I wish I knew," Adrian replied. "All along, my schemes have been half baked at best." He rubbed the side of his nose. "Any suggestions?"

"Listen to your wife," Mathers said. "Her scheme was fully cooked."

"An intelligent woman," Blackwell commented, as he reached them. "Sees a problem and solves it in a straightforward fashion."

"I don't want her involved," Adrian said.

"But she is, isn't she?" Mathers said. "You might recall that she wishes to be involved."

"She is too impulsive to have thought it out fully,"

Adrian said, and wondered why he argued the issue.

"I don't recollect that she sneaked onto the ship, Lord Dane," Blackwell said with an innocent air. "Wasn't it you who carried her aboard and dumped her on deck?"

Tightening his mouth against a scathing reply, Adrian strode to the rail and raised his glass again. Yes, he had carried her aboard, and that was the hell of it. Trying to protect her now was rather like building a ship after the ocean dried up.

"She remains in the cabin," he said curtly, as he gauged the distance between himself and Phillip. "Take us in board to board with *Reckoner*," he ordered, then strode away.

Lorelei bathed quickly, barely noticing that the water was not harsh and scented with salt. She'd willed numbness to shroud her hurt, willed the problem at hand to stand uppermost in her mind. Anger and resolve fortified her. So Dane wanted to protect her. So he regretted the impulse that brought her here. So he wanted to be a hero.

Some other time.

No one knew better than she how impulsive her husband was. Impulsive enough to chase her about Saxon Hill like some satyr chasing a nymph through the woods—she had to smile at that. Impulsive enough to announce their marriage to the world before he'd bothered to ask her, then carry her off to sea— her smile grew at that. But since she'd been willing, those instances had not been matters of life and death. Somewhere between their waltz beneath the stars and an hour ago, she'd realized that her husband's mind was far more creative than practical. Heroics in a garden were romantic, seductive. Heroics on the high

seas with a frigate of the Royal Navy were seldom
practical and rarely healthy. Dane had all but admitted
to her that he didn't know what to do.

She didn't have time to feel hurt.

As she dried and reached into her trunk for a gown,
she repeated it over and over again. No time for anything but what her instinct told her would work. No
one was more proficient than she at bluffing society;
a single sea captain should be no trouble at all. And
she certainly had no time to indulge her fears that
Dane would be done with her after this day's work,
that she was bringing about the end of all that mattered to her.

No time to do anything but what she'd always
done—survive by solving a problem and by consequence, living up to her reputation as a woman who
needed no one but herself. A woman who had too
much of everything—too much body, too much
height, too much audacity—a juggernaut overwhelming everything in her path until others forgot
that she was a woman. A woman who wasn't at all
good at behaving as a woman ought, much less a wife.

If Dane hadn't yet realized that, he most certainly
would by day's end.

She would survive that, too . . . somehow.

Her hands shook as she fastened her gown, an elegant affair—one of the few she possessed that displayed her ample cleavage—of wine red silk overlaid
with a tunic of brocade in a deeper shade that almost
appeared black in certain light. She'd wondered why
on earth Dane had packed virtually everything in her
wardrobe, including her jewels, until she'd recalled
his comment that he might not be able to return to
England.

She reminded herself of it now, assuring herself

that he'd brought her with him for that very reason. That he'd said he intended to be active in their marriage. That even after her hysterics outside the cave, he'd wanted her with him enough to cripple himself carrying her to the ship.

It took three attempts to fasten her rubies around her throat and fasten more in her ears. Adding gloves and a bracelet, she stepped back and surveyed as much of her appearance as would fit in the square mirror above the small table holding a bowl and pitcher. The clothing was elegant, the jewels a statement in wealth, the bearing it had taken her years to perfect a confirmation of her breeding.

Impressive . . . perfect. If ever she was to intimidate someone, it had to be now.

Chapter 24

Adrian was going to win . . . again. The moment the crew of *Reckoner* had heard Phillip say Adrian's name and realized the vessel closing in on them was a Rutland ship, they'd stood by, refusing to obey his order to ready a cannon and fire across *Bifrost*'s bow. Phillip had chosen his crew for their loyalty to the family but had failed to consider that Adrian was head of that family. Adrian was the one who insisted on continuing to pay their wages even if their work had been suspended until the end of the war.

Phillip watched unblinking as the *Bifrost* continued to approach *Reckoner*. *Falcon* had sailed out of cannon range and now circled them like a buzzard anticipating the presence of carcasses.

At least *Falcon* wouldn't press any advantage she might have. Phillip's first order had been to heave the Portuguese flag he carried with many others. Adrian flew the British flag along with the Dane colors and Wyndham crest. Just like Adrian, to avoid a fight.

What was he going to do—pull rank and hope it was enough to get Steven off the *Falcon*?

He didn't think so. His cousin might be in his own skewed world most of the time, but he wasn't crazy. Adrian would have a plan.

Phillip quickly thought through the dozen different plans he'd made, but none would do him any good until he knew what Adrian was about. Continuing to curse a blue stream, Phillip wished he had the guts and the hatred to blow *Bifrost* out of the water. But he didn't, and even if he hated Adrian, he wouldn't be able to bring himself to destroy his cousin, much less the most incredible ship he'd ever seen.

Like it or not, they were now allies. Steven was within reach, and for the moment, all that mattered. One way or another, he would have his revenge on Adrian . . . but not today.

"Damn him to hell," Phillip cursed, as *Bifrost* continued to close in. Dear God, what a magnificent ship she was—long, low, and lithe, like a woman reclining on the waves. And no wonder she was so fleet. She lacked the height, multiple towering decks, and broad beam of other vessels, cutting through the waves rather than heaving against them like a battering ram, her huge expanses of sail billowing above and over her like a pompadour of blue-white hair.

"He's coming in board to board on the port side, sir," his first mate said.

Phillip closed his eyes at the sudden suspicion that Adrian had gone mad, after all. He wouldn't put it past his cousin to try to leap from his ship to *Reckoner*—

Phillip blinked and blinked again, unable to decide whether to believe what he was seeing. A woman appeared on deck, gliding across the boards, as tall as the masts, as abundantly formed as the sails on *Bifrost,* and a bit broad in the beam as well. So imposing was she that he wondered if Adrian had somehow brought a figurehead to life to intimidate *Falcon*'s crew.

But no, she was real, and rigged out as if she were the queen of England.

Phillip's last thought before *Bifrost*'s hull bumped against *Reckoner* was that his damned cousin had brought her along as a secret weapon.

Chapter 25

Lorelei had pushed trepidation aside as she stepped into the companionway, left second thoughts behind as she'd walked to the poop deck, swept away doubts as she smoothed her skirts and approached the rail where *Reckoner* loomed alongside. But now they all caught up with her, shouting to be heard as she slid her hand in the crook of Dane's arm, feeling him immediately stiffen, seeing his brows lower in displeasure.

"Later, you may roar in masculine outrage and I can weep in feminine contrition, Dane," she said, firmly ousting uncertainty as her knees threatened to give way and her heart climbed into her throat. "Later, I will do anything you ask, but for now, you will have to trust me." She quickly turned her gaze across and up to the deck of the ship they were literally against, the sides bumping one another. She shoved a waistcoat and stock at him. "And you must put these on."

He allowed them to fall to the deck.

A man stood glaring down at them from the greater height of the frigate.

"Are you, Phillip?" she called.

"Damn it, Adrian, get the hell away from my ship," the man shouted, ignoring her.

It had to be Dane's cousin. He had the same tall, lanky build, and there was something familiar about the mouth. "Sir, I suggest you come down here immediately," she said imperiously, and pointed to a net that had been lowered over *Reckoner*'s side—she still didn't know all the names for parts of a ship. "You can climb down that." She scanned the horizon for *Falcon*, relieved that the British ship was on their other side and far enough away that many of their movements would not be immediately noticeable.

"Lorelei," Dane gritted out. "You have no idea what you are doing—"

"I most certainly do." She sighed and stepped as close to him as she could. "Have *you* a plan?"

"No, goddammit!" He glared at a point over her shoulder with a fury that frightened her.

"Then you have nothing to lose," she said crisply, then softened her voice. "Please, just this once, trust me." She clutched his arm. "Dane, please look at me."

He stepped back, saying nothing as he glared at her.

"I know I am a woman and ill versed in situations such as this, but I know I'm right in what I do." Her voice thickened and she visibly struggled to keep it firm. "Dane, I beg you to trust me. I will get down on my knees, if necessary."

He stiffened as if something shook and rattled and cracked inside him and he held together by will alone. "You have never begged in your life," he gritted. "I will not have you do so now. Not even to save my pride or satisfy my sense of right.'' He raked his hand through his hair. ''You ask much of me, Lorelei, but trust must begin with one of us. Perhaps my trust in you will provide an example you will follow in future.''

She flinched and dropped her hand from his arm. ''I trust you, Dane. You have no idea how much,'' she said in a choked voice, as the enormity of what she was doing struck her. ''Please remember that I do not disobey and challenge you lightly. If I am wrong . . . if my plan fails''—she swallowed hard and looked away—''if my plan fails—oh, blast it, Dane, I love you. . . .'' She pressed her lips together and breathed deeply. ''I love you so much,'' she repeated in a soft voice, ''and I need you to know that. I would not arbitrarily risk your life for the sake of proving a point. I believe strongly that I know what I am doing.'' She met his gaze and held it, as she squared her shoulders and lifted her chin. ''And I do it because I would rather risk your leaving me than lose you to death.'' Having had her say, and feeling completely foreign to herself, she quickly stepped back, shaking her head as Dane opened his mouth to speak. ''I don't want to hear what you have to say right now, Dane . . . I cannot. Let us just do what we must and sort it out later. Your cousin is what is important now.''

Dane frowned and reached out to her, but a young man jumped to the deck from the nets with a reckless air about him, landing between her and her husband. He was taller than Dane, and had blond hair and a tight expression. ''I can get Steven back, Adrian,'' he said fiercely. ''He's my brother. There's no reason for you to be involved.''

''No?'' Dane said, as he clenched his fists at his sides. ''And if you should lose the battle?''

Phillip's face paled.

"Damn it, Phillip, you never think things through or consider consequences," Dane said, his voice strained with frustration and temper. "The captain of *Falcon* is most certainly a seasoned fighter. The only thing you are seasoned with is rum." He stepped nearer his cousin, grasped his collar, and shoved him against the rail. "Am I to stand by and lose you also?"

"Why not?" Phillip said bitterly. "Losing someone does not overtax *you* as it does most mortals. You simply go on, never speaking of it again—out of sight, out of mind. Especially me."

Dane jerked away from him to stand out of reach, his hand lowering to his side, his expression twisted with some emotion Lorelei could not decipher. "Then let us say that I have no wish to lose the frigate you stole from our shipyards."

Phillip balled his hands into fists and advanced on Dane.

Lorelei stepped between them. "Phillip, I am Lorelei, Dane's wife."

He halted in his tracks. "Wife? You?"

Dane made a sound in his throat, like a growl. "Be careful, Phillip."

"Yes, me. Difficult to believe, I know," she said smartly. "I collect you have unfinished business with my husband."

"I'd like to rip his head off."

"If that were true, sir, you would have attempted it by now . . . and you would not have succeeded." Lorelei reached out and solicitously patted his arm. "Dane can be quite maddening at times, and I agree you must settle accounts between you," she said in a rush, not at all liking the temper Phillip displayed.

Unlike Dane's, it was wild, unfettered, and all consuming, allowing no room for reason. Dane always had room for reason, even at his most furious. "But surely that can wait until we free your brother."

"Get the hell out of my way," Phillip snarled.

"So you can haul out your cannon?" Dane said. "Over my dead body, Phillip."

"If necessary," Phillip said.

"I assure you it will be," Lorelei said. "Our countries are at war. *Falcon* will have no choice but to try to sink you, or take you as a prize, at the very least. And if you fire on her, you will be risking Steven's life, as Dane said. You will be risking Dane's, as well, and I will not have that." She wanted badly to look at Dane, to soothe his fury that seemed to writhe like a live thing behind her.

Phillip leaned back against the rail and crossed his arms, his mouth set in a mutinous line, but again his face paled and his suddenly stricken expression reflected in his gaze.

"She's right, boy, and you know it," Mathers boomed, as he took a position by Lorelei's side.

Phillip closed his eyes and his arms fell to his sides. "Oh, God. I didn't think ... I should have and I didn't."

"Dane has told me what a good mind you have," Lorelei said, "an opinion I am persuaded to believe comes out of his love for you rather than fact."

"A good mind," Phillip said bleakly. "That's why I didn't think things through and might have gotten my brother killed. That's why Adrian doesn't trust me to free Steven, or do anything else, for that matter."

"Trust means nothing when it is forced upon you," Dane said, his voice dripping disgust. "Earn it and I'll give it gladly."

Again Lorelei flinched, certain he spoke to her as well as his cousin. Her declaration of trust meant nothing to Dane. Why should it, when she had made such a point of actions being louder than words?

Mathers glanced from her to Phillip. "What's done is done. I suggest we get you out of here, and after this is over, you and Adrian can beat each other to a pulp—and maybe high time, too."

"With pleasure," Phillip said, though some of his belligerence seemed to drain out of him. "I suppose my cousin has a way to free Steven."

"No," Dane said, as he took a stance on Lorelei's left. "But my wife has. I suggest you listen carefully, and with respect."

Had anyone else heard the edge in Dane's voice? Lorelei wondered, as her head began to feel too heavy to hold erect and a dozen doubts began to whittle away at her determination. Still, she had come too far now to stop. The damage to her marriage was done, perhaps beyond repair.

Taking a deep breath, she launched into her plan. "Phillip, your crew is ill . . . with something highly feared and contagious. Cholera, I think."

"Why not plague?" Dane offered, with a hint of sarcasm.

"Fine," she snapped. "Your ship is riddled with plague, Phillip. Do ships carry a flag signifying quarantine? If so, fly it. Dane has provided you fresh water and sent you on your way. We will take care of the rest without bloodshed, and hopefully without risking Dane's position."

"Just like that, I am to sail off?" Phillip asked snidely, "and put my faith in a woman I don't know?"

"You have no choice," Lorelei said. "I'm certain

Captain Mathers can be persuaded to put you in irons, or whatever it is captains do, if you refuse to cooperate.''

"I expected you to marry some sweet flower of society, Adrian," Phillip scoffed. "I'd never have thought you would saddle yourself with an overbearing bitch.''

Dane lunged forward.

Lorelei grabbed him around the waist and hauled him back, for once thankful for her size. "I care not what you think of me, Phillip," she gasped as Dane escaped her hold without hurting her. "My only concerns are the release of your brother and my husband's well-being . . . so help me, Dane, if you do not stop I will sit on you.''

Dane stilled and stepped back, a small twitch at the side of his mouth.

She planted her hands on her hips. "Yes, I am a bitch when necessary, one that is quite capable of becoming rabid if any member of my *pack* is threatened.'' She gave him what she hoped was an evil smile. "You, on the other hand, appear to care about little but your own dissatisfaction with your lot in life, which I will be happy to see reduced to that of a trapped animal if you continue to provoke me.''

Phillip glared at her, tilted his head in the same way Dane often did, then grinned. "I take what I said back, ma'am. Any woman who can hold her own with any one of the Rutland men, as you just did, deserves respect.''

Dumbfounded at the abrupt turnabout in his attitude, she could only stare at Phillip and absently wonder if all Rutland men were so unpredictable as Dane and his volatile cousin.

Phillip jammed his hands into the pockets of his

loosely fitted trousers and sighed, his mouth working as if he struggled with a thought. ''And as usual, my cousin is correct, as you are. I didn't think things through. I could have''—he swallowed and seemed to strangle for a moment—''I could have gotten my brother killed, just because I wanted to best Adrian.''

Dane's mouth worked and his jaw clenched as he turned sharply away.

She wanted to go to Dane and hold him against the hurt Phillip inflicted upon him. And she wanted to go to Phillip as he stood there looking like an abandoned child. Remembering something Dane had once told her and what Phillip had said a few moments ago, she wondered if he didn't feel abandoned—

Phillip faced Mathers, ignoring Dane. ''My men are ill,'' he said in a monotone, reciting her earlier instructions, ''and I am taking my ship north, where we will all die and *Reckoner* will become a ghost ship haunting the seas.''

Mathers loudly cleared his throat. ''There is a cove on the north shore of Corvos in the Azores. We will rendezvous there.'' He clapped Phillip on the shoulder. ''And for all our sakes, boy, stay away from enemy ships.''

Phillip's expression vacillated between a grimace and a plea. ''All I want is my brother back, sir,'' he said subdued.

''Phillip, we will get Steven back,'' Dane said, then turned to face his cousin. ''And then you and I will either talk or fight—whatever will end this war between us.'' Meeting his cousin's gaze, he began to take another step toward him, then abruptly crossed the deck to the port rail.

A yearning such as she had never seen crossed Phillip's face. Embarrassed to witness his vulnerability, she averted her gaze to Dane, hunched over the rail.

Phillip pivoted sharply on his heel and reached for the heavy rope net draped down the side of his ship.

"Phillip," Dane called, straightening and angling his head to look at his cousin over his shoulder.

Phillip stiffened and paused, one foot on the net.

"Take care," Dane said wearily. "Please," he added, undiguised love and anguish battling in his expression.

Not waiting for Phillip to leave, Lorelei swept up the clothing lying in a pile on deck and whirled toward Dane, fighting the thickness in her throat, the burning behind her eyes at such blatant evidence of love between the cousins—a love so private and so complete that even with the hostility between them, neither could harm the other. She knew so little about such emotion and was again acutely aware of the hole inside her. A hole that only Dane could fill. In that moment, she wished for his love harder than she'd ever wished for anything in her life. . . .

Too late.

She wanted so badly to stand close enough to her husband to touch him, to tell him how much his protectiveness meant to her, to explain again that she was only trying to do the same for him. But she stood apart from him, too far away to reach, yet not far enough not to be heard. She swallowed hard and willed away the tears only Dane could inspire. "I know I am overbearing and far too bold, and unbelievably spoiled," she said, hating the tremble in her voice. "I know I am not at all a proper wife, and you must be quite disappointed—"

"I think it wise," he interrupted brusquely, as he ambled closer to her, shrugged out of his coat, laid it over the rail, and took the waistcoat and stock from her, "for you to tell me your plan, Lorelei, before we confront *Falcon*."

She stared at him, feeling so separated from the man who had taught her more about closeness and family than she'd ever thought to experience, knowing it was too late to put her understanding into practice.

Sighing, she took the neckcloth from his hands and wound it about his collar in one of Beau's favorite knots, carefully adjusting the folds and placing the ends just so as she quickly outlined her plan to him.

He expressed neither approval nor argument, but listened intently, standing still for her ministrations, which she drew out as long as she could, fiddling with the knot of his stock, then holding his coat while he shrugged it on. Such wifely things to do that never would have occurred to her not so long ago. Things, she realized, that grew from the seeds of love. Small things that were a bittersweet comfort.

She stared at Dane's face, feeling suddenly awkward. He met her gaze, holding it, his eyebrows quirked up at the inside corners, his mouth in the half-smile she loved . . . so much.

"The *Falcon* is closing in," he said, reminding her of why a distance yawned between them, why she had trampled his pride—thoroughly but not thoughtlessly. Reminding her of all that he had given her in such a short time and that it was too late to wish for more.

Chapter 26

"It is too late to back down now, Lorelei," Dane said, as he situated her on the plank seat that would transport her from *Bifrost* to *Falcon.* Granted, the ships were almost as close to one another as *Bifrost* and *Reckoner* had been, but she couldn't imagine the bosun's seat could possibly support her an inch, much less several feet over and many more up.

"I cannot swim," she said. "Dane, this will not work."

He covered her hands on the ropes holding the seat. "Trust me, my Lady Lorelei, and hold tight."

"I do trust you, Dane; it is this dratted thin piece of wood I hold suspect."

"One question." He steadied the motion of the seat—what had Dane called it?—and raised his brows in inquiry. "Why are we dressed in evening clothes?"

Suspecting that he was trying to divert her mind and thinking it was a splendid idea, she gave him a patient, slightly indulgent look. "Because they are grand and display our wealth and positions more vividly than garments we would wear during the course of an ordinary day. It is very important that we intimidate the officers of *Falcon* so they will bow and scrape and perhaps not realize they are being gulled.''

Dane shook his head in mock reproach. ''My wife has a criminal mind,'' he commented to no one in particular and released the ropes supporting her insubstantial seat.

Before she could protest further, the seat swayed and began an angled ascent toward the knot of men waiting on the deck of the *Falcon* for her and Dane to transfer over from *Bifrost.*

The captain of the frigate had invited them over after Dane had all but insisted, shouting that he was not about to strain his voice explaining about *Reckoner* across the distance between ships. In any case, his wife wished a tour of a warship.

A blur of motion sped through the air beside her and she knew it was Dane leaping to the net. Frantically she wondered what shipbuilders had against ladders . . . or stairways built on the outside hull of a ship. For that matter, why hadn't Dane built his ship of a height with all the others roaming the seas?

She squeezed her eyes shut and held on for dear life, not wanting to see the depth of the drop to the water, much less her husband scaling the net. *Why couldn't he have used the seat also?* she wondered hysterically. He was fully rigged in evening wear—hardly the proper attire to be behaving like a seaman. He probably looked quite dashing, and under other circumstances she would watch avidly and become agitated in intimate places. She pictured him in her mind instead: his broad shoulders straining, his muscles swelling beneath his coat—she hoped he did not

rip a seam—his marvelously long legs bending, flex-
ing beneath his fitted trousers.

She moaned as her stomach turned topsy-turvy and
seemed to rise and plunge inside her like a ship tossed
about on an agitated sea. This was not the best time
to discover she did not like heights.

Strong hands gripped her waist, steadying her, then
swung her to her feet on a solid deck. She opened her
eyes and focused on the face directly in front of her.
Dane's face. Dane's slanted smile. Dane's expressive
eyes behind the spectacles she'd insisted he wear—to
make him seem more harmless than threatening, she'd
said—that even now slipped down his nose. How had
he climbed the net so quickly?

"If I break your nose," she said conversationally,
"you will then have a bump to keep your spectacles
firmly in place . . . and I will have the satisfaction of
having my revenge on you."

He chuckled as he turned her to face the men clustered about. "Captain, may I present my intrepid wife,
Lady Dane?"

"Captain Preston-Barnes, at your service, my
lady." A man of average height and exaggerated curls
à la Titus plastered around his face with an excess of
pomade clicked his heels and bowed smartly. So
much gilded braid adorned his uniform, he fairly twin-
kled in the sunlight. "I do believe we have met before. Baroness Winters, isn't it?"

Her stomach still swaying high above the water, she
peered at him more closely, at the patch—of all
things—stuck on his cheek. She knew that patch—

"Freddy?" she said, startled to find a fashion tulip
of the first water commanding a warship. "Lizzie's
brother? It's been a veritable age since I have seen

you—five years or more, isn't it?'' she gushed. ''This is too delightful.''

''One and the same, Baroness.''

She elevated the tip of her nose in the air as she took her husband's arm. ''Viscountess Dane now, Freddy—or must I address you as Captain Preston-Barnes?'' She gave him an imposing glare. ''Really, it is such a mouthful. And since Lizzie and I are such friends, you must call me Lady Lorelei.''

He cast a glance at *Reckoner*, growing smaller as she sailed north. ''We have not had the opportunity this morning to break our fast. I assume you have been similarly deprived, and will be most honored if you would join me in the officers' dining room.'' He gave her an ingratiating smile—the pompous man—and held out his arm, gesturing toward the doors beneath the quarterdeck, leading, she assumed, to the saloon and officers' quarters.

She accepted the captain's escort. ''How good of you to think of it, Freddy. I vow Lord Dane and I are famished after all the excitement. You and my husband did introduce yourselves, did you not?'' she prattled on. ''Have you heard from Lizzie? She and your mama were at our wedding just a few weeks past, you know. She didn't mention a word about your commission . . . imagine our Freddy being such an important man.''

Gratefully she sat in the chair Freddy held for her and slipped an inquiring glance at Dane. He shook his head slightly. No sight of Steven yet.

''I do hope you will forgive our attire, Freddy,'' Lorelei said. ''We always dress for dinner—you know how I love fashion—and when we sighted yours and that other boat, we quite forgot to retire for the night and remained on deck.''

''*Ship*, darling, not boat,'' Adrian corrected her, as he sat back with no small amount of awe at her chatter, giving ''Freddy'' no opportunity to reply before flitting from one subject to another.

''Ship,'' she repeated dutifully. ''We just missed you in the Azores, you know,'' she said with feigned regret. ''How lovely it would have been to linger there, but Dane is so fond of sailing his boats that he was annoyingly restless in port.''

Dane threw a male look of exasperation at Freddy at her second mention of ''boats.'' Freddy returned it with the disgusted look men exchange when women say something they deem foolish.

''He has, however,'' Lorelei continued, ''promised me that we might stop there on our way home and perhaps stay awhile. Have you any pineapple from those lovely islands, Freddy? I am so fond of pineapple, and we gave all we had to those poor unfortunates on the other boat.''

Freddy nodded to his aide and immediately passed a plate of pineapple chunks to her. ''Pray, tell me about the other *ship*,'' he said. ''I can't imagine why you stopped for her before coming to us.''

Lorelei slid all of the pineapple onto her plate and tucked into it with relish. ''Why, because it was closer to us than you, of course . . . oh, you don't mind if I take all this, do you? I see no point in disguising my appetite when it is legend among our circle.'' She popped a chunk into her mouth. ''Anyway, Dane was curious . . . 'something did not seem quite right with her,' he said.'' Rolling a bite around her mouth, she closed her eyes and sighed in ecstasy as she slowly chewed and swallowed.

Adrian bit the inside of his cheek to keep from laughing as she savored every bite. His wife had not only a criminal mind but a vicious streak as well. A week from now the officers of *Falcon* would be deeply regretting their generosity in offering her their fruit.

"And was something amiss, Lord Dane?" Freddy asked.

"I'm afraid so, poor devils," Adrian said, with the distraction of which the *ton* accused him. Behavior contrary to his reputation might raise suspicion once Freddy returned to England or received a letter from his sister, whichever came first. He wanted nothing returning to haunt him later. With that thought, he realized that Lorelei's carefree manner was a talent she'd doubtlessly developed in order to fit in. She likely dragged it out of the wardrobe, donning it as she did her almost unorthodox gowns for social occasions like a knight of old donned his armor. Thank God and heaven above that she did not carry on like this with him. . . .

The revelation stunned him. *She didn't carry on like this with him; she never had.* Which meant that whether she knew it or not, she was at ease with him as she was with only a few others. He'd had the thought before, but it had been offhand and taken for granted. He was himself, regardless of who was about. Lorelei shared little of herself with others even as she freely dispensed advice, comfort, and warmth to all who crossed her path. It was quite a talent she had— combining personas so skillfully that he wondered if anyone in her circle, other than Lady Harriet and Brummell, knew anything at all about her.

What a precious gift she had given him—

"Lord Dane," Freddy said, with barely concealed

impatience, "you were saying that something was amiss on the Portuguese frigate . . . ?"

"What? Oh yes," Dane said, pushing up his spectacles for effect. "They have what appears to be plague. The captain said one of the men had been bitten by a rat in the cargo hold, which would bear that out."

"Plague?" Freddy exclaimed, his face blanching. "I saw no quarantine flag."

"Of course you didn't, Freddy," Lorelei chirped. "It wasn't there. They didn't have one, you see. Dane gave them ours, along with fresh water. Evidently they haven't been able to put into port."

"You didn't touch them, did you?" Freddy asked, alarmed as he wiped his hands on his napkin and slid his chair back a foot.

"Don't be absurd. Dane sent a boat over with water and what food we could spare, and told them to keep the boat or burn it . . . rigged it with ropes somehow so none of our men would have to man it." She glanced at Dane with a look of pride. "So very clever is my husband."

"It was wise of you to circle well out of the way," Dane said, as he raised his cup of tea to his mouth.

A flush climbed Freddy's face. "Yes, well, you *did* reach them first," he said quickly. "My duty was to a ship flying the flag of England, and I felt it prudent to hang about to make certain you were all right."

"And we do *so* appreciate it, Freddy," Lorelei said dryly.

Adrian nudged her foot under the table in warning. "How do you like my ship?" he asked, deciding it would be better to be obvious about the uniqueness of *Bifrost* than to raise questions later. Since his secret was out, it made little difference now. "You know, as everyone does, that I once owned a shipyard in the Colonies. When I left to pledge my allegiance to England, I brought it with me . . . thought I'd tinker with the design a bit, perhaps offer it to His Majesty when it meets my standards . . . for the tea trade, I thought.'' Setting his cup down, he launched into a discourse of technicalities that had put more seasoned seafarers than Captain Preston-Barnes to sleep.

Freddy's eyes took on an unmistakable glaze of boredom.

"Really, Dane, must you go on about it now when I am so anxious to have a tour of Freddy's boat?'' Lorelei said, with a glare in his direction. She favored Freddy with a smile. "You will allow me to poke about, won't you? I cannot imagine how a boat—a ship, I mean—this large can possibly float when I sink like a stone in a mere puddle.''

Adrian restrained himself from leaping out of his chair. It had been all he could do to keep from craning his neck to study the men who came and went outside the officers' dining room. And the longer they remained, the more chance there was of making a blunder.

Freddy rose quickly and all but yanked Lorelei's chair out. "My pleasure, Lady Dane.''

"Lady *Lorelei*,'' she chided.

Adrian smothered a laugh of pure relief at how easy it had been as he rose and offered his arm to Lorelei. She latched onto it as if it were a lifeline—the first indication she'd given him that she was rattled. He covered her hand with his, reassuring her in the only way he could at the moment.

But later . . . later he would have a great deal to say to her, and she would listen if he had to sit on her.

*   *   *

"Over five hundred men?" Lorelei said. "So many. How do you keep track of them all, Freddy?"

Adrian had long since shut out Lorelei's questions and the captain's explanations as they strolled with agonizing slowness from stern to stem of the *Falcon.* He'd noted only what was important—the faces of each seaman and marine they encountered, and that Freddy, for all his pomposity and pretension, ran a tight, clean ship. The men appeared healthy and in decent spirits, given the drudgery and tedium of their work.

"Over five hundred men . . . imagine," Lorelei repeated, in a tone Adrian translated as dispirited. "I vow we've seen twice that many."

Thrice, Adrian corrected silently, feeling as wretched as Lorelei sounded. There had been no sign of Steven. All that was left were the men up in the rigging, and if worse came to worst, he would damn well ask to climb the ropes—just for the pleasure of it, of course.

"I've heard horrible stories about the need for strong discipline at sea," Lorelei commented. "Do you have to lock men up, Freddy?"

Good girl, Adrian thought, as he gave her hand a pat of congratulation for thinking of it. The brig was the only place they hadn't visited during their tour. He stared up at the sails, unable to make out faces of the men climbing and swinging through the jungle of rigging and canvas.

"I'm blessed with a crew of good lads," Freddy replied, "and have had little cause to implement such measures. My father—second son of the Earl of Frampton—was an admiral, you know, and it was his belief that if one fed his men well and treated them with respect, they would not disappoint. I have found that he was right.''

And Freddy's penchant for carousing in every port might have something to with it, Adrian thought, though his estimation of Captain Preston-Barnes climbed to considerable heights as his hope of finding Steven hale and whole revived. Still, illness and accidents were not uncommon at sea, and dread was settling in his gut like a ball of lead.

A man stumbled and sprawled on the deck beside Adrian. Instinctively he halted, about to offer the seaman a hand up, remembering just in time that an English noble did not do such things.

''Begging your pardon, ma'am . . . sir.'' The man struggled to his feet and removed his knitted cap in deference to Lorelei while giving Adrian a hard stare.

Adrian squeezed Lorelei's hand twice in their prearranged signal as emotions toppled over one another in a rush to escape. He held his body stiff and erect, forced himself to nod imperiously, studied the features beneath the unfamiliar beard—

''Oh, my heavens!'' Lorelei cried, as she tore away from Adrian's hold and rushed to the seaman, peering at him this way and that and going so far as to part his beard to get a better look. ''Steven, it is you, isn't it? What on earth are you doing here? Why aren't you in the Indies, purchasing a plantation?''

Steven opened his mouth, breath whooshing out as she embraced him with all her strength. ''I expected to hear from you long ago. Why haven't you—'' She broke off and whirled on the captain. ''Freddy, what is my cousin doing here?''

''Your cousin?'' Freddy sputtered. ''I have no idea . . . you have a cousin?''

An officer rushed up to them. ''Here, now, what

are you doing?'' he demanded, as he reached for Steven.

Freddy frantically waved him away.

"Of course I have a cousin," Lorelei said, as the officer backed off to stand nearby. "Doesn't everyone? And I repeat: why is *my* cousin dressed as a common seaman on your ship?" She leaned toward the captain with an intimidating frown. "He left for the Indies to purchase a plantation—an investment for me." Straightening, she lifted her chin to glare down her nose at both captain and officer. "If you tell me you impressed him, I will be very put out, Freddy. A word to George Brummell means a word to the Regent. . . ."

Feeling superfluous—and to his surprise, not minding it—and fascinated in spite of his urgency to get Steven away, Adrian swiveled his head from his wife to Freddy to Steven, following the conversation.

"His Majesty's navy does not impress men, Lady Dane," Freddy said stiffly, his complexion turning a sickly white.

Lorelei turned back to Steven. "Don't tell me you are here on a lark, Steven. I know you like to sail, but this is ridiculous. All you had to do was ask and I would gladly have presented you with a boat as a gift."

Adrian thought he saw Steven's mouth twitch as he lowered his gaze to the deck. "No, not a lark," he said in a muffled tone.

"Perhaps his ship met with bad fortune . . . a storm . . . ?" Adrian suggested, then smiled congenially, feeling anything but. "So you are the cousin Steven that Lorelei"—he emphasized her name— "has been fretting about. I am Viscount Dane, by the way."

"*Did* your ship sink, Steven?" Lorelei asked gently. "You poor man. What you must have gone through."

"I recall little of what happened . . . Lorelei," Steven murmured, obviously getting into the spirit of the thing, though Adrian observed that Steven had locked his knees and his knuckles were white as he tightly held his cap. He raised his head and gave the captain a steady, angry glare. "I remember little except that I was taken off my ship and handed over to *Falcon.*"

"You were taken?" Lorelei gasped.

"I am not aware of how this man came to be among my crew," Freddy said as if he were choking, and cast a glance at his officer. "Mr. Briggs?"

The man shrugged and averted his gaze.

Adrian turned so that only Steven could see the warning in his expression. *Let it go, Steven,* he ordered silently. "You were abducted by a crimp?" he said, more statement than question.

"Yes, yes, I'm certain that was the way of it," Freddy said quickly, his gaze skipping everywhere, as if he searched for a bolt hole while his hand moved to the hilt of the sword he wore. "Such miscreants are plentiful on docks all over the world, taking honest men and selling them. I'll look into it right away. Perhaps my first mate became overzealous in acquiring crew. We were a bit shorthanded on our last run to the Indies." His smile flashed and disappeared. The men in proximity had halted their activities and closed in a loose circle around them, apparently sensing that their captain felt threatened.

Adrian could almost feel the stir of hostility in the air and knew that if they did not resolve the problem to everyone's satisfaction, *Bifrost* and her crew could very well meet with an "unfortunate accident," never to be seen again. With the threat of being publicly denounced by a viscount, and by extension the Marquess of Wyndham, as well as a peeress with very lofty connections, Captain Preston-Barnes faced disgrace followed by exile into anonymity. He had little to lose by eliminating his accusers in a scandal England wished to avoid—

"A crimp . . . is that what happened, Steven?" Lorelei asked as she, too, faced him, revealing to him her panic.

Steven ripped his stare from Freddy, whose hand had tightened on his sword to look at Dane, then Lorelei. His mouth tightened as if he were about to press the issue. He sighed instead. "Yes, a crimp," he said flatly.

Freddy sagged in relief.

"Oh, well, we can hardly blame dear Freddy for that," she said, the panic subsiding in her expression. "Dear heaven, Steven, what you must have gone through. We will get you to Dane's boat immediately and see that you get plenty of rest."

"Sir, this man is a member of our crew. We cannot—"

"This man," Freddy said coldly, "is the cousin of a peeress, Mr. Briggs, and as such has no place in my command. Is that clear?"

The officer's mouth flapped like laundry in the wind.

Lorelei turned back to the captain. "Freddy, I think quite enough has been said on the matter, don't you agree, Dane?"

"I do," Adrian replied, not trusting himself to say more.

"I cannot tell you how grateful I am that Steven ended on your ship, Freddy," Lorelei said, filling in the gap Adrian left with his silence. "Otherwise, I'm certain he would have been subject to dangers I cannot imagine. I will find a way to show you my gratitude when next you are home."

Freddy bowed slightly. "No need," he said, trapped so neatly that there was little else he could do. For once, Adrian was thankful that governments had a habit of denying questionable activities. Captain Preston-Barnes could hardly protest their removing Steven from *Falcon* without admitting to practices his government vehemently denied. In fact, the captain appeared frantic to get them all off his ship.

"We really must go, Freddy. I would offer you the hospitality of *Bifrost*, but Steven's mother has been quite overset since we have had no word from him in so long. I've done my best to reassure her, but she and I never got on well together. Perhaps by bringing Steven home, I will find some favor in her eyes." She smiled sadly. "They—Steven and his mother—are my only family, you see."

"Of course," Freddy said, then rapped out orders to his officer to lower a boat.

"No really," Lorelei interrupted, and swallowed as if a cannonball was lodged in her throat. "I will take the chair back, if you don't mind. Climbing down to a boat would be rather awkward." She cast a tender look at Steven. "My cousin appears fit—thank you for looking after him so well, Freddy—and I'm certain he can go with Dane down that net, can you not, cousin?"

Steven nodded.

"Then I suggest we take our leave and allow these gentlemen to get about the business of war," Adrian said, taking Lorelei's arm in one hand and Steven's in the other and pushing them toward the rail. Turning, he clapped Freddy on the shoulder. "You have my gratitude as well, Captain. Your honorable actions will not go unremarked in London."

Freddy blustered and mumbled, saying nothing that could be translated into a proper sentence.

"Oh, drat," Lorelei whispered, grabbing his attention. She stood staring at the bosun's chair suspended by ropes, then closed her eyes. "Now, Dane, before I lose my nerve."

"You?" he whispered in her ear as he helped her onto the seat. "You, my Lady Lorelei, have enough nerve for an entire country."

Her eyes flew open, staring at him with a sadness he couldn't fathom as the seat swung out over the water.

Chapter 27

Lorelei stood at the rail on *Bifrost*'s deck, maintaining appearances, waving at *Falcon* as she resumed her course and sailed toward the Indies. Captain Mathers immediately set their course back to the Azores, where they would meet Phillip and send Steven home with his brother.

Steven and Dane, too, maintained appearances as they silently flanked her, barely moving until the warship looked like little more than a toy boat on a pond in the distance. Still they were unnaturally calm, and Lorelei wondered if the men felt as weak and spent as she did.

"I'm sorry I almost bungled it for you," Steven said quietly. "I knew better but couldn't see past my anger until those men began closing in."

"It's all right," Dane said. "It was all I could do not to take them all on. If it weren't for Lorelei, we'd both likely be hanging from a yardarm."

"Freddy would have killed us, wouldn't he?" she asked, trembling from the inside out.

"He would," Dane sighed, "if we had pressed the issue. If he'd found out that Steven was *my* cousin from America, most certainly. He could have said we were spies and a potentially embarrassing situation would have become Freddy's heroic act."

"Well, it is over now and everyone is safe," Lorelei said wearily, as she wrapped her arms around her waist, trying to still her shaking.

"It's over," Steven choked and shook his head as if reaction had just set in. "Oh God, I had almost stopped believing." He straightened and strained to look at Dane over Lorelei's head. "Catherine?"

"Mad as hell and ready to take on the whole Royal Navy," Dane said.

Utterly drained, Lorelei stepped out of the way of their reunion, feeling every inch the gooseberry. Everything was over. All that was left was for her and Dane to decide what to do about it. *Later*, she thought. Later, when she wouldn't feel as if she would shatter at one word or one look that hinted at disaster.

Ever since they had boarded *Falcon,* she'd felt as if time had stopped, as if nothing was real. Her mind refused to function, refused to settle on any thought of significance beyond her need to retreat to the cabin and sleep, hopefully until they reached home, except that she wasn't certain where home *was* anymore. She wasn't certain what to do but stand there and listen to Dane and his cousin exchange information.

"The children?" Steven asked.

"They are all well, Steven."

"What of Phillip?"

"He is captain of the frigate we encountered earlier this morning."

Steven paled. "That frigate—I thought it was ours but couldn't be sure. Thank God you came along.

Phillip would have been too quick to light the fuses on his cannon.'' He hesitated as if reluctant to say more. ''Was he drunk?''

''To my knowledge, Phillip hasn't had a drink for a year,'' Dane said. ''It may be that he is trying to put himself to rights.'' He grinned at Lorelei. ''If not, Lorelei has displayed a remarkable talent for giving him a set-down that he respects.''

''Lorelei,'' Steven said as he, too, looked at her, ''is a most remarkable woman. Imagine having two such tigers in the family. We will never get away with anything.''

''Catherine is Steven's wife,'' Dane explained, ''better known as Mama Tiger by us all.''

Lorelei managed a smile and a nod. ''I'm sure she will be ecstatic to have you back, Steven. It must have been torture for her, not knowing where you were.''

''Home . . . life as it should be . . . as I thought to never have it again.'' Steven closed his eyes, then made a strangled sound.

In the next moment Dane and his cousin were holding one another, patting one another's back, their shoulders heaving, breath shuddering as their voices choked and thickened. Captain Mathers joined them, a hand on the shoulder of each of the larger men, his eyes bright and blinking furiously.

She saw tears in Dane's eyes as he gave her a look full of gratitude and held out his arm, asking her to join them.

She shook her head as she backed farther away, then whirled and stumbled to the companionway leading down to the cabin, not wanting Dane's gratitude, hating it.

*　　*　　*

"I hate this," Adrian said, as he stared after Lorelei.

"Hate what?" Steven asked.

"Something is wrong, yet I don't know what it is. I can't imagine what it is."

"Just think about it for a while and it'll come to you, boy," Captain Mathers said.

Raking his fingers through his hair, Adrian took a step toward the companionway. "I'm not inclined to wait that long," he muttered.

Steven gripped his shoulder, stopping him. "I don't know what troubles her, or you, but you'll settle nothing with emotions running high. She needs rest; she could barely stand straight. Let her sleep and have a good meal at the end of it, then talk to her, after she realizes the world is in its proper place again."

"I wasn't aware that it was misplaced," Adrian said, leashing his impatience as he glanced at the sun, shocked to find that it was quickly sinking into the horizon. Another day gone, when it seemed like only moments ago that he and Lorelei had boarded the *Falcon*.

"Of course it was," Mathers said. "What has transpired since we sailed from Spindrift has hardly been normal. Lady Lorelei might be a strong, intelligent woman, but she is also a new bride. Come to think of it, I'll wager nothing has been normal for either of you from the minute you met—a little over a month ago, wasn't it?"

"A little over a month ago," Steven repeated. "Damn, Adrian, you really shouldn't drag your ass when changing your life from the inside out," he said dryly, as he clapped a hand on Adrian's shoulder and grinned. "The old salt is right, Adrian, and so am I. Let her sleep—no doubt you haven't allowed her much peace. In the meantime, I need a brandy and a complete explanation of how I acquired my most extraordinary new cousin.''

Calling himself a hundred kinds of coward, Adrian allowed Steven and Mathers to lead him around while they sought out Blackwell and left him again when he declined their invitation to join them, saying he might ''come round later to see who requires aid in finding their bed.''

They argued over the best place to settle. The saloon was the most obvious, but it occupied the bow right next to the captain's quarters, where Lorelei was hopefully sleeping. Finally they sprawled on the deck near the pigpens, presently occupied by only one sow. Mathers had suggested the chicken pens, but decided that the constant clucking would remind him too much of the housekeeper who saw to his needs when he was at home in Connecticut.

The cabin boy approached them slowly, carefully balancing a tray from the saloon loaded with a bottle of brandy, glasses, a tower of sandwiches, and cigars. ''Anything else, sirs?'' he asked.

''Pillows,'' Adrian said, wincing at the offense of hard deck on his back. It would, he feared, never be the same again. But then, neither would he, and he'd be damned if he could find a single reason to complain.

The moon grinned down on them as the night aged, unnoticed. All but the men on watch had long since retired to their bunks, and those required to remain on deck skirted the group by the pigpens. Someone below played a wistful tune on his harmonica, the perfect accompaniment to Adrian's tale of seeing Lorelei and immediately falling head over heels for her. He told it all from beginning to present, leaving nothing out, and adding snippets remembered with every swallow from his glass.

"I love her, you know. I'm foolish with love for her. It's not fashionable to be so taken with one's wife." Adrian sprawled on the pillows young Joseph had fetched, listening to the snores and grunts of the sow in her pen behind him. Holding his snifter up to the sky, he peered at the moon, distorted by liquid and glass. "Why is it that women have no trouble discussing their lives, yet men require a state of drunkenness in order to express themselves?"

"It's an unwritten law," Mathers said with a belch. "Men do one thing and women do another. It maintains some sort of cosmic balance."

"Balance," Adrian scoffed. "I've been unbalanced since I met Lorelei. It isn't fair when *her* wits seem firmly in place. Every time I think she is as unsettled as I am, she manages to collect herself before I can take advantage of her momentary lapse." He focused on his cousin. "Steven, you've been married since you were out of short pants. Does Catherine always get the better of you?"

"Always," Steven said. "I spent the first four years—or was it five?—of our marriage feeling as if I *still* belonged in short pants and wanting to throttle her for reducing me to such a state. I should have realized what I was in for when *she* proposed to me."

"I had to coerce Lorelei into marrying me," Adrian said glumly. "Announced it to a hundred members of the *ton* without asking her . . . and she took it."

"If you boys wanted sweet hothouse blossoms of society, you wouldn't have picked Lorelei, and Steven wouldn't have said yes to Catherine," Mathers pronounced, as if it were the wisdom of the ages. "If you'll recall, your fathers also married women as strong and stubborn as they were, preferring partners and mates to slaves and porcelain bric-a-brac to decorate their lives. Good thing, too. The Rutland empire wouldn't exist if it weren't for them standing behind the men, prodding them along.''

Steven drained his glass and sighed in contentment. "Catherine says that all men are dreamers but it takes a woman to make sense of what we dream for.''

"Behind every great man, there is a greater woman to kick him in the arse,'' Blackwell said, as he joined them with a bottle of rum in his hand.

"But they're subtle about it,'' Steven added. "I never know I've been booted until two days later.''

"Lorelei isn't subtle,'' Adrian said, as he beat Steven to the last sandwich and bit into it.

"Forthright and honest, she is,'' Mathers commented.

"She's unhappy.'' Finishing off the sandwich, Adrian studied the pattern of crumbs on his chest. "I don't know why. Don't know what to do, either.''

"There's rainwater left,'' Mathers said. "Send her a hot bath in the morning and a plate of pineapple to nibble on. Then go in and help her wash. My Matilda liked that, God rest her soul.''

"Can't,'' Adrian said, wondering if it was his imagination or did the crumbs on his coat really form the constellations?

"Course y'can,'' Blackwell said, as he lit up a cigar.

"Can't,'' Adrian repeated, and stuck his cigar between his teeth, forgetting to light it as visions of bathing Lorelei teased him without mercy. He could almost feel the satin of her flesh beneath his soap-slicked hands, her breasts swelling and pouting at him, her belly so soft, then contracting with pleasure, her thighs cushioning his hips—

Mathers snored loudly and his head lolled to the side.

"Why can't you?" Steven asked.

Sobering and with the cigar still clamped between his teeth, Adrian brushed the crumbs away as he remembered their first night—their only night—at Spindrift, how Lorelei had confided to him, how she had told him that she did not know if she would ever be agreeable to displaying her abundance, for obvious reasons. How she expected him to understand that. It occurred to him that such expectations were both unreasonable and complimentary.

"I love you, Dane . . . so much. . . ." She'd said it without warning, giving him all that mattered, and then asked him not to respond—afraid perhaps that he wouldn't respond in the way she wished? If she only knew—

Mathers jerked and opened his eyes to slits. "Tell her, boy. Tell her everything. She'll find out sooner or later anyway. Women are smart that way." His head nodded again and his eyes closed. "Just rip out your heart and lay it at her feet. It's better than having her pry it out of you."

"More dignity that way, too," Blackwell said sagely. "At least you'd be doing it of your own free will. It's not any harder than telling us how much you love her."

Adrian stared at Blackwell and then his cousin, both close to joining Mathers in drunken slumber. He frowned and swept his gaze toward the bow, toward the captain's quarters, where Lorelei lay—

Something glided over the deck. Something white and flowing. Something tall and well rounded. He squinted and stared hard, catching the shadow of plump limbs beneath the flowing white. Legs, he thought. Lorelei's legs.

Had she come to fetch him to bed, as wives were wont to do from time to time? Had she missed him? But if she had, why was she returning to their cabin without him?

He struggled to his feet, intent on following her and giving her a dressing down for venturing on deck in her nightgown with only a large shawl thrown over her shoulders, but his legs folded beneath him, too soggy with drink to hold him upright. He slid down the front of the pigpen as his head swam and the brandy seemed to be flooding his brain, washing away thought. His eyelids wouldn't stay open, dropping closed as if they were weighted. He gave up the battle and sighed as one last thought swam to the surface.

He could smell carnations; Lorelei *had* been here. Why? And how much had she heard?

Lorelei shut the door very gently, very quietly, and paced the length of the cabin, circled and quartered it, then paced the length again. She'd been concerned about Dane when she hadn't heard the hum of men's voices coming from the saloon and had gone in search of him, telling herself that she was hungry and would find something in the galley to tide her over until morning. It was a reasonable excuse to wander the deck in the infant hours of morning. An excuse she could live with, since she was almost certain that she didn't really want to see her husband, that she wasn't really concerned about him. He was a grown man who had gotten along very nicely for thirty years without her help. Just yesterday, he'd made it bitingly clear that he neither wanted nor needed her aid.

He had the annoying habit of reacting like a typical man, infuriating her; then, after a while, he'd capitulate without warning, disarming her. He was always doing that—catching her off guard, confusing her, making her question her choices and her beliefs until she didn't know what was up and what was down.

Like when she'd reached the pigpens and heard him mention her name. She'd almost run. To hear Dane speak of her in an adverse way would have torn her apart. But then she'd heard his voice, wistful and bemused. He'd said a word she'd never thought to hear from him or anyone else. A word she'd learned to distrust and fear until tonight.

Love. . . .

He loved her. He was foolish with love for her. She'd heard him say it to Steven and Captain Mathers. Surely he wouldn't lie to them.

Dane never lied.

She'd been rooted to the spot, wanting to hear more, craving to hear more, believing without question what he'd said. She didn't know why, when she'd sworn never to believe such a thing again, but she did. She'd continued to listen, fascinated that three such men would give women so much credit, amused by their resignation, and indignant—but only slightly so—at their insinuations that they were victims down to the last man.

And then she'd seen Dane glance her way. She had turned and run then, a coward who felt as if she were floating above the cool wood of the deck, completely swept away. The melancholy that had gripped her since Dane had become so remote the night before sank into some pit and remained there. Her certainty that she had quenched Dane's interest in her once and for all hung in the air without a single good reason to support it, and likewise fell into the pit. Dane had known what she was like before he married her. She'd given him more than one demonstration of her bold nature. He was an intelligent man, a thoughtful man who saw more deeply than others. A man who was not like others, and who she sometimes thought belonged in armor, charging after a dragon. A man who, conversely, was incredibly progressive in his attitudes toward women. A man like no other.

And he was her man; he'd said as much.

She trusted him to know his own mind, his own heart.

He was honest and honorable. Of course, he'd practiced deception on the *Falcon*, but that hardly counted. He'd merely fibbed, and then only by omission. He openly displayed his feelings for his cousins and his uncle and his friends. More than once he'd openly displayed his admiration and respect and liking for her.

And Dane didn't lie.

She trusted him!

The revelation plunked her back to solid footing again. He loved her. Wonderful. She trusted him. Fine. She thought it would be even more fine and wonderful if he told her face to face without her having to kick him from behind.

Chapter 28

Lorelei was sorely tempted to prod her husband into action—any action—by the time they reached the island of Corvos and joined *Reckoner* in the small secluded bay to reunite Steven with his brother. For the past three days she'd spent a great deal of time chatting with Steven, hearing about his wife and his children and his concerns over Phillip. She'd enjoyed every minute of it, even as she'd wished that it was Dane she spoke with. More often than not, Captain Mathers and Mr. Blackwell would join them with their own memories of family to share.

She understood now what Dane had told her about the many bonds that forged love and formed a family. Harriet and Beau were her family of friends, which had expanded to include the men who sat with her in the saloon or strolled with her on deck. Captain Mathers treated her with a paternal gruffness as he taught her the parts of a ship, interspersing the lessons with words of encouragement to be patient, and small squeezes of the hand to reassure her—of what, she wasn't certain. It didn't seem to matter. Those warm gestures convinced her that she was not, and would not, be alone again unless she chose to be.

It amazed her how easy it was to make true and honest friends when she wasn't directing her energies toward convincing everyone, including herself, that they couldn't possibly want her company.

Mr. Blackwell treated her with a quaint charm that both flattered and comforted her. Always, he had a casual comment concerning her appearance that altered her perceptions of the reflection she saw in the looking glass. Often, he discussed politics and business with her, reminding her that she had a quick mind and did not always offend when she used it. His attitude was not one that would be embraced by society any time soon, but it hardly mattered. She had no desire to alter the *ton's* opinions of her. What on earth would they find to whisper about if she did?

Steven, too, treated her with respect and admiration, frequently remarking on how much she and his wife had in common, which led to wry quips and a long-suffering roll of the eyes that men seemed to master immediately after birth.

Dane was polite and solicitous and said as little as possible, spending his time observing every function of *Bifrost* and making copious notes on the ship's performance as well as detailed draughts on possible changes in the design. Out of desperation, she'd taken to following him about, asking questions and shamelessly showing off the knowledge she'd gleaned from Captain Mathers. Dane had been patient in both listening and explaining. Yet for all the conversation they'd had, he'd not said a word she wanted to hear.

He had, on the other hand, seemed uncharacteristically awkward, often tripping over his own words, impersonal as they were, then staring at her with a bemused expression that tipped his eyebrows, quirked his mouth, and formed a vertical crease just above his nose, like a dimple of thought rather than of amusement.

Strangely enough, she would realize at odd moments that she did not feel abandoned by him, nor did she question whether or not he cared for her. No longer did she fear that he would leave her, disillusioned by her true nature. It really was a strange feeling, like suddenly realizing that a once excruciating pain had suddenly lifted, no longer trapping her in misery and fear. Somewhere along their course from England to the middle of the Atlantic Ocean, the child that lurked inside her, always wary, always suspicious, always defensive, had simply gone to sleep with a contented smile on her face.

Lorelei did not fool herself into believing that child would not awaken from time to time, but she thought that with each instance, it might be easier to soothe her cries of fear and mistrust and put her to sleep again. To believe in the woman she was becoming.

Nevertheless, her patience had worn thinner than cheesecloth. And she would have to hold it together a while longer whether she liked it or not, for she was determined, for once in her life, to wait patiently rather than charge ahead. Besides, Dane had another battle to fight, another wrong to right, with Phillip.

After speaking with Steven, she'd completely lost her annoyance with Phillip, understanding what drove him even though she was appalled by the directions in which he chose to go. Given Dane's preoccupation, growing more extreme the closer they had come to Corvos, she reckoned that her husband had enough to work out without her interference.

But now that they were moored in the sheltered little bay on the most isolated island of the Azores, she reached the end of her tether. He and Phillip had had twenty years to sort themselves out and hadn't. She wasn't about to wait another twenty for her turn at having Dane's attention.

She stood at the window, staring at the small crescent of a beach and beyond that levels upon levels of dark volcanic rock and dense sections of lush foliage. How she would love to walk there with Dane, perhaps find a soft patch upon which to lie with him beneath the sun and talk about things that mattered.

Behind her, Dane and his cousins sat at the dining table in the saloon while the crew discreetly found duties at the opposite end of the ship. Dane and Phillip spoke to one another with stilted politeness without saying anything of merit. Steven spoke not at all except to answer a question directed to him. Phillip formally thanked Dane for rescuing Steven and Dane replied with a cliché. Dane inquired as to Phillip's future plans, and Phillip responded with a shrug.

"Damn it, Phillip, when do we all stop having to pay for mistakes I made twenty years ago?" Dane shouted, alarming her. He never shouted.

"You never make mistakes," Phillip shot back.

"I believe, Phillip, that Dane has been trying quite hard to admit to you that he does," Lorelei said sharply, as she turned on them, vexed beyond recall that their bullheadedness once again prompted her to meddle. "And Dane, I believe that Phillip feels that his future is not in his hands, but yours."

"Lorelei, stay out of this," Dane said wearily.

"It is none of your concern," Phillip said sullenly.

"I beg your pardon, but if I am to watch my husband torture himself over the rift between you, then it most certainly *is* my concern.'' She placed her hands on her hips and faced Dane. ''And if I am truly a member of this family, then I cannot stay out of it.''

Dane gave her a startled glance that softened into an expression that glowed with tenderness, then seemed to heat and smolder with something intimate and promising. ''She's right, Phillip,'' he said, in a tone that sounded like a low growl—or purr—of satisfaction, as if something had been suddenly resolved to his liking.

It would be nice if he shared it with her.

Dane sat back and extended his legs in a sprawl, his smile on her small and private even as his brows arched in challenge. ''It occurs to me that the enmity between us might be vanquished once and for all if we allow my wife to do the talking. I, for one, am . . . curious as to what she has to say.''

''It can't be resolved,'' Phillip said with a stubborn thrust of his jaw. ''It's too late.''

''Too late my . . . my''—Lorelei fumbled for a word to replace the one that had so readily leapt onto her tongue and failed—''my arse! Dane made a mistake by refusing to discuss the death of his father and to address the guilt you all felt, yet only you cling to. He has been trying—clumsily, I might add—to admit that. Are you so small-minded that you will carry that to your grave? Are you such a child that you will have your revenge no matter what?'' She reached across the table and grasped Phillip's arm to keep him from rising and leaving the saloon.

Phillip averted his gaze.

''Phillip,'' she said gently, ''you needed to talk about it, didn't you? You needed to speak of the guilt you felt, and the remorse. You needed to feel like an equal, to accept your part of the responsibility, though

I fail to see how any of you could have been responsible. Dane's father was ill. He was a grown man who made his own decisions. You and Steven and Dane had nothing to do with it.''

''And instead,'' Dane said with a wealth of regret in his voice, ''I refused to speak of it, to listen to you.''

''You left me alone, damn it!'' Phillip said as he lunged forward, glaring at Dane. ''And every time I made a mistake or did something wrong, you did it again, taking responsibility until all I felt was guilt, all the time. There was no room for anything else.'' He sat back and ran his hand down his face. ''I wish you had shouted at me when I fouled things up. I wish you hadn't taken the blame for my mistakes. I wish you would at least have allowed me to make them right. But you didn't. You said you never wanted to talk about it. You said it was too late to talk about it. If it was too late, why did it hurt so much? Why did it keep hurting?''

So swiftly that she didn't realize what was happening, Dane lunged from his chair, grabbed Phillip by the neckcloth, hauled him out of his seat, and slammed his fist into his face. She stared in disbelief as Phillip staggered back against the bulkhead, shook his head, and slid down to sit on the deck, blood streaming from his nose.

Steven rose and pulled back his arm, ready to strike Dane. Instinctively, Lorelei wrapped her hand around his fist and shook her head. ''Let them be, Steven. This has been delayed dangerously long already.'' She pried his hand open and pushed on his shoulders until he sank back into his chair, his expression anguished, twisted.

Dane strode toward Phillip and stood over him, his

fists clenched at his sides. "That is what I should have done more than once, damn you. I wanted to beat the life out of you for throwing tantrums until Father agreed to the hunting trip. I hated you then." He reached down and jerked Phillip to his feet, pressed his forearm against Phillip's throat to keep him from moving. "I hated you for not seeing that he was ill. I hated you for assuming the blame when it was too late to do anything about it."

Abruptly Dane released Phillip and walked to the window, his back to all of them. "It terrified me to feel like that. I didn't understand how I could hate you and love you at the same time. I was enraged that I loved you at all." He pivoted and glared at Phillip. "Don't you understand?" he shouted. "I couldn't say anything. I didn't know what to say. And if I had opened my mouth I would have howled like a rabid animal. I couldn't hit you because I was afraid I'd never stop."

Lorelei stood back, barring the entrance to the saloon, watching and listening with morbid fascination, certain in one moment that she witnessed a family destroying itself, realizing in the next that she was wrong, yet unable to fully comprehend why.

Phillip remained against the bulkhead, his expression stunned as he wiped the blood from his face with his sleeve.

Dane plowed his hand through his hair, lowered his voice. "I loved you too much to hate you, Phillip. You were five years old. You didn't do it on purpose. I took it for granted that you would realize that."

"Why aren't you angry at me, too, Phillip?" Steven asked. "I didn't speak of it either, even when you tried to tell me how you felt. And later I kept silent while you beat your head against a wall trying to be like Adrian just so you could best him.''

''Not best him,'' Phillip said with a heaving sigh. ''I wanted to make it all up to him by helping. Our parents had just died. Uncle John was all we had left. We depended on him and he died, and then Adrian stepped right into his shoes. He held us together.'' He raised his head, met Dane's gaze. ''*You* didn't need to cry. *You* weren't afraid. *You* took care of us and I wanted to help. I wanted to prove that I could. That I could be as strong as you were.''

Covering her mouth with one hand, Lorelei watched Phillip and thought of the child that often wailed inside her, lost and alone and so very afraid. A similar child was in Phillip's expression of confusion and doubt and guilt. She'd heard another child in Dane's voice as he'd spoken of grief and anger and fear. She saw yet another in Steven's slumped posture, his head lowered in shame and regret.

But children could learn. And they became adults. Her husband had become one far too soon. Phillip was still trying. Steven was caught between, his loyalties divided between a brother he loved and a cousin he loved—as wrenching as Dane's loyalties divided between two countries, and as difficult to resolve.

Lorelei breathed deeply, feeling helpless against the emotions that awakened and rattled the bars of the cage she'd placed them in so long ago, shaking all the parts of herself and rearranging them.

She walked to the table and picked up a napkin, dipped it in a glass of water, and approached Phillip. ''I know nothing about families except what I've learned from Dane and from you and Steven,'' she said very carefully, concentrating on each separate word to keep from losing control, to keep from weep-

ing with the sheer joy of comprehension—so much
comprehension that it overwhelmed her.

She held Phillip's chin with one hand and cleaned
his face with the other. "I do not claim to understand
what I've learned, except that families—whether
comprised of relatives or friends—are made up of
people. People make mistakes. They hurt one another
without meaning to or realizing it. It doesn't mean no
one will care about you as a result of your error. It
doesn't mean that you are beyond redemption. It simply means that you make mistakes."

She glanced at her husband, at the arrested expression on his face, then flipped the napkin and used a
clean corner to remove the last of the blood from beneath Phillip's nose. "I have learned that family is
something we must trust to forgive us and to continue
loving us even when we do not behave as we should."
Again she met her husband's gaze. "If we force ourselves to behave as we think others expect, then we
are not trusting their love for us or ours for them."

Frowning, Phillip gave her a long, dazed stare.

She dropped the napkin on the cabinet built into
the bulkhead beside her and placed her hands on Phillip's shoulders, afraid to let him go, afraid that if he
denied her the opportunity to share her thoughts with
him, final understanding would escape them both. Understanding that needed a voice to be real. Too much
was in turmoil inside her for her mind to work it out
silently.

"Dane, when did you stop hating Phillip? When
did your anger with him fade?" she asked.

He hesitated so long, she feared he wouldn't answer. "I don't know," he finally said. "Not long after
we buried my father, I realized it had disappeared."

"But not your love for Phillip?"

"No," Dane said softly.

She sniffed and felt wetness on her cheeks, ignoring it. "Phillip, you have made many mistakes in your attempts to prove yourself. But what were you trying to prove—that you were worthy of Dane's forgiveness, or that you didn't deserve it?" She sobbed as he made an animal sound in his throat. Reaching up, she caressed his cheek, wanting to soothe him. "Don't try to lie to me. I am far too experienced in trying to prove I don't deserve anything but what I provide for myself to be fooled." She swiped at her eyes with the back of her hand and sniffed again. "And Dane is quite proficient at proving that I am foolish and wrong and wasting my effort on him. If you have any sense at all, you will trust in the forgiveness he gave you a long time ago, and then you will forgive yourself."

She released her hold on his shoulders and backed up toward the entrance to the saloon. "And you, Dane, will stop indulging Phillip's tantrums. Trust him to choose his responsibilities and then fulfill them rather than merely tossing him a task here and there with the expectation that he will not accomplish it. I have discovered that we are all prone to meeting expectations at the level upon which they begin. You have taught me that it is desirable to begin at the highest level and work to live up to it."

Steven cleared his throat and regarded her with his head tilted—surely a Rutland trait. "Have you any wisdom for me? I'm feeling quite left out."

She stood in the threshold now, knowing that silent tears ran down her face for more reasons than she could count, none of them bad. "Go home to your wife. For every moment you are not speaking with her, or holding her, or ripping out your heart and laying it at her feet, she is most likely devising diabolical ways to pry it from you.''

Steven choked on a laugh.

Dane abruptly lowered his gaze, but not quickly enough to conceal the flush creeping up his neck. ''Last night . . . you heard everything.''

''I certainly did, and was immensely heartened by it. I'd never realized how much power men believe we women possess. It is my intention to cultivate that belief for the rest of our lives together.'' She backed up another step. ''As gratified as I would be to witness proof that my meddling has accomplished something, I would also feel quite put out by your displays of affection toward one another when I have not received affection from my husband in what seems like ages.'' She backed up a bit more, trembling again, fighting fear again that she had gone too far, that she had done the wrong thing. ''I will leave you three to sort yourselves out.'' She fluttered her hand. ''Embrace one another, or resume fighting, whatever it will take to end this thing once and for all. I am going for a walk to clear my head and decide whether I actually did dispense wisdom or whether I've made a complete fool of myself.''

She walked until she ran out of deck, then turned and stared blindly at the island, remembering the way Dane looked at her at the last, wondering if he'd been glowering or simply wondering what to make of his slightly mad wife.

She wasn't at all certain she wanted to know.

Adrian slowly strolled toward Lorelei, grimacing at the grit of sand that had crept into his shoes. When Lorelei had said she was going for a walk, it hadn't occurred to Adrian that she'd meant on the island.

He'd spent an hour searching the ship before Mathers had deigned to tell him that one of the crew had rowed her ashore. And for three hours before that, he and Phillip and Steven had followed Lorelei's advice as far as they comfortably could for the moment.

She'd wandered a distance inland and found a pretty knoll with bushes scattered like plump cushions over the ground. Late summer flowers decorated the landscape with vivid colors. A view of the ocean spread out like a rippled carpet from the opposite side of the island, the sun hanging suspended above the horizon, spilling melted gold light over the water and gilding the tips and curls of the waves.

Lorelei sat on the ground, her back against a depression in the rise as if she sat in a well-worn chair, her knees drawn up, her arms around her legs, looking as if she had been just like that for a long time. She watched him with an unwavering gaze, both wary and expectant.

"That was quite a soliloquy," he said.

"Did you talk or fight with Phillip?" she asked softly.

"We talked, resolving some issues, leaving others to work out as we go along. It will take time for us to adjust to new insights and learn how to deal with old hurts."

"You will succeed," she said. "I'm sure of it."

He strode to a tree near her, propped his elbow on the trunk, and rubbed his forefinger back and forth over his chin. "From the moment I first saw you, I wanted to be a hero. I didn't succeed at that."

She smiled slightly and rested her cheek on her knees, watching him. "You saw me and wanted me in spite of it."

He shook his head. "Because of it," he corrected

softly. "Because of what I saw and what you revealed to me in a very short time."

"All right, Dane. Because of what you saw. That in itself makes you quite extraordinary, though others might consider it strange. And you were strong enough to overlook my foolish attempts to show you why you couldn't possibly want me. You have tried to protect me—"

"Instead, you protected me," he said with a mirthless laugh. "I was as bad as Phillip, not thinking things through, sailing off to save my cousin without any idea how. You saved us all, my Lady Lorelei."

"I suppose I did," she mused. "Fancy that."

He gave another mirthless laugh.

"Dane, I did it at the expense of your pride. Yet you didn't hold it against me."

"I behaved like a beast to you."

"Only a little," she admitted. "I don't imagine heroes take too well to having damsels trying to organize their quests."

"Damsel," he said with a snort. "Too tame a description for you." He crouched at the base of the tree, facing her as his hands idly sifted through the grass. "You are a woman in every sense of the word." He squinted, trying to see her more clearly, but he was too far from her and her features were indistinct. Pulling his spectacles from his pocket, he slipped them on. "Whoever heard of a hero wearing specs?"

"It distinguishes you from all the other gallants."

"As a boy, I was always running into things and stumbling because I couldn't see properly. I hated having to wear these. I hated not being able to read more, so I wore them."

"I doubt you were ever clumsy when it mattered.

Certainly I've never seen you stumble or falter.'' She rose and took a few steps toward him. ''Dane, your words and your actions with me make you the most magnificent of heroes. You've wrought so many miracles for me, showing me in small ways what you see when you look at me, what you learn as you listen to me. You made me learn about myself—all the things I didn't want to know for fear they would confirm what I didn't want to believe—that I am unappealing and completely unwanted by anyone. When I was a child, I believed that my parents left because I was so large a baby. I believed they left because they didn't want me, because they were embarrassed by me.''

''They were selfish,'' he said harshly. ''They saw only what they wanted. They didn't see your incredibly beautiful eyes, or the trust and dependency that only a child can give without fear. They denied themselves the pleasure of seeing your smile that is like a warm embrace to anyone upon whom you bestow it. They missed the pride they would have felt watching you grow into a most extraordinary woman with a fine mind that is always firmly rooted in common sense.'' He grinned up at her. ''Well, most of the time. On occasion you do venture into foolishness.''

''Like trying to discourage the love of a man who saw all those things about me and made me see them, too?''

''Like that,'' he said gravely, wanting so badly to go to her, to hold her and make love to her. But not yet. Not until he said all things she had a right to hear and never had, not even from him. ''You have a strong spirit and a generosity that humbles me. You have an ability to adapt that is rare. You have a beauty that shines more brightly than your smile, and a womanliness that is only enhanced by your form and your softness and your grace. And you have a wisdom that is frightening. No one in this world is more worthy of love than you. No one in this world is more fortunate than I to love you and have your love in return.'' He pinned her with his gaze, willing her to hear and to believe him. "I love you, Lorelei. I'm foolish with love for you," he said hoarsely.

He saw her body shudder and her hands tremble and her lips press together tightly. He heard that small whimper that came from a well somewhere deep inside her—vulnerability and need stifled.

"Heroes are never frightened by a woman's strength," she said thickly. "As you were never frightened by me."

"Then I suppose that perhaps I am a hero after all."

"Dane, I love you so much I don't know what to do with it all."

He angled his head back to look, unseeing, at the sky, at the changing light of day's end. He'd wanted to hear those words spoken in her voice, from her heart. They sank into him, filling him with hope for a future he'd never thought was possible. "Thank you, my Lady Lorelei. I realize how difficult it was for you to say it, to admit it to me as well as yourself, and to trust that I would not use the words against you. I needed to know that you trusted me enough to tell me. . . ." He began to straighten from his crouch, but she held out her hand.

"Please, Dane. Stay where you are for just a little while longer. There is something else I must do . . . another way in which I must give you my trust." She kicked off her shoes, then bent over and reached beneath her gown, removed her stockings one by one, showing him brief glimpses of long, rounded leg. She lifted her skirt and untied her petticoat tapes, slid the garment down, her hem dropping along the way, again concealing her hips and thighs and ankles.

He couldn't breathe for the emotions crowding in his throat, for the anticipation of the gift she was giving him as she released the ribbon that gathered her bodice into a half circle below her neck, slid it over her shoulders—pretty shoulders that were round and soft—and down her arms—long enough to embrace the biggest of fools—one at a time, holding it up to cover her breasts.

"I will likely spread out even more with each child we have, you know," she said in a high voice as apprehensive as her expression. Her forced smile quivered.

He fell back on his seat, stunned by what she'd said. The last thing he'd ever expected her to say. "You said you didn't want children. You don't have to—"

"No, I don't have to," she replied with her familiar air of independence. "But I think we might be very good parents, Dane. The world needs good parents, and I need to share this love that fills me with someone who needs it. Children need love. They deserve it." She straightened to her full height as she pulled the pins from her hair with one hand, the other still holding her gown up. Strands of rich brown touched with gold fell around her shoulders and down her back.

"As I said: I will likely spread out with each child I carry. I have a bit of a belly, and my thighs are . . . dimpled. My waist will thicken with age and no doubt disappear altogether. My . . . my breasts will most certainly sag in time—"

"Shut up," he said with a croak. His mouth felt

dry and full of pebbles. His forehead beaded with perspiration. His arousal, with no regard for moments of such profound emotion, swelled and rose to new heights of awareness, painfully rigid.

She released her gown so quickly it startled him, baring her body in a single downward drift of fabric. "You have given me everything I'd ever wished for, Dane—more than I'd ever dared to wish for. I wanted to give you a promise that I will not keep even my most shameful secrets from you."

He stared at her every curve, absorbed every detail of long neck, large breasts puckered from the kiss of air, cushioned belly and wide hips, dimpled thighs and sturdy calves, slender ankles and feet disproportionately small. Her face was pale but for a bright flush staining her cheeks. Her hands were clenched at her sides as if she struggled not to cover herself. Her toes curled into the grass as if she could barely stand.

But stand she did, her body framed by the sunset sky, brilliance radiating across it like colors refracted through a cosmic crystal. But not as brilliant and vivid as she, and not nearly as beautiful in his eyes.

"There are many things I would say in this moment if I could find the wits and words to express what I feel, Lorelei. I am wearing my spectacles and see you clearly and am speechless with wanting to touch and hold and taste the beauty I see." He spread his hand in the air in front of his groin. "If I thought I could move, I would come to you." He angled his head. "Will you come to me instead?"

She closed her eyes and gave that little whimper again, then opened them and fixed her gaze on his face as she walked toward him, kneeled before him, opened her hand over his cheek, then his chest, then down to below his hard stomach. "Only in my dreams did I ever believe a man would look at me as you do,'' she said in a broken whisper. "Only in my dreams did I ever believe in anything at all, especially myself.'' She swallowed and dashed a tear from her eye, never once taking her gaze from him. "Adrian, I see myself in your eyes, and I *am* beautiful. I believe it just as I believe you love me . . . that I deserve your love.''

He smiled and pulled her to him, wrapped his arms around her, crushed her against him. "You called me Adrian.'' He kissed her ear, her neck. "I didn't realize how important it was to me.'' He caressed her breasts between them, lowered his head to taste them, to inhale the spring scent of her. "It was a barrier you erected, a formality you observed to keep a distance from me.''

She shuddered at his every touch, at the press of his lips and the stroke of his tongue over her flesh, then leaned back and traced his wide mouth with her finger, pressed her palm to his chest. "You have taught me that love has many forms. That passion and friendship are two parts of a whole in marriage. As we are two parts of a whole, husband and wife, friends and lovers . . . hero and heroine. You have proved to me that love by any name is still love.''

She smiled and the sun sank into the sea, leaving only her brightness, only her beauty. It was more than enough to light his way.

He lowered her to the ground and removed his clothing as he stared at her lying before him, open and welcoming him with the desire for him that brought her body to life. "Adrian,'' she whispered, as she reached for him, urged him with hips and legs to sink into her, took him inside her, and moved beneath him. "Adrian, dance with me again beneath the stars.''

Dear Reader,

Julia Quinn is quick becoming a rising star here at Avon Books, and next month's Avon Romantic Treasure TO CATCH AN HEIRESS shows why. A case of mistaken identity provides Caroline Trent with the escape she needs from her stuffy guardian. But Caroline escapes right into the very strong arms of sexy Blake Ravenscroft. Julia is pure fun to read, and if you haven't yet joined in the fun you should!

Lovers of Regency period romance shouldn't miss Suzanne Enoch's BY LOVE UNDONE. Four years ago, Madeline Willits was found in a compromising position. Now she's rusticating in the country, but when handsome Quinlan Bancroft arrives at the estate she's once again caught up in passion and discovered in *another* compromising position! Poor Maddie...all she ever seems to do is fall for the wrong man—but then Quinlan proposes marriage...

If you're hooked on THE MEN OF PRIDE COUNTY series by Rosalyn West, then you know you're in for a treat with next month's THE OUTSIDER. Starla Fairfax has returned to Pride County with a secret. She accepts northerner Hamilton Dodge's proposal of marriage for one reason only: he can protect her from her past. But Dodge has more in mind than a marriage of convenience...

Contemporary readers: be on the lookout next month for Hailey North, an exciting, new writer. Hailey's got a winning writing style, and in BEDROOM EYES, her debut book, she's created a magical, sensuous love story. A prim-on-the-outside attorney, Penelope Sue Fields has dreams of finally meeting Mr. Right. But lately all the attention she's getting is from Mr. Wrong—ex-cop Tony Olano. Will Penelope ever find true love?

Enjoy!

Lucia Macro

Lucia Macro
Senior Editor

AEL 0698

Avon Romances—
the best in exceptional authors and unforgettable novels!

TOPAZ
by **Beverly Jenkins**
78660-5/ $5.99 US/ $7.99 Can

STOLEN KISSES
by **Suzanne Enoch**
78813-6/ $5.99 US/ $7.99 Can

CAPTAIN JACK'S WOMAN
by **Stephanie Laurens**
79455-1/ $5.99 US/ $7.99 Can

MOUNTAIN BRIDE
by **Susan Sawyer**
78479-3/ $5.99 US/ $7.99 Can

A TOUGH MAN'S WOMAN
by **Deborah Camp**
78252-9/ $5.99 US/ $7.99 Can

A PRINCE AMONG MEN
by **Kate Moore**
78458-0/ $5.99 US/ $7.99 Can

THE WILD ONE
by **Danelle Harmon**
79262-1/ $5.99 US/ $7.99 Can

HIGHLAND BRIDES: THE LADY AND THE KNIGHT
by **Lois Greiman**
79433-0/ $5.99 US/ $7.99 Can

A ROSE IN SCOTLAND
by **Joan Overfield**
78007-0/ $5.99 US/ $7.99 Can

A DIME NOVEL HERO
by **Maureen McKade**
79504-3/ $5.99 US/ $7.99 Can

Discover Contemporary Romances
at Their Sizzling Hot Best
from Avon Books

SIMPLY IRRESISTIBLE *by Rachel Gibson*
79007-6/$5.99 US/$7.99 Can

LETTING LOOSE *by Sue Civil-Brown*
72775-7/$5.99 US/$7.99 Can

IF WISHES WERE HORSES *by Curtiss Ann Matlock*
79344-X/$5.99 US/$7.99 Can

IF I CAN'T HAVE YOU *by Patti Berg*
79554-X/$5.99 US/$7.99 Can

BABY, I'M YOURS *by Susan Andersen*
79511-6/$5.99 US/$7.99 Can

TELL ME I'M DREAMIN' *by Eboni Snoe*
79562-0/$5.99 US/$7.99 Can

BEDROOM EYES *by Hailey North*
79895-6/$5.99 US/$7.99 Can